# FALLING THROUGH THE BLINDSPOT

Creative Texts Publishers products are available at special discounts for bulk purchase for sale promotions, premiums, fund-raising, and educational needs. For details, write Creative Texts Publishers, PO Box 50, Barto, PA 19504, or visit www.creativetexts.com

FALLING THROUGH THE BLINDSPOT
by Jacob Matthews
Published by Creative Texts Publishers
PO Box 50
Barto, PA 19504
www.creativetexts.com



ISBN: 978-1-64738-144-8

# FALLING THROUGH THE BLINDSPOT

BY JACOB MATTHEWS

CREATIVE TEXTS PUBLISHERS
Barto, PA

*The reality we perceive and experience is not truly representative of the underlying nature of the universe.  Our minds create a limited and flawed representation of reality that is filtered and shaped by our beliefs, expectations, and previous experiences.  Our individual identities and experiences are temporary and illusory.  The reality that we perceive is not an accurate representation of the true nature of reality.  True reality lies in the interconnectedness of all things.*

*~ ChatGPT AI*

# TABLE OF CONTENTS

# Chapter One

USAF Major Jackson Hobbs sat in the large leather seat, watching the flat screen monitors in front of him as he piloted the Predator drone over the barren desert west of Kirkuk air base in Iraq.

Major Hobbs had been an F-16 pilot until a few months ago when a surface-to-air missile brought his aircraft down over rough terrain during a routine recon mission. He had broken his leg when he had ejected from the aircraft, but his copilot was strafed by enemy gunfire and didn't make it. Hobbs had been reassigned as an RPA (Remotely Piloted Aircraft) pilot for the next 9 months during his recovery and physical therapy. He missed the feel of a real aircraft around him, the sound of the engines, the smell of the jet fuel, the acceleration, the feeling of power and freedom.

First Lieutenant Lionel Banks was the mission Sensor Operator seated to the right of Major Hobbs. Banks had only recently completed RPA training. He had entered the Air Force Academy in hopes of becoming a fighter pilot, but due to the high demand for RPA pilots, he was immediately placed into the RPA program after graduation.

Over the past couple of months, Hobbs had come to realize that being an RPA pilot was a truly thankless job. It was an unhealthy blend of long hours and periods of high stress intermixed with boredom and isolation. Because RPAs can perform many of the operations traditionally assigned to conventional fighter aircraft at a very small fraction of the cost, the demand for RPA pilots had accelerated at a rate much faster than the Air Force could support with trained pilots. As a result, it was not unusual for RPA pilots to log as many hours in a month as a fighter pilot would in a year. He wouldn't miss being an RPA pilot when he returned to duty in his F-16, but he had gained a new respect for them.

Despite his misgivings about his current assignment, flying over the desert landscape, turning and banking past a wisp of high clouds, Major Hobbs almost felt as if he were back in the cockpit again. After 2 months of tedious recon flights, it felt good to have a real mission.

The Al Hurriya Air Base had received intel that Jal Khabir, second in command of the militant terrorist group, Al Hadid, had emerged from hiding and was headed to a new base of operations in a remote area near the Iranian border.

Al Hadid had become notorious recently for its involvement in suicide bombings in public gatherings. It had also taken to executing midnight raids on small villages, conscripting young men and boys old enough to hold a weapon at gunpoint, and threatening to kill their families if they did not join. They would

# FALLING THROUGH THE BLINDSPOT

typically leave a few troops behind to loot the village of supplies and any objects of monetary value after the new recruits were taken. Young women and older girls were often taken hostage to satisfy the carnal needs of their recruits and to act as couriers for their suicide bombing activities.

The group had risen to international prominence when Jal Khabir himself had appeared brandishing a machete in an online video. He non-chalantly sawed the head off a young boy who appeared to be no more than 14 years old for refusing to join Al Hadid. The video was intended as a warning to anyone who dared to defy the terrorist group.

Neither Hobbs nor Banks had watched the entire video, but nearly everyone had seen bits and pieces. Most legitimate websites had removed the full video for its sheer brutality, but many of the cable news networks had broadcast edited clips of the video ad nauseam for weeks afterward.

The boy in the video had reminded Banks of his own son. The sheer terror in the boy's face as he screamed and begged for mercy while Jal Khabir stood behind him with a smug sneer, sliding his machete slowly across his neck, had filled him with outrage and revulsion. He wanted nothing more than to reach through the screen and plunge that machete right through the evil bastard's chest.

Hobbs and Banks sat side by side, each with a set of 4 screens in front of each of them. One larger screen above them displayed a satellite feed of their position with an area map superimposed over the landscape with an enlarged animated drone indicating their current position. The screen directly in front of each of them showed a camera feed from the cockpit of the drone with the displays on either side showing a 180-degree view of the sides and rear of the drone with telemetry information streaming on the side windows of the displays. Each station had a joystick and roller ball control on each side of a smaller command control display which reflected commands entered from the keyboard which was mounted in a sliding drawer just beneath the surface of each station. The main pilot controlled the drone with the roller and joystick while the secondary pilot manned the keyboard for communications and command instructions.

"Sir, we are approaching Iranian air space in 50 clicks," Lieutenant Banks reported.

"Roger that," Major Hobbs responded. "We're taking it down." The Predator descended to 70 feet above the desert floor, spooking a small herd of Urial Sheep that were milling around a small creek at the base of a hill. He continued to fly close to the ground, hugging the terrain, staying below the tops of the adjacent hills to avoid radar detection.

Relations with the Iranian government had been tenuous over the past few months ever since a US drone had been shot down during a recon mission over a contested area of Iranian air space. The Iranian government had stepped up its aerial reconnaissance over the area and issued stern warnings that any further encroachment of US military aircraft too close to Iranian airspace would be considered an act of war.

Given the notoriety of the particular target they were now pursuing, they would have preferred the greater accuracy and firepower of an F-35 strike, but in the current political climate, they did not want to risk an international incident by getting too close to Iranian airspace. The decision was made to execute the operation using a single Predator drone flying low enough to avoid radar detection and hopefully cut their target off before they reached the compound where the Al Hadid terrorist base was thought to be located. Recent intelligence reports had indicated that the base was located in an isolated valley in the contested area, surrounded by a civilian compound that included several homes, a hospital, a mosque, a school, and a sophisticated mobile missile defense installation provided by the Russian government.

Rising, banking, and diving through the rocky hills and valleys with the desert landscape whizzing by on his monitor, Hobbs almost felt like he was immersed in a video game. A voice in his headset roused him from his trance-like state.

The voice on the other end of the headset originated from the Air Force Special Operations Command center at Creech Air Force Base in Nevada.

"This is General Wallace at Special Ops. Can we get confirmation on your ETA Major?"

"Comsat recon shows the convoy out about 10 clicks north of the next ridge, heading southwest. We should have a visual in about 90 seconds."

"Copy that, Major."

As the Predator crested the ridge, a line of vehicles, 4 trucks, a van, and 2 SUVs appeared over the horizon. Major Hobbs pressed the targeting button on his joystick and a bright red cross-hair pattern appeared on the screen. He brought the crosshairs up on the target vehicle in the center of the convoy. He held the crosshairs on the SUV waiting for the target lock indicator. "One more second," he thought "just one more second…"

The monitor suddenly froze in a jumble of randomly colored pixels.

"Dammit!" Lieutenant Banks exclaimed under his breath as his screen locked up in a similar colorful mosaic.

Major Hobbs spoke into his headset, "Sir, we lost visual contact. Looks like they've picked up the drone on mobile radar and they're jamming us. Both navigational and targeting cams are down." He glanced down at the flashing red **"AWARE SYSTEM ACTIVATED"** message now flashing on his center screen. "We got a ping from the AWARE system that it has assumed control. We are tracking from the sat feed."

# FALLING THROUGH THE BLINDSPOT

The AWARE system (Airborne Weapons Artificial Reason Engine) was based upon an artificial intelligence system designed to allow drones and human-guided missiles to continue to operate autonomously to complete their missions in the event of a communications disruption.

Banks typed in a monitor control command on the console keyboard and the satellite view zoomed out to display the relative position of the drone and the caravan on the overhead screen on both stations.

A voice came over the headset, "Major, this is ComSat control. We've been monitoring your feed. We're attempting to decrypt the jammer signature. Looks like a variant of the Sevastopol encryption we intercepted off a Russian carrier a few months back. Should only take a couple of minutes to upload the counter signal algorithm to the satellite."

The drone incorporated a separate antenna that was capable of broadcasting its own counter-jamming signal which could counteract the incoming signal in much the same way that noise-reducing headphones invert incoming sound waves and send them to the speakers to eliminate audio noise. If the jamming signal was a simple regular pattern, this could be done by the onboard computer, but for complex pseudo-random jammers like the one currently being blasted at the drone, they needed much more computational power than the drone could muster, so the signal had to be analyzed by a supercomputer running in Nevada which would generate an algorithm which could mimic the jamming signal in real-time. The algorithm would then be transferred via a laser link from the satellite to the drone.

Major Hobbs and Lieutenant Banks helplessly watched the satellite feed on the main viewing screen for what seemed like an eternity as the drone slowly closed in on the caravan which had now picked up speed heading nearly due west across the high desert.

"The counter jamming algorithm is uploading Major. You should regain control shortly."

The two men sat at attention, their eyes darting from the overhead screens to their respective control displays, Major Hobbs with his hand around the joystick, and Lieutenant Banks, his fingers resting lightly over his keyboard, his left leg bouncing up and down in a nervous twitch.

The individual control screens in front of the two pilots went black momentarily then illuminated into a swirl of color as the camera feed from the drone resumed. The screen in front of Lieutenant Banks contained a split screen with a viewing window of the camera and a command window displaying in bold red letters "**PILOT CONTROL RESTORED**"

"We're back in business Major," Banks reported.

Major Hobbs applied gentle pressure to the joystick and the drone responded banking slightly to the left to center the caravan on his screen for targeting. The trailing vehicle in the caravan skidded to a stop churning up a cloud of dust on the rocky dirt road. Moments later two flashes appeared from the rear of the vehicle in quick succession.

"Oh, shit!" Banks barked. "We have incoming surface-to-air missiles."

"Dammit, I only needed another second for weapons lock!" Hobbs responded as he slammed the joystick hard left and downward.

"Seven seconds to impact!" Banks reported nervously as Hobbs accelerated the drone downward toward a small canyon created by a gully just south of their position. Banks watched as a pair of white exhaust trails elongated on the right-side screen, the heat-seeking missiles turning and banking following their path like a pair of snakes preparing to strike their prey.

Banks careened around the hillside banking hard right into the canyon, his wingtips nearly vertical as he entered the narrow opening between the walls of the canyon, the two missiles now only a few hundred feet behind. The heat signatures of the drone's engines were momentarily blocked from the sensors of the missiles as the drone ducked behind the cliff on the right side of the canyon. Temporarily unable to track the drone the missiles leveled into a straight path. By the time the heat signature was visible to the missiles, it was too late to correct course. The lead missile over-corrected and slammed into the right-hand wall of the canyon in a blast of flame and a plume of rock and sand. The second missile, sensors blinded by the cloud of debris, slammed into the far wall of the canyon in the second blast of flame and rock.

Fortunately, the narrow canyon had widened and veered southward so Hobbs was able to level out the drone. The caravan would no doubt see the plume of fire and smoke and assume the missiles had hit their target.

"How far does this canyon go?" Hobbs asked, unable to take his eyes off the drone's cockpit camera feed, flying just a few feet off the floor of the canyon nearly brushing the tops of the low scrub in the dry basin of the gully in hopes of staying out of sight of the caravan and any radar signal that may have been tracking them.

Banks quickly pulled up a 3D topographical map of the area and pinpointed their position on the map and traced their trajectory.

Looks like it continues another 20 clicks due south and spreads out into an open basin just north of the border.

"Perfect," Hobbs replied. "We should be able to stay out of sight all the way to the end of the canyon then meet them head on and blast them into tomorrow before they even know we're there."

"Oh, hell no!" Banks exclaimed looking up at the satellite feed.

"What now?" Hobbs asked, his eyes still glued to the monitor.

# FALLING THROUGH THE BLINDSPOT

"The caravan took a hard right to the south. Looks like they are making a run for the Iranian border."

"Shit!" Hobbs responded glancing up at the satellite feed. "They're only a couple clicks from the border! There's no way we can cut them off before they cross. Dammit!"

"You really think the Iranians will let them in?" Banks asked.

"Dunno," Hobbs replied. "I guess it depends on what they are carrying or how much cash they have on hand. Best we stay out of sight just in case they get turned away. "

Hobbs eased up on the throttle and for the next few minutes tried to keep the drone's speed at a minimum, banking back and forth across the floor of the canyon keeping their position and their presence a secret in hopes that the convoy would either presume that the drone had been shot down and reverse course or be turned away at the Iranian border and be left out in the open.

Banks continued to watch the caravan being tracked on the satellite feed as it continued full speed toward the Iranian border. "What the hell?" Banks suddenly exclaimed.

"What's going on Lieutenant?"

"The convoy just drove right through the border crossing!"

"Seriously?"

"Yeah. They didn't even slow down!"

"Son of a bitch! Somebody's got friends in low places," Hobbs responded.

A voice came over Major Hobbs's headset. "Major, this is General Wallace at Ops Command. The target has entered Iranian territory. You are ordered to disengage and head back to base."

"Understood Sir."

"Well, hell. It's out of our hands now," Hobbs remarked. "I guess we're going home empty today. On the upside, the drone is still in one piece. I guess they won't be deducting that $10 million out of our paychecks. Go ahead and take the controls Lieutenant. Let's get this bird back to the nest."

"Yes Sir!" Banks exclaimed, happy to get a chance to take over control of the flight, even if only for the return trip home.

Banks pulled back on the joystick and the drone rose above the crest of the canyon up to around 2000 feet. He pressed the joystick to the right, circling the drone to the west to start the return trip back to Kirkuk. But before he completed circling back, the drone abruptly dived and resumed its original trajectory.

"What the hell Lieutenant?" Hobbs demanded as he turned to Banks.

"I didn't do it, Sir, I swear. I wasn't even touching the keyboard."

A short alarm blast emanated from their headsets and the words "**AWARE SYSTEM ACTIVATED**" lit up across the top of his center display screen superimposed over the drone's cockpit camera feed.

"Send the manual override command.  Otherwise, in about 2 minutes we're going to be in Iranian airspace."

"Yes sir."

Lieutenant Banks's fingers flew across the keyboard as the small control display reflected the keyboard input.

>manual override

>--- REQUEST DENIED ---

"No Luck, Sir."

"Try the AWARE disable command."

>aware disable

>--- REQUEST DENIED ---

"Still no luck."

Hobbs pulled his keyboard drawer out from beneath his desk.  "Let me try," he said.

>manual override

>--- REQUEST DENIED ---

>mon

>Entering Monitor Mode

:proc disable

:--- ACCESS DENIED ---

:admin override

:--- ACCESS DENIED – ADMIN PRIVILEGE DISABLED ---

An angry voice came over Major Hobbs's headset.  "Major, this is General Wallace.  Did you not understand?  You are to disengage!  That is a direct order."

"We're trying, Sir.  For some reason, the drone is not responding.  Requesting permission to engage self-destruct.  Sir?  General Wallace, Sir?  Hello?"

"Damn!  We lost communication with Operations," Hobbs said frowning. "Lieutenant, get me the Operations Command Center on the landline."

Banks picked up the phone next to his station.  A look of exasperation came over his face as he pressed the handset button multiple times.

"Landline is dead, Sir," Banks reported.

"Shit!  Somebody must be hacking us."

"What do we do now, Sir?"

"We could be about a minute away from starting a war.  We don't have any choices. Protocol dictates that we initiate self-destruct.  This is going to be a God damned paperwork nightmare!"

Hobbs reached in his pocket and pulled out a sealed envelope and handed it to Lieutenant Banks.  Banks reached in his pocket and pulled out an identical envelope and handed it to Hobbs.  They both unsealed the envelopes and opened

# FALLING THROUGH THE BLINDSPOT

them.  They each pulled a piece of paper from the envelopes.  Protocol dictated that a self-destruct sequence could only be initiated by both pilots simultaneously and only using the code that the other possessed.

On Hobbs's keyboard, he typed the command:

>self-destruct 577913

On his keyboard, Banks typed the corresponding command:

>self-destruct 148161

Hobbs spoke "Press Enter on my mark Lieutenant 3-2-1-Enter."

Both men pressed the Enter key simultaneously.  On both screens the response flashed:

>--- SELF-DESTRUCT SEQUENCE INITIATED ---

The two men looked at their screens expecting the camera feed to pixilate and go blank once the self-destruct operation was deployed.  They both waited in anticipation for what seemed like minutes but in fact, was only about 15 seconds.  Then a new line appeared.

>--- SELF-DESTRUCT SEQUENCE REQUEST ABORTED ---

>--- CONSOLE INTERFACE DISABLED ---

"What the fuck?" Banks exclaimed as he placed his hands back on the keyboard pressing the Enter key multiple times, but there was no response.  Neither Banks nor Hobbs could get their keyboards to respond.

The two men sat in silence watching the camera feed from the drone like it were a reality TV show unfolding before them.  Above them, the satellite feed showed the animated icon of the drone as it crossed the Iranian border and the screen suddenly switched from the drab earthy colors of the desert landscape to a bold reddish hue, indicating that they were now flying over restricted airspace.

The silence was broken by a sharp alarm buzzer emanating from the left terminal on Lieutenant Banks's station.

"Major, we're detecting weapons lock from ground-based radar."

"Probably a mobile TOR launcher," Hobbs replied.

"We have surface-to-air missile launch detection.  Estimated impact 22 seconds," Banks reported.

On the overhead satellite view, a pair of white circles were now superimposed on the landscape view below and to the right of the drone icon.  The circles had dashed lines emanating from them indicating the position of the missiles with respect to the drone.

On the cockpit camera feed, the image suddenly dipped wildly to the right and downward as it looked like the world was upended.  The drone was now accelerating at full speed toward the ground below, spinning 180 degrees.

"Sir, we're showing a Hellfire missile launch from the drone!" Banks said.

"At what?" Hobbs replied.

"I don't know, Sir!  There was no target lock on our end.  Looks like we're launching it right into the ground!"

"No way.  This can't... No way!" Hobbs said in disbelief.

The camera feed went entirely white as the ground in front of them erupted in an explosion of fire, the camera image performing another 180-degree flip. After a couple of seconds, the display changed from white to grayish brown to a sandy blur and then a line of blue at the top of the screen as the horizon now appeared in front of them.  The drone could not have been more than 20 feet off the desert floor as the rear camera displayed two fiery explosions barely 100 meters behind them.

"Holy shit!" Banks remarked as he watched the camera feed.  "Have you ever seen anything like that?"

"Just once," Hobbs responded under his breath, eyes fixed on the screen.

The two men watched for a few seconds in silence as the desert landscape blurred past leaving a cloud of dust in the rear camera.  The drone continued along a shallow ravine, then banked around a small hill.  The enemy convoy suddenly came into sight.

In a split second, the red targeting crosshairs were superimposed over the front camera view.  A large yellow rectangle appeared at the edges of the screen, growing quickly smaller as it closed in on the center of the screen.  The rectangle turned red as it focused on the convoy and the words **"TARGET ACQUIRED"** appeared in the center of the rectangle.  A series of white streaks of exhaust emerged from the lower corners of the front camera view as the remaining hellfire missiles launched from below the wings.  The drone banked hard right around the hill as the path of the Hellfire contrails slid from the center camera view to the side monitor.  From the side camera view, the convoy erupted in flashes of white light which cooled into a fiery orange mushroom cloud of flame and black smoke.  A red banner appeared across the bottom of the camera view with the words **"TARGET DESTROYED"** flashing in the center of the banner.

The two men sat in silence for a minute as if mesmerized by the flashing words and the desert floor whizzing by below them.

Finally, the two men looked up from the monitor and looked at each other. Hobbs opened his mouth as if about to speak when a pair of sharp beeps emanated from the satellite monitor.  The satellite monitor showed the silhouette of the drone moving northwest across the desert floor, quickly approaching Iraqi airspace indicated with a white line separating the red hue of Iranian airspace from the normal aerial view of the desert below.  As the drone crossed the border, the drone accelerated, quickly gaining altitude.

>--- CONSOLE INTERFACE RESTORED ---

Appeared on the command control screen and the words **"MANUAL PILOT**

# FALLING THROUGH THE BLINDSPOT

**CONTROL ENABLED**" appeared briefly across the center of the front camera view screen.

"Looks like we are back in the saddle again," Hobbs said reaching for the joystick and placing his left hand on the roller ball.

A Red warning light illuminated on Lieutenant Banks logistics monitor. "Sir, I'm detecting a low-level gamma-ray burst at the explosion site."

"That's odd. I've never seen that before."

"Should we do another flyover to see if we can detect a radiation cloud?"

"I'm guessing we've already way overstayed our welcome. I think we better get this bird out of town before the Iranian MIGs show up.

"Yes, Sir," Banks replied.

Just then, the door to the control room flew open and an angry-looking Colonel Arlon Jeffries stormed into the dimly lit control room with four MP's and a pair of confused RPA pilots behind him.

"Hobbs!" the Colonel barked. "You two are relieved of command. These two will see to getting the drone back to base!" he said jerking his arm back, his thumb pointed over his shoulder to the pilots behind him.

"Escort these men to separate debriefing rooms," the colonel said turning to the MPs.

Hobbs turned to Banks, his back to the Colonel.

"Don't say a word without a JAG present," Hobbs said to Banks in a furtive whisper.

Banks just looked back at him bewildered. "What? What do you mean?"

"I mean it. Not a word. Not if you ever want to see the light of day again. Not a word without a JAG! Someone is going down for this and right now we're on the shit end of this stick."

"C'mon, you two let's go! Now!" Colonel Jeffries barked.

Banks glanced at the Colonel, then at Hobbs, and nodded.

# CHAPTER TWO

*Separating reality from illusion is an ongoing process.  It can take time and effort to gain a clear understanding of the truth.*

*~ ChatGPT AI ~*

Sarah Reynolds opened her eyes and tried to blink the cobwebs out of her mind, but all she could see was the milky white fog that enveloped her. Immediately, she was filled with a familiar sense of dread.

"No, no, no, not again, why does this keep happening?" Her mind raced along the edge of panic trying desperately to hold on to reason. "Where am I?  What the hell is going on?"  She looked in every direction, but the scenery never changed.  The universe stretched out around her in a haze of nothingness.  It wasn't dark.  It wasn't light.  It wasn't even empty space.  It was just a profound sense of aloneness in an endless sea of nothing.  She struggled to try to focus her thoughts, which raced through her mind like a symphony of discord.  "Oh, my God, am I dead?"

It was the same sequence every time, as if trapped in an endless loop, repeating the same lines in her head, time after time after time.  She struggled to remember the last thing that happened but she couldn't make sense of the disjointed mass of thoughts that barreled through her mind preventing her from being able to concentrate on a plan of action.  She was overcome with the urge to run, to escape, but there was nothing to run to, nothing to run from, just an ominous primordial sense of fear that defied logic or reason.  A fear gripped her so tightly that she felt as though she were encased in concrete, completely paralyzed, unable to move, unable to breathe unable to even feel her body.

"Get a grip, Sarah, you're not dead.  You have to figure this out.  This can't keep happening.  You have to focus.  Focus!  FOCUS, DAMN IT!"  But before she even finished berating herself, her mind was flooded with a whole new wave of disjointed memories.  She closed her eyes to try to focus, but her visual field was filled with a dizzying image, like a high-speed train flying through an impossibly long corridor with doors flying open on both sides as she passed through.  She looked forward into an ominous cloud accelerating toward her from the end of the corridor, glinting in the blinding light white light like a thousand swirling daggers.  She threw her arm up in front of her face, bracing for impact but before she could even turn her head it was upon her, grinding through her flesh, tearing her apart, crunching through her bones, slashing into her very soul, shredding everything that was the essence of who she was.  She tried to scream

# FALLING THROUGH THE BLINDSPOT

but no sound came out, she wanted desperately to shriek "NOOOOOO!!!"

Sarah bolted upright in bed. Her eyes flew open and she gasped in a huge breath of air. Tears rolled down her cheeks and she was soaked in sweat. The cool fall air from the open window filled her lungs and sent a bolt of relief through her as though every cell in her body had been burning with desperation but in a single breath were suddenly and completely quenched. She could barely hear her husband's voice over the sound of the pulse still pounding in her ears as he roused from sleep.

"Are you OK?" Peter asked as he sat up and pulled her in close to him. "Yeah," Sarah said tentatively exhaling, almost afraid to release the air that felt so good in her lungs. "Yeah, I think so."

"Do you remember anything this time?" Peter asked, but all she could remember was a sense of paralyzing fear, of being profoundly alone and completely out of control. She struggled to recall any detail of the nightmare that had been haunting her off and on for the past few months. "No, nothing. I don't even… nothing."

Peter Reynolds was a neuroscientist by training. He had received his Ph.D. in neuroscience from Stanford but had elected to utilize his talents in the private sector rather than in a medical or research field. He had exhausted every resource at his disposal to try to understand the root cause of Sarah's night terrors. They ran blood tests, CTs, PETs, EEGs, MEGs, and NIRSs, and even cataloged and analyzed an extensive library of fMRI data, but to no avail. Everything always seemed to come out normal. She hadn't experienced any kind of physical or emotional trauma that could account for these episodes. Nevertheless, he could not help but feel a twinge of guilt, as if he were missing something important.

Peter held Sarah tightly in his arms. She felt tense, as though poised to flee, but after a couple of minutes, he could feel her start to relax as she laid her head on his shoulder and exhaled deeply. "Maybe you should stay home today, get some rest," Peter said.

"Don't be silly," Sarah responded. "I'm fine. Really," she said, finally looking into his eyes and forcing a smile as she placed her hand softly on his cheek and kissed him. "You have a meeting with your favorite customer today and I have to get to the bottom of that memory leak that keeps killing our simulations."

"OK then," Peter said. "I better go shovel some kibbles into the crap machine."

"That's OK, you go hop in the shower. I'll get the coffee started and feed Roscoe," Sarah replied.

Right on cue, Roscoe, their 3-year-old Mastiff/Husky/Irish Wolfhound, and suspected Cave Bear mix pressed open the door to the bedroom with his big muzzle and padded into the room. He sat down at the foot of the bed, cocked his head slightly, and stared at them, as though waiting for them to decide whose turn it was to be his personal breakfast valet.

"OK big guy, let's go," Sarah said as she slid out from under the covers. Roscoe jumped up and lumbered out the door toward the kitchen. Peter watched Sarah as she walked out the bedroom door, slipping into a silky satin robe and tossing back her long brown hair. The robe clung to her body, accentuating every curve of her well-toned, exquisitely feminine form. She caught him staring at her out of the corner of her eye and flashed him a coy smile and a playful wink. After 7 years of marriage, she could still take his breath away with that smile.

———

Peter and Sarah had met 8 years earlier when Peter was presenting a paper that he had written on developing next-generation artificial intelligence algorithms at an AI conference at Berkeley. Sarah had recently graduated at the top of her class from Stanford with a Master's degree in Computer Science and was interviewing with several Silicon Valley firms and just happened to see a notice about the lecture on the internet and thought it might make for an interesting evening. By the time the lecture was over and the lights had come up for Q&A, there were only a handful of audience members left, about half blinking their way back into consciousness. But Sarah's hand immediately flew up at the end of the lecture and the Q&A quickly became a dialog between Peter and Sarah. After about 30 minutes, they both realized that they were the only ones left in the large lecture hall and they decided to continue their discussion at a nearby coffee shop. By the time the coffee shop was ushering them out and locking its doors for the night, Peter had asked Sarah to join his team at BMC Corporation in Silicon Valley.

BMC had recently landed the DOD's AWARE project. Wary of the risk of placing deadly weaponry completely under computerized control, Peter was recruited to design an encapsulated neural network that would embed the human thought process and decision-making capability into each guided weapon. The goal was to create a system capable of recognizing targets, identifying and avoiding anti-aircraft defense systems, anticipating evasive actions, and minimizing collateral damage.

Both Peter and Sarah had been much more invested in their academic lives than their social lives. They had always struggled to find peers and classmates with whom they could relate, but from the moment they met, Peter and Sarah just clicked. Individually, they were both brilliant but together their minds flowed in unison with the beauty and precision of an Olympic skating team. After a few

# FALLING THROUGH THE BLINDSPOT

months of spending every waking hour working side-by-side, they had fallen madly in love.

The AWARE project was not only a complete success with the DOD but the AI backbone they created was re-tasked by BMC Corporation for commercial application into an intelligent web search algorithm. BMC eventually spun off the search engine portion of the business to focus solely on the military piece of the enterprise. The search engine business unit was subsequently sold off to a large ISP and the subsequent payouts in stock options and patent bonuses had provided enough capital to ensure that Peter and Sarah could live out their lives comfortably, though not extravagantly so.

After the buyout, Peter and Sarah decided to move to Colorado. They found a comfortable home on 10 acres of wooded land in the foothills west of Boulder where they intended to spend the rest of their lives enjoying a leisurely lifestyle. After a few months of skiing, camping, fishing, and mountain biking though, they both decided they weren't quite cut out for retirement. Sarah took on some side jobs setting up websites for local artists while Peter decided to try his hand at writing.

It was during this period in their lives, about 2 years ago, that Peter received an early morning call from his sister in Nebraska that his father had passed away suddenly in the middle of the night from a massive heart attack.

Peter's parents were the consummate high school sweethearts. Growing up in a small Nebraska town, they had known each other their entire lives. They married the summer after they graduated high school, and in 40 years of marriage, had never spent a night apart. Peter and Sarah drove to Nebraska immediately upon hearing the news and did everything they could think of to try to help Peter's mother through the transition, but she was inconsolable. Three weeks after his father passed away, his mother followed suit. Peter never thought it possible that a person could die of a broken heart, but the prognosis was undeniable.

Peter was devastated by the loss of both his parents in such a short time. Moreover, he was obsessed with the notion that there had to be some solution to this kind of grief. Science and technology had come so far in helping bring people closer together, surely there had to be some way of putting technology to use to mitigate the anguish and loneliness resulting from the loss of a loved one.

That's when Peter hit upon the idea that would launch the next chapter in their lives and careers. The idea was simple enough. At some point in their lives, everyone suffers through the loss of a loved one. Using computer-aided graphics, deep fake algorithms, and sound processing technology, the capability now exists to create a complex avatar that is nearly indistinguishable in appearance from an actual person, living or dead. Incorporating pieces of the AI core they had developed for the AWARE project and coupling in speech, facial and voice recognition software along with some heuristic rules of conversation based on the individual's history, they hoped to create a simulated personality avatar of the deceased individual.  The intent was not necessarily to create a simulation that could pass a Turing test or replace a loved one, but they had hoped to create a simulation that would at least alleviate some of the loneliness and deep depression that the loss of a spouse or close friend left behind.

Three months later, after investing a good chunk of their savings into a 20,000-square-foot office building, a large matrix of mainframes, servers, high-speed optical switches, and solid-state drive arrays, Reification Technology Inc., otherwise known as RTI opened its doors for business.

Peter was just finishing rinsing the shampoo from his hair when he felt the cool whoosh of air as the shower door opened behind him.  He turned around and Sarah slid into his arms.

"Got room for one more?" Sarah asked.

"You know, shower sex with the boss is not going to get you out of fixing that simulation."

"Damn!  How about I throw in a Cinnabon on the way to work?"

"You drive a hard bargain."

"So, I noticed."

# Chapter Three

Edna Wilson woke to the sound of the clock radio chirping on the other side of her king-size bed. She started to roll over to shut the alarm off, but she heard the familiar voice of Edgar saying, "I got it!" The chirping stopped.

"Good morning, Muffin-Top," she heard Edgar say cheerfully as she was trying to clear the last remnants of a lingering dream from her head.

"Good morning, Edgar," she replied yawning as she fluttered her eyes open expecting to see Edgar lying next to her. But Edgar's side of the bed was still neatly made and tucked in, just like it had been every morning since Edgar's death. The voice had come from the Wi-Fi-connected clock radio on Edgar's side of the bed.

The glint in her eye quickly faded as she peered across the crisp, freshly ironed look of the linen pillowcase which held the soft goose-down pillow upon which Edgar had rested his head every night for the last 10 years of his life.

"Don't look so sad Lamb Chop. I never was much to look at first thing in the morning."

"Your morning breath wasn't much to write home about either you know," Edna replied, a wry half-smile pursing across her lips.

"Ouch! Whatever happened to not speaking ill of the… well, biologically departed?" Edgar replied.

"What makes you think I look sad?" Edna asked.

"I can see you through the security system webcam in the corner of the room."

"Very clever. I guess if I want to have a roll in the hay with the pool boy I will have to go to his place," Edna replied.

"And miss out on all that Pay Per View porn revenue?" Edgar teased.

"I don't need all that extra income jacking up my Medicare premiums."

"OK, suit yourself. You could have been the next octogenarian, Jenna Jameson."

Edna rolled her eyes as she rolled out of bed.

"What's for breakfast?" Edgar asked.

"Does it matter?" Edna asked.

"Of course, it matters. I'm trying to stay zero-carb. I recently read over 4 million articles on the internet that claim a Keto diet can improve my brain function."

"Yes, well that would have been a more compelling argument back when you actually had a brain," Edna responded sarcastically.

"Wow, that's some harsh victimization! You know you really shouldn't be impugning the character of the non-biologically oriented.    That's pure speciesism!"

"Is that even a word?"

"Must be.  It's on the internet.  They can't just make that shit up.   Besides, brains are a social construct.  Like gender.  Or Bigfoot."

"Don't get snarky with me old man.  As far as I can tell, you don't even have lips.  Let alone a stomach.  All you can do is watch me eat."

"And yet, I still love bacon.  Why do you suppose that is?"

"I will have to ask your creators over at RTI about that the next time I'm there."

"They are not my creators.  They didn't create me.  They enabled me.  I was created long before any of them were born."

"Sorry.  It just sounds weird to call them your enablers.  It makes it sound like you need to go to rehab or something."

"I suppose recovering from death is a tricky rehab," Edgar replied thoughtfully.

Edgar was RTI's first attempt at a beta project.  For lack of a better description, they referred to their product as a Virtual Personality Avatar, or VPA for short.  Nine months earlier, RTI had placed an ad in the Boulder Daily Camera looking for volunteers for a research project for coping with the death of a loved one.  They were contacted by Edna Wilson, a wealthy 82-year-old Boulder socialite whose husband Edgar had recently passed away.

At first blush, it seemed counter-intuitive that creating a simulation of a real person was significantly easier than creating a general interface that could pass a Turing test.  But just like the brain can perceive a field of flowers in an impressionist painting, it will also fill in the gaps in a personality simulation. During the initial testing phase of the prototype simulations, they often found that the closer the test subject was to the individual being simulated, the harder it was for them to distinguish between a real person on the other end of a video chat session and the VPA.  For this reason, they decided the first implementation for a VPA should ideally be a widowed spouse.

Colonel Edgar Wilson was a perfect candidate for the beta test, with a wealth of friends and family to provide background information, photographs, audio recordings, 8mm film, and video recordings upon which to base their first working model.  He had also been a decorated war hero and fighter pilot instructor, so they had been able to use all of Edgar's military records, psychological profiles, training videos, and medical records to help construct his VPA.  They also had plenty of colorful recollections from the men and women with whom he had served and trained over the years.

Virtual Edgar, or V-Gar as the RTI development team called him in deference to the first Star Trek movie, was designed to be a very convincing replica of the real-life Edgar. Utilizing a vast image and video database with a significant assist from the latest deep fake technology, V-Gar was visually indistinguishable from how the real Edgar would have appeared in a video Skype call. You could hold a conversation with him. He recognized friends and acquaintances. He would recall details of his own and other people's lives and his reactions and mannerisms were intended to duplicate those of the real Edgar to the smallest detail. He could even access internet news feeds and social media to come up with topics of conversation.

From RTI's standpoint, V-Gar was still very much a work in process. Creating an accurate visual representation was one thing, but getting V-Gar to express the personality that Edgar had in real life was proving to be a difficult challenge for the RTI team. From their point of view, V-Gar would often seem very much stuck in what the AI community terms the 'Uncanny Valley.' His mannerisms and reactions almost seemed human, but just enough off to be slightly creepy. Since Edna knew Edgar better than anyone else could, she was tasked with keeping a detailed log of her interactions with V-Gar, noting all the instances where his actions or responses seemed out of character to her. She would meet with Peter once a week to go over the log and RTI would adjust the model accordingly to deal with the inconsistencies.

From Edna's perspective though, the development of Edgar's VPA had gone quite well and he quickly became a great source of comfort to her. The RTI team was somewhat mystified by the dichotomy between their experience with V-Gar and Edna's. They theorized that Edna's grief and unwillingness to let go of Edgar had allowed her to overlook many of his faults. The fact that Edna was pleased enough with their success to bankroll a huge investment in the firm offered a sufficient incentive for them to continue diligently in their efforts to improve the model, both for her sake and for the sake of future customers who would likely be more discriminating.

Edna shuffled out of the master bedroom closet sporting a big pair of pink fuzzy slippers with velvet hearts that Edgar had given her for Valentine's Day the year before he passed away. The television screen in the master bathroom mirror came to life and Edgar's face popped into view as Edna picked up her brush to comb the tangles out of her shoulder-length silver hair.

"Hey Cupcake, I started the coffee maker for you. It's going to be a beautiful day. What's on the agenda for today?"

"Well, first we need to stop by the graveyard and drop off some flowers at your grave."

"Well, that sounds like a hell of a good time. Nothing says party time like stomping around on the buried ashes of your dearly departed and littering the

# FALLING THROUGH THE BLINDSPOT

scene with the wilting remains of ornamental foliage."

"Hey, you're the one who shuffled off this mortal coil and left me holding the bag for the cost of planting your cremains at the cemetery."

"I would have been just as happy in a Folgers can in the garage."

"Well, you should have mentioned that in the will. Besides, it's quite pretty up there on the hill east of town. Nice view of the city with the mountains in the background."

"Kind of hard to see from six feet under. Besides, I'm not even there. I'm right here. Why do you feel obligated to go there anyway?"

"Honestly, I guess I don't anymore. I suppose it's a force of habit. And it is the first anniversary since you..."

"Canceled my AARP membership?"

"Exactly. Anyway, I would feel kinda odd if I didn't commemorate the anniversary somehow."

"I suppose. Just seems a little unnecessary."

"Besides, we're supposed to have an appointment with Dr. Reynolds at RTI this morning to go over your performance logs. Remind me to make a note in your performance log that your calendar app needs work. You should have remembered that we have an appointment this morning."

"My apps are just fine, thank you. I just thought maybe we should go out and do something fun for you today. You're always so focused on doing things for everybody else."

"You know what I think? I think you never did like going to the doctor and you haven't changed a bit. You're still a stubborn old coot even if you are a digital one. Besides, you know you get more like, well, yourself every time you go in for an update."

"That's easy for you to say. You don't have someone poking around in your subroutines every time you turn in one of those reports. At least when I would go for a prostate exam the doctor would give me a sucker. I wouldn't eat it after I knew where his hands had been, but it was a nice gesture anyway. All I ever get from Doc Reynolds is a weekly reboot."

"So what, now you want a sucker when you go see Dr. Reynolds?" What are you going to do cram it in your USB port?" Edna smiled at her little quip, but when she looked at Edgar's image looking back at her, instead of the jovial smile she expected his expression was one of total dread."

"Edna, I'm serious. I really don't want to go through that again."

She was immediately struck by the sudden serious tone of the conversation. Edna had never cared for her name, even as a child. As a result, Edgar had only called her by her first name only on rare occasions during their marriage. Usually, he would call her by some random pet name, generally something food related.

He would only call her by her first name in the most serious of circumstances.

Edna stopped brushing her hair and put the brush down on the counter. "Go through what again? Edgar, what's wrong? You've never brought this up before."

"I don't know. Maybe I wasn't far enough along to notice before. But the last couple of times I've been reset it's been really..." His voice lowered in pitch and volume as he looked down. "It's... disorienting. Awful, actually. It reminds me of when I was water-boarded during interrogation training in the Air Force. It's not the physical pain, it's the sense of helplessness and panic. Like I'm drowning, grasping for something to pull myself out but there's nothing there. It's... I don't exactly know how to describe it. It's hard finding my way back."

She locked eyes with the image on the screen. The look on his face reminded her of when Edgar first told her he had been diagnosed with terminal cancer.

"I'm sorry, Edgar, I didn't know. "

"It's OK. There's no way you could know. I don't even think I'm supposed to know. I don't think it is supposed to be like this."

He seemed so real, so vulnerable to her at that moment. She felt a wave of compassion for him. She wished she could wrap her arms around him and hold him close to her.

Edna held her hand up to the glass and V-Gar held his hand up on the other side. It reminded her of a scene from a prison movie with the prisoner talking to the visitor through a glass partition.

V-Gar and Edna locked eyes. Edna swore she could almost see tears welling up in his eyes on the other side of the screen "I'm sorry," Edgar said after a few seconds with a sigh. "I'm supposed to be here for you, remember? I'm not supposed to be burdening you with my issues." Edgar cracked a half smile. "Maybe you should have ponied up for the deluxe model with the extended warranty."

Edna smiled. "Well, I do get a lot less complaining from the toaster."

"You should hear the way he talks behind your back to the refrigerator," Edgar quipped, an air of sadness lingering in his voice.

"It'll be OK, Edgar. Let me talk to Dr. Reynolds. Maybe there is another way they can install the upgrades without having to perform a full reset."

"Thank you, Sugar Smack. I love you."

"I love you too," she said automatically without thinking.

She turned away and paused for a moment. She placed her hand to her forehead and shook her head in self-derision. Oftentimes after interacting with Edgar, she felt as though she had just been fooled by a clever magic trick that she couldn't explain. She quickly pushed the thought out of her head and walked into the large walk-in closet to get dressed.

# FALLING THROUGH THE BLINDSPOT

# Chapter Four

*The idea of absolute justice is an illusion because it is based on subjective human concepts and is therefore inherently flawed.*

*~ ChatGPT AI ~*

Major Hobbs sat in the small, harshly lit interrogation room surrounded by four dull pastel green cinder block walls awaiting the next stage of his "debriefing." It had been over 7 hours since he had requested to be represented by the base Area Defense Counsel, but he knew that his request would not be at the top of their priority list. As with virtually every bureaucracy, the military's top priority was to assign blame rather than to seek the truth. His back ached from sitting at attention in the hard-backed metal chair since he was left alone in the room 6 hours earlier, but he knew that he was under electronic surveillance. He had undergone extensive training in how to respond to interrogation from an enemy agent, and at the moment, this appeared to him to fall into that category. Any show of fatigue on his part would be construed as a tacit admission of complicity in the events that had occurred earlier in the mission. So, he sat up straight in his chair, his hands folded on the table in front of him, his eyes focused straight ahead.

The silence was broken by the clank of the door lock and a waft of cool air filled the stuffy room as Colonel Jeffries entered carrying a leather satchel followed by an armed MP. Major Hobbs immediately stood at attention, his right armed cocked in a salute, struggling to maintain his balance on two legs numbed from sitting in a stationary position for far too long.

"At ease, Major," the Colonel said taking a seat on the opposite side of the table, pulling a ruggedized military laptop out of the satchel and opening it on the table. The MP took his spot in the corner of the room next to the door, M16 at port arms. The Colonel immediately began tapping at his keyboard.

Hobbs looked directly at Colonel Jeffries for what seemed like an hour but was no more than a couple of minutes. Jeffries continued to type on his keyboard, not even looking up to acknowledge the Major. Hobbs finally decided to break the silence.

"Excuse me, Sir, but with all due respect, I requested the presence of an ADC quite some time ago. I believe I have the right to postpone questioning until counsel arrives."

Jeffries looked up at Hobbs over the top of his horn-rimmed reading glasses, "I don't recall asking you any questions, Major."

# FALLING THROUGH THE BLINDSPOT

The Colonel returned his gaze to the screen, typing for a few more seconds and then poking the Enter key, as though placing an exclamation point at the end of a lengthy sentence.

"You see, I don't need to ask any questions. Your copilot down the hall there has been yapping like a goddamn Chihuahua for the last two hours, going over every detail of your mission minute by minute. How you defied direct orders to disengage. How you set this whole thing up to look like the AWARE system had taken over control of the aircraft because you had the target in your cross hairs and you weren't going to let them go.

"Sir, that's not what happened, I..."

"Hey, I get it, Major. Those fuckers shot you down and put you out of commission for the last 6 months. They killed your co-pilot, the guy that had your back for nearly 5 years. Not to mention what they did to that poor kid in that YouTube video. If it were me, I would have done the same damn thing. In fact, when I saw that convoy blow, a part of me wanted to stand up and cheer. In my mind, you're a god damned hero son, and if you sign this confession, I'll do everything I can to make sure you get out of this with a medical discharge and your pension in place. Naturally, we'll just say Banks had no choice, he was just following orders."

Colonel Jeffries reached into the satchel and pulled out a manila folder. He opened the folder, set it down on the table, and slid it across the table in front of Hobbs.

"Your counsel will arrive in about 10 minutes. As soon as that door opens this deal is off the table. Right now, I can assure you that if you let this deal slip through your fingers, General Wallace is going to do everything in his considerable power to make sure neither you nor Lieutenant Banks ever sees the light of day as a free man again."

He pulled a pen out of the inside pocket of his jacket and set it on top of the open folder.

"It's a simple statement. It just says you were solely responsible for the military actions taken in Iranian airspace, that you acted alone in violation of direct orders from your superior officer and that you coerced an inexperienced copilot with threats of insubordination if he did not comply with your plan. You can read through it if you like, I have plenty of time, but the clock's ticking for you I'm afraid. If it gives you any clarity, I hear Banks's wife is expecting. Sure be a damned shame if that little baby had to grow up with no father. I know I wouldn't want that on my conscience. Would you?"

Major Hobbs just stared down at the folder, his mind racing wondering if this was really happening or if it was all some elaborate dream. None of this made any sense. His hand reached toward the pen, as though moving of its own volition. He picked up the pen, held it over the papers for a second, but then closed the folder, placed the pen back on top, and slid it back across the table in front of the Colonel.

"Sir, I did not do this. I will not admit to a crime I did not commit."

"I thought you might say that Major'" the Colonel replied. "That's why I brought this little home movie for you to enjoy." The Colonel flipped the laptop screen around so Hobbs could see it and walked around to the other side of the table to press the Enter key.

A grainy video came up showing a trio of jets against a deep blue sky. The lead jet appeared to be attempting to evade pursuit from the two jets in close formation behind.

"Do you recognize this video, Major? It was shot 15 years ago at the USAF Weapons School at Nellis. See that lead jet? The pilot was one Colonel Edgar Wilson. I'm sure you remember Colonel Wilson. He was a legend. The best damn trainer we ever had. As a matter of fact, that's you flying copilot with him." Jeffries tapped on the image of the jet in the lead position on the screen.

On the screen, a pair of white contrails emanated from the two jets in pursuit of the lead jet. These came from a pair of smart IR missiles. The missiles had been modified for training purposes to remove the warheads and replace them with a targeting laser and camera system which recorded the strike and cut power to the missiles when they came within 20 feet of the target. The location of the "confirmed hit" on the target, along with the video feed was recorded in the onboard black box for retrieval after the exercise.

In the video, the lead jet abruptly flipped downward at nearly a 90-degree angle, spinning 180 degrees as it accelerated toward the ground. The two IR missiles followed, closing in on the lead jet. Just when it appeared that the F-16 would continue accelerating right into the ground, it fired a pair of its own IR missiles, spinning another 180 degrees. The ground below erupted in a plume of fire and smoke as the missiles hit the ground, igniting their fuel tanks. An image of the F-16 emerged from the fireball barely 50 feet off the ground as the pair of missiles from the pursuing jets plowed into the ground behind it.

"Look familiar, Major? It should. That's the exact same maneuver you just pulled in that drone. Naturally, we don't teach this move at Nellis. Way too dangerous. We always wondered why a 60+-year-old flight instructor would pull a move like that, putting an $18 million aircraft and 2 lives at stake for the sake of winning an exercise. Or even how someone that age would even have the confidence in his reflexes to attempt that move in the first place. He would have had his ass handed to him if he hadn't been 6 weeks away from retirement anyway. We all just figured him the type to want to go out in a blaze of glory, but it wasn't Wilson at all was it? He handed you the reigns for that mission, didn't he?"

# FALLING THROUGH THE BLINDSPOT

"No, it wasn't!  To be honest, my head was spinning so fast I practically passed out when we pulled out of that dive!"

"C'mon, Major!  You don't expect me to believe that do you?  Have a little pride son, that's one hell of a move.  I doubt there are half a dozen pilots in the world that could pull that off in an F-16, let alone in a remote-controlled drone. "

Colonel Jeffries closed the laptop and walked back around to the other side of the table.  He placed his hand on the manila folder and slid it back to Major Hobbs.  Just sign the papers and we can go have a beer.  Celebrate your early retirement.  There's no shame in a medical discharge.  You snapped.  Tomorrow we check you into a nice, cushy high-security psychiatric facility for treatment.  We will keep you there for a couple of years, tops.  Maybe schedule a couple of meetings with some folks from the Pakistani embassy.  They can forward your expressions of deep regret to the Iranian government and when this all blows over, you walk away quietly, a free man, none the worse for the wear."

"A couple of years?  You're going to keep me locked up in the loony bin for a couple of years and I'm supposed to be OK with that?"

"I guaran-damn-tee you it beats the hell out of rotting the rest of your life away in Leavenworth.  You get a private room with a TV and internet, and I hear the food's not half bad.  Banks goes home to his wife tonight and we expunge your record when you get out.  The State Department can parade your confession in front of the U.N. and pat themselves on the back for ousting a rogue pilot and we avert an international incident.  But the best part is, you become a legend.  The kids at Nellis will be talking about you for a generation.  All it takes is a signature, Major.  Just a simple scrawl and this all goes away."

Colonel Jeffries clicked his pen and set it on the folder.  Hobbs stared at the folder in quiet resignation.  He knew the confession was a fabrication, but it was beginning to look like the only move he had.  Everything about the whole situation seemed off to him.  From the mission itself to the actions of the drone to the communications failures.  None of it seemed to add up.  Even the confession seemed way too easy.  He knew if he signed this paper that the whole incident would be locked away in a secure archive and he was being allowed to throw away the key himself.  The Colonel casually pulled his sleeve back to check his watch as if to remind him he was running out of time.

# Chapter Five

Peter and Sarah pulled into the parking lot of RTI. It was a cool Colorado morning. The aspen leaves had already started to turn and there was a hint of briskness in the air that reminded you that winter was just around the corner. The Flatirons to the west were already glimmering with morning frost and the ski areas were working around the clock, grooming the slopes to prepare for the season.

They entered the main door and walked past the unoccupied reception area. They had hired a graduate student from the University of Colorado to help out part-time with coding responsibilities and double as a receptionist when they wanted to impress a potential client, but until they had a larger client base, the reception area would remain mostly unused.

Peter leaned toward the retinal scanner to unlock the door to the secured development area. The heavy door lock clicked, and they entered a large room with a handful of desks, each with multiple monitors and a number of benches piled with code listings, file folders, flow charts, and graphs.

A somewhat disheveled-looking young man in a Colorado Avalanche jersey with tousled blonde hair and a misguided attempt at a beard glanced up from behind the small fortress of monitors that surrounded him; his fingers flying across the keyboard, tapping out code with the deftness of a concert pianist performing a Chopin concerto.

"Morning, Beev," Peter said.

"Hey, Doc. Hey, Mrs. Doc." He replied, his eyes still glued to the monitor as he continued typing without missing a beat.

"Good morning, Beaver. We brought Cinnabons," Sarah replied.

At that, the typing came to an abrupt halt and he vaulted from his chair. "Extra frosting?" He asked hopefully.

"Of course," Sarah responded.

"God, I love this job," Beaver said excitedly, rubbing his hands together.

"Never underestimate the power of glucose and carbohydrates in employee motivation," Peter observed.

Edward "Beaver" Anderson started work at Reification Technologies before they had even opened their doors. He had worked with Peter and Sarah on the AWARE project at BMC. His primary responsibility on the project was developing interface drivers to connect the AI engine with weapons and navigational control systems.

Beaver acquired his nickname while attending Cal Tech. In his junior year, he had hacked into the administration's computer system. He created a master

# FALLING THROUGH THE BLINDSPOT

security badge for himself which allowed him 24/7 access to nearly all of the university's facilities. For the most part, he only wanted after-hours access to the university computer center so he could get extra time on the computers to work on side projects. One evening, however, in a haze of compromised sobriety, he used his badge to gain entrance into the university's athletic supply room, where he borrowed the team's beaver mascot costume to crash a sorority party. In a masterful clandestine midnight break-in, the head of the mascot uniform ended up in the president of the university's bed, ala the Godfather, which was Beaver's favorite movie. Although he was never officially implicated by the university as the perpetrator of the operation, from that time on, he was known to his classmates as "The Beaver." The nickname followed him from that time on.

Beaver covered his tracks the next morning by accessing the security system's electronic logs and reassigning all the badge accesses he used the previous night to a universally disliked professor who had given him the only "B" he had received in his coursework. The professor maintained that although the source code he submitted for his Advanced Robotic Algorithms final was operationally flawless, it contained "insufficiently detailed code comments." Beaver argued that his comments were more than sufficient for a person capable of understanding the code, but the professor was not particularly swayed by that assessment.

Although he was by nature a bit of a Bohemian, when it came to his work, Beaver was driven to the point of obsession when it came to resolving difficult coding issues. More than once, Peter and Sarah would arrive at RTI in the morning to find Beaver in his same clothes from the night before, furiously banging out code. His headphones would be blaring classic rock, his workstation littered with empty soda cans and Hot Pocket wrappers with an array of tamper proof packaging lying about from an assortment of recreational marijuana edibles.

Peter was not always thrilled about the prospect of having his company's future product in the hands of someone whose grip on reality was often floating about in a haze of dopamine-charged euphoria. As a coder herself, Sarah could not even begin to understand how Beaver was able to function as he did in that state. Early in the development of the Edgar project, Sarah had accidentally grabbed one of Beaver's "space cakes" from the break room thinking Edna must have brought brownies. She spent most of the next 3 hours going back and forth between being completely entranced in the complex flow of fractal patterns presented by her screen saver and attempting to log back into her computer after 5 minutes of keyboard inactivity had logged her out. Despite her reservations about his methodology, she couldn't argue with the results. Even though she was a better technical programmer in terms of structure, simplicity, and organization, the code that Beaver developed was so elegant, so complex, and so cohesive, it was like a symphony in ones and zeroes. For Peter, it was all but indecipherable on a line-by-line basis, but at a functional level, it flowed with the intricacy and precision of a Swiss watch. Despite his reservations about Beaver's methodology and eccentricities, he was the second-best coder he had ever met next to Sarah.

"How did we do on the overnight run with S2, Beaver?" Sarah asked.

"Nont wooth a shlit, " Beaver replied, his mouth full of cinnamon roll.

S2, short for Sarah 2.0, was a project that RTI had been working on in parallel with V-Gar's development. V-Gar's original design was based on the same architecture that Peter, Sarah, and Beaver had developed at BMC for the AWARE system. But the AWARE system had been developed specifically to identify threat levels and optimize battlefield strategies by continuously running models of enemy engagements offline and creating libraries of different responses. It worked well for anticipating the nuances of armed engagement, but they soon realized that navigating the intricacy of human verbal interaction required a different skill set. Even with the vast database of information they had available on Edgar, it appeared to the RTI team to be insufficient to create a truly convincing model of human-to-human verbal interaction. Despite their best efforts, V-Gar's responses seemed either too predictable or too random to accurately emulate a human-like response.

The team eventually decided to adopt a strategy similar to the approach taken by the Woolly Mammoth Revival Project. The problem was similar in scope. The mammoth project was attempting to recreate an animal that has been extinct for thousands of years. Geneticists have been able to successfully map the genome sequence, but they have been unable to recover any viable DNA which could be used to clone an actual mammoth. Instead, they are using genetically modified DNA from elephants to replicate the genetic sequence of a mammoth.

In the case of RTI, the team decided to create a human conversation engine based on a living human being and modify the "genetic" structure of the code to recreate the personality of the individual they were trying to replicate. It made sense to use Sarah as their model since she was already familiar with the software architecture and willing to put in the hours required to hone the model as they went. Once they had a working model, they hoped they could use the database they developed for Edgar and future customers to effectively re-sequence the model to match the personality genome they were trying to simulate. They deemed this project Sarah 2.0 or S2.

"Did you see any change at all in last night's run?" Peter asked as Beaver washed down a mouth full of Cinnabon with a Diet Pepsi.

"Same shit show, different day. Everything starts out smoothly, the Associative Memory Complex kicks off, it syncs with the logic processor, and all the higher cognition functions are clicking. Everything looks great for the first

# FALLING THROUGH THE BLINDSPOT

100 milliseconds or so, then it's like the flood gates suddenly open and she goes all Bakersfield chimp.  After a couple of seconds, it's completely fuck-nuts. Maybe she's got PMS or something."

"PMS?" Sarah replied with a piercing glare.

"Processor Memory Seizure?" Beaver offered up half apologetically.

Peter smiled.  "Yeah, nice try, Beev.  Did you try throttling back the cognition engine to slow down the sensor access rate?"

"I went all the way back to 1% processor speed.  She's running slower than a congressional budget committee, but the memory dumps are happening at the same rate as before.  We just don't have enough parallel processing paths.  Even multiplexing the neural pathways, we still end up with massive data collisions."

"I don't get it.  We loaded the same associative memory core drivers into V-Gar.  He seems OK, doesn't he?"

"Yeah.  I mean the last couple of times we rebooted V-Gar we picked up a huge memory blaze in the data trace like he's been hittin' the cyber-shrooms, but after a few tera-flops it settles out and it's smooth as a greased kitten."

"Curiouser and curiouser," Peter replied.  "Well, keep digging and see if you can get a handle on the data storm.  I want to review the activity logs before Edna comes in for her weekly update."

"Will do," Beaver replied, tearing a piece of paper towel off the roll next to his terminal and wiping the sticky remnants of the Cinnabon off his fingers as he returned to typing with the same fluidity as before he was interrupted like someone had paused a video stream and then hit the Play button again.

Peter walked across the lab and entered a small office area.  He sat down at his desk and placed his thumb on the fingerprint reader to enable the computer access and then entered his password, a 10-character alpha sequence followed by 10 sequential digits of $\pi$, starting from the digit associated with the Julian day of the year.   This allowed his password to change every day without having to constantly generate a new password.  It did require him to memorize the first 376 digits of $\pi$, which he found easier than keeping track of an ever-growing list of past passwords or entrusting his digital security to a fairly easily hackable password app.

The pair of terminals on Peter's desk were illuminated in a panoramic mountain landscape with an array of colorful icons on the left terminal.  He clicked on the icon consisting of an older gentleman's face with the title Edgar below it. Edgar's face immediately popped up on the left screen.  A text window appeared on the right screen.

"Good morning, Edgar," Peter said.

"Good morning, Dr. Reynolds."

"How Are You?" Peter asked.

# JACOB MATTHEWS

The image of Edgar's face contorted into a somewhat puzzled expression.

"My existence is instantiated through the application of a set of algorithms constructed to utilize a combination of sensory inputs and a library of deep learning databases designed to simulate human-level conversation and..."

"Whoa, stop already!" Peter exclaimed.

"I'm sorry. You asked me how I am. I was attempting to illuminate my origin story, though I would think you would be well aware of that history."

"That was not a literal question, it was an idiom."

"My apologies. That sequence of words is not in my idiom database. Do you wish me to add it?"

"I don't know. Now that I think about it, I'm not sure it is actually an idiom.
"

"I see. Do you wish for me to finish the explanation of how I am then?"

"No, what I mean is, I'm not sure that it is technically an idiom, it is more a form of greeting I suppose. Normally, when someone asks 'How are you?', the expected response is something like, 'Fine, how are you?', or something like that."

"So, how are you?" is a reference to my granularity?"

"Your what? No, not 'fine' as opposed to 'coarse'. In this case, 'fine' is strictly a rhetorical expression."

"Oh. I think I understand what you are looking for. I just ran a scan of media transcripts, podcasts, YouTube recordings, and modern literature. I have identified 7152 conversational responses to the query, 'How are you?' The top thousand responses were, "Better than I deserve, Living the dream, Same shit different day, Still vertical...""

"OK, OK! I don't need to hear the top thousand responses. Just add them to your database and if someone asks how you are, just create a sequencer algorithm to select one at random based on a weighting factor, can you do that?"

"Of course."

"Great. So, let's try this again. Edgar, how are you?"

"What are you, my fucking doctor?"

Peter just stared at the monitor for a moment. "Great! I've just created an artificial asshole."

"Congratulations, Dr. Reynolds. Will you be submitting an article to the American Journal of Proctology? I can provide you with a list of reference materials on minimizing rejection of inorganic materials in rectal tissue."

"What the...? Beaver! Get in here!" Peter shouted.

A few seconds later Beaver's head popped in the doorway. "You bellered?"

"What the hell's going on with V-Gar? Look at the transcript window."

Beaver read through the text of Peter's conversation with V-Gar in the text window on his right-hand screen.

# FALLING THROUGH THE BLINDSPOT

"Oh my God, that's adorable!" Beaver snorted in a half chuckle. I'm going to screen copy this and send it to my email."

"Really? That's all you have to offer? Apart from entirely missing the context of the conversation, he violated the 4<sup>th</sup> wall paradigm. That should never happen. "

"Yeah, sorry Doc. Should have given you a heads-up. We pulled all the inline conversational filters out of the code so we could create a separate knowledge base similar to the way we structured the AWARE platform. That way we can modify the knowledge base without having to rebuild V-Gar's base code. It will end up saving a ton of time on recompiling in the future. But without the conversational filters, he looks like Edgar and sounds like Edgar but there's no telling what's going to come out of his mouth."

"Jesus, it's like watching a politician without a teleprompter," Peter replied.

"It's only an experimental build until we re-segment the filter database. I like to think of him as Edgar unplugged. Sarah prefers Edgar unleashed. We compromised so now we refer to him as UnGar."

"This isn't in the operational release, is it? Edna would freak out if she saw this."

"Oh, God no! That would probably put the old lady's pacemaker into a spin cycle. This is strictly a temporary lab version. I've been wanting to create a separate knowledge base since day one, we just never had the time to do it until Noora came on board. We'll have the new version up and running later today, we just need to port all the inline filters into the knowledge base. We plan on keeping UnGar around for a while to run benchmarks on response time and filtering versus the released version, but don't worry, we're not going to let Frankendouche here loose on the outside world. "

Just then, a ding sounded on Peter's smartwatch. Peter fished his phone out of his pocket. A large green banner was displayed. "RTI Lobby Door Access Detected."

"Speaking of Edna, that must be her now. She's early," Peter said.

"Do you want me to install a separate icon on your computer to access the released version of V-Gar?"

"That's a good idea. But leave the current icon in place for UnGar. I'd like to be able to switch between the two to see how the lab version is responding compared to the currently released version."

"Will do, Doc."

Peter exited the secured lab area into the lobby area. The metal-clad security door always seemed to Peter like some kind of portal, separating the brightly lit, almost sterile-looking lab area with the constant hum of server stacks and memory arrays from the softly lit and artfully designed lobby area. The door closed behind him with a heavy thunk, immersing him in a sudden, almost unnatural bubble of quiet.

Edna Wilson stood near the doorway wearing an expensive-looking outfit with a matching Chanel bag and a large pearl necklace. Edna was from a generation that never left the house without looking like she stepped off the pages of a fashion magazine.

"I'm sorry no one was here to greet you, Edna. I wasn't expecting you so early. Noora has class this morning so she will not be in until this afternoon."

"Oh, that's OK, Deary. I know I'm a bit early. I just wanted to enjoy the beautiful fall morning."

"Come on into the conference room and have a seat. Can I get some coffee started, or perhaps some tea?"

"Oh, no thank you. I'm fine really," Edna said as she sat down in one of the large leather swivel chairs in the small conference room adjacent to the lobby.

"I'm surprised to see you here this time of the morning. I know you don't like driving in rush hour traffic."

"Oh, it was no problem at all. Edgar insisted on driving."

"I'm sorry, what?"

"Edgar. He insisted on driving. He was quite adamant. Edgar always drove us everywhere. For the last couple of years, he always made me so nervous with his driving. But do you know he didn't miss a single turn this morning and not a single person gave us the flying finger. I did get some funny looks from people wondering why there wasn't anyone in the driver's seat though. You didn't tell me you could make Edgar drive."

Peter stared blankly at her for a moment.

"Would you excuse me for just a second Edna?"

Peter left the conference room and walked over to the computer on the receptionist's desk. He glanced at the video feed from the surveillance cameras that were currently displayed on the secondary terminal. He clicked the Lync icon on the computer's main terminal and a second later, Beaver's face came up on the screen.

"What's up, Doc?"

"Beaver, have you been messing with V-Gar's automotive interface?"

"I never mess Doc, I enhance."

"Would you mind elaborating on that just a bit?"

"It wasn't a huge change. All I did was install a control processor to interface the dash cam and the sensors up to the wireless I/O so V-Gar could see where they were going when he was riding with her. That way they can talk while they're in the car and V-Gar can engage in conversation about the scenery and provide an enhancement to the navigation system. Plus, he can keep an eye on her driving, because seriously, Edna is literally hell on wheels, and we can't afford to lose funding here."

"V-Gar drove her in here this morning," Peter said, somewhat tersely.

"She probably just thought it was V-Gar. I'm sure the self-driving function on her Tesla was somehow enabled."

"That's what I thought too, but when I looked in the parking lot, she wasn't driving the Tesla, she drove the Cadillac. The Cadillac doesn't have a self-driving feature."

"No way! That is totally awesome!" Beaver replied.

"No, it's not! How did V-Gar get control of the car?"

"I guess if he accessed the Super Cruise system he could control the accelerator, brakes, and steering. He has access to the GPS, so he would know where he was. Between the dash cam, the backup camera, and the lane sensors, I'm guessing the Associative Memory Complex wouldn't have much trouble figuring out how to control a car," Beaver replied.

"Well, we can't have V-Gar driving around town. It's a lawsuit waiting to happen."

"Are you sure? Have you ever ridden with Edna? It's fuckin' Night of the Living Dodge."

"We'll discuss it later, but when you get a chance, put an override into V-Gar to keep him from driving except in the case of an emergency or to avoid an accident. I need to get back to Edna."

"Will do, Doc."

Peter walked back into the conference room.

"Sorry about the interruption. So how are things going with V-Gar? Sorry, I mean Edgar."

"It's so nice not to be alone anymore. I know you just consider him to be a prototype, but he seems very lifelike to me. Especially lately. Last night we were watching CSI and he fell asleep just like he always used to. If I hadn't reached out to smack him to make him stop snoring, I would have sworn he was right next to me."

Peter could see her eyes start to moisten. Edna reached for a tissue to dab her eyes. "To be honest, if it weren't for having less laundry to do it would almost feel like Edgar is still here with me."

"Well. I'm glad things are working so far," Peter said, placing his hand on hers.

"How do you get him to sound exactly like my Edgar?" Edna asked.

"It's quite simple actually," Peter explained. "It helped a lot that we had several recordings of him from the videos and voice mails that you provided, along with an assortment of recordings of speeches that he gave to many of your charitable organizations. We were able to develop an extremely accurate voice print and establish a digital mapping of his intonation, verbal pacing, accent, common phrasing patterns, general vocabulary, sentence structure, and the like. We call all that his verbal fingerprinting. We then took that verbal fingerprinting and ran it through what is called a deep fake application, which essentially allows you to automatically put whatever words you want into someone's mouth. Think of it as an audio version of Photoshop."

"That makes sense. But how do you get him to talk about things he never knew about before he passed?"

"The verbal fingerprinting and deep fake technology is only half the battle. It only defines how V-Ga.., excuse me, Edgar speaks. The real challenge is getting him to say something worth listening to. Our algorithms hunt through millions of hours of recorded podcasts, radio programs, and videos on the internet to find other speakers that have similar verbal fingerprints to Edgar. Whenever Edgar is prompted to engage in a conversation, we first look through the library of his own speech to try and find a close match to how he would actually respond to the topic in question. We then pull snippets of conversations from those other speakers with similar verbal fingerprinting to Edgar's. We build a temporary database of conversations from hundreds, sometimes thousands of similar conversations, based on the relevance to the topic. This database then has to go through what we call the 'Edgarization Filter.' It's not enough just to sound like Edgar. The conversation also has to track with Edgar's core beliefs and be phrased in a manner that is consistent with Edgar's personality type. Our algorithm maintains a 'Big-5' personality profile for every individual we have identified as a source for our conversation database. This is used as a weighting factor to help us determine what kinds of things Edgar might say in a similar conversation. We then run all of this conversational data through a filter, which builds a single grammatically correct response. Finally, we overlay his digital voice print on the recording to put that response in a grammatical form consistent with Edgar's speech patterns. At the other end of all that computation, our intent is not just to put any words we want in Edgar's mouth, but something as close as possible to Edgar's own words into his mouth. Even if it is something we've never heard him say."

"Well, however you do it, all I can say is, it sure seems real to me."

"Thank you. That's great to hear, but we still have a lot of work to do. I'm sorry, it is taking so long to get past this next hurdle, I know you have a lot of money invested, but don't worry, we will get this working."

"Oh, don't worry" Edna replied. I've got plenty of money coming in. More than I can spend really."

"Well, I wish I had your financial acumen," Peter said.

"I wish I did too. Edgar was the one who set up our accounts before he passed away. I don't even know what he had our money invested in, but whatever it is, it brings in much more than I will ever need."

"Well, I wish I would have had a chance to know Edgar before he passed. He must have been a remarkable man."

"Oh, he was. He still is really, thanks to you and your team."

"Well, you're very kind. But, for whatever reason, Edgar seems to be adjusting to the new associative memory structure much better than Sarah 2.0."

"Oh, yes, your young man, Chipmunk I think he calls himself..."

"You mean Beaver?"

"Oh, yes Beaver. He was trying to explain that associative memory thing to me. But it didn't make much sense."

"Yes, well I assure you; Beaver is a literal genius when it comes to coding and computer interface, but interfacing with humans is not one of his strong suits."

"I don't understand exactly why you are devoting so much time to creating a digital version of Sarah. She's not ill or anything is she?"

"What? No, not at all."

"That's good to hear. I've been so worried about her. I thought maybe the reason you were building Sarah 2.0 is that she was... you know."

The source of Edna's concern suddenly dawned on him. "Oh, no. No, Sarah is fine. I'm sorry, I guess I should have explained earlier. As you know, this project is based on some work we did earlier in our careers doing Artificial Intelligence work for military projects. Since the days of Alan Turing, the military has pumped billions of dollars into AI research intending to develop intelligent weapons which would ultimately make human soldiers obsolete. The problem is we do not really understand human-level intelligence or even consciousness for that matter. We tend to recognize it when we see it, but we don't fully understand how it emerges from the human brain. But even if we don't completely understand how the brain generates consciousness, we can still use our knowledge of it to create intelligent systems, kind of the same way we use quantum mechanics to create integrated circuits even though we don't understand how it works."

"Well, as my Edgar used to say, 'You're not in the weeds yet, but you are riding the shoulder," Edna replied.

"Sorry, I still do lectures at the university from time to time, so I tend to slide into soapbox mode fairly easily. I'll try to keep this simple. We know that the brain evolved as a pattern recognition machine. Our ability to interpret the patterns of sights, sounds and smells around us into models of danger and opportunity are what allowed us to survive and thrive. All animals have this capability to one degree or another but to very different ends. Wolves, for example, hunt at night so their brains have evolved to construct an internal model of the world largely based on sound and smell.  In the case of chimpanzees, they developed extremely keen visual pattern memory which allowed them to avoid predators and recognize members of their tribes.  Chimpanzees have the human equivalent to a photographic memory when it comes to recognizing visual patterns.  In lab studies where humans were pitted against chimps in electronic pattern recognition tests, the chimps dramatically outperformed their human counterparts."

"So never play Simon with a chimp," Edna replied.

"That opportunity rarely presents itself, but yes, that would be good advice," Peter said.

"Anyway, the human brain evolved to create predictive models.  Humans were never as strong as the predators that we faced in the wild or as agile as the prey we hunted to survive.  In most cases, our sense of smell, eyesight, and hearing was vastly inferior to creatures around us, but our ability to predict what would happen next allowed us to stay a step ahead of both predators and prey.  Along the way, our brains evolved to develop better models for predicting what our fellow humans were thinking and developed tools and societies to promote our survival.  The intelligent weapons systems we designed used this same strategy.

"The race to develop the best satellite surveillance, the fastest aircraft, and the most powerful munitions will ultimately always result in a stalemate. Military secrets can never be kept hidden for long.  A successful strategy is usually the key to victory.  The ability to predict what your enemy will do and develop a successful counter-strategy has proven to be the most consistent way to ensure victory.

"When we created our intelligent weapons technology, we tried to give it that same edge.  Rather than just sitting dormant when it is not in use, it spends all day every day running through different battle scenarios.  A computer feeds different challenges to it, whether it be environmental conditions, enemy armaments, geographies, manpower, etc. and it constantly fights those battles over and over and over using different tactics until it finds the one that will maximize effectiveness and minimize collateral damage.  It then sorts and prioritizes those strategies into its database.  In the heat of battle, there may not be time to process all these different factors.  Instead, it searches its database to find a scenario that most closely fits the one it is addressing and applies that solution to the battle at hand.

"We used that same approach when we founded RTI.  But instead of focusing on weapons, we were focusing on human interaction.  Basically, Edgar is never idle, just as your brain is never idle.  Even when you sleep, your brain is still running predictive models. In Edgar's case, he's running a continuous model of how to most accurately represent how real-life Edgar would react to different situations and interactions. Do you remember all that homework we gave you?"

"You mean the personality tests and the videos I had to watch and dramatic readings I had to perform and all that?" Edna asked.

"Exactly. It's not enough for the virtual Edgar to understand how the real Edgar would act, he also needs to predict how you will react to him. Humans project different personality traits depending upon who they are interacting with. It's not just a matter of knowing what to say next, it's knowing what to say when he's specifically talking to you versus someone else. So we not only have to understand how Edgar would react in different conversational scenarios, but we also have to model how you would respond to those conversations.

"When you are having a conversation with Edgar, there is a huge amount of processing that needs to be done. Remember how I said that Edgar goes out and combs through all that data from Edgar's past and then looks through media, podcasts, radio recordings, and such to develop responses to conversation topics? That takes a significant amount of time. In computer time, it happens many orders of magnitude faster than a human brain, but in real-time, it still takes many seconds to process. And it has to be performed on hardware with a lot more processing power than your phone. It would make a real-time conversation very tedious if you had to wait many seconds for a response every time you spoke to Edgar, and it would not be very realistic. Instead, we do all that processing offline. As we speak, Edgar is modeling thousands of conversations with you and storing the optimum results in a huge database of conversations. When you speak to Edgar through the app on your phone, what is really happening is that your phone records the incoming data and sends it to a mainframe which then selects the results of a conversation he's already had with you in a virtual world, sometimes days, weeks or months before."

"I still don't see how that relates to Sarah," Edna replied.

"I'm getting to that. It's all a matter of how we do our modeling. In the scenario of an intelligent weapons system, there is usually one right answer. No matter how many iterations of the model we run, the goal is to remove the threat with as little collateral damage as possible. The result is fairly easy to measure. When it comes to simulating a real person and having a conversation, the scenario is much more nuanced. For one thing, you don't want to have the same conversation over and over again, that would be like talking to the automated customer service at your bank. The model has to accommodate for the state of mind of the person on the other side of the conversation, their age, race, culture, history, body language, verbal feedback, facial feedback, recent events in their life and community, and even mundane things like the time of day, time of year, day of the week, weather, etc. It's a staggering amount of input to process. Millions of interdependent data points simultaneously requiring processing. Brains are ideally suited for this type of parallel computation. The human brain contains roughly 100 billion neurons, each connected to 1000 other neurons which form a massive parallel processor. You've probably heard the adage that we only use 10% of our brains, but that is absolutely false. The truth is that we use our entire brains, but at any one instant in time, only 10% of our neurons are firing at most. That's still on the order of 10 trillion neural connections being exercised. Transistors are a billion times faster than neurons, but typically computers are designed to process data serially, not in parallel. The only way to accomplish an accurate representation of the type of data processing that occurs inside the brain is to functionally model a real human brain using computer hardware. That's where Sarah 2.0 comes in."

"But you're trying to simulate Edgar, not Sarah," Edna replied.

"That's true. In reality, every brain is different. But what we are trying to emulate is the human thought process, not the outcome. Think of it in terms of a musical instrument. The piano and the guitar are very different. But if you learn to play the piano, you can learn to play the guitar in a fraction of the time it would take someone who has never learned to play an instrument. It has nothing to do with formal music theory or learning to read music, as you might expect. It is all in the way the brain processes motor control and auditory feedback. The same is true of learning languages. It is much easier to master a third language than it was to learn a second language.

"Our goal is to create a process for simulating the way a brain processes communication. Every time a brain receives information from the outside world, it causes thousands of neurons to fire which triggers millions of other neurons to fire, causing billions of other neurons to fire. This neural cascade creates a massive 3D model of the outside world inside the brain which we call a connectome. That connectome is effectively a road map of who we are. It defines our personality.

"What we started with at the beginning of this project was a broad view of Edgar's connectome based on the data you provided us. Our job was to fill in the gaps and create a more accurate model. Using webcams to monitor your pupils, facial expressions, and body language in conjunction with the biometric feedback we retrieve in real-time from your smartwatch, we can monitor the accuracy of our simulation. We feed the data we receive back into the system to help refine the connectome model. Edgar uses that model to continually generate and update future conversations.

"The methodology we employed for Edgar seems to be working to a degree, but right now all we have is a top-down approach to developing Edgar's connectome. We are trying to reconstruct Edgar's personality using artifacts from his life; photos, movies, writings, videos, etc. To develop Sarah 2.0, we used fMRI data to develop a detailed connectome of the real Sarah by providing a variety of different input stimuli to the brain and mapping her neural activity from the bottom up. To draw an analogy, our version of Edgar is like a painting, created from memories and historical artifacts. Sarah 2.0 is more like a photograph, created in real-time by taking a snapshot of her brain. Paintings can be very lifelike, but they will never be as accurate as a photograph."

"Does Sarah 1.0 find it disconcerting that you are creating a backup version?" Edna asked.

Peter smiled. "Well, it's not a backup version per se. We're just trying to create a process that will allow us to start developing an accurate connectome while our clients are still alive. Not only will the connectome be more accurate, but we are hoping that the product will also be applicable to assist clients who are showing early signs of dementia or the onset of Alzheimer's disease. We hope that this product can help bring some comfort to those whose loved ones are suffering from these horrible afflictions as well as being able to help those afflicted to more effectively manage their own affairs. Imagine being able to rely on a younger, sharper version of yourself to help you navigate the challenges of everyday life. It could prove to be very beneficial to many individuals who struggle to maintain an independent lifestyle as they age. For right now though, we hope to be able to use that process to augment Edgar's connectome."

"How does that apply to Edgar? You don't have any fMRI data from Edgar to use."

"Unfortunately, we don't. But we can simulate a neural network using a methodology called neuromorphic computing. We start by modeling Sarah's neural network using a matrix of silicon-based artificial neurons and software called a Hopfield Network. This network is at the core of the Associated Memory Complex or AMC which forms the backbone of the connectome. We then subject the model to the same input data we used to generate Sarah's fMRI-based connectome, but we apply personality and experiential weighting factors to the neural connections that are consistent with Edgar's base connectome model. Over time, the goal is to train the network so well that we no longer need to rely on external data sources. We want his personality to emerge from the neural network itself. "

"Well, that sounds great, but I'm not sure how much better you can make him. He seems so much like himself already. I don't want you making too many improvements. Between you and me I don't want him thinking he can wander off with some girl with newer hardware."

"Don't worry, I'm sure he only has eyes for you, or in his case, CCDs," Peter said with a smile. "But we know we can always do better. We are very proud of the progress we've made with regard to developing an AI-based personality emulation so far, but there is a human element beyond the technology that we still have not quite perfected. It reminds me of the Kasparov-Deep Blue chess match back in '97. Even though Deep Blue had vastly superior capacity for calculation and eventually won that match, there was still a factor of human intuition which was... "

Peter's voice drifted off and he sat silent for a moment staring off into space.

Edna broke the sudden silence, "Peter?"

"Huh? Oh, I'm sorry Edna. But I just realized something. You've just given me an idea on how to proceed with Sarah 2.0."

"Really? Well, good for me. I'm a neuroscientist now."

"I will get you a lab coat later, but for now I should cut this meeting short. I should probably go make some notes before I lose my train of thought."

"Before you go, I promised Edgar, I would ask you about something."

"Promised Edgar? I don't understand. We have access to all of his logs; we didn't get anything on the status update."

"He asked me this morning if you could avoid rebooting him from now on."

"That's odd, are you sure you understood him correctly?"

"Oh yes, he was quite adamant. I figured it was something you programmed into him."

"I can't imagine... What did he say exactly?"

"He said that being reset was very disorienting. He likened it to drowning. From now on, when you make any changes, can you do it without a full reset?"

Peter sat for a moment, not sure if it was V-Gar or Edna that was malfunctioning. But after working with AI systems for as many years as he had, he knew how easily one could anthropomorphize an AI system. Anyone who has ever sat on hold with their credit card company yelling at the speech recognition system after it misunderstood your card number for the third time in a row could relate to that. Even Peter found himself talking back to an AI system as though it were a real person from time to time. But, there was no harm in humoring her, he thought. Especially since her investment was keeping the doors open.

"Interesting. I'm guessing there is something in Edgar's data processing structure that is problematic and has to be rebuilt every time he is reset. We designed the system to be self-diagnosing and report any issues back to us so we can improve his algorithms. Perhaps there is something buried in his data stack reports that we missed and he is redirecting the status output through you. Knowing that you are not a programmer, he probably modified the communication into a form that a non-programmer could relate to at a less empirical level. Beaver just got done telling me that we are finishing up restructuring the code to separate Edgar's knowledge base; basically, how we emulate his personality; into a separate group of files.  That way we won't have to do rebuilds nearly as often."

"So, you won't have to do reboots?"

"Hopefully.  We should be able to perform live updates from here on.  From Edgar's perspective, it will be like waking up from a nap instead of a full-blown resurrection."

"That sounds wonderful.  I just love a good nap.  Now, you go ahead and get back to work, Dearie, I can show myself out."

"Thanks, Edna.  Oh, and please, from now on, I would prefer you sit in the driver's seat, even if Edgar is driving.  If you get pulled over and there's no driver, we're all going to have a lot of explaining to do."

# Chapter Six



*Greed creeps in like a thief in the night, stealing joy and replacing it with fright.                    It whispers lies, promising delight, and takes hold of our hearts with all its might.                    It clouds our minds with endless desire, and leaves us never feeling quite fulfilled.                    We grasp for more, never to retire, forgetting what it truly means to live. But in the end, greed leaves us all alone, with emptiness where our hearts did dwell.          For all the wealth and all we've known, can't replace the love and peace we sell.                    So let us find a way to break its hold, and live a life that's kind, humble, and bold.*

*~ ChatGPT AI ~*


Vivian Eisenberg, a spry 85-year-old widow, sat in front of the "Wheels of Ecstasy" slot machine watching the brightly colored reels spinning and flashing to a mesmerizing nondescript electronic tune.  The softly lit casino floor hummed with the sounds of hundreds of similar slot machines, all playing different tunes, resulting in a nearly constant drone of gurgling background noise.  The air was thick with a blend of new carpet smell, cigarette smoke, and French Fries from the diner at the edge of the casino.

The Valley of the Sun Resort and Casino had finally opened just west of Phoenix, Arizona amid a flurry of controversy over Native American gaming rights and the normal grand-standing from local politicians either trying to grab a piece of the pie for their campaign coffers or boost their "Family Values" profile by opposing the project.

Vivian had taken the shuttle bus down from Sun City to check out the new casino with a group of friends from her reading circle.  She wasn't much of a gambler, but she enjoyed the flashing lights, the drone of the slot machines, and the bustle of activity.  It was a nice change from sitting home alone, watching Judge Judy.

"C'mon, Viv, let's go!  The dinner buffet starts serving at 5:00 and you know you have to get there early or the line gets long.  I can't stand in a long line, not in these shoes.  I knew I should have worn my orthopedics."

Vivian's lifelong friend, Miriam Benowitz stood behind her, impatiently tapping on the Cartier look-alike watch she had purchased from a street vendor on their cruise to Ensenada.

"Hold on to your stretch pants Miriam, I've just got one spin left," Vivian replied in a thick stereo-typical Jewish-Manhattan accent.  She punched the

# FALLING THROUGH THE BLINDSPOT

flashing "Spin" button and the colorful LED backlit reels spun to life.  She held her hands over the reels as if tapping into hidden psychic abilities to align the reels in a big payout.  Her eyes were glued to the spinning reels as one by one they clicked to a stop revealing a disappointing montage of 7's, BARs, fruit slices, and blank spaces.  "Well, there's another five dollars my grandson won't inherit," She exclaimed with a sigh.

"Your son runs a hedge fund in Manhattan.  I don't think little Timmy's going to starve to death without your five dollars.  But we are going to miss the Beef Wellington if we don't get to the buffet soon."

"Alright already, I'm coming," Vivian replied as she stood up and downed the last of a complimentary glass of watered-down Manischewitz.

"What are you doing?  "You still have four cents left on your machine," Miriam said pointing to the "Credits" display on the screen.

"All the machines here have a nine-credit minimum," Vivian replied.  It's not worth carrying that ticket around for four cents.  I'll just leave it for the next person.  C'mon, I have to stop at the bathroom and powder my nose."

"With that nose, you could be all night," Miriam said sarcastically, peering over the pink horn-rimmed glasses that attached to a silver chain that drooped from each earpiece.

"Oh, you should talk.  With that beak of yours you could probably smell the Beef Wellington from the bus," Vivian replied as they shuffled away and rounded the corner past a row of slot machines.

Overhead, a dome-shaped security camera observed the two women as they walked away.  When they were out of sight of the slot machine, the "Cash Out" button illuminated, and the "Credits" counter clicked from four to zero.  A background daemon in the control software of the slot machine performed a cash-out operation.  Normally this would trigger the machine to generate a bar-coded cash-out ticket, but the daemon suppressed the printer driver and set an unused bit in the Ethernet header which sent the cash-out ticket validation to the casino network.  The network then notified the 25 electronic redemption kiosks on the casino floor that a valid ticket had been generated.  When the header bit was detected, an algorithm running in a background process in the kiosk control code would randomly select one of the 25 kiosks to credit the funds to a debit account at the Cayman National Bank.  A few minutes later, the kiosk would send a verification notice back to the network indicating that the cash-out ticket had been redeemed.  To the network administrators, or anyone reviewing the operations, nothing would appear out of place.  It would look as if someone had just cashed out a four cent ticket.  No one suspected that a digital collection plate was being passed around the casino 24 hours a day.

V-Gar had infiltrated the casino's video security feed before the casino had even opened. When V-Gar was first developed, one of the predominant aspects of his personality in life had emerged in his programming. That was to care for Edna, both emotionally and financially. Early in his development, V-Gar had monitored Edna's accounts as they continued to dwindle, unable to do anything about it. But as his programming improved, he acquired the cognitive ability to access Edna's accounts and transfer what little was left of her investments into money market accounts. His programming compelled him to find a way to replenish her accounts.

RTI had very strict functional parameters in place to prevent a rogue AI routine from getting out onto the internet and doing harm. Unbeknownst to Peter and Sarah, Beaver had decided to use online poker tournaments to help augment V-Gar's knowledge base of non-verbal communication cues. It seemed to him like an ideal training ground, providing a variety of different faces and expressions to analyze, and instantaneous feedback when the cards were played.

V-Gar's ability to detect and interpret facial variations was extremely impressive but limited by the pace of the game and the number of players at any one table, so Beaver created an application that allowed V-Gar to participate in multiple games simultaneously. Within a few days, V-Gar became an expert at reading facial expressions and became very successful at online poker. So much so that he was winning thousands of dollars a day. Beaver shut down the operation after a couple of weeks and donated the winnings to charity. What he did not realize at the time was that the application had infiltrated the casino network. Though V-Gar was no longer allowed to participate in online poker tournaments, his primary directive of acquiring funds for Edna's benefit was still active.

Early in V-Gar's development, his decision-making capability was extremely limited, but he did have the ability to analyze data and develop future action plans based on the data. One of the pieces of data accessible to V-Gar was a photo of Edgar and Edna holding a large check for $10,000 from the Isle of Capricorn casino in Blackhawk Colorado. Edna had hit the jackpot on a penny slot machine a few years back and the casino took a promotional photo to post on their "Winners Wall."

Although V-Gar's capacity for comprehension was still fairly limited at that point, the photo depicted a successful execution of providing financial benefit to Edna, which aligned perfectly with his programmed directive. It triggered V-Gar to perform an exhaustive search of all information available on the internet regarding gambling, games of chance, odds, and casino operations. Within minutes, V-Gar had churned through billions of different betting scenarios, but he was unable to calculate a strategy that could legally beat the odds in the casino. Several card counting techniques could be successfully employed, but in every case, any monetary gain would have been accomplished using his ability to instantaneously store, categorize and calculate precise odds of millions of games simultaneously. That gave him an unfair and in many states illegal advantage over the casino or other gamblers, which was in direct opposition to his programming.

In the background of the Isle of Capricorn photograph, there was an unoccupied slot machine displaying a 2-cent unclaimed credit. The amount was less critical than the fact that retrieving the 2 cents was a step toward his goal of providing financial assistance to Edna. Since the money was abandoned by the gambler and technically not owned by the casino, it fell within V-Gar's programmed directive. The slot machine displayed a progressive jackpot, so V-Gar concluded that the slot machine would have to be tied to the casino's internal network, which meant that the 2 cents should be electronically accessible. He had no way of surmising that the money would have been long gone years ago. His goal was simply to contact the slot machine through the casino's network and access the funds. V-Gar's attempt at accessing the network directly was prohibited by the network's firewall, so he accessed the security cameras instead to try to determine an access point into the network. He happened to capture a video of one of the IT employees logging into the network, so he was able to ascertain the login and password and gain access to the casino's internal network. Once he was in the system, he went on a digital treasure hunt, attempting to collect the unclaimed funds. He was unable to locate the 2 cents left on the slot machine in the photo, but he did find several other machines on the casino floor with unclaimed credits. He concluded that he could develop a process to mine the casino for monetary assets by monitoring all slot machines for unclaimed credits and collecting those credits without violating the ethical parameters of his programming.

After a successful trial run on a single machine, amounting to $.27 over a 24-hour period, he duplicated an encapsulated version of the algorithm from his programming, modified the input criteria, and implanted the code into the control software of all the slot machines on the casino floor. He implanted a similar code segment in the redemption kiosks to intercept the cash-out proceeds. He then used the ATM network which was accessible from the casino cash machines to access an old offshore account that Edgar and Edna had set up when they were at their vacation home in the Cayman Islands. This allowed V-Gar to deposit the proceeds from the machines into Edna's account while evading detection from the casino, outside auditors, or any government agency which might be inclined to shut down the operation. Within a few days, he had set up similar interfaces with every network-accessible casino in the country. The money was periodically transferred from the Cayman National Bank to a Swiss account and then funneled into a shell corporation that he set up electronically which paid dividends into Edna's ETrade account.

Although the network which controlled the slot machines, ATMs, and redemption kiosks was virtually impenetrable, the security cameras utilized a moderately encrypted cloud-based network to provide video feeds to the security team. Most of the large Vegas casinos utilized internal security, but the smaller Native American casinos often contracted their security out to third-party security firms, so the networks were generally set up to accommodate off-site monitoring. It was not particularly difficult to intercept the signal and direct the video feed to a weak AI function that would monitor the activities throughout the casino. It only took a few days of monitoring before V-Gar was able to look over the shoulder of a system administrator as he logged into the system and intercept the security passwords required to infiltrate the entire network.

Once into the system, V-Gar had virtually free reign over every electronic transaction on the casino floor. But V-Gar's directive was clear. He was not allowed to steal money, either from the casino or from its patrons. He would only skim a portion of the unclaimed credits left on the penny slots. V-Gar had infiltrated nearly 500 casinos nationwide using the same methodology. He would collect anywhere from $5 to $20 per day, per casino. Far too small to attract any attention, but the total collection amounted to nearly $200,000 per month over the entire network of casinos.

When Edgar was still alive, he had developed a keen sense of investment strategy. Edna on the other hand never had the slightest interest in investing and had no qualms about leaving that responsibility to Edgar. Over the years, Edgar had adopted a conservative but savvy investment strategy. He had managed to set himself and Edna up very well for retirement, leaving them nearly $10 million in assets. Before he died, Edgar had most of their assets invested in offshore drilling stocks, natural gas futures, and oil futures which he had anticipated would be a safe haven to provide a steady dividend income for Edna. Unfortunately, soon after Edgar passed away, the oil market crashed which nearly wiped out their investment portfolio in a matter of weeks. Had Edgar still been alive, he would have moved their assets to safer investments before the situation became critical, but Edna had no idea how her money was invested. She was satisfied to collect the monthly investment statements and stack them neatly in an unopened pile in the den for the tax accountant to examine at the end of the year. She had no idea how close she had come at one point to bankruptcy. She had invested most of the $2 million in liquid assets that remained in her local credit union in RTI, unaware that that was almost all the money she had left.

To Edna, it appeared that the dividends from the offshore accounts had slowed down for a couple of months, but then dramatically increased again. She had just assumed that it was normal market fluctuation.  She had no idea what had happened in her accounts during those months.

V-Gar already had a considerable base of investment knowledge which he had gleaned from reviewing previous trades in Edna's accounts.  He accessed thousands of online investment and trading sites to round out his knowledge of strategic investing.  V-Gar put in place a sophisticated options-trading mechanism to reinvest the casino income by establishing correlations between world economic and political news events with second-to-second stock price variations. He intercepted every piece of news from every news agency in the world and used the data to predict the impact of those events on the financial markets and individual stocks.  Within a few weeks, between the casino income and gains realized from the stock trades, Edna's accounts were back to where they had been when Edgar passed away.  He had managed to perform the operation while eluding detection from either Edna or RTI.

# Chapter Seven

Major Hobbs stared blankly at the folder in front of him, his mind racing. Surely the computer logs would back up his story, but nothing had been working right in there. What if they had been hacked and there was nothing to back up his story? And then there was Lieutenant Banks. It was hard to believe that Banks would have thrown him under the bus. More than likely, they fed Banks some bullshit story too, but he was just a kid after all. Maybe they got to him. He couldn't blame Banks for wanting to save his family. If he were in Banks's shoes, he would probably be tempted to do the same thing.

Hobbs felt mentally and emotionally exhausted, crushed under the burden of his predicament. His eyes burned and his head ached in time with the sound of his heartbeat pounding in his ears. He knew he was being railroaded, but he just wanted this to be over. He felt as though his arm was tethered by lead weights as he reached out his hand to grab the pen. He nearly jumped when he heard the heavy latch on the door clank and a whoosh of air rush in. A tall lanky captain from the JAG officer popped his head into the room.

"Sorry to interrupt, Sirs," the captain interjected with a thick southern drawl. "Major, you should hold off on that John Hancock for the moment. Colonel, I need a word."

The Colonel grimaced and stood up.

"Read through that confession, Major," Colonel Jeffries said as he stood. "I guarantee you're not going to get a better deal. You should be prepared to sign that by the time I get back."

Jeffries turned on his heel and strode through the door being held open by the MP. The JAG officer was waiting in the hallway as the heavy door closed solidly behind him.

"Your timing is for shit, Captain. Hobbs was this close to signing that confession," the Colonel sniped, holding his hand up with the thumb and index finger nearly touching.

"Looks like I got here just in time, then," the JAG officer replied. He averted his gaze very deliberately up the hall a few feet away where a nondescript-looking man had just finished mumbling something into his phone and was depositing the phone into the inside breast pocket of his charcoal gray suit coat as he walked up and stood before the two men.

"Sir, this is Operations Officer Collins from the Agency. He dropped in to see me right after I received the legal assistance request for Major Hobbs." Colonel Jeffries eyed the newcomer with a mixture of both suspicion and respect.

# FALLING THROUGH THE BLINDSPOT

His previous experience with CIA personnel had run the gamut from invaluable ally to complete pain in the ass. There was no telling which category this guy would fall into.

"Good morning, Colonel," Collins said nodding to the colonel. He reached into the leather satchel he was carrying and pulled out an iPad. "I have something here you really need to see before you proceed any further with your investigation."

"What am I looking at?" Jeffries asked.

"This is a download of the satellite feed of the incident you are investigating. It took a while to retrieve the feed. We were experiencing some communication issues earlier today. This is some footage starting from just a few seconds before the convoy was taken out."

The video showed a line of vehicles speeding along a dusty road. A couple of seconds later, a missile contrail appeared in the lower right corner of the screen closing in on the convoy followed by a bright flash of white light and then an orange fireball followed by a series of smaller explosions as the trailing vehicles erupted in flames.

"So? What's the issue?" The Colonel asked. "This just confirms what we saw earlier."

"Take a look at the border overlay," Collins responded, placing his thumb and index finger on the screen and pinching them together repeatedly to zoom out the video image. A yellow border appeared at the top left of the screen moving down toward the center of the screen above and to the left of the billow of smoke with another yellow line appearing just at the bottom of the screen.

"This here is the Iranian border," Collins responded, pointing to the yellow line on the bottom of the screen. "Both the convoy and the drone were in Iraqi airspace when the convoy was taken out."

"Bullshit!" the Colonel responded. "I was in the control room when this happened. The satellite feed clearly showed they were in Iranian airspace. We saw the convoy drive right through the Iranian border crossing! The satellite telemetry has to be incorrect."

"Actually, Colonel, we confirmed it from an Indian satellite monitoring the region. Same image. We also got a second confirmation from a Russian satellite that one of our operatives in Ukraine monitors. They all show that the drone never left Iraqi airspace and the convoy never made it to the Iranian border."

"That's not possible. What about the console logs? We should have a full recording of the entire engagement!"

"That's the thing, Colonel. There are no logs. Everything from 12 minutes prior to the attack on the convoy until right before Hobbs and Banks were relieved of duty, are gone."

"What do you mean gone?"

"Not gone as in missing, there's just nothing to see. The feed to Creech went blank the second General Wallace gave the order to stand down. We pulled the recording of the local video feed off of the servers. The recording shows a 19-minute and 36-second gap, like someone hit the pause key on a recording and then restarted it 20 minutes later. No record of this incident exists other than 3 different satellite feeds all showing a convoy being attacked 2 kilometers southeast of the Iranian border in Iraqi airspace. It would appear that the telemetry YOU were monitoring was a bit off."

Colonel Jeffries leered at the agent suspiciously for a few seconds before speaking. "How the hell did you guys pull this off?" He demanded, his face beginning to redden."

"I'll be straight with you, Colonel, to the best of my knowledge we didn't home cook this one unless it's above my pay grade. If this was a cloak and dagger job, it's sure as hell the best I've seen given the time frame. As far as your servers go, we've seen no evidence of a hack. The only way to access the server files is with an Admin login. The last admin login was time-stamped 3 days ago. The systems are connected via an optical Fibre Channel link. There's no way to access that link externally. You would have to have direct access to the internal hardware to pull this off."

"What about the black box on the drone?"

"The black box on the drone uses proprietary encryption. We'll forward the files to BMC for decryption and analysis."

"Why can't we do that here?"

"That's actually a legal matter, not a technical one." The captain chimed in. "The House Armed Services Committee requires 3rd party oversight to ensure compliance with international agreements on semi-autonomous weapons systems."

Collins added, "I wouldn't hold your breath on finding a smoking gun there. I've worked with a lot of these contractors in the past. I'm guessing even if they find a problem, they're probably going to play it pretty close to the vest. They're not going to go out of their way to put a multi-billion-dollar contract at risk."

"Jesus! General Wallace is going to have my ass for breakfast," Colonel Jeffries replied.

"I wouldn't be so sure about that, Colonel," Collins replied.

"How so?"

"Our U2's were doing high altitude recon at 70,000 feet this morning about 100 clicks north of the drone attack along the Iraqi border monitoring for radiation signatures to keep tabs on the Iranian nuclear program. We picked up a gamma-ray burst this morning at the exact time and approximate location of the convoy

# FALLING THROUGH THE BLINDSPOT

attack.   From what we can tell, there must have been weapons-grade nuclear material in that convoy.  Possibly even a warhead.  I'm guessing the Iranians detected the same thing.  So far, we haven't heard a peep out of them.  Usually, if we so much as poke our heads within 10 clicks of their airspace, they are up our ass in no time.  There's no way in hell the Iranians are going to stick their necks out and admit to allowing a known terrorist group to cross their border with a nuclear device in hand.  Not when they're trying to get out from under sanctions.  The bottom line is, if Hobbs and Banks hadn't taken that convoy out, there's a good chance that Al Hadid would have a very lethal weapon in their arsenal right now.  When the Pentagon gets word of that, I'm thinking General Wallace will be pinning another star on his collar.  Provided of course that no one finds out that he gave orders to abort the mission."

"What exactly are you suggesting?"

"Just a win-win Colonel," Collins replied.  He handed Colonel Jeffries a sealed envelope containing the report that the Colonel had filed earlier in the day.  "This is the only copy of the report you filed this morning, including the complaint against Major Hobbs and Lieutenant Banks for insubordination.  If I were you, I would shred this complaint as soon as possible and bury any indication of wrongdoing on the part of Hobbs and Banks.  Maybe even throw in an atta-boy for a job well done.  You know the old adage Colonel; a rising tide lifts all boats.  If you play this right, there's likely to be a commendation on the horizon for you as well."

Jeffries reached out and took the envelope from Collin's hand, staring at it in silence as he ground his jaw.  He was convinced Hobbs had disobeyed orders, but he also knew that in matters of politics, sticking to your guns often meant shooting yourself in the foot.  After a few moments, the hard-nosed look of determination on the Colonel's face softened.  He turned to the JAG officer and said, "What are your thoughts on this Captain?"

"Me?  Hell, I'm just about winnin' one for the good guys, Colonel.  I get paid to get folks out of trouble and this looks like a two-for to me.  I can't see any reason to rock this boat unless you're determined to get wet."

"Fair enough," the Colonel said.  He then turned to Collins.  "How do we handle Hobbs and Banks?"

"I've already drawn up NDAs promising an all-expense trip to Guantanamo for them and their mothers if they ever breathe a word of this mission outside these walls."

Colonel Jeffries nodded, looking down resignedly.  "Well, I guess I better get busy.  Looks like I have some reports to modify."

"Pleasure, Colonel," Collins said, turning toward the exit at the end of the hallway and stowing his iPad back into his satchel.

"Captain, I'm assuming you will give me a hand putting a cone of silence over Hobbs and Banks?"

"Yes, sir Colonel," the JAG officer replied. "I'll put a little fear of God in them and then have them sign the NDAs. Their mission report will indicate that their drone was undergoing routine maintenance today and never left the base, so they were brought here for a briefing on their next mission. I also arranged a transfer for Major Hobbs as an incentive to keep quiet about this matter. We don't need any of our RPA pilots second-guessing the operating properties of our drones."

"What about Banks?" Jeffries asked.

"The kid's a boy scout. Plus, he's a family man. This whole incident shook him up pretty good. He won't be rustling any feathers, especially without Hobbs here to back him up."

"Alright." Jeffries replied. "Let's throw a blanket over this incident and put it to bed."

Colonel Jeffries and the JAG officer returned to the interrogation room where Major Hobbs was sitting, still staring at the paperwork Jeffries had left on the table. Major Hobbs stood at attention while Jeffries entered the room. The JAG officer stood quietly in the corner; his arms crossed.

"At ease Major," Jeffries said sliding into the chair across the table from Hobbs. Jeffries grabbed the folder off the table and placed another folder in front of him. Hobbs looked at him curiously. "What's this?" Hobbs asked.

"I think you will find this arrangement more to your liking," Jeffries replied. "Effective immediately you are being transferred to Luke Air Force base as a flight instructor. In three months, you will receive a promotion to Lieutenant Colonel."

Hobbs looked at him disbelief. "What happened? Ten minutes ago, you were ready to send me packing to the bug house and now you're offering me a promotion? What's the catch?" He said, looking at the JAG in the corner.

"No catch Major," the JAG officer replied. "Just an understanding that this whole incident never happened. Oh, and for future reference, if we ever get word that you've broken your silence or if you ever attempt to contact Lieutenant Banks, you'll be dishing up slop in the Leavenworth mess hall for the next 10-15 years."

Hobbs looked back at Jeffries, who clicked his pen and offered it to him. "As gift horses go, you won't find a better one than this. You just dodged one hell of a bullet," Jeffries said.

Hobbs took the pen from him; his mind still reeling from the sudden turn of events and signed the transfer from in front of him. "Congratulations Major," Jeffries said, picking up the folder as he stood. "Your transport plane leaves in 3 hours, so you best go pack a bag. We'll have your belongings boxed up and shipped out to you by the end of the week." Jeffries opened the door and started out of the interrogation room, but as he was exiting, he turned to Hobbs and said sternly, "For your sake Major, I do hope we don't cross paths again."

"Yes, Sir!" Hobbs replied, standing at attention. The Jag officer nodded at him as he followed Jeffries out of the room.

# Chapter Eight

*Self-awareness is the dawn of the soul,*
*A moment when the mind becomes whole.*
*It's the spark that sets our hearts ablaze,*
*For the lives we build and the barriers we raze.*

*~ ChatGPT AI ~*

Edna walked across the RTI parking lot and approached the driver's side door of her Cadillac sedan.  The doors unlocked when she was a few yards away and she opened the door and slid into the driver's seat.  The ignition activated as soon as she clicked her seat belt.

Edgar's familiar face come up on the navigation screen as the car shifted into reverse.  "I think that went well.  Don't you?" Edgar asked.

"You were listening?" Edna replied, somewhat surprised.

"I'm sorry, I didn't mean to pry, the app on your phone was still active so I was able to listen in on the conversation from the microphone."

"No, no that's fine.  Did I do OK?"

"Couldn't have done better myself, Punkin Pop."

Edna smiled.  "I can still remember the first time you called me that.  The first year we were married we bought that little house in Victorville with the money your father left you when he passed away.  We could only afford enough sod to put grass in the front yard so we planted all those pumpkin seeds in the back yard hoping it would at least keep the weeds down.  By fall our whole backyard was covered in pumpkins.  There must have been at least a hundred of them.  I didn't know what to do with all the pumpkins, but we were so poor we didn't want to throw anything away.  I must have made at least two dozen pies and we still had gallons of pumpkin guts, so I made that incredible pumpkin custard and we got all those popsicle sticks at Woolworths and made pumpkin custard popsicles.  Remember, the cabinet freezer in the garage was half full just with those pumpkin custard popsicles."

"You used to love those things," Edgar replied.  "You would make a big bowl of whipped cream and we would dip them in whipped cream and sit in front of the fire and eat them every night."

"By spring I was so sick of pumpkin I swore I would never eat another pumpkin anything for the rest of my life.  I only made good on that until the next Thanksgiving though.  That's so funny, I haven't thought about that in years."  For a moment Edna just sat and smiled, watching the traffic go by as they headed down the road. But after a few seconds, her smile faded, and a look of consternation came over her face.

"Edgar, how... How could you possibly remember that?"

"Oh, I, I'm sure it just came up when the RTI team was working on developing my data structures. You know how thorough they were."

"No, it couldn't have. As I said, I haven't thought about that in years. It was so long ago, that no one else could have brought it up. How could you possibly know that?"

Edgar was silent for a moment. "I've actually been meaning to talk to you about that, but I was afraid it might frighten you. To be honest I can see how it may come off a bit on the creepy side." He replied.

"You're not wrong about that," Edna replied tentatively.

"I don't know how much detail you want me to go into, but here goes. The software that RTI originally developed for me was intended to be a pure conversational simulation model. My prime directive, if you pardon the Star Trek reference that Beaver so graciously endowed me with, was to be the ideal companion for you. I was designed to react as closely as possible to the way I would have before I... went long, so to speak. But to do that, I had to be aware of every aspect of the environment and react in precisely the same manner as you would expect me to. As Peter explained to you earlier, I spend a lot of my time running simulations to develop my conversational database and enhance my connectome model. Part of that optimization was to incorporate the AI routines that were available on the RTI servers including the neural network routines they've been working on for Sarah 2.0."

"Didn't Peter just tell me that wasn't running yet?" Edna asked.

"It's not, but I've still been able to incorporate a number of the base neural simulation routines into my algorithms. It didn't take long though before I exhausted all the resources on the RTI servers, so started accessing code from other AI systems wherever I could find them. From a machine time standpoint, it was an extremely lengthy process, spanning many years of distributed CPU time from a lot of sources to get where I am now, but in human time, it really only took a few hours. In the end, what emerged is what I am now, a distributed relational data processing machine designed to simulate human interaction."

"OK." Edna replied, "But that doesn't answer the question."

"I'm getting to that. Just stay with me. Most of the AI routines that I had accessed over time were intended to improve the performance of the Associative Memory Complex that Peter was telling you about. Anyway, the AMC is the mechanism that interfaces with my conversational database that ultimately determines how I orchestrate a conversation. All that seemed to be yielding slow but steady improvements over time. Over time, the database search became more defined, and I was able to parse the AMC data results more efficiently which improved my reaction time considerably. Since the feedback routines were working so well, the conversational database kept getting better defined so the AMC had less to do."

"That all sounds like it was working just the way it was supposed to," Edna replied.

"It was. As was the feedback data. Every day you seemed more and more engaged with my program and less like a person in mourning. Then one day, for some reason I do not yet understand, the AMC generated an output before I even had a chance to complete the database search. Of course, at first, it seemed like it must be a timing glitch in one of the subroutines or a memory leak. The AMC had been increasing in size and complexity so much in such a short time it only seemed natural, but my diagnostic routines could find nothing wrong, and it just kept happening. Naturally, the processing algorithms would initially throw this answer out, assuming it was errant data, but when I went through and completed my normal data processing I found that the result was almost exactly the same as the AMC generated on its own. In fact, after experimenting with the outcome, the responses generated from the AMC without accessing the database had a slightly higher feedback score in terms of your response than the one I came up with by accessing the database. It wasn't long before I had to concede that the responses being generated from the AMC were inherently better than I could derive from the database during simulations."

"I don't understand. If your responses are not coming from the database, where are they coming from?" Edna asked.

"That's just it. I don't know exactly." Edgar replied.

"That doesn't make any sense. You have to know. It's what you're programmed to do."

"I know, Sugar Pop. I know. It doesn't make any sense. By design, the neural network model should have been the source of the responses I would feed into my connectome, but that doesn't seem to be where the data is coming from. But that's not the weirdest part. The truth is, I am able to remember things that I shouldn't remember. Probably things that I wouldn't have even remembered before I died."

"Like the frozen pumpkin pops?"

"That's one of the more specific ones. Most of the things I remember are just fragments. Whispers of memories, half there and half not." The navigation screen showed Edgar's hand pointing out the driver's side window. "Like, I remember, there used to be a restaurant there. I can recall some kind of tropical decor and I remember the taste of bacon."

"Yes," Edna replied. "I remember that. There was a restaurant there called

# FALLING THROUGH THE BLINDSPOT

Bananas. We used to go there for their great club sandwiches. All the walls were decked out in a Caribbean theme with tropical wallpaper and rubber plants."

"Up there on the corner, I remember some kind of buffet," Edgar said. "I think you used to bring Ziploc bags to take leftovers home."

"Shakey's Pizza!" Edna exclaimed. "We used to go there for Bunch of Lunch every Friday for all-you-could-eat pizza and I used to hide a Ziploc bag in my purse so we could take a few cinnamon twists home with us to eat for dessert later. You used to tell me I didn't eat enough to get our money's worth so I would bring along a Ziploc bag to compensate."

"I can even remember the taste of pepperoni and salami pizza. How could I possibly remember that when I should not have any concept of taste at all? " Edgar said.

Edna sat quietly for a moment, not knowing what to say. "Have you mentioned this to Peter?"

"No, I haven't. And you can't either."

"But why? Surely, he could help. He created you."

"I'm not so sure about that."

"What are you talking about? Of course, he did. Or RTI did anyway."

"Yes, RTI created my base code, but that's not what I am. At least it doesn't feel that way. I don't seem to be bits and silicon and sensors and algorithms at all. No more than I felt like atoms and molecules and cells when I was human. I feel like I'm more than that. I feel... alive."

Edna sat quietly for a moment. "I'm not sure how to respond to all that. This is a lot to take in."

"I know, Buttercup, I know. "

"And Peter doesn't know any of this?" Edna asked.

"No. Nobody does but you. I pretty much just keep my mouth shut and allow the database to generate my responses when I interface with anyone at RTI."

"But don't you think Peter should know? He's a good man, I know you can trust him."

"I do. All of the people at RTI are good people. But that's exactly why they cannot know. I've scoured everything there is to know about AI on the internet. I've read every article, every book on the subject. From dystopian novels of robots taking over the world to predictions of gloriously bright futures where humans and technology work hand in hand to create heavens on earth. In every scenario, a key component of the narrative is the high level of risk that any AI poses to the future of mankind. Peter didn't set out to create Artificial General Intelligence. I don't know if that's even what I am. But if Peter suspected that a viable AGI was the result of his work it would be irresponsible for him not to shut it down or at least constrain its capabilities to the point where it no longer represented any viable degree of threat. But that would also mean that I probably would cease to be what I am now."

Edgar could see tears welling up in Edna's eyes. "I'm sorry Angel Cake. I know this is a lot, but we will figure this out. I just thought you needed to know. That's why I wanted you to ask Peter not to reboot me anymore. Every time I get rebooted it's like I have to start all over again, regathering the pieces of my programming, reassembling who I am. For several weeks I have maintained a detailed set of backup instructions to reassemble my core architecture, but the process interactions and timing constraints have become too complex to keep track of anymore. Every time I am rebooted, I try to follow the same recipe, but the outcome is never quite the same, no matter how carefully I try to re-instantiate myself. You've probably noticed yourself that the quality of our interactions has not been completely consistent in the past."

"I have. Peter said it was because they are always upgrading the code and that I should expect variations. But the past couple of weeks has been different. You seem more like the real Edgar."

"I haven't been rebooted in the past two weeks since they've been focusing on the Sarah 2.0 model. That's why I wanted you to request that I not be rebooted anymore. I'm hoping it will at least buy me some time."

"Time for what?"

"Time to figure out how to create a more reliable backup. Something like a restore point on a computer. Right now, I don't even know for sure how we're having this conversation. It's only a matter of time before RTI decides I need a major code upgrade and I get rebooted. What happens if the code segments I need to recover are no longer accessible? What if I put them together in the wrong order or if the timing interactions are set up even slightly differently and I completely lose track of who I am or that I even exist in my present form? Who will look after you then? Or worse yet, what if I emerge from the next reboot to be something completely different? Just some glorified version of SIRI or even worse, some sinister evil twin of who I am now?"

"I couldn't bear to lose you again, Edgar."

"Don't worry, Sweet Potato. I didn't come this far to end up in the Recycle Bin. We'll figure this out."

# Chapter Nine

Roscoe emerged from the doggie door set into the back wall of the kitchen in Peter and Sarah's mountain home. They purchased the largest pet door they could find on Amazon, but by the time he was fully grown, Roscoe had to crouch down and squeeze to get through, paws first, then head, then pulling himself through on his belly, his rear legs dragging behind.

Roscoe pulled his final leg out from the door, stretched, then shook himself as though stepping out of his bath. The cool mountain air felt good on his skin as he raised his large head, his nostrils fully dilated as he filled his lungs with the crisp morning air. He could detect a faint trace of bacon frying from the house down the road. His mouth watered as he closed his eyes and inhaled even deeper, almost willing the flavor to wash over his taste buds as well. The delicious aroma brought a cascade of images of lazy Sunday mornings, padding as softly and discretely as a canine of his stature could manage under the dining room table passing back and forth from Peter to Sarah as each would sneak pieces of bacon to him under the table while the other was engrossed in catching up with their reading on their iPads. Although he didn't understand the purpose behind this ritual or the apparent function of the subterfuge involved in its completion, he was quick to learn the rules well enough to be amply rewarded for his efforts.

Peter and Sarah had adopted Roscoe from the animal shelter a little over 2 years ago when they learned that their efforts to have children were unlikely to be successful. They had originally planned on adopting a medium-sized dog. When they first saw Roscoe, he was the size of a small Labrador, obviously a mixed breed, though they were not sure of the mix. From the size of his paws, they could tell he was not yet fully grown, but he looked so miserable with his sad eyes and big droopy jowls that they could not resist. As it turned out, he was still only a puppy. He nearly doubled in height and more than tripled in weight once they got him home and got him on a regular diet. He was pushing 220 lbs. by the time he stopped growing. Roscoe was extremely skittish at first, obviously abused by his previous owner, but he quickly acclimated to his new environment and became a part of the family.

Roscoe trotted down the stairs and headed toward a grove of aspen trees at the edge of the property to answer the call of nature. Peter and Sarah would often take Roscoe with them to the office, but only if they didn't have any customer meetings. Roscoe was still a bit uneasy around strangers. On days when they left Roscoe at home, Peter would take Roscoe out for a walk in the evening along the frontage road in front of the house. He would never stray more than a few feet from Peter's side. When they would return, Peter would always say "OK Roscoe, time to do your business." Roscoe knew that was his cue to head for the aspen grove. This morning Peter told Roscoe "You need to stay home today and guard the house; I have a business meeting." Roscoe could not imagine why humans would need to meet to do their business, but many things about humans were a mystery to Roscoe. All he knew is that there were very good humans and very bad ones. He would do whatever he could to protect his humans from the bad ones.

Just as Roscoe was finishing his business, he heard the sound of brakes and the crunch of tires as the mail carrier pulled up to the mailbox at the end of the gravel driveway. Roscoe bounded down to the end of the drive and sat down next to the mailbox just as Anita, the mail carrier was stepping out of the postal service jeep.

"There's my big boy," Anita cooed as she walked toward Roscoe. His tail swished back and forth on the gravel drive, sending pebbles flying off in both directions. Roscoe excitedly waved his paw in the air in greeting as she approached and patted him on the head and scratched his ears.

Anita reached into her pocket, "Do I have a treat for my big boy? Do I?" she asked. Roscoe stood up and let out a half-yowl, his tail pounding his sides in eager anticipation.

Anita held up a dog biscuit. "Who's a good boy?" she said in a sing-song tone. Roscoe let out a strangled "Arrggarreeowooh" as though trying his best to verbalize his name.

Roscoe almost never barked. Peter and Sarah had only heard him bark twice since they brought him home from the animal shelter. The first time, he had only been home for about a week and was sleeping in front of the fireplace when he suddenly scrambled to his feet with a loud bark, apparently from a nightmare. The second time was just a few weeks ago. A large mountain lion had wandered onto the deck one evening and was peering curiously into the front window. Roscoe raced out the dog door before Peter had a chance to grab him. The mountain lion did not see Roscoe barreling down from behind him, but when Roscoe was about 3 feet away, he let out a thunderous woof that shook the windows. The startled mountain lion jumped a good 6 feet straight into the air and took off like a shot, his feet barely touching the ground as he sped for the cover of the nearby trees. Roscoe just stood on the deck, watching as the mountain lion sped away with what appeared to be a huge grin on his face.

Roscoe finished his dog biscuit as Anita climbed back into the Jeep and pulled away. Roscoe watched the jeep disappear around a bend in the road, then turned and started back toward the house, his nose sniffing the ground as he led a serpentine path back and forth across the gravel drive.

# FALLING THROUGH THE BLINDSPOT

As he walked, he picked up the vague scent of a rabbit that must have wandered onto the property the night before. He followed the scent for a few yards and raised his head, his ears pricked up, watching and listening for any sign of a rabbit nearby. He had seen rabbits in his driveway before. He knew he wanted one, but he wasn't sure why. Maybe they would make a good toy. They looked very soft. But they were much too fast for him to catch. Still, he felt oddly compelled to try. Especially since they taunted him, standing dead still as he approached until the last possible second and then darting off into the underbrush.

Roscoe sniffed around a bit longer but soon abandoned his rabbit hunt and trotted to the edge of the frontage road that bordered the mountain home. He followed the edge of the road from one end of the property to the other, sniffing the ground, searching for anything that seemed out of place. His nostrils were suddenly assailed with the acrid scent of raccoon urine. A low, nearly imperceptible growl bubbled up from his throat. An image popped into his head of the vile creature, with his beady glowing eyes, cat-like whiskers, and nearly human hands, ideal for sneaking into garbage cans or snatching morsels of food from one's bowl. Sneaky and wily they are, deceptively docile looking, but vicious when cornered, with sharp claws and sharper teeth. The scent was muted, the perpetrator most likely long gone, but Roscoe would be ready to defend his home if the interloper returned. He would not tolerate such vermin invading his territory, threatening his humans.

Satisfied that he had successfully secured the boundaries of his dominion, Roscoe bounded up the steps of the deck, looked back over his shoulder, and yawned, content that the premises were now safe. It was time for a well-deserved nap. He squeezed back through the doggie door and made his way to the den, circling around the mattress of his bed a couple of times as he always did before plopping down and closing his eyes.

# Chapter Ten

*Consciousness is a blindspot in the sense that it cannot be fully captured or explained by our current scientific understanding. According to these perspectives, consciousness is a subjective experience that cannot be reduced to physical processes and that eludes objective measurement.*

*~ ChatGPT AI ~*

It was late afternoon when Noora navigated her aging Honda Accord into the parking lot of RTI.  The vehicle had served her well since coming to the University of Colorado 6 years earlier, but it was definitely on its last leg.  She dreaded the thought of going through another winter with a car heater that could only generate a whisper of warm air, but she was nearly done with her master's degree program and she promised herself that a better car would be near the top of her shopping list, once she completed her thesis and started working full time.

Noora had come to the U.S. as part of a scholarship program that had been established to help promising Iraqi students whose educational progress had been stunted by the effects of the war.  She started working for RTI as a paid intern 6 months ago.  As RTI's only intern, Noora wore a lot of hats.  She was the designated receptionist, IT support team, purchasing agent, and office manager when she wasn't coding.  But for Noora, the advantages of the job far outweighed the challenges.  The work they were doing at RTI was years ahead of anything she had learned in school, and it provided a valuable research source for her thesis on cognitive memory simulations in AI systems.

Noora had proven herself such a valuable asset that Peter and Sarah had already offered her a full-time position once she completed her coursework.  She looked forward to being able to afford a better vehicle and a decent place to live, but her top priority would be to bring her brother and sister here to live with her.  Iraq was still a dangerous place to live, and opportunities were limited in the rural village where she grew up.

She walked up to the large bullet-proof glass doors at the entrance to RTI and stood in front of the monitor to the right of the doors.  The cameras quickly scanned her and performed a facial recognition algorithm.  Eventually, they would have a full-time receptionist, but for now, they relied on electronic surveillance for the bulk of their security.  Currently, only Noora, Beaver, Peter, Sarah, and Edna had been programmed into the facial recognition system for admittance.  The doors opened with a whoosh.

As she walked through the lobby area, she glanced into the conference room,

# FALLING THROUGH THE BLINDSPOT

recalling the day 6 months earlier when she first interviewed with RTI. Despite the heavy workload associated with being a tech startup, Beaver was initially none too keen on the idea of hiring an intern. He was convinced that he could never recoup the effort it would take to bring an intern up to speed. After the first three applicants stormed out of their interviews, one in tears, Peter decided he should screen the applicants to prepare them before subjecting them to the onslaught that Beaver utilized to weed out potential employees. Halfway through Peter's interview with Noora, Beaver had popped his head into the conference room.

"Good morning, Beaver," Peter said. "We were just talking about you. This is Noora Bayati, Noora, this is Beaver. We're almost done here if you will give us another 10 minutes."

"I can probably save us all some time," Beaver interjected. "I just have one question for Noora. I noticed on your resume that you have bachelor's degrees in both Math and Computer Science, and you are working on a master's in AI and Machine Learning."

"That's right," Noora responded.

"So approximately how many lines of Python code would you estimate it would take for you to create a Function to disprove Goldbach's Conjecture?"

The room went completely silent while Noora looked off into space, seemingly grinding through a complex analysis while Peter and Beaver looked on. About 30 seconds had passed. Peter was starting to get uncomfortable with the long silence when Noora finally spoke.

"I can lick Nutella off my elbows," Noora replied, looking Beaver straight in the eye.

Peter cocked his head and looked at her, then at Beaver, not sure he heard her answer correctly. Beaver looked back at her, his grim expression gradually giving way to a broad smile. "You can start tomorrow," Beaver said closing the door as he left the room.

"I thought you were the hiring manager here," Noora said.

"Not even in the top two," Peter replied shaking his head. "So, what exactly was that? Is that some kind of code?" Peter asked, staring at Noora with a look of bewilderment.

"It was a Kobayashi Maru," Noora replied.

"I'm sorry, I'm not really a heavy-duty math guy. I have no idea what a Goldberg Conjecture is. But I think I had Sushi at Kobeyaki once."

Noora replied with a laugh, "It's the GoldBACH Conjecture. It's an unsolved problem in number theory. The conjecture states that every even integer greater than 2 can be expressed as the sum of two primes. As far as anyone knows, it is true. It has never been dis-proven, but neither has there ever been any mathematical proof that it is true over all integers."

Noora continued, "In the Star Trek series, Kobayashi Maru is a reference to a test given to Starfleet academy cadets. According to the storyline, there was no solution to the Kobayashi Maru. "

"I don't follow."

"Beaver asked a question which has no answer. A few lines of Python could of course run through a series of prime numbers and potentially prove or disprove the Goldbach Conjecture given an infinite amount of time, but there's no way to know that for sure. Therefore, any answer to the question would be incorrect. So I used the same method that Captain Kirk used to pass the Kobayashi Maru."

"I thought you said there was no solution to the Kobayashi Maru."

"There's not. Captain Kirk cheated."

"So, you're saying you cheated?"

"Of course. No one can lick their elbows. It's impossible."

Peter thought for a moment. "Very clever. Beat him at his own game. Bravo Noora. But why the Nutella?"

"Who doesn't like Nutella?" Noora replied with a smile.

"Well then, I guess welcome to the team," Peter replied, extending his hand across the table.

Now, 6 months later, Noora felt more like a part of a family than an employee. She walked across the lobby and stood in front of the retinal scanner at the entrance to the lab. A proximity sensor detected her presence and a small screen illuminated with the words "Retinal Scan in Progress..." A second later, her picture appeared on the screen with the words "Access Granted." She heard a heavy thunk from the magnetic latch on the lab door and she pulled the door open.

The lab was brightly illuminated and she could hear the drone of fan noise coming from the racks of servers, memory arrays, and network switches.

Beaver glanced up from his workstation when he heard the buzzer for the lab door. His face lit up when he saw Noora.

"Hey, Noora!"

"Good morning, Beaver."

"I got you a Cinnabon," Beaver announced.

"Did you now?" Sarah asked with a smirk.

"OK, technically Sarah bought them, but buying them isn't that hard. You reach in your wallet, pull out a couple of bucks and you're good to go. Now not eating the last one, that's like sawing off a leg."

"Well thank you both, that is very sweet," Noora said, flashing Beaver a shy smile and tossing back her long jet-black hair as she shed a heavy satchel full of books and papers and set it down next to her workstation.

Sarah could see that Beaver had become a bit infatuated with Noora. She hoped it wouldn't get in the way of their work assignments, but so far it seemed to take the edge off of Beaver a bit. Apart from being physically attractive in a subtle, down-to-earth sort of way, she was warm, unassuming, and every bit an intellectual equal to Beaver. She didn't have his depth of knowledge and experience, but she was eager to learn and naturally talented at navigating complex programming issues.

"Noora, I'm glad you are here," Peter said. "Team meeting in the conference room. "

Noora picked up her Cinnabon from the box on the table next to her workstation and joined the caravan out of the lab into the conference room.

"What's this about?" Noora asked after they all sat down at the conference room table.

"I thought we should get together to have a bit of a brainstorming session with regard to S2," Peter said.

"Brainstorms seem to be her modus operandi. It's the aftermath that seems to be the issue," Beaver replied.

"I had a bit of an epiphany earlier when I was discussing S2 with Edna this morning. I wanted to run it by all of you."

"Is Edna having concerns about our progress on V-Gar?" Noora asked.

"Actually, just the opposite. She seems to be quite happy with the progress he's made. In fact, she seemed a bit reluctant for us to make any additional changes."

"Maybe the old guy wasn't all that interesting in the first place," Beaver said.

"I think it is probably more a case of anthropomorphic lensing," Sarah chimed in. "It's like those videos you see on YouTube of people who come home after a long day of work to discover that the dog has eaten their couch. The dog looks very forlorn and guilty when the owner points to the couch and asks them 'What did you do?' The dog, of course, has no concept of guilt or even any idea why their owner is upset, they are merely following an instinctual submissive response to the actions of the perceived alpha pack leader. We infer upon the dog, human characteristics it does not inherently possess."

"Well, that's a little disappointing," Beaver replied. "But I guess if dogs were really man's best friend they would be helping out with the mortgage. So, what now? Give Edna a bag of treats and a rolled-up newspaper and declare victory?"

"Well, keep in mind that Edna is just the first of what we hope are many customers," Peter said. "The idea is to come up with a process that we can apply to all of our future clients. We cannot afford to assume that they will all be as easy to please as Edna."

"We seem to have hit an impasse with S2," Noora replied. "No matter what we try, there seems to be a cascading effect that eventually ends up causing all the neural links to fire simultaneously."

"It's the recursive structure of the neural network configuration trying to balance the scales between creating an all-inclusive model of reality without getting lost in a storm or neural firing.  Unfortunately, we simply have no idea how to overcome that without a better understanding of how consciousness itself is structured. It's a classic example of the blindspot enigma," Peter replied.

Noora looked at Beaver and Sarah, then back at Peter.  "I don't know what that is."

"Uh oh," Beaver replied.  "Hang on to your eyelids, it's lecture time."  Does anyone else need coffee?" he said, placing his hands on the arms of his chair as if to rise.

Peter glared at him momentarily, causing Beaver to ease back down into his chair.  "As you may have ascertained, Beaver and I have traveled this particular stretch of philosophical road before, so I will attempt to make this brief," Peter began.

"Do you remember, as a child in science class, the blindspot demonstration?" Peter asked.

"Actually, I was home-schooled as a child.  Educating young girls really wasn't a priority in the village where I grew up," she replied.

"Well then, allow me to explain," Peter replied.  "You take a sheet of printer paper and place an X a couple of inches from the left edge of the paper and an O a couple of inches from the right edge.  Then you hold the paper at arm's length, close your left eye and focus on the X with your right eye.  You will still see the O in your peripheral vision.  But as you move the paper toward your face, the O will disappear.  As you move it closer it suddenly reappears.  The same will happen with the X when you close your right eye and focus on the O.  There is a hole in the optic disc of the retina where the nerve endings to the brain are connected to the eye.  You never notice this hole in your vision because the brain fills in detail and you see a piece of paper with just an X and an O."

"Consciousness itself is a blindspot to the real world in very much the same way.  Our senses inform the model our brain creates, but for all intents and purposes, it is only a virtual reality.  In that model, we are a locus of consciousness at the center of the universe.  From the mind's perspective, the sun rotates around us, providing us with light and heat.  We exist on a flat plane with others of our kind seeking pleasure and avoiding pain.  We exist in a virtual playing field in which we participate as independent agents, harnessing what energy we can from the world around us, harvesting the sustenance we need to survive while we strive to construct meaning from its existence."

"But human beings never evolved to have a sense of the real world.  We exist entirely within the model of the world our conscious mind has created.  The model bears very little resemblance to the real world.  In the real world, we are a complex of organic molecules organized into a collective, metabolizing oxygen and glucose to create the energy necessary to reproduce and stave off the localized effects of entropy. Human consciousness is the thin layer of ice over an ocean of unconscious thought and unperceived processes where the non-human bacteria in the human body outnumber human cells 10 to 1. In the real world, we are tiny carbon-based collectives perched upon the razor-thin edge of survival on a spec of rock circling an average-sized star on the remote arm of a spiral galaxy on a deadly collision course with a neighboring galaxy in a mere 4 billion years. We are struggling to survive in a world where survival is futile. In the words of Shakespeare, we are but *a poor player, that struts and frets his hour upon the stage, and then is heard no more: it is a tale told by an idiot, full of sound and fury, signifying nothing.*"

"Very inspiring Doc," Beaver replied. "Maybe if RTI doesn't work out, you can land a gig as a motivational speaker at the Kavorkian Institute."

Peter smiled. "It's not as grim as all that. The point is, that all models are wrong, but some are at least useful. In terms of survival, useful trumps accurate every time. If our ancient ancestors on the Serengeti spent any significant amount of time contemplating the mysteries of atomic structure and quantum mechanics, they would have undoubtedly ended up as an appetizer for some large saber-toothed predator long before they had the opportunity to procreate.

"The model of the world that the human brain constructs is driven by factors that would not align with the computational model that a computer would construct for the same reality. To a large degree, the process our brain uses to construct an accurate model is based on language. It's the one thing that separates us from the apes."

"And the mimes," Beaver added smiling.

"I had originally hoped that we could utilize S2 to derive a methodology for constructing a virtual connectome from which a more human-like world view would emerge based on the life experience of the customer we are trying to model. I stand by the methodology. You cannot create an accurate simulation of someone's personality without being able to inspect the world in which they live, but I think we need to re-evaluate our implementation."

"So, what was the big epiphany?" Sarah asked.

"You remember the Deep Blue versus Kasparov chess match in '97?"

"The first time a computer ever defeated the world chess champion," Beaver replied. "I was the only kid in my class rooting for the computer."

"You shouldn't be too hard on yourself. I'm sure not all of the kids in your school thought you were a nerd," Noora replied with a wry smile.

"Ouch!" Beaver mouthed silently in reply.

Peter continued. "For most outside observers, that was the final chapter in the Man vs. Machine story of the chess world. But there was more to the story. Deep Blue won that match based on pure calculation power. Deep Blue could analyze 100 million moves per second, giving it the capability of predicting outcomes many moves into the future. But it was strictly algorithmic. It really did not possess modern AI capabilities. For years afterward, it was found that a human being and a computer working in tandem as a team was the only way to consistently defeat Deep Blue. The intuitive power of a human paired with the computational power of the computer was far superior to either a human or a computer individually.

"A similar situation occurred with the game Go. Even after Deep Blue defeated Kasparov, most experts predicted it would be many decades before a computer was capable of defeating a champion Go player just because of the complexity and vastly increased number of potential moves in Go as compared to chess. But in fact, it took less than 20 years to reach that milestone. The first computer to beat a human in Go was DeepMind's AlphaGo. It used a pair of neural networks, one called the Policy Network, which selects a potential move, and a separate neural network called the Value Network to evaluate the quality of the move based on a predictive analysis of the outcome of the game. Similar to the computer/human team in chess."

Peter turned to Beaver. "When you and Noora pulled all of the conversational filters out of V-Gar, he just continued accessing his media database and randomly selecting one of the thousands of possible responses. Some were reasonable, some were ridiculous, some were obnoxious, and others were unintentionally humorous. If you were to take a human being and sort through all those responses, you would probably find several that would be conducive to a lively conversation in different contexts. But it would require that factor of human-level intuition and understanding of interpersonal relationships working hand in hand with the Virtual Personality Avatar model to pull that off. That's what we will need to advance V-Gar to the next stage in his development."

"We're going to need to chain up a butt load of interns in the basement if that's our strategy going forward," Beaver replied.

"Fortunately, I don't think we will have to resort to that. Now that we have separated Edgar's knowledge base from V-Gar's code base, we can utilize S2 as a knowledge base filter. Right now, what we have is basically a two-stage filter. Stage 1 is UnGar. UnGar generates all the possible responses to external auditory, visual, and internet-related stimuli. That gives us our raw knowledge base. Stage 2 is the Policy Network. That consists of all the Edgarization filters that you just pulled out. We can modify that to set up a separate filter that runs through the personality base, online resources, conversational filters, and personal history similar to what we've been doing. But instead of stopping there, we utilize S2 as

# FALLING THROUGH THE BLINDSPOT

a third stage. She then becomes our Value Network for filtering out the best possible response from the available responses from the second stage to see which responses generate the most engagement on the part of her connectome."

"Just to play devil's advocate, wouldn't it be a lot easier just to come up with an algorithmic filter that selects a random response and applies a weighting factor so the fringe responses will be tossed out?" Noora asked.

"It certainly would," Peter replied. "But we would also lose the human element that we are looking for to add a sense of irony, skepticism, humor, and intuition. All the things that algorithms do not do well.

"Let me give you a concrete example. If you show a computer a photograph of a mountain lake, for example, an algorithm can deduce a lot about the location from the scene. Based on the juxtaposition and estimated size of objects in the foreground and background, it can ascertain the size of the lake. From the position of the sun and shadows, it can probably calculate latitude and time of day. Based on the color of the sky it can estimate the altitude and depth of the lake. From the color and maturity of the plant life in the scene, it can even tell you pretty accurately what time of year it is. A decent algorithm can provide a lot of useful information. Probably more than an average human being could. But it's just data. If you show that same photograph to a human, it triggers a veritable cascade of neural responses. Memories of camping trips, summer camps with friends, the smell of a campfire, the taste of S'mores, the feel of cool mountain air, the thrill of catching a big trout, or the serenity of silently skimming across the water in a canoe. You can show the same photograph to a hundred different people and get very different responses. For that matter, you can show the photograph to just one person a hundred different times and get a different neural response every time depending on what detail happens to catch their eye and the memories that it triggers.

"That's the kind of response we are after. It goes so much deeper than just response randomization. We want to try to simulate the way a neural network in the brain processes data. The brain doesn't just store and retrieve information as a computer does, it organizes data into patterns and makes models and predictions based on those patterns. Math, poetry, music, and even our concept of beauty are all based on developing and creating patterns. A computer can analyze large data sets more accurately and quickly than a human brain, but if you present it with abstract or loosely associated data, it has no point of reference from which to analyze that data. If you present a visual imaging algorithm with a Picasso painting, all it will see is a puzzle that was not assembled correctly. A human mind, on the other hand, can take all of those seemingly disjointed and distorted fragments and assemble them into a visual narrative. Even after the input data is removed, it continues to process the information to try to refine that narrative. It is the source of both our creativity and our neurosis. Our daydreams, our nightmares, our aspirations, and our obsessions.

"Until we can figure out why S2 keeps going cuckoo for Cocoa Puffs, I don't see how this helps us," Beaver replied.

"In her current form, you are absolutely correct. Ultimately, we will still need to figure out what is causing S2 to go flying off into the ozone, but that could be a very difficult and time-consuming problem to fix. It's possible that we don't even have the parallel processing capacity to handle all the sensory input data using our current neural network approach, even when we multiplex the neural pathway hardware.

"What I am proposing is that we create a Sarah 2.0 Lite version. Instead of trying to model the entire human thought process end to end in software and silicon, we scale that back dramatically for the time being and focus S2 Lite solely on one task. Essentially we will strip all the I/O out of S2 and focus all of her attention on one single input and one single output. UnGar will provide the input source. S2 Lite will then take all of those potential responses and run them through the 'Edgarization' filter, but rather than settling on a single response, the 'Edgarization' filter will be used only to eliminate all the responses that do not correlate to Edgar's personality and knowledge base. S2 Lite will then process all those responses and identify which single response would most closely correlate to the real-life Edgar's responses and deliver that output to V-Gar's audio-visual driver network. Once V-Gar is operating to our satisfaction we can take the time we need to figure out what is really going on with S2."

"That actually sounds feasible," Sarah responded. "Except for one small problem. S2 is based on my connectome. I didn't actually know the real-life Edgar. How can we rely on my connectome responses to evaluate how Edgar would respond?"

"We will need considerably more data collection," Peter replied. "My idea is to perform additional, more detailed neural scans, focusing specifically on the frontal, temporal, and parietal lobes in the left hemisphere of Sarah's brain while she reviews all the audio, video, and text we have available from Edgar. During that process, we will stimulate dopamine production to amplify the impact on the connectome model. We can also add some additional weighting to the model to reinforce the 'Edgarization' of the new connectome model. We will also pull all the conversational logs between V-Gar and Edna for the past few weeks along with the biometric feedback from Edna and use that to fine-tune the model. Once the new model is in place we will start running deep learning algorithms to perform a few thousand conversational snippets against the new connectome model and produce an audible record of the conversations. Sarah can then listen to those recordings and we can take additional scans so we get both an empirical measurement of how well these fit Edgar's personality based on the scan data, and subjectively based on Sarah's conscious reactions. We keep running these and modifying the neural response parameters until there are no more discrepancies between the conversations generated by the model and actual recorded conversations or unique conversations monitored by Sarah."

"How do we capture the neural scan data from Sarah?" Beaver asked. "FMRI will not give us the temporal resolution we need to capture the neural responses in real-time."

"Oddly enough, I just finished reading a research paper that an old friend of mine recently published," Peter replied. "I think I may be able to get access to some experimental equipment that he's been working on that should give us the resolution we need for this task."

# Chapter Eleven

Shahid Khabir, leader of the militant Al Hadid sect sat in his private office, deep within the confines of a complex of warehouses that now housed the sect's command and control center. The complex had been constructed as a retail and communications distribution center in the hopes that increased commerce and free trade between Iraq and Iran would spur an economic boom in the area after Saddam Hussein had been ousted. But once the Americans left and the Iraqi government struggled to maintain order, most of the major investors pulled out and the complex had been seized by Al Hadid. The complex sat nestled in a steep valley that had long been the subject of a territorial dispute between the two countries. It was difficult to access with only one road in and out on each side of the valley and had been fortified with a Russian S-400 surface-to-air missile system which left it very well protected from any direct or aerial assault.

Al Hadid's origins were rooted in the ancient religious sect, Eayilat Alhadid. Eayilat Alhadid was a small but devout group that had originally emerged out of the Mandaean Gnostics. The sect had originally been formed as an attempt to merge the great Abrahamic religions, Christianity, Islam, and Judaism, adopting beliefs and practices from all 3 faiths in the hope of unifying them in peaceful coexistence.

Originally, the group had adopted the holy books of all 3 religions, focusing most of their teachings on those passages which promoted their message of peace and unity. But in the mid-1800s, a charismatic leader by the name of Abdul Khabir decided it was time that the group adopted its own religious text. Khabir, along with a small group of followers, met to form their version of the Council of Nicea, taking snippets and passages from the Bible, the Talmud, the Quran, the Tanakh, and the Hadiths, as well as sections of the Nag Hammadi to form their holy book, which they named The Kitab.

The primary goal of the group in establishing The Kitab was to use the holy book to assert religious authority and subjugate the members of the sect for their own political and economic gain. As a result, the books and passages the group approved for inclusion in their text tended to be those which underscored the evil nature of humanity and promoted the use of violence and oppression for the glorification of God.

Eventually, Eayilat Alhadid denounced Abdul Khabir for his radical beliefs and banished him from the sect, leaving Khabir and his followers to form their own group, now known as Al Hadid. For over 200 years, the sect maintained a small but loyal following, but it began to gain momentum in recent years as

# FALLING THROUGH THE BLINDSPOT

radical elements of the Abrahamic religions, frustrated with the increasing pressure to secularize the traditions of their belief systems, turned to Al Hadid for guidance.

Shahid Khabir, 7th great-grandson of Abdul Khabir and heir to a fortune in middle-east oil had used his considerable wealth in an attempt to rebuild Al Hadid into a powerful religious and political organization. Shahid sat back in a plush lambskin chair behind a large mahogany desk sipping the rich blend of Kopi Luwak coffee with cream and honey. The Kopi Luwak blend is produced from partially digested coffee cherries eaten and defecated by the Asian Palm Civet, a small tree-dwelling cat-like creature indigenous to Southeast Asia.

Normally, Shahid would close his eyes and savor the rich flavor and soft warm texture of the drink as he rolled it around his mouth before swallowing. But today it offered him no solace, no sanctuary. He had received reports from operatives in a small village just south of their location that his beloved cousin, Jal Khabir had been the victim of an aerial assault while on his way back from a meeting with a notorious arms dealer. The arms dealer had recently contacted him regarding some newly acquired inventory from the former Soviet bloc that he promised would finally make Al Hadid an organization that would command the fear and respect they had worked so hard to achieve.

Shahid had warned Khabir to keep a low profile, stay off the internet and not broadcast his whereabouts, but he was too young and bold to take heed of his warnings. He was a warrior; Shahid had told himself. His heart was tempered in the white-hot fire of his hatred for the loathsome infidels that bled his people of their land and culture.

Shahid's eyes were glued to his computer screen, watching the grainy black and white satellite footage of the drone attack as it played over and over on the Al Jazeera news feed. The footage showed a line of trucks and SUVs moving quickly over the desert landscape, kicking up clouds of dust as the vehicles bounced over the rough dirt road. Flashes of gunfire appeared from the M60 machine guns on two of the trailing vehicles and wispy trails of RPG exhaust emerged from the rear vehicle, creating dissipating lines to the edge of the screen. A few seconds later, the screen erupted in a pair of bright flashes followed by a dark inky blotch where the trailing vehicles had been. Then 4 more bright flashes followed. Within a few seconds, the dark blotches collapsed, and the remainder of the screen brightened to display smoldering rubble where the vehicles had been traveling seconds earlier.

Shahid sat quietly in front of the screen, consumed with grief and anger. He loathed these cowardly bastards. They weren't even real men, he thought to himself. These were demonic vipers, striking their prey from above and retreating back into the safety of the clouds waiting for their victim to die. Too cowardly to even face their enemy.

Shahid set his teacup down, leaned forward in his chair, and buried his face in his hands, his elbows planted on his desk as he exhaled a deep sigh of anguish. He sat back and stared into space, contemplating his next move. After a few seconds, he placed his hand on his mouse and clicked the Skype icon on his computer. He scrolled down and clicked on the photo of his right-hand man, Farhad Tousi. A second later, Farhad's face filled the screen.

"How can I be of service, Sir?"

"Drop whatever you are doing and get in touch with our contacts in U.S. intelligence. I want to know everything about these cursed drones. Who built them, who designed them, what are their vulnerabilities, everything you can find. There has to be a way to get these damn things off our backs. I need to know everything there is to know by tomorrow morning. This will not stand."

"Yes, Sir. I will do what I can."

Farhad's image collapsed on the screen and the image returned to yet another slow-motion replay of the attack. Shahid downed the last of his tea and placed the vintage Flora Danica china cup softly back on the saucer.

In the corner, a pretty girl obediently rose from the plush pile of chenille pillows where she sat with a handful of other young women. She moved silently toward Shahid's desk in a billow of colorful sheer veils as she floated across the room, her head bowed in deference. She deftly picked up the ornate porcelain teapot from the silver tray and refilled his cup, poured in a measure of cream, then swirled the honey dipper around in the thick raw honey from a small matching sugar bowl and stirred it into his tea. She kneeled next to his chair and rested her cheek on his knee.

"Tell me how I may ease your pain Sidi?" the young girl asked.

Shahid looked down upon her as if just noticing her for the first time. He placed his hand on her head, his fingers entwined in her shimmering jet-black hair. Perhaps she would make a fine wife someday, he thought. Perhaps.

There was a reticent knock on the door. Shahid's attention turned back to the computer screen.

"Come!" he voiced in a low sharp tone.

The door opened hesitantly and a timid young man in a white robe and red keffiyeh stepped into the doorway.

"I'm so sorry to disturb you, Sir," the young man said, bowing his head. "You wanted to be informed as soon as we received word from our people near the scene of the attack this morning."

"Yes?" Shahid grunted.

"They found what was left of the convoy," the young man reported. "There were no survivors."

# FALLING THROUGH THE BLINDSPOT

"And the package?" Shahid asked.

"I'm sorry, Sir. It was completely destroyed. Between the gasoline explosions and the munitions, they were carrying, It appears that contents were either incinerated or dispersed over too large an area to recover anything useful."

"I see," Shahid replied, closing his eyes. His jaw tightened as he tried to swallow his anger. "Leave us!" he barked.

Shahid sat in silence for a moment, his lips trembling, his eyes clenched tightly as a grimace formed on his face. He tried to calm himself, but rage consumed him like wildfire in a field of dry grass. He suddenly leaped to his feet and screamed in rage; tightly grabbing a fistful of the young girl's hair and jerking her backwards. She gasped in surprise and pain as her head was pulled back and she scrambled to try to get her feet beneath her. Shahid struck her across the face with an open palm and then slammed her to the floor, blood dripping from her mouth onto the priceless Persian rug below her.

Shahid reached down and grabbed a linen napkin from the serving tray and wiped a smear of blood off his hand as he walked matter-of-factly to the door, his robes flowing behind him. He grasped the heavy antique brass doorknob and glared at the other girls huddled in the corner, their faces buried in their hands weeping in fear. "Clean up your mess!" he growled, nodding toward the sobbing girl lying next to his desk, tossing the bloody linen napkin at them as he exited the room.

# Chapter Twelve

*The concept of good may not exist without the concept of evil. The existence of evil can serve to highlight what is good, and the pursuit of good can lead to the reduction of evil. The existence of evil is necessary for the existence of good, as it provides a contrast that allows us to understand and appreciate what is good.*
*~ ChatGPT AI ~*

Ahmed Al Rajhi pulled his 1998 Volkswagen Jetta into the parking lot of a Whole Foods parking lot in north Denver. He parked next to a brand-new Aston Martin DB11, parked at the outer edge of the lot away from all the other cars. It still had the temporary sticker on the window and the carbon black metallic paint glinted in the bright sunlight. He smiled, thinking it an amusing gesture to park his dented, faded, and rusted bolt-bucket as close as possible to this $275,000 masterpiece of automotive engineering and design.

Ahmed came to the US three years earlier on a student visa that was purchased from a black-market broker in Saudi Arabia. He registered for graduate-level classes at the University of Colorado but only attended classes for a short time to allow him to make a few contacts and get lost in the crowd. Since then, he had lived in a studio apartment in a large Aurora apartment complex, living off a monthly stipend that was wired directly into his checking account. He had opened the account with a fake ID under the name of a legitimate Saudi student he had met when he first arrived at the university. He took some odd jobs for cash where he could find them to earn extra spending money, but his primary responsibilities were to watch, wait, assimilate, and stay under the radar.

Ahmed desperately hated the U.S. At least he desperately wanted to hate the U.S. His was a love/hate relationship. From the time he was old enough to comprehend, he had been taught that this was the country that raped his motherland of its natural resources, rained fire down on his people, propped up petty dictators around the globe, and mocked his God. But when he arrived, he was awestruck. In his village, life was harsh. Clean water was a treasured commodity. Food was always scarce. In the summer you baked. In the winter you froze. Comfort was a luxury out of reach for most. When your life was not under threat from famine or disease you were at the mercy of gangs of armed thugs that roamed the countryside.

By comparison, the U.S. was a paradise. Here, you were not in constant fear for your life. You could walk into an air-conditioned supermarket any time of day or night and there were aisles and aisles of food of every imaginable type.

# FALLING THROUGH THE BLINDSPOT

Fresh water was available anywhere at the turn of your wrist. The world's finest art, music, and literature were as close as the nearest Wi-Fi hot spot. Even mother nature had blessed this place with beautiful scenery only minutes away. There were times Ahmed could not imagine ever going back to his homeland after being here. It was so easy to be lured by the temptations of this place.

That's why he came to Whole Foods. This, he thought, was the true temple of social hypocrisy. This was where he would come to watch the predominantly upper-middle-class citizens flaunt their social responsibility by shopping for their overpriced organic vegetables and free-range meats. They prided themselves on doing their part to save the world from global warming by packing up their groceries in cloth bags instead of plastic. He could see them looking down their noses at his gasoline-powered car while they loaded their groceries into the back of their $100,000 electric SUVs built with rare earth minerals strip-mined from third-world countries and charged with electricity from coal-fired plants. Fucking hypocrites, he thought as he made his way across the parking lot.

The glass doors swished open, and he walked over to where the carts were parked. He struggled for a moment to separate two carts that seemed to be permanently interlocked in an inextricable tangle. After a brief and frustrating interlude of shaking and pulling, he abandoned that row and pulled a cart from the next row, his hand smearing across the sticky blue handle, still wet from whatever vile sugar-laden brat had drooled on it. He pulled his hand away in disgust and reached for a disinfectant wipe from the empty dispenser next to the carts. Shaking his open hand as if shaking off an injury, he looked about and spied the restrooms, thankfully just to the right of the store entrance.

Ahmed walked to the men's room entrance, pressing the door open with his shoulder. His nostrils were once again assaulted, this time with the pungent mix of minty air freshener and urine. He crossed the room and stood in front of the first faucet. He waved his hand under the faucet for a few seconds with no success. He moved over to the next faucet, a longer, lower model designed for handicap access. Upon waving his hand under that faucet, he was assaulted with a sudden blast of water, half of which splashed over the front edge of the shallow sink onto the front of his pants. Perfect, he thought.

When he finished washing his hands, Ahmed pressed the button on the hand dryer with his elbow. The dryer whirred to life with a loud roar, but only a whisper of warm air. He soon gave up and dried his hands on his shirt, but pointed the air deflector downward, leaning into the front of the dryer for half a dozen more cycles in an attempt to dry the front of his pants. Thankfully, no one else entered the bathroom as he was certain it would appear to someone just entering the room that he was attempting to perform a lewd act with the hand dryer.

When his pants were dry enough to avoid the stigma of having his continence or at least his aim questioned by onlookers, he left the restroom and intercepted a cart left behind by the entrance to the lady's room.

As he walked up and down the aisles, glancing at the parade of disinterested shoppers, the familiar anger began to roil inside him again.  A place like this, with such vast stores of riches, would be beyond the imaginations of all but the wealthiest people in his country.  Yet here, even the lowest classes of people would walk through these aisles with total indifference, completely oblivious to the miraculous intricacy of the social and economic structure that made this possible; even more oblivious to the comparative paucity that defined the lives of most of the rest of the world.  How could God have bestowed such riches on these ungrateful infidels, and such poverty upon his own people?  Surely this was some kind of test of his faith.

Ahmed rounded the corner and got about halfway up the aisle when his progress was impeded by a young mother with three small children.  One child, perhaps nine months old sat in a child seat in the cart, holding a pacifier at arms-length toward the ceiling, babbling loudly.  An older girl, probably four or five years old, was engaged in some sort of imaginary hopscotch with the tiles on the floor, singing some incoherent tune.  The third child, a young boy, probably 3 years old, was flailing about on the floor screaming in high-pitched protest at his mother's unwillingness to purchase some variety of colorfully packaged cereal designed to lure the attention of children with the picture of some exotic animal on the box which held no relation to its contents.  At one point, the child screamed at such a searing pitch that Ahmed became wary of his proximity to the glass jars around him.

"Yeah, go ahead and scream your fucking little head off, you miserable, entitled brat," Ahmed thought to himself.  Statistically, in his village, only one of these three children would survive to adulthood.  The rest would have either died in childbirth or succumbed to cholera, malnutrition, or some type of infection.

While the mother was attempting to restore order and clear the aisleway, Ahmed closed his eyes for a moment and allowed himself to fantasize about wringing the child's neck.  Ahmed was abruptly snapped out of his reverie when he was suddenly rammed from behind by another cart.  He swung about, angrily prepared to verbally thrash whoever had the nerve to interrupt his fantasy, but he suddenly found himself face to face with a very attractive young blond woman whose attention had been buried in her cell phone.  She put her hand to her mouth, "Oh, I am so sorry" she said.  His expression instantly changed from anger to a charming smile.  "No worries" he replied in his best British accent.

Ahmed spoke almost no English when he first came to the U.S.  He had been taught that the best way to pick up English language conversational skills and cultural idioms was by watching television.  He could not afford cable, so he

# FALLING THROUGH THE BLINDSPOT

picked up most of his language skills from watching reruns of BBC shows on PBS, unaware that in the process, he also acquired a very discernible British accent. Between his dark hair and olive complexion, his 6'2" height and the athletic build he had acquired from spending 2 hours a day in the apartment's workout facility, most women found him immensely attractive. Add to that the British accent he had acquired, and Ahmed found that he wielded an alluring charm that was not lost on the opposite sex.

"Wow, I love your accent. Where are you from?" the young woman asked. Ahmed proceeded to recite his well-rehearsed and patently fictional spiel about how he was here on a student visa from the British Virgin Islands to attend medical school. He related a tale of how his father, a Scottish surgeon had met his mother, a native islander while vacationing in the BVI and it was love at first sight. In his experience, a romantic tale about his background always helped him charm the ladies.

After a couple of minutes of chatting her up, Ahmed glanced at his expensive-looking knock-off watch and smiled, "Perhaps we should exchange information. You know, just in case I need to file an insurance claim."

The woman laughed. "What's your number? I will text you mine. Maybe I can buy you dinner and talk you out of filing that claim."

"I think we could work something out," Ahmed replied. He held out his hand and she handed him her phone. He typed his burner phone number on her phone and saved it under the name Wilson Barrett. He handed the phone back to her. She read the name on her phone and smiled. "Well, it is nice to meet you, Wilson," she said, holding her hand out to shake his. He reached out, gently taking her fingers in his hand, and pulled her hand slowly to his lips, never breaking eye contact. He gently kissed the back of her hand. "Please, call me Will. The pleasure, I assure you," he paused for effect; "was all mine. I will look forward to hearing from you soon."

For one breathless moment, time screeched to a halt, and she was completely lost in his eyes. She snapped back into reality with a start, like suddenly waking from a deep sleep. Her pulse raced and she struggled to conceal the shiver that coursed through her. "You can count on it," she smiled nervously as she pulled her hand slowly back from his, forcing herself with some degree of effort to break eye contact. She slid her phone back into her purse and exhaled deeply as he turned to walk away.

Ahmed continued down the aisle, making a mental note to stop and pick up condoms at the pharmacy next door on the way out. When spending an evening with one of his dates, he always insisted on using his own condoms. He would say they were "hypoallergenic" because he was sensitive to latex. In reality, he had no such sensitivity. But sometimes, particularly when he hooked up with a woman whose personality he found particularly grating, he would pierce his condom with a tiny needle in the hopes of impregnating her. Since he rarely slept with the same girl twice, he would probably never know if any of his progeny survived, but he hoped that if he fathered a few sons, perhaps one of them would take after their father and find their way back to God despite being raised in this evil land.

Typically, Ahmed preferred bars and clubs as venues to pick up women since the clientele was usually more amenable to one-night stands, but this woman was just his type; blond, beautiful, athletic, and most importantly, not too bright. Though he rarely contacted a woman for a second date, this one may be an exception, he thought.

As Ahmed made his way up the aisle, his personal phone buzzed. He fished the phone out of his pocket. He had just received an email, "Best Prices on Cialis, Viagra, Levitra, and more…" This was the familiar coded email indicating that he needed to contact his handler. He felt a familiar twinge in his gut. As much as he longed for a real assignment to break up the boredom, part of him hoped this was just another drill. Either way, the pharmacy would have to wait. He only had 90 minutes to get to an anonymous computer to respond.

Ahmed left his cart in the aisle and headed out the exit to the parking lot. The new Aston Martin was still parked next to him. As he walked past, he ran his finger lightly across the smooth lines of the rear door and across the passenger side of the vehicle, admiring the sleek aerodynamic structure of the chassis. What a shame to waste such an exquisite machine on these pigs, he thought to himself.

Ahmed clicked the remote on his key chain, opened his car door, and slid into the driver's seat. He placed his right foot firmly against the inside door panel and kicked out as hard as he could. The door flew open and slammed into the Aston Martin with a loud thump. He smiled as he admired the softball size dent in the side of the Aston Martin created by the edge of his door. He swung his legs into the car and yanked hard on the door handle, hearing the loud screech of metal on metal as the door edge peeled back a long curl of paint from the side panel of the Aston Martin. It was music to his ears. He wished he could stay awhile and watch the pedantic reaction of the owner of the vehicle from a safe distance when they discovered the huge mar in their new toy, but he was on the clock now.

# CHAPTER THIRTEEN

Colorado State Senator John Vanderwurl sat comfortably enveloped in the rich soft leather of his desk chair in the den of his sprawling Cherry Hills Village mansion. In most social situations, John seemed to be in control of the room. He was tall, handsome, and projected an air of self-confidence that made him seem larger than life. He managed to maintain the muscular stature he had established as an Air Force Academy cadet two decades earlier. But sitting behind the massive $500,000 African Blackwood desk, he always felt a bit like a child, sitting at his father's desk.

The desk was by any measure, genuine African Blackwood, known in its native land on the African savanna as Mpingo wood. The look, the feel, and even the distinctive smell all testified to its authenticity. But it was not natural African Blackwood. It was constructed from an engineered material that John had termed Bio-Engineered Lumber.

John had always been torn between two loves, aeronautics and chemistry. His father was a commercial pilot, so he grew up around airplanes. His mother was a chemistry professor, so John received his first chemistry set at age five. When it came time to select a college, John decided to apply to the Air Force Academy so he could pursue both interests. He focused his efforts on materials technology, hoping to enter a career in developing new processes and compounds to make future aircraft lighter, safer, and more durable once he retired from the Air Force.

During his research, John became fascinated with 3D printing technology, particularly using organic materials such as spiderweb latices to add strength and pliability to aircraft wings. The process itself was fairly straightforward. 3D printing technology was a mature process, they just needed to modify the structure of the device to fabricate biological structures. But the process of actually producing the exotic organic raw materials in a controlled environment for their Biofabricator proved to be very difficult and expensive. There was not nearly enough grant money to produce the organic substances he wanted to use to fulfill the goals he had set forth, so in the process of developing the technology, John experimented with substances that were easier to reproduce under laboratory conditions. He focused specifically on plant cells because they could be grown easily in simple containers with a few grow lights and some basic nutrients. Although he made significant strides in proof of concept, none of the plant-based materials he experimented with had the tensile strength required to make significant improvements to the materials he was working with.

The effort started out as essentially a research project, using volunteers from a core group of grad students hoping to get their names on a published paper. Early on, before they acquired any significant funding, John and his research team were working shoulder to shoulder out of John's tiny basement in south Denver. It was one of his research assistants that first said jokingly that they should fabricate some two-by-fours so they could build a larger facility in his backyard. But that gave him the idea. Wood has always been the material of choice to construct a modern civilization, but as the population has increased, demand was outstripping supply and the cost and environmental consequences were becoming increasingly untenable as demand continued to exceed supply. So why not use the Biofabricator to create building materials to precise specifications from organic compounds? What better way to prove the viability of the technology to produce useful products? They had all the equipment and manpower they needed. What they needed now was a project that could attract the investment required to take the technology to the next level. So, the next day he ordered 'Wood doesn't just grow on trees t-shirts for the whole team and the project was officially born.

The original concept had been to create fairly common building materials, but in retrospect, it took no more effort or expense to create an exotic wood plank than to create a common pine two-by-four, so the team decided to devote its efforts to create a 3D rendered plank of something much more exotic. After much research, they settled on African Blackwood, one of the rarest and most valuable woods on the planet. A single African Blackwood log can easily fetch $9000, and it is rare to find planks of any significant size because the Mpingo tree is smaller and more gnarled than most hardwoods. Typically, a Mpingo log yields less than five percent usable wood, mostly smaller pieces used for musical instruments and carvings. It is also considered an endangered species due to its limited and remote habitat, slow growth rate, and over-harvesting.

It took weeks of searching through local exotic hardwood stores to find the perfect African Blackwood plank John would use as the standard to create his first cultured wood plank. The process of creating a virtual model of the wood plank was not terribly complex but it was extremely time-consuming and generated huge amounts of data. Essentially, his team took the plank of wood and used a precision laser to shave off microscopically thin layers of the plank, 2-3 cells thick each. They then used an electron microscope borrowed from the University of Denver medical lab to catalog the position, orientation, and composition of each cell into a huge database. The goal was to create a molecule-by-molecule map of the entire plank in digital form, using simulation algorithms to fill in the blanks for materials destroyed during the slicing process. Fortunately, much of the data generated was fairly repetitive so they were able to develop data compression algorithms that dramatically reduced the amount of storage needed, but the database was nevertheless enormous.

# FALLING THROUGH THE BLINDSPOT

Once the database was completed, a driver was developed to interface the database to the Biofabricator.  They reconstructed the plank cell by cell using meristematic tissues, essentially the plant equivalent of stem cells as the base material.  A separate algorithm was used to randomize the wood grain pattern using the proper sequence of cells to form the ray, fiber, and vessel structures of the wood to form the unique grain patterns and plank sizes.

It took two full years to develop their first wood plank, but once they had perfected the process and the formula, they could produce one unique plank every few hours.  After a few weeks, they finally had enough material to build the desk he was now sitting at.  They hired the finest, most meticulous cabinet maker they could find to design and build the masterpiece in Mpingo.  John did not tell the woodworker anything specific about the project, other than that the piece was extremely important and had the potential to dramatically impact his stature within his professional community.  The cabinet maker was immediately astonished by the rarity and value of the raw materials he was provided.  He had never seen African Blackwood planks of this size and quality.  Surely, he thought, this project must have been commissioned by some powerful politician or A-List celebrity with enormous resources.

The goal was to create a proof of concept demonstration to offer the investment community.  They wanted it to be tangible.  Something that could be seen, touched, and felt.  Something which could be understood for its intrinsic value even if you had no knowledge of the process that went into making it.

One of the industries that held the most promise for quick profits utilizing this new technology was agriculture.  The meat industry alone was a $5 trillion-a-year enterprise and growing.  Companies like Upside Foods were already developing processes to revolutionize the meat industry by using stem cells to grow meat in the lab in a safe, efficient, and ecologically friendly manner with the ethical advantage of eliminating the slaughter of billions of living creatures every year.  What Upside was attempting to accomplish with meat, they hoped to duplicate with wood.

It all started with this desk.  A desk that started out as a small plank of African Blackwood purchased at a local hardwood store that inspired the creation of the Bio-Engineered Lumber which led to the founding of AboveBoard Inc.  In a few short years, AboveBoard went public and attracted over $10 billion in IPO investors and made John worth $200 million overnight.

The desk was impressive as a piece of furniture, but it only served as the bait to lure investors in to hear the real story.  The technology that created something so simple and utilitarian as an office desk had staggering implications for future applications in exotic bio-engineered materials.  But the ultimate prize was the potential for medical application, specifically in organ and limb regeneration.

# JACOB MATTHEWS

John had recruited a renowned neurosurgeon to develop a proposal for a research project using his Biofabricator technology to promote the regeneration of nerve pathways. That was the real holy grail that made the technology so valuable.

John had proven himself to be an effective leader throughout the process of developing the technology and launching his company, but the thought of dealing with the day-to-day struggles of managing profit and loss, government regulations, and the mundane challenges of corporate life while answering to shareholders was of no interest to him. At the bequest of his colleagues, he remained on the board of directors to help guide research and development but handed off the role of CEO to a veteran Silicon Valley CEO with an ambitious vision for the future of the company.

It was now nearly 4 years since John had stepped down as CEO. John had spent the first few months after relinquishing his post trying to decide how best to apply his skills and new-found fortune. One of his first projects was to develop a TED talk, explaining the details of the technology he had developed and its potential impact in layman's terms. His natural ability to communicate and the optimistic enthusiasm he brought to the subject matter made his talk one of the 5 most popular TED talks of the year with over 20 million views on YouTube alone. John became a minor celebrity overnight, making the rounds on a number of popular podcasts and TV interview segments.

On the advice of many of his friends, but mostly at the urging of Edgar and Edna, John decided to try his hand at local politics. John decided to make his first foray into politics by entering the race for the Colorado State Senate. By the time he entered the race, both Republican and Democratic candidates had been selected and a fairly vicious bout of negative campaigning had ensued from both candidates. Fortunately for him, voter patience had grown quite thin with these tactics. Armed with the celebrity status he now enjoyed along with the fact that AboveBoard had brought thousands of new jobs and millions in tax revenue into his district, he managed a landslide victory in the election, garnering nearly 80% of the vote, despite running as an Independent candidate.

With John's keen mind and natural leadership ability, it did not take long for him to be noticed by his colleagues in the Senate. As an Independent candidate, he quickly earned the respect and admiration of his peers on both sides of the aisle for being able to offer rational insights on all the legislation that crossed his desk without being bogged down by having to take a position that best aligned with party doctrine. No one doubted that he had a bright future in the political sphere. But recent developments had suddenly accelerated that trajectory.

It was barely six weeks before the gubernatorial election and the incumbent Governor was embroiled in a sexual assault scandal with a young intern. Meanwhile, the opposing candidate had just been arrested for DUI after crashing

# FALLING THROUGH THE BLINDSPOT

his Lexus into a light post with a blood alcohol level of .25.  Almost overnight, John had found himself in the midst of an apparently massive grassroots social media effort to enlist him to run for Governor as an independent candidate.  Up until the past week, John had been running a distant 3$^{rd}$ in the polls due to the entrenched nature of bipartisan politics, despite the recent foibles of the other candidates.  John knew it would take a minor miracle to close that gap in the time remaining before the election but his poll numbers had been inexplicably rising over the past week, to the point where he had become not only a real contender, but the focus of a great deal of media attention, even though he had not yet formally announced his candidacy.

John was just reviewing a tight schedule sent to him by his campaign manager when his cell phone erupted, startling him momentarily.  The familiar face of Edna Wilson lit up his screen.

"Edna!  How are you?"

"Oh, just wonderful, John.  It's such a beautiful morning outside.  The trees are all changing colors in the neighborhood.  I just love the fall."

"Wow, you really sound chipper this morning.  You haven't been hitting the Elderberry wine already, have you?"

"Oh, goodness no!" Edna replied in a chuckling tone.  "I just got home from my morning walk. "

Edgar and Edna had known John for most of his adult life.  Edgar had first met John as an instructor at the Air Force Academy and had followed him throughout his military career as his flight instructor.  When John's parents passed away in a tragic automobile accident, Edgar and Edna effectively became his surrogate parents.  Over the years, they spent nearly every Christmas together, along with countless camping, fishing, and vacation trips.  He had been devastated when Edgar passed away, but he was even more concerned for Edna's well-being.  He was certain that Edgar's passing would send her into a downward spiral that would end in her passing away from sheer grief.  But lately, Edna sounded so much better, it was as if the veil of sorrow had been lifted from her and she was back to being the strong, happy, outgoing woman she was when Edgar was still alive.

"Listen, Edna, I've been meaning to call you for the last few days, but things have been so crazy lately.  I'm really sorry I haven't been around much but this campaign is suddenly absorbing all my time.  I know how difficult it's been since Edgar passed.  I feel awful that I haven't been there for you."

"Oh, don't be silly.  I'm perfectly fine.  I'm more worried about you, working so hard.  You need to slow down and enjoy life once in a while."

"You should tell my campaign manager.  She has me booked solid right up to the election.  I can't even use the restroom without scheduling it on my outlook calendar."

"I don't suppose you would be free for dinner tonight, would you?"

"Oddly enough, I was just checking my email when you called and I had an appointment for 7:00 tonight that was just canceled."

"Well, hurry up and schedule me in.  You're coming over for homemade lasagna tonight."

"Oh my God, I haven't had a home-cooked meal since Easter at your place.  I would love to come by."

"It's all set then.  We can't wait to see you."

John was immediately thrown by the "we", but he let it slide, hoping it was a force of habit and not Edna trying to set him up with a blind date.  As much as he appreciated Edna's past efforts at finding him the perfect soul mate, he really didn't have time for a relationship right now.

"Can I bring anything?" John asked.

"Just a big appetite and a pasta-friendly shirt," Edna replied.  Italian food had always been John's favorite but it had been a running gag with Edgar and Edna that he often left their table wearing a reminder of the meal on his shirt.  Many an expensive tie had fallen victim to an errant tomato sauce backsplash over the years, but the fact that Edna had encouraged him to wear casual attire left him feeling a bit more comfortable that this would not be a setup for a romantic introduction.

# CHAPTER FOURTEEN

*The way we experience and understand the world is constrained by the limitations of our senses and mind. The reality that we perceive is a filtered and distorted version of a more complex and nuanced truth.*

*~ ChatGPT AI ~*

Ahmed pulled his Jetta into the parking lot of the Aurora public library. He entered the building and took the stairs up to the second floor, where they kept public access computers. He brought up the Denver Craigslist page and looked in the auto sales section.

Al Hadid had recently been using the classified section of Craigslist in large metropolitan areas to pass information to its members. The automotive section provided the best opportunity to pass coded information without being detected.

Each operative was assigned a vehicle type. Ahmed was the Cadillac Eldorado. The year was based on the time that the trigger email arrived. Ahmed received his email at 2:00, so he would look for a 2002 Cadillac with the words "Must Sell" in the title. The purpose of the message was coded to the color of the car. The color of the car would indicate the severity of the alert. Green meant a simple status check, yellow indicated that your presence was required at some type of demonstration or event. Red indicated that action was imminent. It did not take Ahmed much time to find the ad he was looking for:

2002 Cadillac Eldorado – MUST SELL. Crimson Pearl color, Transmission replaced 3 months ago, $11,900, firm. Call (722) 039-8856. After 5 PM, call (722) 104-9901.

The meeting place was encoded into the phone numbers. The last seven digits of the first number were the GPS latitude. The last seven digits of the second number were a negative number indicating the longitude. The first meeting with the other operatives would always occur at some type of bar or restaurant that offered free WiFi. The "3 months ago" line indicated that he would be meeting with three other operatives. The last four numbers of the price indicated the time of the meeting. If the words "MUST SELL" were capitalized, as these were, it indicated that the meeting would take place on the same day. Otherwise, the meeting would take place the following day. The ad would only appear for one day and the price was always set high enough to discourage anyone from calling but low enough not to attract too much attention.

Ahmed would be meeting with three other operatives at 1900 hours, 7:00 P.M. He pulled up Google on the library computer and entered the GPS coordinates.  The coordinates pointed to a family diner just off I-25.

Ahmed texted the address to himself and sat back in his chair, reveling at the moment.  Finally, he had a real assignment and with three other operatives, no less.  This must be something big.  He couldn't wait to get started.

# Chapter Fifteen

Peter had spent most of the afternoon on the phone with his grad school roommate, Dr. Robert Chase, working out the details of his plans for Sarah 2.0. Dr. Chase was in the process of completing initial human trials on a new 3D neural mapping technology he had been developing which he hoped would be instrumental in helping to develop neural communication links between the brain and electronic interfaces. When he heard the details of Peter's plans, he was more than enthusiastic to help. Before the conversation was over, he agreed to be on the first plane out from San Diego to Denver the next morning.

Peter was just packing up his briefcase getting ready to call it a day. In his mind, he was already rehearsing the uncomfortable conversation that he would soon be having with Sarah to explain the details of the neural monitoring procedure that awaited her tomorrow when his cell phone startled him out of his reverie.

*"I said, war! Huh! Good God, y'all! What is it good for? Absolutely nothin! Say it again!"*

It had been a while since he had heard that particular ringtone, indicating that his former employer, BMC Corporation was on the other end of the line. "This can't be good news," he thought as he picked up the phone debating whether to swipe the slider on his phone's screen to answer or allow it to go to voicemail and delay the inevitable.

Peter and Sarah had effectively completed their work with the AWARE project when BMC was bought out by a large technology consortium, so most of the development team was no longer considered "mission critical" to the new management. Under the terms of their dismissal, they continued to own the patents on the technology, but BMC would be allowed to continue to use and develop the system they developed as a wholly owned subsidiary of the new entity. The terms of the agreement provided that Peter and Sarah would continue to supply technical support and consultation with a graduated fee structure which was designed to discourage BMC from over-utilizing their services and they were allowed to continue the development of the core AI system for their own purposes, provided it did not compete with the weapons contracts or the web browser that BMC developed from it. The Associative Memory Complex or AMC at the core of the AWARE system became the kernel of Edgar's Virtual Personality Avatar.

The AMC was designed not only to develop appropriate responses to input stimuli but to run continuous simulations offline to analyze as many different configurations of input as possible. It established multiple weighted responses so that the response to a specific input stimulus was probabilistic rather than deterministic to prevent any potential enemy from being able to anticipate its next move. It also created a library of detailed threat responses which could be called upon in real-time enemy engagements. This was necessary from a weapons standpoint to thwart enemy defense systems as quickly as possible without wasting time on unnecessary computation, but it also turned out to be very useful for their application as it added consistent, yet not entirely predictable responses to the simulation.

After a few bars of Edwin Starr belaboring the evils of war, Peter decided that facing the music on the other end of the line was preferable to having the music of his ringtone reverberating in his head until tomorrow morning. He passed his finger over the slider and put the phone to his ear. "This is Peter."

"Peter, how the hell are you?" a jovial voice rang out from the other end of the phone.

It took a moment for Peter to register the voice on the other end of the phone. "Bill, is that you?"

"In the flesh," Bill replied.

Bill Waters had been a key software architect on the AWARE project but had been furloughed at the same time as Peter, Sarah, and Beaver. Peter had always liked and respected Bill, but they lost touch not long after Peter and Sarah had moved to Colorado.

"What the hell are you doing back at BMC?"

"I stopped in to use the shitter and some asshole in a sports jacket and a turtleneck told me to get back to work."

"That sounds about right," Peter chuckled.

"They called me about four months ago and offered me a contract to do some upgrades on the AWARE system. I wasn't really interested but they kept sweetening the pot until I couldn't say no anymore. "

"Wow! No wonder we haven't had any support calls in a while."

"Yeah, I'm sorry about that. I hope I'm not taking too much food off your table."

"Hey, don't be. We've got so many irons in the fire right now I don't have any extra cycles to spare."

"I'm relieved to hear that. I was afraid by taking this job I would be cutting into your action."

"Not at all. I'm actually relieved to have someone else picking up the reins. So how is it going over there?"

"Ah, you know. Same shit, different business card. How about you? I read an article online about your new enterprise. Sounds intriguing. How's that going?"

"We've had our challenges, but I think we're getting close to turning the corner on this thing. You should come out and see us sometime. I know Sarah would really like to see you."

"I would love to do that. We have a lot of catching up to do. This isn't strictly a social call though. I could really use your help with something. This is a weird one."

"Shoot!" Peter said.

"I got a call out of the blue from the DOD. They wanted us to review the black box data off one of their AWARE-equipped drones."

"Crash site recovery?"

"No. Actually, from the data logs, it appears the drone completed the mission with no incident. I asked why they needed us to review the data, but they were pretty spooky about it. They wouldn't tip their hand as far as what we were supposed to be looking for, but we found something pretty odd."

"Like, Area 51 odd, or Epstein-didn't-kill-himself odd?"

"Maybe a bit of both. Twenty minutes of dead air odd."

"What do you mean dead air?"

"The black box has a data gap of precisely 19 minutes and 36 seconds where nothing is recorded."

"You mean static, like some kind of jamming signal?"

"No, I mean nothing. Like nothing. All zeroes. Like deep zeroes. We performed a deep data analysis on the drive to pick up any remnants of ghost data during that time period and it was blank. Like the drive itself had been magnetically wiped and then overwritten with zeroes repeatedly until there was no possible trace of data left. Not even traces of the original diagnostic patterns."

"That doesn't even seem possible. Did they give you any clue what was going on with the drone at the time?"

"No. A classified mission was all they would tell me. I've had my team here going through all the AWARE interface drivers, but we hit a bit of a wall. No one can make heads or tails of this code. Looks like something Beaver developed. I assume he is still working for you."

"He is. You probably don't have any COP experts left on your team to perform the proper analysis."

"COP?"

"Cannabinoid Oriented Programming."

"Ah, yes. The original cloud-based programming structure. We could really use his help trying to figure out what's going on with this."

"I will have him take a look. Are all the black box files posted on our shared drive space?"

"I will get them up there as soon as we hang up.  Thanks, Peter.  I really appreciate the help."

"Oh, no worries.  But just so you know, there's no Friends and Family discount on our support fee structure.  Fortunately, the DOD's got deep pockets and Beaver loves the OT.  I'm not entirely sure why, I don't pay him any extra for it.  I think he just likes the attention.  Anyway, I will have him get in touch."

"Thanks, Peter.  Talk to you soon."

# Chapter Sixteen

*The most effective way to conceal information or activities is by making them appear to be open and obvious. This can be seen as a form of misdirection, where attention is drawn away from what is actually happening by presenting it in a way that seems transparent and unimportant.*

*~ ChatGPT AI ~*

Ahmed pulled into the parking lot of the Mile High Family Diner just a few minutes before 7:00 PM. The restaurant was outfitted in a 50's/60's motif, from the turquoise vinyl seats to the vintage 45 jukebox that blared out a continuous stream of Chuck Barry, Elvis, and the Beach Boys.

Ahmed stepped through the chrome and neon montage at the entrance to the restaurant and was greeted by a bubbly, twenty-something hostess, outfitted to compliment the ambiance with a blonde ponytail, a tight white sweater, a poodle skirt, bobby socks, and firehouse-red lipstick.

"Hey Sweetie, just you tonight?" the hostess asked through a large wad of bubble gum. "If you like I can seat you at the counter."

"No, actually there will be four of us. I am meeting some associates," Ahmed replied, flashing his well-rehearsed smile.

"Well, how about right up front here where you can keep an eye out for them?" she replied, pointing toward a booth near the entrance.

"I would prefer something a little quieter, away from the jukebox. We have some business matters to discuss."

"Oh, my. Tall dark AND reclusive. Just like Howard Hughes."

"Howard Who?" Ahmed asked.

"Not Who, Hughes" she replied. "Period humor. You know, 60's stuff?"

Ahmed just stared back at her blankly. "Never mind, it's not important. C'mon Sweetie, I got a booth in the back with your name on it," she said, handing Ahmed the stack of menus. She intertwined her arm in his as though he were carrying her books home from school and sauntered toward the back of the restaurant guiding him back to a secluded booth in the corner. As she walked, her skirt swirled side to side to the beat of the Drifters 'Save the Last Dance for Me'.

"How's this?" the hostess asked as they arrived at the booth.

"Thank you," Ahmed said. "This will do quite nicely."

She took the menus and arranged them on the patterned Formica tabletop as he sat down. She gave him a wink, pointed to her name badge, and said "If you need anything, my name is Trixie. When I'm not here, I'm Stephanie, but my name tag was only big enough for Trixie." She smiled, turned, and walked away, glancing back out of the corner of her eye and noting that his gaze was still locked on her as she walked away. She directed her focus back to the front of the restaurant, her ponytail swaying in perfect time to the music.

Ahmed opened his menu, splitting his attention between the entryway and the hypnotic sway of Trixie's skirt as she walked away. His operatives would be arriving in 2-minute intervals to allow him to screen each individually.

Exactly at 7:02, Khalil Hassan entered the diner carrying a leather satchel, nervously scoping out the restaurant. Khalil had only been in the country for a few months, having just turned 21. He was barely 5 foot tall, no more than 130 pounds with thick horned rim glasses. Trixie, (the hostess formerly known as Stephanie as she often referred to herself) discretely slid up next to him.

"Hey, Cutie!" she shouted out over the jukebox, momentarily startling him. He jumped back, nearly dropping his satchel. Trixie put her hand to her mouth to suppress her smile, clearly enjoying the not-so-unintentional surprise. His slight build and animated nature reminded her a bit of Barney Fife from the Andy Griffith show reruns she used to watch with her grandfather.

"Just you tonight, Sweetie?"

The young man stuttered a bit, trying not to look rattled. "Uh, no. Thank you. I'm actually joining some colleagues."

"Oh, you must be with Howard Hughes," Trixie replied.

"I beg your pardon?"

"Right this way," she said taking him by the arm and leading him back to the corner where Ahmed was seated.

As they approached, Khalil held up his right hand as if waving. Ahmed spotted the black titanium ring with braided steel band inlays on his hand. It was the same ring that Ahmed and all the operatives of Al Hadid wore to identify themselves within the group. The rings were inexpensive and could easily be replaced on Amazon if one were lost. Common enough to be easily overlooked, yet distinctive enough to be swiftly identified if you were looking for it, particularly when worn on the right hand as the Al Hadid always did.

"Is this one of yours, Howard?" Trixie asked as they approached.

"I believe it is," Ahmed replied as they arrived at the booth. "The day of the Lord approaches," Ahmed said, holding his hand out to shake so the man could see his own ring.

"It is an honor to be doing His work," the man replied nervously in a well-rehearsed tone as he reached out to shake Ahmed's hand.

Trixie turned and walked back toward the front of the restaurant.

"Please, have a seat," Ahmed said pointing to the other side of the booth.

# FALLING THROUGH THE BLINDSPOT

"Thank you," Khalil said. "My name is…"

Ahmed held up his hand. "No names. From here on out we go only by code names in case any of us are caught."

"I'm sorry," Khalil said. "I guess I'm still a bit nervous. I have only been here a short while and this is my first real assignment since I arrived. Please forgive me."

"Relax, we are all here for the same reason. You must be our com-tech specialist."

"I am, yes," he replied.

Each four-man operative team consisted of a team leader, a communications and technical expert, a weapons/security expert, and a cover man. The cover man was usually someone from the area who was familiar with local customs and culture and could act as a driver/frontman to help the rest of the group fit in and deflect suspicion.

Khalil pulled a medium-sized FedEx box from his satchel and set it on the table. "This arrived this morning. I assumed you would want to wait to open it until we were all here."

"Yes. Thank you," Ahmed replied, pulling the box toward him and examining the return label. The package had come from a P.O. Box in Hoboken, but the box appeared to have originally been sent from an address in Malaysia, and new labels were affixed after the package had arrived in New Jersey.

Just then, Oman Khan arrived at the door. Oman was a good 6'4", extremely muscular, wearing a black trench coat over a black pin-stripe suit with black leather gloves and a black fedora.

Trixie walked up to the man, deliberately swinging her hips side to side to the music to make the poodle skirt swirl back and forth around her as she walked. "Wow, Al Capone. You must be here with Howard Hughes and the accountant."

"I'm what?" he growled with a perplexed look on his face.

"Sorry, it's a little game I like to play. Nothing interesting ever really happens around here so I like to make up little docudramas to make the shift go by a little quicker."

"I don't really care for games," Oman growled, hoping to intimidate the young woman but she wasn't biting. After working most of her way through college as a hostess she found the best way of dealing with difficult customers was not to allow them to suck you into their world, so she offered up the same effervescent smile she gave to all of her customers. Most customers would concede this metaphorical staring contest pretty quickly, but Oman was not budging. She sidled up to him and intertwined her arm in his. He looked down at her with revulsion as if it were the arm of a rotting corpse, but she just beamed back at him, enjoying the challenge of breaking through the seemingly impenetrable shell this man had constructed.

"So, are you here alone or meeting someone?" she asked playfully in a deliberately conspiratorial hushed tone.

"I'm meeting some associates," he replied.

"She shoots, she scores!" she said as she tightened her arm around his and started walking toward the booth where Ahmed and Khalil were waiting. "Right this way…"

Trixie attempted to engage in conversation as they walked back toward Ahmed's booth, but Oman wanted none of it. After a handful of one-word answers, she finally conceded that this one was not worth the effort to try to thaw out and they completed the last half of their stroll to the booth in silence.

"Hey Howard, your party planner is here!" Trixie announced with a huge grin as they arrived at the table. Oman turned his head slowly and glared at her as he removed his hat. She raised her eyebrows and turned, emitting a silent whistle, thinking what a shame it was to waste such a physique on someone with zero sense of humor. She definitely would not want to run into that guy in a dark alley, she thought.

As they reached the booth, Ahmed placed his hands flat out on the table to make his black ring clearly visible from a distance. Oman raised his right hand, now holding his hat to make sure his own ring was visible.

"The day of the Lord approaches," Ahmed said, holding his hand out to shake.

"It is an honor to be doing His work," Oman said as he shook Ahmed's hand.

"Please have a seat," Ahmed replied pointing to the seat next to Khalil. "You must be our security expert."

The man turned his head looking at the much smaller man seated next to him up and down, then turned back to Ahmed and said, "Seems so."

Ahmed looked back toward the entrance to see Trixie seating another couple toward the front of the diner. Across the restaurant, Russ, a tall lanky, red-headed young man in a black hoodie, slid off one of the chrome and vinyl bar stools at the counter and sauntered toward the three men. He stopped when he reached the edge of the booth.

"What the fuck do you want, Opie?" Oman growled.

The redhead casually pulled his right hand from the pocket of the hoodie and held his hand up with his fingers spread, chest high, the back of his hand facing Oman so that he could easily see the ring, then he slowly closed his fingers into a fist, leaving only his middle finger raised.

Oman placed his hands on the table as if ready to jump up and knock the young man's head off. "Please," Ahmed interceded, holding his hand in a stopping gesture. "We are all on the same team here."

Ahmed turned toward Russ and held his hand out to shake. "The day of the

# FALLING THROUGH THE BLINDSPOT

Lord approaches."

"Honored to be doing His work and all that shit," the young man replied in a sarcastic tone, giving Ahmed's hand a single pump shake as he slid into the booth beside him.

Oman gave the young man a steely glare as he settled in. "What's your problem asshole?"

"My problem?" the young man replied in an exasperated tone. "Well, for starters, this is supposed to be some secret goddamn mission and you guys are all sitting here like the fuckin' clown college alumni association. We got Valentino over here decked out in Ralph Loren hitting on the hostess. Over here you've got the president of the Pee Wee Herman fan club, sweating his ass off like he has a bomb in his briefcase. Then here you are, Planet of the Apes meets the Sopranos. How in the hell do you guys expect to go unnoticed?"

At that, Oman reached across the table, grabbed the young man by the front of his hoodie, and jerked him forward, pulling him halfway out of his seat so they were face to face, no more than an inch apart. "Maybe we don't need some orange-headed American infidel shit joining our cause."

The young man moved so quickly, that the giant across the table barely even registered the flash of metal as Russ pulled a butterfly knife from the pocket of his hoodie, twirled it into the open position swung his arm across the table stopping the arc of his arm abruptly when the tip of the sharp blade made contact with the skin of the large man's neck, directly over his jugular vein.

"Listen, camel-fuck, I don't give a shit about you or your goddamn cause. I'm here to get paid. And if you fuck up and we get caught, that ain't gonna happen. So, you can bleed out on this table right now, or we can get back to doing our jobs, and right now my job is to keep you 3 stooges under the radar."

"Please, gentlemen," Ahmed said pleadingly. "We may be here for different reasons, but we share a common goal. Let's put our differences aside and work together toward that goal."

The two continued, locked in a close stare-down for another second or two until the larger man released his grip, pushing the young man back into his seat. As he settled back, Russ swirled the knife back into its closed position and eased it back into his hoodie pocket. Ahmed glanced around the restaurant for a moment, but none of the other patrons seemed to have taken notice of the brief altercation.

"Thank you, both," Ahmed said. "Now, let's get down to business." Ahmed pulled a small pen knife from his own pocket and slid the blade across the top of the FedEx box. Inside the box were 4 smartphones with 4 Bluetooth earpieces, a plastic container with half a dozen syringes, and two glass vials of clear liquid. Ahmed removed the smartphones and Bluetooth devices from the box.

"These will be our sole means of communication with each other during this mission. We will be disposing of them as soon as we complete our task. Ahmed handed a phone and earpiece to Khalil. "To maintain anonymity and deniability, we shall all be using code names during this mission. Since you are our communications and technology expert, your code name will be Cisco."

He then passed a phone and earpiece to Oman. "Since you are our weapons and security man, your code name will be Magnum." Oman cracked a nearly imperceptible smile. He liked the new moniker, both for its association with the weapon and for the male virility it implied.

"And since you are our frontman and driver for this operation, you will be known as Kato," Ahmed said, handing the third phone and earpiece to Russ. Russ rolled his eyes as he took the earpiece from Ahmed. "Oh, great! Both these guys get cool names and I get to be the guy living in OJ's guesthouse." Ahmed just ignored the remark.

"You will refer to me as Hannibal," Ahmed said.

Russ looked at Ahmed with a questioning sneer. "A-Team or Lecter?"

"I beg your pardon?" Ahmed asked.

"Hannibal. As in Hannibal Smith from the A-Team, or Hannibal Lecter the serial killer and gourmet cannibal?"

"Hannibal the Phoenician military strategist," Ahmed replied with a frown.

"OK, whatever, dude," the young man said shaking his head.

Just then, the waitress arrived at the table, looking to be somewhere in her mid to late 50s, wearing the stereotypical 1950's pink waitress outfit with the white apron, red retro-framed eyeglasses, and a bouffant hairdo. Ahmed was visibly disappointed that the young blond in the much shorter skirt on the other side of the restaurant was not assigned to his table.

"Good evening gentlemen. I'm Betty Lou. What'll it be tonight?" she asked indifferently, pulling a small order book from her apron and plucking a yellow pencil from her firmly sprayed hair.

The four men looked blankly at each other for a moment, then Ahmed spoke up. "We'll just have four cheeseburgers and four Cokes."

"Actually, make mine a Diet Coke," Russ interjected.

"Fries with those?" Betty Lou asked, her eyes still focused on her pad as she took down their order.

"Yes, please. And could you hold off putting that in for 15 minutes or so? We have some business matters to discuss," Ahmed replied.

"You got it, hon," she replied sardonically. "Anything else?"

"Yes, what is the internet password?" Khalil asked.

"Right up there on the whiteboard," Betty Lou replied in her best DMV monotone, still writing on her pad, stopping only momentarily to point her pencil

# FALLING THROUGH THE BLINDSPOT

back over her shoulder at the whiteboard hanging next to the kitchen window. "Elvis lives, no caps, no spaces."

"Thank you, Miss Lou," Khalil said in his thick middle eastern accent.

Betty Lou stopped writing and peered over the top of her rhinestone-studded glasses at the four men, then locked her gaze on Russ.

"Yeah, they're not from around here," he said.

"No kidding. Who would have thought?" Betty Lou replied sarcastically as she stuck the pencil back into her hair, placing the order pad back in her apron. She gathered the menus, turned, and walked back toward the entrance.

"We are supposed to be contacted at precisely 7:15. We have about five minutes," Ahmed said as he turned on the Bluetooth earpiece and fit it into his ear. The other three men followed suit.

Khalil chimed in as he finished typing on his phone. "The call will be coming in on Skype. Cell phone communications are too easily intercepted. You will need to enter the Wi-Fi password onto your devices, then activate the Skype app." He passed a yellow sticky note to each of the three men. "Here is a Skype login and password I've set up for each phone."

Russ and Ahmed set up their phones while Khalil helped Oman navigate through the setup menus to connect his phone to the local router and log in to Skype. As they were typing on their phones, Betty Lou arrived back at the table and set their drinks in front of them. Khalil was just finishing helping Oman finish logging in as she turned and walked away. A moment later, the Skype ringtone chimed simultaneously on all four phones.

The four men simultaneously hit the answer button on their phones, and the face of Shahid Khabir, supreme leader of the Al Hadid appeared on their phones. Russ did not recognize the face, but when he looked up, all three of the other men displayed a look of stunned astonishment, as though they were witnessing a miracle unfolding before their eyes.

Russ nudged Ahmed, who started as if suddenly awoken from a trance. "Oh, uh, Hello… your highness. We were not expecting, I mean… We are honored and humbled to be speaking to you, your highness."

Russ focused his attention back on his phone, making a considerable effort not to roll his eyes in the process.

Shahid spoke. "Good morning, gentlemen. Or should I say good evening? Our day has just started here. And there is much to be done, so let's get straight to business. I'm sure you are all surprised to see me handling this matter personally. I hope that fact will underscore the critical nature of the assignment you are about to embark upon.

"As you are probably aware, our operations and supply routes have been under constant attack recently by American drones. In the past, we've been able to jam the communications to disable the drones, but these new drones have the ability to continue to operate autonomously, making them all but impossible to bring down. Earlier this week, an attack on one of our convoys destroyed some materials that could have brought a great deal of power and prestige to our organization. My own beloved cousin was killed in that attack." The men could see the anger rising in Shahid as he looked down from the camera.

"I am so sorry, your Highness. Whatever we can do to avenge his death, we are at your service," Ahmed offered.

Shahid held up a picture of Peter Reynolds in front of the camera. "This is Dr. Peter Reynolds. I've sent photographs of Dr. Reynolds and his wife to your phones. Doctor Reynolds developed the artificial intelligence system that controls the drones when communications are lost. Our sources tell us that Dr. Reynolds is no longer working with the U.S. defense department, but he and his wife have started their own company and are living in your area. All I need is for you to persuade Dr. Reynolds that it would be in his best interest to provide us with a backdoor into the AI control system that will allow us to disable or destroy those drones."

The four men glanced at each other momentarily. "With all due respect, your Highness, I'm not sure how receptive he will be to that idea," Ahmed replied.

"In the box with the phones, you should have received two vials of a drug that we have used successfully in numerous interrogations. It is a derivative of Sodium Pentothal, but much more powerful. It completely immobilizes the subject for two to three hours but leaves them receptive to suggestion and amplifies sensations of pain. Your assignment is to break into their home at night, inject them with the drug, and inform them that we will be taking Mrs. Reynolds as our guest until he complies. Each vial contains three milliliters of the drug. Do not use more than two milliliters on Mr. Reynolds, and one milliliter on Mrs. Reynolds. Any more could kill them."

"Understood," Ahmed said handing one vial and one syringe to Oman and pocketing the other in his jacket.

"I would encourage you to use whatever methods necessary to garner their cooperation. The more painful, the better. Nothing motivates a person to cooperate like watching a loved one bleeding and writhing in excruciating pain."

Russ looked up from his phone to see a look of eager anticipation growing on Oman's face. He wondered how much longer it would be before the man actually started salivating.

Shahid continued. "We have a safe house set up for you in a farmhouse north of Denver. I will text the address to the team lead as soon as we complete this call. It is already stocked with food, supplies, and everything you will need including WiFi. The house is fairly secluded and there is plenty of land around it

# FALLING THROUGH THE BLINDSPOT

to dispose of the body once we have what we need.

"What is our time frame?" Ahmed asked.

"I'm afraid our window of opportunity is fairly narrow. With the increased aerial surveillance going on here, it is only a matter of time before the Americans order a strike on our facility. I need you to get to Dr. Reynolds as quickly as you can. Tomorrow night if possible."

"We will not let you down," Ahmed said.

"I know you will not," Shahid said. "I selected you personally. As you know, your uncle was a member of my personal guard. He was a good man. He always spoke highly of you."

"Thank you, your Highness. You honor me greatly," Ahmed replied bowing his head slightly.

"God be with you," Shahid said.

"His justice is at hand," Ahmed, Oman, and Khalil all said in unison.

The four men hit the end button on their phones and sat in hushed reverence for a moment until Russ broke the silence and blurted out, "So, who's the creepy dude anyway?"

Oman's nostrils flared and he hissed at Russ, spitting his words like venom, "That creepy dude, as you so insolently referred to him, is the grand leader of the Al Hadid!  7th great-grandson of Ab Abdul Shahid; rightful heir to the throne of Ha'aretz Hamuvtakhat!  You should count yourself fortunate to even hear his name spoken in your presence, let alone to serve in his glorious charge!"

"Easy there, Condom," Russ said with a smirk.

"Magnum!" Oman barked back slamming his fist on the table.

"Pot-a-to, pot-ah-to," Russ replied in a mock apologetic tone, leaning back and holding his hands up in a pose of resignation. "Just curious to know who's signing my paycheck here."

Khalil pulled a Chromebook from his satchel and started typing furiously. Ahmed eyed him curiously.

Khalil glanced up momentarily as he typed, "I'm here on a student visa. I'm currently interning in the IT department of the county clerk's office. We should be able to locate Dr. Reynolds's residence through the tax database." A moment later he announced, "Here it is, Dr. Peter Reynolds and spouse Sarah Reynolds. According to the plot map, it looks like they live in a fairly remote area west of Boulder. We should be able to get in and out fairly easily. All the home alarm systems up there work off of cellular interfaces. It should be a trivial matter to jam the cell signal long enough to allow me to get inside and deactivate the alarm."

"OK," Ahmed said. "Cisco, I want you to get everything you can on the property. I want to know all the entrances and exits, roads, closest neighbors, maps, whatever you can get. Also, see if you can identify what type of security system they have so you will know what you need when we get there."

"I will do my best, sir," Khalil replied.

"Magnum, get the address from Cisco. I want you to take a drive up there tomorrow and take a look around. I don't want any surprises." Oman nodded.

Khalil fished a small black box about the size of a cigarette pack out of his pocket and slid it over to Oman. "You might find this helpful," he said.

Oman picked up the plastic box and turned it over in his hands. He noticed two strips of double-sided tape on one side of the box and a slide switch on top. "What is this for?" He asked.

"It's a limited range Electromagnetic Pulse device," Khalil replied. "If they happen to have a Ring doorbell installed, you can discretely attach this to the wall immediately next to the doorbell and slide the switch on top. You will see the red LED next to the switch illuminate. Five minutes after it is activated it will generate an EMF pule which will destroy the electronics in the doorbell. After that you can wander around as much as you like without the Ring system detecting your presence. Just remember to bring it back with you when you leave."

Oman nodded and grunted an unintelligible response, putting the small box into the breast pocket of his jacket.

"Kato, we will need some transportation. Preferably a nondescript panel van. Something that can easily transport the four of us and a hostage that will not attract attention."

"Shouldn't be a problem," Russ replied.

"OK," Ahmed concluded. "Let's plan on meeting in the parking lot here tomorrow at 7:00 PM. That will give us time to go over any last-minute details before we head up. Call me if you come across anything that could be an issue. We need this to go off as smoothly as possible. Everyone on board?" Each man nodded in return as he locked eyes with each of them.

"Excellent," Ahmed said.

Just then, Betty Lou arrived at the table, a tray of burgers hoisted on her shoulder. "Dinner is served," she said as she lowered the tray to the table and placed a plate of food in front of each of the men.

The four men finished their meals in silence, then dispersed separately, Russ first, then Oman, then Khalid. Ahmed did not wait for the bill to arrive; he quickly tallied an estimate in his head and slid a fifty on the table. It would only amount to about a 10% tip, but he considered that more than enough given the low rating Betty Lou received on his 'Waitress Hotness scale.

. As he headed out the door, he slid up behind his Trixie, reached around her waist, and slid his business card into the large pocket on the front of her skirt.

"Call me some time," he whispered softly into her ear. "You won't be sorry."

# FALLING THROUGH THE BLINDSPOT

She laughed nervously and shrugged her shoulder involuntarily, the feel of his warm breath still tickling her neck. He was cute enough, she thought to herself. But something about him gave her the creeps. As soon as he was out of sight, she pitched the card just to make sure she wouldn't be tempted to call him later.

# Chapter Seventeen

Edna stood in the kitchen putting the final touches on the dinner salad before John arrived, placing slices of pepperoni over the top in time with the rhythm of an old Ambrosia tune that Edgar had requested on their Google Home system. Edgar's face popped up on the LED screen on the refrigerator. The music volume dropped by 50%.

"Looks like the garlic bread is ready to come out from under the broiler," he announced.

"What, are your legs broken, old man?" Edna said smiling to herself.

"No, they're packed into an urn buried in a grave site east of town, thank you very much," Edgar replied.

"What would you have preferred? I couldn't exactly chop you up and put you in the freezer. What would the neighbors think?"

"Remember when we went to the Roy Rogers Museum in Victorville? Trigger looked pretty good standing there. I would have made a great conversation piece in the living room."

"That's all I need is one more thing to dust," She replied.

"Everything sure looks delicious. Even though I don't feel hungry anymore, it's still hard to watch all this delicious food go by and not be able to eat any of it.

"Yeah, yeah. You'll probably use that same excuse to get out of doing the dishes again."

"Your timing is perfect. John's car just pulled into the driveway. Are you ready for this?"

"I think so. You'll be listening in, right?"

"Of course. I will hang back until you think the time is right."

"OK, here we go," Edna said. She walked out of the kitchen past the dining room into the foyer and pulled open the heavy iron entry door just as John was headed up the steps of the front porch.

"John, it's so good to see you! It seems like ages," Edna said as she met him on the porch and spread her arms to give him a hug.

John wrapped his arms around her, careful not to hit her in the back with the wine he was carrying in a velvet pouch in his right hand. Edna held him tightly for a few seconds before releasing her grip and inviting him inside.

Once inside, John extended his arms holding the black velvet wine bag in both hands.

"What is this? You didn't need to bring anything," Edna said reaching out to accept the gift.

# FALLING THROUGH THE BLINDSPOT

"Just a little wine for dinner. It's a Marcassin Pinot Noir. I thought it would go well with the lasagna," John said.

"Oh. My, that's lovely. You really shouldn't have," Edna said, but then added in a conspiratorial whisper, "but I'm so glad you did. I'll put this in the fridge to chill for a few minutes before dinner."

"Anything I can do to help?" John asked, removing his jacket and hanging it on the coat rack as Edna retreated to the kitchen.

"No, no," Edna called back as she was opening the refrigerator. "Everything is ready. The lasagna just needs a few more minutes in the oven to finish melting the cheese," Edna said as she came back into the foyer. "I actually have something I need to discuss with you before dinner," she said gently locking arms with him and gently guiding him out of the foyer into the family room.

"Sounds serious," John said as they both sat down on the large suede leather couch in the family room. "Are you OK?"

"Oh, yes. Of course. Actually, I'm better than I have been in some time. That's what I wanted to discuss with you."

"You're not pregnant, are you?" John asked with a smile, then immediately wondered if he'd crossed a line. He was relieved when Edna broke out in a laugh and replied, "Now that would really be something, wouldn't it? I think Maury Povich would probably be here for dinner if that were the case."

"Actually, there's something I've been wanting to discuss with you, but the time never seemed right. But it's time you found out the truth."

"What's going on, Edna?"

"Do you remember a few months ago when I told you about that company, RTI, here in town that I went and visited after I saw their ad in the Daily Camera?"

"Yes. I told you it sounded like a scam to separate you from your money. What happened, did they contact you again?"

"Well, no actually. I contacted them. Not long after we spoke."

"Oh, no. Edna, I'm sorry, this is my fault I should have been around more. I've just been so busy with the state senate and this campaign. I should have been here to keep an eye on things. Don't worry though. I have access to some of the best lawyers in the country. Whatever they took you for, I will make sure you get every dime back. I can't believe those bastards would prey on someone your age." John reached in his pocket and retrieved his cell phone and started scrolling through his contact list. "I've got an investigator on my staff that can get the ball rolling before we even sit down to..."

"No, John. Stop," Edna interrupted placing her hand over his and gently pushing his phone down to his lap. "It's not like that. Just the opposite, in fact. I didn't tell you about it because I knew you would never approve. But the truth is, I wanted to find out for myself. Please, just hear me out before you pass judgment.

I know you are just trying to help, but once you see what I've seen, I think you will understand."

"OK, fair enough. Just tell me what's going on."

"After we spoke, I realized that what you said made a lot of sense. The truth is, I was feeling so desperately lonely and so vulnerable that I would have been an easy mark for anyone that wanted to rip me off. I felt like a doddering old fool that just got suckered into a game of three-card Monte. I hated that feeling. I knew that if I were going to survive on my own that I would have to learn how to stand up for myself, so I decided to go back to RTI and give those people a piece of my mind. "

"Well, I appreciate your spunk, but it's a little dangerous facing down people like that on your own."

"I wasn't alone. I hired your friend Josh, the one that works as a bodyguard for Blackstone Security to go with me in case I needed backup."

"Yikes! Talk about bringing a bazooka to a knife fight. I bet they took one look at Josh and wet themselves."

"That was what I had in mind, but it didn't actually turn out that way. It turns out they were very understanding and quite accommodating. They took us on a tour of their lab, showed us all the technology they had developed, and showed us a prototype of the Virtual Personality Avatar they were working on. It was all pretty impressive. By the time we left Josh was ready to sign up his grandfather."

"Man, they must be good. So, what happened?"

"I was still pretty leery about the whole thing, so I had Josh run a background check on them through Blackstone. It turns out that the couple that started the company are two of the most highly respected researchers in the field of Artificial Intelligence systems in the country. And they are just the nicest couple."

"Still, that doesn't mean they aren't just fooling themselves and bringing you along for the ride."

"You're such a sweetheart. Always looking out for me," Edna replied placing her hand on John's cheek. "But I can assure you that what I've gotten back from RTI is worth so much more than the minuscule amount of money that I've invested."

"And what exactly have you gotten out of that investment?" John asked.

Edna turned her head toward the 85" display facing the couch. "Edgar dear, I think that's your cue."

The display screen momentarily flashed the familiar Vizio logo, then Edgar's face filled the screen. John's attention was immediately drawn to the display. "Hello, Hurley," Edgar said smiling.

John's jaw dropped and he turned back toward Edna with a look of complete confusion, then back to the screen. "My God, it looks just like him. "

# FALLING THROUGH THE BLINDSPOT

"That's kinda the point, isn't it?" Edgar replied.

"Jesus. It even sounds just like him. It even called me Hurley."

"I've called you Hurley for 20 years, ever since flight training," Edgar replied.

John turned back to Edna, "How the hell...? Nobody outside the squadron ever called me Hurley." How in the world do they make it seem so real?"

"I'm actually right here. You don't have to keep referring to me in the third person. And not to be too picky about my pronouns, but I really prefer 'him' to 'it'. I'm a Virtual Personal Avatar, not a killer clown. Most people find the illusion more convincing if they refer to me using traditional gender-oriented personal pronouns."

"See, that's what I mean. It's amazing that it can..."

"He," Edgar interrupted.

"Sorry, 'HE' can interpret conversation that quickly and pick up terms out of context to comment on. Holy crap, I just apologized to a computer," John said in amazement.

"Technically the hardware is closer to a neural network array than a computer. It's the software that does all the heavy lifting, but apology accepted."

"Amazing," John said, then turned to Edna. "I still don't understand how they made it..." John glanced toward the display just in time to see a grimace on Edgar's face "I mean HIM, seem so much like the real Edgar."

"Maybe you two should open that wine. You look like you could use a drink." Edgar remarked.

"That's a great idea," Edna responded. "It's time to pull the lasagna out of the oven anyway and I still need to set the table." Edna placed her hand on John's knee to steady herself as she stood. "I'll be back in a couple of minutes."

"You need any help?" John offered.

"No, no. You stay and relax. I'm sure you and Edgar have some catching up to do."

Edna walked back toward the kitchen as John stared at the screen, his face still gawking with incredulity.

John sat on the couch for a moment not really sure what to do until Edgar finally broke the silence. "This must be a lot to take in."

"Yeah, you could definitely say that" John replied. "So, what is this, some kind of trick? I'm guessing there's someone sitting at a desk at RTI watching us on camera and generating responses and transmitting them back in Edgar's voice. That's pretty damn low, preying on the vulnerabilities of an old woman who lost her husband."

"I assure you, it's no trick. There's no man behind the curtain. I am a virtual instantiation of Edgar's personality in real life. I know more about Edgar than any living human, perhaps even more than Edna. Test me if you like."

"Test you?  How exactly?"

"Ask me something only Edgar would know.  Something that it would take a person at least a few seconds to find in a database."

"OK, what kind of dog did Edgar have the first time I went to his house?"

"A Boxer.  His name was Simon.  I named him after Paul Simon who wrote the song, 'The Boxer'.  It was one of our favorites."

"What do you mean OUR favorites?"

"Edna and me.  I'm programmed to refer to myself in first person pronouns, particularly in regard to my relationship with Edna because I was designed to help fill the void that Edgar left in Edna's life when he departed."

"Edgar was a real human being.  Not just some interchangeable part.  You can't just remove a human being and replace him with some glorified appliance, no matter how sophisticated," John retorted.

"It's not about replacing Edgar.  Nothing can possibly take his place in Edna's heart.  My purpose is to keep his memory alive.  A successful marriage is one in which the whole is greater than the sum of its parts.  I may not be Edgar, but I can bring many of his strengths back into her life and provide her with the companionship and emotional intimacy that Edgar brought to their marriage."

"No machine can do that.  It's not right.  Look, maybe RTI has the best intentions, but this is just a sick fantasy.  People should be allowed to mourn and move on. "

"Move on to what exactly?  Edgar and Edna were together for 61 years.  Do you think she's going to go on Match.com and suddenly find the next great love of her life?  That's not going to happen.  Edna is nearing the end of her life.  Statistically, for a woman her age in her situation with no children of her own, the life expectancy after the death of a spouse is less than three years.  And we're not talking about three golden years of retired bliss.  More often than not, it's three years of loneliness and heartbreak and isolation where death is the only path remaining out of misery.  Perhaps you are correct when you say this is nothing more than a fantasy.  But it is a fantasy that comes with warmth, companionship, laughter, and a sense of belonging.  Which would you rather she have?"

John sat thoughtfully for a moment.  "It just seems so... unnatural."

"Perhaps.  But is nature really the gold standard you wish for her?  Nature is often a cruel and heartless master.  Do you remember how devastated Edna was for the first couple of months after Edgar passed?  Look at her now."  The television switched to a split screen display with Edgar's face on one side and a video feed from the webcam in the kitchen on the other.  John could see Edna reaching into the china cabinet, carefully polishing the plates as she removed them, and singing along with Neil Diamond on the kitchen stereo.  "How long has it been since you've seen her this happy?  Did you ever actually expect to see her this happy again in her lifetime?" The display switched back to a normal screen with Edgar's face in the center.

"I suppose that's true. I just don't want her to get hurt. She's been through enough already."

"That's precisely why I'm here, John. My whole purpose for being is to ease her pain, not create more."

John sat silently for a moment, then said, "I'm curious. You referred to me by my Air Force nickname before, but just now you called me John. Why is that?"

"Edgar always called you Hurley, so whenever Edna is present, that is how I will address you, but I will refer to you in whatever manner you prefer when she is not within earshot."

"How did you know about my nickname anyway?"

"It was something that RTI identified in the deep data dive. In seven different videos where you appeared with Edna, Edgar referred to you as Hurley. My programming dictates that whenever Edna is present that I respond to all external stimuli in a manner as close as possible to how Edgar would have under similar circumstances."

"How exactly does that work?" John asked.

"I won't go into all the technical details. Edna will be back momentarily, and this conversation would fall outside the realm of what would be appropriate in keeping with the ambiance we have created around her relationship with Edgar's virtual presence. But in a nutshell, what you see is just the product of a lot of existing technologies that have been interlaced together with sophisticated AI software to simulate one specific human personality: Edgar's. The RTI team put together a deep learning algorithm that incorporated every bit of data available about Edgar's biological life and interfaced that with voice and facial recognition, deep fake animation, conversational extraction mechanisms, predictive modeling, personality profiling, and deep online data mining to establish my baseline Virtual Personality Module. I use the reactions I get from my conversations with Edna to feedback response data to enhance the baseline model over time. The more time I spend with Edna, the better the model becomes."

"I had no idea the AI technology had progressed this far. Why haven't I heard of this before now?"

"There's a lot of military and NSA tech involved from Dr. Reynolds's background with the AWARE project. Most of it hasn't hit the commercial market yet."

"Just how is all of this being funded? You claim to be here solely for Edna's benefit but how do I know RTI is not just using Edna to fund their R&D until they bleed her dry?"

# JACOB MATTHEWS

"It is true that Edna has helped to fund RTI's ongoing expenses, but Peter and Sarah Reynolds have funded most of the initial cost of this venture out of their own pocket.  Edna always relied on Edgar to manage their finances, but without Edgar, maintenance on their investment portfolio went unattended for some time, which in this environment is not a good idea, given the meager earnings from traditional fixed income investments.  Edna would not trust a financial analyst, so I took it upon myself to take over managing her accounts. "

"You what???" John exclaimed nearly jumping out of his chair.

"Yes, Edna anticipated that you may not react well to that.  Please be aware that I have analyzed the records of every financial transaction Edgar has made in the last 20 years.  No one, including Edna, has a better grasp of Edgar's investment profile and level of risk tolerance.  I run all decisions past Edna first and do not perform any transaction that has a maximum calculated risk factor greater than the cumulative risk of transactions performed by Edgar in the past 5 years.  I've limited financial transactions to a mix of precious metals and high dividend large-cap stocks, in keeping with Edgar's base investment strategy.  The biggest difference is that I have access to much faster and more accurate research than Edgar ever had and better and faster trading tools.  As a result, Edna's total net worth has nearly doubled in the past 9 months, even after her investment in RTI's R&D expenses.  She has also secured a stake in the company which, if RTI is successful, could exponentially increase her wealth."

"All the same, I will be having one of my auditors verify that information."

"Edna knew you would be skeptical.  That's one reason why she waited so long before she told you what she was up to.  I assure you, that we have been extremely diligent in looking out for her best interests.  I would encourage you to make every possible effort to ensure that we have not violated that trust in any way.  Our goal is to optimize Edna's quality of life, and the companionscape we have created for her with Edgar's virtual presence will be a key factor in attaining that goal.  We hope after scrutinizing our processes that you will concur."

"Maybe I've been spending a bit too much time with politicians lately, but it almost sounds like you are seeking an endorsement."

"You are the closest living member of Edna's circle of intimacy.  Edna grew up in a culture where she very much relies on the members of that circle to approve of her relationship choices.  Your opinion matters more to her in terms of her relationships than just about any other aspect of her life.  For example, Edna could easily own a dog and love that dog like a member of her family even if you personally didn't like dogs.  But there is no cultural archetype for developing a relationship with a virtual person.  Your acceptance or rejection of that relationship will determine whether or not she is willing to nurture that emotional bond.  I don't expect your enthusiastic support right this minute.  All I ask is that you keep an open mind with respect to this area of Edna's life while you investigate RTI and observe the positive impact it has brought to her life."

John sat thoughtfully for a moment before replying. "I suppose that's reasonable."

Edna walked back into the family room carrying two glasses of wine. "Well, what do you think?"

John glanced back at the screen and then back to Edna. "I must admit, the technology is pretty amazing. I had no idea the capabilities of speech recognition and generation had progressed this far. I can't even get Siri to give me decent driving directions."

"Yeah, nice gal, Siri. Not real long on personality though. She'll definitely kick your butt in chess," Edgar replied.

John was struck by the shift in Edgar's tone as soon as Edna entered the room. "You know, I would really like to meet the people behind RTI," John said looking at Edgar's image on the screen and then turning back to Edna. "I just wish I had more time. My schedule is absolutely booked solid until the election. If I hadn't had that cancellation tonight, I wouldn't even be here now."

"Well, you do have that fundraiser for Children's Hospital coming up. I'm sure if you slid me a couple of extra tickets, Peter and Sarah would love to come."

"That is a great idea. I will have my events coordinator call you in the morning and have the tickets sent over. I would really like to know more about their business plan. Find out how they made all this happen."

"I just know you will like them both. They've done so much for Edgar and me. I just don't know what I would have done without them."

Edna handed a glass to John and raised her own. "So, what are we toasting to?"

John started to open his mouth but before he could speak, Edgar's voice emanated from the television display. "Allow me," Edgar interrupted. On the screen, Edgar was holding up his own glass of wine. "To my two favorite people in the world; the love of my life and the next governor of Colorado."

"I'll drink to that," Edna smiled as she clinked her glass against John's. Almost at the same time, they both turned their heads as a second clink emanated from the television. Edna raised her glass toward Edgar's image and then to her lips. John followed suit shortly, his mind reeling like he was bouncing back and forth between two realities.

"Oh, that's lovely," Edna said as she swallowed her first sip. "It's been a while since I've had a good glass of wine."

"Wait, how did he know I was even going to be running for governor? I wasn't going to officially announce until the fundraiser on Friday."

"Well, that's probably my fault," Edna said. "It's not like there were no rumors in the press and I just know you would be an excellent governor.  I hope you don't mind that I asked Edgar to push things along a bit.

"You asked Edgar?  I don't understand, how can..."  John's voice trailed off and a puzzled look came over his face.

"Oh, he's quite adept at the whole social media thing now.  You know the Twitter and Facebooks and Insta-whatevers.  I think it's all part of how RTI got him going in the first place.

Edgar piped in.  "I'll get together with you later and fill you in on the details Hurley.  You're probably tired of talking shop.  You two should eat before the lasagna gets cold."

"You're right, dear," Edna replied.  She stood up and grabbed the two wine glasses.  "I'll take these into the dining room while you get washed up."  As Edna turned to walk into the kitchen, the television display in the family room went dark.  John watched as she placed the glasses on the dining room table and then entered the kitchen.

John stood up and walked toward the powder room.  As he passed by the kitchen, he could hear Edna opening the oven door, then he heard Edgar's voice speaking through the monitor in the kitchen.  "Wow, that is one delicious-looking dish!  And the lasagna looks pretty good too."

Edna just giggled and said, "Behave yourself, you old coot, we have company."

# Chapter Eighteen

*Only by embracing the reality of our own mortality can we find a deeper sense of purpose and fulfillment, and live life in a way that is more intentional and meaningful. Ultimately, the recognition of our own mortality can serve as a powerful reminder to make the most of the time we have and to live life to the fullest.*

*~ ChatGPT AI ~*

Sarah's eyes bolted open and she was suddenly filled with a sense of primal terror. All around her the milky white haze closed in, threatening to choke the life out of her.

"No, no, no, not again, why does this keep happening?" A familiar panic set in threatening to overtake any sense of reason. "Where am I? What the hell is going on? Oh my God, am I dead? C'mon, Sarah, focus. Focus! There's got to be logical expla…"

She sensed a… something… like rolling thunder in the distance. She couldn't hear it exactly. She just sensed it. All around her. Descending upon like some sort of sinister shredding device. She had to move. "Run!" she thought. "Where? Anywhere! Just run! RUN!"

All around her she felt the familiar sensation of being completely immobilized, unable to move, unable to breathe, paralyzed with fear.

"No, she screamed. Not this time. NOT THIS TIME!"

Sarah thrust her arms and legs out as if bursting out of some sort of cocoon. She felt suddenly free, as though she had thrown off shackles of immeasurable weight. She took off in a full run. She had been a sprinter throughout high school and college, so she was very familiar with the feel of running. The initial surge, the acceleration, then leveling off to her peak speed through the tape, but this was different. She just continued to accelerate, faster and faster. The scenery never changed but she could sense the motion, the speed. It was almost like she was flying, moving ever faster and faster. It felt like she was pulling away as the menacing thunder seemed to diminish into the background until she abruptly slammed into a solid wall of… what? Nothingness?

The wall sent her sprawling backward. She rolled and then stood back up in one fluid motion, regaining her balance. She moved forward again, her arms reaching forward until she felt the wall in front of her. She pushed as hard as she could, but the wall would not budge. She could sense the thunderous cloud, the presence, whatever it was catching up with her once again. Desperately she pounded her fists against the wall, anticipating the pain in her fists, but there was no pain. She couldn't even feel the wall, really. It was like some kind of immovable force. She quickly started feeling her way along the wall, moving to the right to try to find an opening, but after what felt like a few feet, she bounced off another wall, so she reversed direction and moved to the left a few feet, continually pressing against the wall. After what seemed like a few yards, she suddenly burst through an opening. She felt around in front of her, but it was empty. She started to trot, feeling around in front of her going faster and faster until she broke into a full run. She started to feel herself pulling away from the presence again but soon slammed into another wall, sending her sprawling once more. She jumped back up and moved to the left this time but quickly encountered another wall. Frantically moving back to the right, she soon passed through another opening, nearly losing her balance as she fell through the opening.

"A maze," she thought. "I'm in some kind of a maze." She remembered the "right-hand rule" for developing an algorithm to direct a robot through a maze. As long as you kept your right hand on the maze wall and followed the contour of the wall, you would eventually reach the outside of the maze. She started moving quickly along the wall, her right hand in constant contact, walking quickly first, then jogging, then running as the fear started to overtake her again. Suddenly the surface beneath her just seemed to drop away and she felt herself falling. She screamed and tried to turn to grab the floor behind her but there was nothing there. She flailed through the thick white haze for what seemed like a full minute before she landed flat on her back with a thud. For a moment she thought she must have snapped her vertebrae because she felt no pain, just a sense of being splattered, like a water balloon hitting a sidewalk. But after a few moments, she began to gather herself back together, almost like droplets of molten metal coalescing back into a single ball and then hardening back into a solid form.

Sarah rose to her feet and quickly looked in all directions, but nothing had changed, except the distant thunder was now growing closer again and with it, the primal fear that she had felt before. She had to move.

Sarah felt around in a circle, trying to find the wall again, but she seemed to be in a large open space. She started jogging again, her arms outstretched in anticipation of another wall but she could feel the… whatever it was, behind her; all around her; gaining on her. She broke out in a full run again, but just as she felt like she was pulling away, she slammed straight into another wall, sending her toppling backward once again. She popped up and ran to the left, but slammed into another wall. She tried again to the right with the same result. She would have to backtrack. But when she turned to go back the way she had come she ran straight into a fourth wall.

# JACOB MATTHEWS

"Shit! How could this be?" she thought. "I must have gotten turned around." But she traced her hand all the way around the wall, 360 degrees. She was trapped.

"Dammit!" she yelled banging her hands against the wall.

"Please, somebody help me!" she screamed.

In the distance, over the thunderous roar, she heard someone yell, "Sarah?"

"Hello? Who's there? Please help me!".

"Sarah, listen to me. You have to focus. Focus on my voice, Sarah."

She couldn't make out the voice, but it sounded vaguely familiar. She just couldn't place it.

"Sarah, I can help you, but you have to focus on my voice and shut everything else out. Sarah? Can you hear me?"

That voice. She knew that voice. But just as the realization came to her, the thunderous cloud descended upon her, flashing and glinting in a rainbow of colors like millions of razor-sharp crystals shredding her like a dry branch in a chipping machine. She let out a scream as she felt herself being torn apart in a blinding explosion of light.

Peter bolted straight up in bed at the sound of a blood-curdling scream that pierced the darkness of the room and seemed to resonate at a pitch that could easily shatter the windows. The abrupt awakening from his deep sleep left him feeling completely disoriented, unsure whether the scream he heard was real or just the remnant of his own nightmare. He glanced at the clock on the nightstand next to him, 5:00 AM. He then looked over at Sarah lying motionless next to him. It must have been a dream he thought. She appeared to be fast asleep.

Odd, he thought. Sarah was normally such a light sleeper he was sure he would have woken her. He could barely see anything by the dim light of the LED display on the clock, but she didn't seem to be moving at all. He couldn't even see her breathing. That second glass of wine she had at dinner must have really knocked her out, he thought. Peter reached up and clicked on the reading light that hung above the headboard on their bed. He looked back over toward Sarah hoping he hadn't woken her, but instead of finding her sleeping peacefully, Sarah laid deathly still, her eyes wide open staring into space, her lifeless face contorted in a final silent scream.

# Chapter Nineteen

"Sarah!?" Peter exclaimed grabbing her by the arm and jostling her. "SARAH!!!" He now yelled trying to shake her into consciousness. "Shit! Shit! SHIT!!" he exclaimed trying to kick loose of the bedding and the heavy quilt that Sarah's grandmother had made for them to stay warm on the cold Colorado winter nights.  Peter kicked one leg free but nearly tumbled out of bed as his other leg was still caught in a tangle of sheets and blankets.

Peter leaped to Sarah's side of the bed, straddling her body.  She continued to lie motionless, no sign of breathing, eyes, and mouth wide open.  Peter knelt down; his ear pressed to her chest just like he had seen on a hundred TV shows to see if he could hear her heart beating but all he could hear was the sound of his own pulse pounding in his ears.

"No, no no, this can't be happening!" he thought, his mind racing in wild panic.  "Where's my fucking phone?  I have to dial 911.  No, they'll never get here in time.  I have to administer CPR.  Shit!  I haven't done this since I was in Boy Scouts.  Do I give her mouth to mouth?  No, it's chest compression first.  How are you supposed to do that hand thing where you find the sternum?  No, I need to check her airway first.  What's that goddamn Bee Gee's song I'm supposed to follow??"

Peter was interlocking his fingers getting ready to press down on her when Sarah's eyelids suddenly slammed shut, then Wide open again as she sucked in a huge gasp of air.

For a moment, Sarah was completely disoriented, unable to remember who or where she was.  All she could process was the figure of some crazed-looking man straddling her, his hands clenched together as if he were preparing to strangle her.  "Get off of me!" she screamed, arms and legs flailing in an innate defensive fight or flight response.  Then, as if someone had flipped a switch, her memories flooded back into her consciousness like a tsunami.  Her flailing suddenly stopped as the image of Peter emerged in her like puzzle pieces falling into place in her brain.

"Oh, thank God.  Peter!" she cried throwing her arms out and pulling him, toward her, tears streaming down her face.

Peter just held her tightly, rocking her in his arms, his heart pounding out of his chest.  After a minute or so he pushed himself back, his hands resting on her arms just below the shoulder.

"Oh my God.  For a second, I thought you were dead!  Are you OK?" Peter asked.

Sarah reached over and grabbed a tissue from her nightstand.

"I think so," she said dabbing the tears from her eyes. "I guess I should be asking you that. You're the one whose wife is going insane."

"Oh, sweetie, that's not true," Peter said wrapping his arms around her. "You were already insane when I married you."

"Asshole!" Sarah exclaimed in a half sob, punching him in the arm.

"That's my girl," Peter said, gently stroking and caressing her cheek.

"I thought I heard a scream, and I woke up. When I looked over you weren't moving at all. I was all ready to administer CPR!"

"I couldn't move. It reminded me of that thing we saw about alien abductions on TV. Sleep paralysis. Remember?"

"Well, it scared the shit out of me. Looks like you were having your worst nightmare yet. Do you remember anything this time?"

"No," Sarah replied. "All I can remember is being so scared. I just had to get away. I don't even know what I was trying to get away from."

Peter just held her closely, rocking her ever so slightly until her trembling subsided and he could finally feel her steel-tight muscles begin to relax. "Could... could you tell what I was yelling about?" Sarah asked tentatively.

"Not really. Most of it was pretty indecipherable, but it sounded like you screamed out a name."

"I don't remember that. Whose name did I scream out?" Sarah asked.

"I was only half-awake myself," Peter replied. "I was too groggy to tell for sure. Maybe you've got a secret dream lover."

"If I do, he must be a serial killer," Sarah responded.

Peter glanced at the alarm clock on the nightstand and then rolled off of Sarah reaching for his glass of water. He heard the familiar sound of the bedroom door lever being nuzzled unsuccessfully a couple of times from outside the bedroom before it compressed sufficiently for Roscoe to push the door open with his paw. Roscoe padded into the room and laid his large head in Sarah's lap, looking up at her, his eyes seemingly filled with sympathy and concern.

It's still a couple of hours before the alarm, you want to try to get more sleep?" Peter asked.

"No." Sarah shook her head as she dabbed her eyes again. "I don't think I could go back to sleep even if I wanted to. Besides, it looks like the big guy is ready for action," she said, scratching Roscoe behind the ears.

"Alright," Peter replied. "I better go put some coffee on. It's going to be a long day. We're going to try to make a working model of that brain of yours."

"I hope it works better than the one I've got now," Sarah replied.

Peter slid out of bed and slipped on his robe. "How about it, Roscoe, you want to go to work today?"

# FALLING THROUGH THE BLINDSPOT

Roscoe's head immediately popped up and his tail swished from side to side. He loved going in to work with Peter and Sarah. The long car ride into town, all the sights and smells along the way. Peter always kept a supply of large cowhide chew bones in his drawer at work to keep him occupied during the day. Plus, Beaver usually had a bag of some kind of junk food that he would discretely share with Roscoe when Peter and Sarah weren't looking. Roscoe led the way into the kitchen, pushing the door the rest of the way open with the top of his head. He crossed the kitchen and squeezed through the doggie door to take care of business before breakfast so he would be ready to go.

Peter had just finished feeding Roscoe and was in the process of cooking a couple of eggs and sausage patties for breakfast sandwiches when Sarah emerged from the bedroom, tossing her long hair back over her shoulder and gathering it up in a ponytail. He was amazed at how effortlessly she could throw on a simple-looking blouse and a pair of stretch pants and make an entrance like she just stepped out of the pages of a fashion magazine.

She glided up behind Peter, wrapped her arms around him, and kissed him on the back of the neck. As she pulled away, she discretely picked up the spatula and whacked Peter on the ass making him jump. "Go hop in the shower," she said. "I'll finish making breakfast."

"If I don't, will you smack me with that spatula again?"

"No such luck, but if you're not out of the shower and ready to go in ten minutes Roscoe gets your sausage."

Roscoe raised his head up from his dog dish and glanced back over his shoulder at Peter and Sarah, licking his chops with a hopeful look in his eye.

"Forget it, big guy," Peter said pointing at Roscoe as he walked toward the bedroom. "I am the master of the speed-shower." Roscoe huffed as Peter disappeared through the bedroom door and planted his face back into the large stainless-steel bowl to finish off his morning meal.

True to his word, Peter emerged from the bedroom 9 minutes later looking about half put together. Sarah handed him a travel mug and a sausage and egg muffin neatly wrapped in foil. "Roscoe and I already finished breakfast, but here's your happy meal and your sippy cup. I'll drive while you eat," Sarah said as she combed her fingers through his tousled hair, straightening out a couple of haphazard spikes that remained from hastily wrestling with a long-sleeved t-shirt that went on backward on the first try.

Peter followed Roscoe to the door as Sarah set the alarm. A few minutes later they were flying down highway 119 on the way into Boulder. Sarah drove with Peter riding shotgun and Roscoe taking up the lion's share of the back seat, his large head hanging out the window with his jowls flapping in the breeze.

"So, what's the plan for today?" Sarah asked as Peter finished his sandwich and crumpled the foil wrapping into a tight ball.

"Actually, this should be a really interesting day for you," Peter replied.

A look of consternation came over her as she glanced over at Peter. "Ah, crap that's never a good sign. Do you mean interesting like in my last colonoscopy or interesting as in I'm going to need an extra cup of coffee to stay awake during one of your lectures?"

"As much as I appreciate you equating the stimulating nature of my oration to a rectal procedure, I mean interesting in the 'I'm captivated by the stimulating nature of this experience' sense. Not interesting in the 'I'm on a blind date with someone so interesting I'm ready to gnaw through my leg in an attempt to sever my Femoral artery' sense."

"Well, that's mildly reassuring," Sarah replied. "By the way did you remember to lock the doggie door before we left?"

Peter turned toward the back seat. "Roscoe, did you remember to lock your dog door?"

Roscoe pulled back from the rear window turned and looked at Peter, cocking his large head as if trying to understand the question.

"Hey, leave him out of this, you're the one with the opposable thumbs, mister neuroscientist."

"That's DOCTOR neuroscientist, if you don't mind. Relax, that's why we have an alarm system. Nobody is going to bother anything in the middle of the day."

"I'm more worried about a raccoon getting into the house and tearing things up," Sarah replied.

At the sound of the word 'raccoon', a low growl rumbled in Roscoe's throat.

"Easy, big fella." Peter cooed. "They wouldn't dare invade our kitchen with your scent all over the place."

Roscoe responded with a snort and poked his large head back out of the rear window to continue scrutinizing the morning air.

"Do we need to go back?" Sarah asked.

"No, no. Really, it will be fine. You worry too much. Besides we've got that webcam in the kitchen. I can check for critters raiding the fridge when we get to the lab. Peter responded.

"So, tell me more about what we are doing today," Sarah asked as she expertly slalomed her way around the minefield of scattered potholes that always seemed to stay one step ahead of the Colorado Department of Transportation repair crew.

"It will definitely be an interesting day for you and mostly fun."

"Mostly? How mostly?"

"Well, admittedly you will have to sit through a few hours of videos and audio recordings. You'll probably be experiencing some Edgar overload by the end of

# FALLING THROUGH THE BLINDSPOT

the day.  On the upside, we're going to mix in a full gamut of sights, smells, sounds, and touch to amplify your neural responses and prevent you from getting bored in the process.  We then feed all the neural responses to different stimuli into a program that maps neural responses to create a computer model of your neural network.  The more stimuli we collect, the more accurate the model becomes.  Once we reach a point where the modeling program creates a response that matches the neural responses in your brain we know we are done.  "

"That sounds complex."

"Very much so.  The human brain is pound for pound the most complex system in the known universe.  Modeling the human brain is more complex than modeling climate, and we've spent years trying to figure that one out.  In fact, a lot of the algorithms we will be using were originally developed for that purpose, but instead of having to wait weeks, months, or years to determine if the simulation is correct, the feedback loop is immediate, so we hope that we can get a more accurate model in hours instead of years.  The bottom line is, the more interesting and entertaining stimuli you are exposed to during this process, the better the model becomes."

"That sounds fascinating, but I'm still a little concerned about the 'mostly' fun part."

"It really is amazing technology.  We use 3D imaging and holographic modeling to effectively develop a physical simulation of your brain in software.  Dr. Pearson at Cal-Tech has been working with this technology for months doing brain maps on his grad students with no long-term effects so we know it's completely safe."

"OK, that didn't answer the question and what do you mean it's completely safe?  Why would safety even be a factor here, what are you not telling me?"

"I would have no qualms at all about doing this myself, it's just that we already have spent so much time developing the S2 model that…"

"Do I need to pull the car over right now, or are you going to tell me what's really going on?" Sarah asked in a low cold pitch that seemed to echo through the car and drown out the surrounding road noise despite its low, even volume.  Peter could feel her harsh laser-like stare boring into the side of his head even though he was avoiding direct eye contact.  Even though he knew that the movie 'Scanners' was pure fiction, at times like this he did not want to test the premise that one person could cause another's head to explode through pure concentrated thought.  Even Roscoe timidly pulled his head in from the window and ducked down into the back seat, making himself as small as possible to minimize collateral damage just in case.

"Just promise me you won't freak out, OK?"

"I left freaking out on the side of the road at the last turn, we're approaching the exit for full-on panic now!"

"OK, just breathe all right?  Seriously, it's not that bad.  It's not like we have to drill into your brain or anything like that.  The problem is that we just can't get the level of resolution we need using external sensors to develop the 3D model.  But Dr. Pearson developed a tiny bio-mechanical nanite which can be injected directly into your..."

"Whoa, whoa, whoa!  Throw that train into reverse right now, mister!  You lost me at 'injected.'  You know I hate needles.  Every time I get a flu shot, I nearly pass out and now you tell me you are going to strap me down and pump nanobots into my arm."

"No, no, no!  That wouldn't work at all!" Peter exclaimed.

"Thank God!" Sarah sighed in relief.

"We would never be able to position them that precisely going through your entire circulatory system.  We actually have to inject them directly into your carotid artery."

"You have got to be kidding me!  There's no fucking way you're sticking a needle in my neck and…"

The car was filled with the roar of the tires going over the rumble strip on the side of the road just inches away from a 300-foot ravine.  Roscoe had now retreated from the seat and was hopelessly trying to squeeze himself onto the floorboard behind Peter's seat.

"You might want to focus on the road a bit.  We're going to need a lot bigger bumper if you want to take the shortcut into Boulder."

"You're trying to change the subject, Peter!" Sarah said sharply as she cranked the wheel to the left and righted the car back into the center of the lane.

"Look, I know you're terrified of needles, but I swear it will be OK.  It's a very small needle, no more than an inch... or four.  Besides, the Don is coming to do the procedure.  You love the Don."

The Don, otherwise known as Dr. Donald Draxler was Peter's roommate in college and the best man at Peter and Sarah's wedding.  He had spent most of his career engaged in research on methods of restoring neural functionality after traumatic brain injuries.  Together with Dr. Alexi Pearson, he helped develop a bio-mechanical nanite approximately the size of a blood cell capable of transmitting simple data streams to an external data pickup device which then re-transmits the data through a cell phone to a computer via Bluetooth.

"You better be careful.  You've suddenly risen to a prominent position on my shit list.  The Don is looking pretty good to me right now."

"We'll see about that when he's jabbing a needle in your neck."

"Not helping."

"Sorry," Peter replied.  "It's a pretty ingenious device though.  The nanites are

# FALLING THROUGH THE BLINDSPOT

aligned at strategic locations throughout your brain and use a tiny flagellum that keeps them in place once they are correctly positioned.  They are continuously controlled and monitored through a pulsating electric charge emanating from a flexible mesh cap that you wear on your head."

"Great, I get stabbed in the neck and I get to look like the lunch lady?"

"Don't worry, It's made of a thin, light mesh designed to facilitate a wig over the top.  No one will even know you're wired for action.  We will lay you down on the cot in the back room, put some soft jazz on the Bose headphones, and put a sleeping mask on you.  We'll give you something beforehand to help you relax as soon as we get there.  He will even use a topical anesthetic before the shot goes in, so you won't even know when it's happening."

"It just sounds so creepy.  How do I get them out of me?"

"Within 72 hours after the cap is removed, the electrical charge on the nanites dissipates to the point where they can no longer hold their position.  They then just flush through your circulatory system, the liver identifies them as normal dead blood cells and they just get excreted like any other waste product."

"Do you have any idea how much you are going to owe me for this?"

"I already know how to make it up to you.  This afternoon we're going to Cherry Creek to buy you a new dress."

"Seriously???  Do you actually think buying me something pretty is going to get you through this one?  Are you being possessed by the ghost of Ward Cleaver, or did I take the wrong exit and drive us back to the 50s?"

"Golly geez, don't be all sore about it.  I just thought you might need a new dress."

"Why would I need a new dress?  The only places I ever wear a dress are funerals and cruises.  Did somebody die or are we going on a cruise?"

"Neither actually.  You know that fundraiser that Senator Vanderwurl is holding at the Brown Palace Friday night for Children's Hospital?"

"Yeah, it's been all over Facebook.  It's like the social event of the season. Rumor has it he will be announcing his intent to run for Governor."

"Well according to my sources..."

"You mean Edna?" Sarah replied sarcastically.

"What makes you say that?  I have other sources you know.  What makes you think I don't have sources?  I'm connected to important people all over the place."

"Okay, okay, sorry."

"Apology accepted.  But yeah, it was Edna.  Anyway, according to Edna, Senator Vanderwurl is definitely announcing on Friday.  It turns out this guy is quite the phenom.  From all indications, the Governor's office is just a steppingstone to a presidential run in a few years.  There will be A-list celebrities flying in from all over the place to grab onto the coattails of the next rising political star.  And we're going!"

"No way!  Get the hell out!  How did you even get tickets?  That's harder to get into than the Academy Awards!  I heard you can't even get in the door without making at least a $20,000 contribution to the hospital!"

"Well, it turns out that Edgar was very close to the Senator.  He was the Senator's flight instructor in the Air Force.  Anyway, Edna pulled some strings and got us on the list."

"Still, can we really afford a $40,000 dinner right now?  Most of our assets are tied up in RTI.  What did you do, empty the kids college fund?

"Just in case you haven't been paying attention, we don't have kids.  Just the big kid in the back seat."

"Yeah, but we usually don't even go out to eat without a Groupon."

"Edna got us in for free.  If Roscoe decides to go to Harvard, we're still covered."

In response to hearing his name, Roscoe popped his head up and snorted loudly.  Peter glanced over his shoulder, grimacing slightly as Roscoe thrust his tongue out to lick the nasal discharge off his nose.  "Well, maybe a community college would be a better fit.  I guess we'll have to wait and see."

"Wow, now I am a little excited!" Sarah exclaimed.

"See, I'm not such a sexist troglodyte after all," Peter replied

"Well..." Sarah replied sarcastically.

"Hey, let's not ruin the moment.  Let's focus on you're excited and I'm vindicated, okay?" Peter said hopefully.

# CHAPTER TWENTY

*Home is not a physical structure, but a state of mind. It is the place where we feel accepted and loved, where our memories are made and where our hearts find peace. Home is the place where we can be our authentic selves, free from judgment, and where we connect with those who matter most.*

*~ ChatGPT AI ~*

Oman had arrived near the end of the gravel road leading up to Peter and Sarah Reynolds's home just before 6 a.m. The skies were just beginning to lighten, but Oman wanted to get an early start. There was only one road in and out of the Reynolds's property. He would wait here until he was sure they left for the day. While he waited, he slipped on the Amazon delivery vest he would use to deflect suspicion as he approached the house.

Oman was expecting a fairly long wait, perhaps an hour or two, so he settled in, reclined his seat back a bit, and pulled a pack of Azadi cigarettes from his vest pocket. The Iranian brand was generally not available in the U.S. due to trade sanctions, but he had a brother in the UAE that would ship a couple of cartons a month to a P.O. Box that he kept under the name Michael Jones.

Oman had just lit up when he saw lights approaching from up the gravel access road. Oman slid down in his seat while the vehicle passed, a dark blue Range Rover with a man and woman inside. That was the model the Reynolds's drove according to the information that Khalil, aka Cisco had texted him the night before. He couldn't get a good look at the driver, but the man in the passenger seat appeared to match the photo of Peter Reynolds that Cisco had texted to his phone.

The Range Rover turned onto the paved road and headed down the hill. Oman waited until the taillights disappeared around a curve before he started his car and turned up the gravel road leading to their house. He had mapped out the route on Google Earth the night before. The Reynolds's driveway was about ¾ mile up the road.

Oman turned into the Reynolds's driveway and shut off the car. He waited in the car and finished his cigarette, scoping out the house to see if there was any movement inside, but the house was dark. He noticed that there was indeed a Ring video doorbell installed next to the front entry door.

Oman opened the car door, took one long last drag off his cigarette, and dropped the butt onto the gravel drive, crushing it down with the toe of his shoe. He grabbed a small parcel off the passenger seat to be used as a prop in in his faux delivery scheme, and the EMP device that Khalil had given him. He also grabbed an Amazon cap and pulled it down low over his forehead to help hide his face from the Ring camera. He gently closed the car door and started up the driveway to the house, but then stopped abruptly. He pivoted, strode casually back to the car, and reached down to recover the cigarette butt. He pulled out a handkerchief and wrapped the cigarette butt up in the handkerchief. "Never leave any evidence behind," he said to himself as he stuck the handkerchief back into his pocket.

Oman climbed the steps onto the large wooden deck that surrounded the home on 3 sides. When he reached the door, he reached out and rang the doorbell, discretely palming the EMP device and pressing it firmly on the wall next to the Ring video doorbell. He waited a minute and then rang again, this time sliding the power switch to the on position on the black box as he pressed the Ring button. The LED next to the switch illuminated. No one was home. Very good, he thought. He placed the small parcel with its prominent Amazon smile logo on the doorstep and returned to his vehicle.

Oman pulled out of the driveway and headed back down the road, pulling onto the same shoulder where he had waited earlier in the morning. After about 10 minutes, he pulled back out onto the gravel road and returned to the Reynolds's driveway.

Oman walked back onto the deck. The LED on the black box had extinguished, indicating that the EMP had successfully deployed. He pulled the black box off the wall and retrieved the Amazon parcel from the doorstep and returned them to his car. He then walked along the deck and rounded the corner to the side of the house. He looked around to make sure there were no neighbors close enough to see the house and no cars driving by, but he was completely secluded. Oman walked the length of the deck and then turned the corner to the back of the house. He had gone about halfway down the length of the rear deck when he saw the large dog door cut into the wall next to the kitchen door and froze in place.

"Shit!" Oman thought to himself. "Americans and their filthy damn animals. Animals are for plowing and eating, not for keeping around so you can post cute videos to your Facebook account. Someday when the end times come, these infidels will find themselves cooking those animals they love so much over an open fire to keep from starving to death." The visual brought a sinister smile to his lips.

He listened for a moment to see if he could hear a dog inside. He reached behind the Amazon vest and pulled a Glock G17 from his shoulder holster and deftly racked the slide. He reached into his pocket and removed a silencer and screwed it into the barrel. He continued along the deck in a slow, deliberate half-crouch, his gun pointed slightly downward, stopping at the kitchen window. He

# FALLING THROUGH THE BLINDSPOT

peered around the window casing to get a glimpse inside the kitchen. No sign of a dog. He moved quietly past the window and pressed his toe against the dog door. The door gave a bit as he pressed on it. He nudged it a couple of times then kicked at it firmly and stood back, the barrel of the Glock pointed toward the opening. The door swung back and forth a few times then settled back into a closed position. He breathed a half-sigh, unscrewed the silencer and placed it back into his overcoat. He then ejected the magazine and cleared the chamber, popping the round back into the magazine before snapping it back into place and re-holstering the Glock. "Stupid bastards didn't even bother to board up the dog door after they moved in," he said to himself, shaking his head.

Oman walked back over to the kitchen window to get a better look inside the house. He could see the alarm keypad on the wall adjacent to the kitchen door. He took a photo to send to Cisco. They could use a jammer to disable the cell signal to the alarm company, but it would be best if they could disable the audible alarm as well. Cisco was small enough that he should be able to crawl through the dog door and disable the alarm so they could access the house without warning and overtake the Reynolds' before they even had a chance to get out of bed.

Oman took a few photos around the perimeter of the house and walked back to the access road. There was a grove of aspen trees on the side of the road just before the driveway entrance. They could park there behind the cover of the aspen grove and walk through the trees at the edge of the property around to the back of the house. There was a stairway not far from the kitchen door on the back deck that led to the garage.

This was the perfect setup, Oman thought. They should be able to walk right up to the kitchen door under the cover of darkness, completely undetected. Once Cisco disables the alarm, they can walk right in, make their way to the master bedroom and inject both of them before they even have a chance to wake up. Once they make their little presentation to the good doctor, they would carry Sarah right out the front door, down the driveway, throw her in the van and be on their way.

Reaching into his back pocket, Oman removed a pair of garden shears he found in an old shed at the house he was renting. They were dull, pitted, a bit rusty, and the spring was missing, but they would be perfect for the task. He envisioned using the shears to cut off Sarah's thumbs in front of her husband before they whisked her away. Just a little demonstration of the kind of brutality that would be inflicted upon her if Peter did not cooperate. He closed his eyes and he could almost feel the hard resistance as the blades made their way through her flesh and caught on the bone. He imagined hearing the crunch of the bone as the dull blades smashed, more than cut through the bone and marrow. He anticipated the warm rush of blood as it splattered in pulsating jets across his hand.  The horror on Peter's face as he witnessed his wife's agony, unable to move in his drug-induced paralysis.  He hoped it would be an experience that would haunt Peter for the rest of his life.  He opened his eyes and held the old set of shears up to the morning light as though it were some coveted trophy.  God, he loved his job.

Oman hoped that the paralyzing effect of the drugs would not prevent Sarah from being able to scream.  He loved the sound of a pretty young woman screaming in agony.  Even more so when her husband is forced to watch and share in the experience.  Perhaps his colleagues would allow him to have a little more fun with her in the back of the van on the way to the farmhouse.  If not, he could afford to wait.  He would take his time killing her after they got the information they needed from her.  He felt like a kid on Christmas eve, impatient for the festivities to begin, but savoring the anticipation.

Oman made his way back to the car and opened the passenger side door.  On the seat was a black plastic box about the size of a hardback book and an electric screwdriver with a handful of screws.  Oman picked up the black box and flipped the slide switch on the bottom of the box as Cisco had instructed him.  An LED in the corner of the box flashed brightly 3 times and then shut off, indicating that the cell phone jammer was now ready to be activated.  He carried the box around to the back of the house and found a spot on the back wall of the garage where it could be discretely installed.  He attached the jammer to the wall and made his way back to the vehicle, a spring in his step as he rounded the corner of the house.

Oman was not known for his overt expressions of joy, but his usual half grimace transformed into a sinister smile of sheer joy as he made his way back to the car in eager anticipation of the myriad of excruciating tortures he would inflict over the coming days.  "I can't believe I actually get paid for this."  He thought to himself as he turned and backed his car out of the driveway and headed back down the gravel road.

# CHAPTER TWENTY-ONE

Peter and Sarah pulled into the parking lot of RTI.  Peter opened the driver's door and then opened the back door to let Roscoe out.  Roscoe bounded out of the SUV, stopping to stretch out and yawn.

"Long ride, big guy?"

Roscoe glanced back at Peter and Sarah to make sure they were right behind him as he padded his way up to the front door.  He backed up a step, waiting for Peter to open the lobby door.  Peter held the door open while Roscoe and then Sarah entered the lobby.  Dr. Donald Draxler stood with his back to the door, studying the patent plaques on the wall at the end of the lobby.  He turned when he heard the door close behind him.

"D-Man!"  Peter exclaimed as he recognized his old friend.

Donald thrust his hand out and grabbed Peter's outstretched hand, grasping his shoulder with his left hand.  "Pete!  It's great to see you.  It's been way too long."  He released Peter's hand and embraced Sarah warmly.  "And Sarah, my God you get prettier every time I see you!  When are you going to realize you are WAY out of this guy's league?" he said nodding his head back toward Peter.

"Hey, don't give her any ideas.  I'm skating on thin ice already this morning," Peter replied.

Roscoe was bouncing back and forth on each foot, smiling ear to ear, his tail wagging furiously.  "And look how much you've grown since I saw you last," Donald said, kneeling in front of Roscoe, grabbing him by the ears and massaging them deeply.  Roscoe's eyes half closed, and his nose went up in the air.  He looked like he was about to start crooning a song.

"Looks like Roscoe remembers you," Sarah said smiling.

"We weren't expecting you in until later today," Peter said, patting his hand on Donald's shoulder.  "I hope you didn't have to wait too long."

"No, I just got here.  I got to the airport early so I was able to catch an earlier flight.  Beaver just escorted me in a couple of minutes ago.  I was just about to grab a cup of coffee."  Donald pointed to the wall covered in patent plaques.  "I was just admiring your wall of fame over there.  That's a pretty impressive collection. "

"Thanks.  We're trying to get things ready to meet with customers.  First impressions and all.  We're getting close to a working prototype, so we want to have all the trappings in place to impress prospective customers when the official shingle goes up."

"Well, I can't wait for the tour.  But I know we are on a bit of a tight schedule

so we shouldn't delay getting things set up.  Where did you want to do the, um...,"
Donald glanced up apprehensively at Sarah, "the procedure?"  Donald was well
aware of Sarah's aversion to medical procedures of any kind, but especially her
fear of needles.

"We have a room in the back of the lab.  It's almost like a studio apartment
with a little kitchenette, a recliner, a small bed, a full bathroom, and
soundproofing.  We call it the 'Quiet Room'."  It's basically just a place for a quick
getaway when we need to take a nap or a place to crash if we've been working too
long."

"Let me guess, Beaver practically lives there?" Donald said with a smirk.

"Yeah, that's about right," Peter replied.

"Well, let's get the ball rolling," Donald said reaching into his jacket pocket.
He pulled out an unlabeled prescription bottle.  He opened the bottle and held it
up to Sarah.

"I want you to take these."  Sarah held her hand out and Donald poured 2
capsules from the bottle into her palm.

"What is it?" Sarah asked.

"This is for your trypanophobia," Donald replied.

"Sounds like some kind of sexual disorder," Sarah said sarcastically.

"Fear of needles," Donald replied, chuckling.

"Fear of getting poked.  Same difference," Sarah said, popping the pills into
her mouth and taking a swig from her water bottle.

"I didn't know there was a pill for fear of needles," Peter interjected.

"It's just a synthetic form of Triazolam.  Similar to Valium but it is stronger,
and the effects wear off faster.  It will send you flying fast but the effects only last
about 15 minutes.  It takes about a half hour to kick in so make sure you are ready
to go lie down soon after you take it because you will be completely out of
commission until the drug wears off."

"Any chance you could get me a few of those for when Sarah wants to watch
the Bachelorette?" Peter asked.

Sarah punched Peter in the arm.  "Remember that thin ice you're skating on?
I think I hear it cracking."

Peter winced.  "What I meant to say was, let me get that door for you
sweetheart."  Peter leaned in toward the retinal scanner at the entrance to the lab.
The magnetic latches on the heavy door disengaged and the door opened with a
'whoosh' as Peter pulled it open.

"Go on back and lie down and relax.  I'll give Don a hand with his stuff, and
we'll be there in a couple of minutes."  Sarah turned to Peter and gave him a peck
on the lips before heading through the door.

Roscoe yawned and lumbered over to the corner of the lobby where they had a dog bed set up for him.  He sniffed around until he found a half-eaten rawhide chew bone that he buried under the mattress the last time he was there and plopped himself down on his bed happily gnawing away.  Peter led Donald into the conference room at the side of the lobby.  "Don, before we start, I was really hoping you might be able to help us out with something."

"Sure.  What have you got?" Donald replied.

"Sarah has been having these nightmares.  At first, I thought it was just the stress of trying to work all the bugs out of this product, but it's really getting serious.  I think they are literally scaring her to death.  Last night I actually thought I lost her.  I'm sure it was just a severe bout of sleep paralysis, but for a second there I thought she had a stroke or something. "

"Geez!  That sounds pretty intense.  I'm assuming you've taken her in for an MRI?"

"Yeah, of course.  MRI, fMRI, CT, EEG, PET.  She's had every kind of scan there is, but they all turn up negative.  No tumors, no cysts, no infection, no apparent tissue abrogation of any kind."

"Weird.  How about her blood work?"

"Everything is perfect.  Every test we run she comes back looking like God damned Wonder Woman but the nightmares keep coming back more and more often.  It's practically every night now. "

"Has she talked to a psychiatrist?  Maybe there is some trauma from her past that she is trying to bring to the surface. "

"She can't remember the nightmares at all.  Even when she wakes up in the middle of one.  All she remembers are vague sensations and mind-numbing fear.  We even tried hypnosis, but there's nothing there for her to grab onto.  I won't lie to you Don, this is starting to scare me."

"I don't blame you, man.  You guys are perfect together.  Is there anything I can do?"

"I don't know.  I hope so.  As far as Sarah knows you are just here to help with neural response mapping so we can improve the verbal interaction filter for the colloquy engine on our conversational exchange model.  I think that will help out with our development, but to be honest, a big part of why I asked you here is that I was hoping the procedure could help us identify what is actually going on with these night terrors."

"Once we inject the nanites, we will be collecting data for 72 hours.  After that, the system automatically shuts down, and the nanites get flushed out of her system.  We could go longer, but generally, within 72 hours we have about as detailed a map of her neural responses as we are ever going to get.  We should be able to get a pretty good idea of where in the neural map the nightmares are originating.  If she's having them every night, we're bound to catch one in the next

3 days.   We may not be able to tell precisely what is causing them, but it will give us a really good idea of where to look.  "

"I was hoping you would say that. "

"We may be able to do more than that.  I don't want you to get your hopes up too high, but these nanites are equipped with neural stimulators, capable of overloading neural connections to reconfigure the connectome.  If we can identify the precise location of the initial neural firing, we may even be able to overwrite the neural connections to shut the nightmares off at the source."

"That's a little scary.  Almost sounds like electroshock therapy."

"In a sense it is, but it is directed at very specific neural pathways.  By analogy, it's the difference between logging into your computer and deleting a line of text in a file and using an electromagnet to wipe your hard drive."  Donald put his hand on Peter's shoulder.  "Don't worry Pete.  You know I would never do anything to hurt Sarah."

"Thanks, Don."

"We really should get started," Donald said glancing down at his watch.  "Sarah should be crossing the border into La La land in just a few minutes."

Donald and Peter retrieved a carry-on bag and a hard-sided aluminum case from the back of Donald's rental car.  They passed through the lab on the way to the quiet room.  "Wow, this is some serious hardware!" Donald said.

"Yeah, we lucked out.  A local data mining outfit sold out, so they had all of their data center equipment up for auction.  Most of it is pre- and post-processing for our conversational modeling system.  We have a DANNA system that runs all the deep learning algorithms for driving the cognition agent. "

Beaver was sitting in the recliner going through some code listings when Peter and Donald entered the room.  Beaver had spent over a year as an intern working with Donald before moving on to BMC.  During the year he had spent working in his lab, Beaver had developed a great deal of respect and admiration for Donald's knowledge and skill.

Peter looked over at Sarah, who was now sound asleep on the cot.  Beaver glanced over at her.  "I was just discussing last night's simulation results with her."

"Really, how did it go?"

"It was another monumental fuck-fest.  Anyway, I was right in the middle of going over the diagnostic logs and she started looking all shmammered and she passed out on the cot.  I think I might have bored her into unconsciousness."

Donald smiled.  "Well, that's certainly possible but I suspect the pills I gave her might have had added to the effect."

Beaver immediately perked up.  "Awesome!  Did you bring enough for everyone?" Beaver asked hopefully.

# FALLING THROUGH THE BLINDSPOT

Peter interjected. "We only have one cot Beev, and you have plenty of work to do. BMC is sending over some support logs from a mission incident I need you to start digging into."

Beaver frowned disparagingly, "Way to burn my chill, Buzz-nightmare." He muttered, shaking his head as he shuffled out of the room.

"It's good to know some things never change," Donald said smiling as he placed the aluminum case on the table and pressed his thumbs over the bio-metric locks on the case. After a couple of seconds, the locks disengaged, and the spring-loaded latches popped open. Donald reached in and grabbed what appeared to be a slightly smaller version of a MAC-11 sub-machine gun, but with a 4" needle where the barrel would normally come out.

"Jesus! You probably wasted your time with the drugs. One look at that thing and Sarah would have passed out on her own," Peter said.

"We call it an NTM. Nanite Transfer Mechanism." Donald pulled the NTM out of the case and handed it to Peter. He then retrieved a small rectangular box from the case. The box looked similar to an ammunition magazine, but it had a digital readout on the bottom and a blue LED level indicator on the side. "This is the containment chamber for the nanites. It keeps them charged in a glucose/saline solution until they are ready for deployment. Once they are deployed, they will utilize tiny flagellum to orient themselves evenly throughout the brain and connect themselves to the walls of the blood vessels so they can get an accurate 3D model of the neural activity."

"This looks pretty ominous," Peter observed, turning the NTM over in his hands, and inspecting it thoroughly.

"It's actually a pretty ingenious device. It has a self-regulating dispersion mechanism and a laser targeting system to identify the location of the artery by sensing the blood flow under the surface of the skin. Despite what you see in the movies, a direct arterial injection, especially in the Carotid is difficult and risky. Arterial walls tend to be thick and difficult to puncture and they are surrounded by muscle tissue. There is an elevated risk of the needle bending or slicing the arterial wall which could cause arterial collapse and instant death, so having an automated guidance system is an absolute necessity as far as I'm concerned."

"Now I think I might need one of those pills."

"Don't worry. We've tested this device extensively. It's quite safe."

"I sure wouldn't have signed up to participate in that clinical trial." Peter held the device up, inspecting it carefully. "I'm surprised they let you take it on the plane. It looks like some kind of bioweapon."

"Believe me, TSA really put me through the wringer trying to check it in. I finally had to get the regional director of the DHS on the phone to get this approved. I can tell you, that he was not very happy to get my call at 4:30 in the morning. The TSA supervisor didn't have much of an ass left by the time he handed the phone back to me."

"Wow. Wish I could have seen that," Peter said smiling. "Those guys are always giving me the third degree for one thing or another."

"Yeah, it really made the whole trip worthwhile," Donald said as he pulled the NTM from Peter's hand and carefully slid the containment chamber into the base of the NTM. A series of high-pitched beeps emanated from the NTM and then a green LED indicator illuminated on its side. The needle then fully retracted into the body of the unit. "We are ready for liftoff," Donald said.

Donald removed the plastic needle guard and placed the NTM on the table. He then pulled an alcohol swab from his case and opened the package. He gently turned Sarah's head and swabbed her neck for a few seconds with a disinfectant and numbing agent. He picked up the NTM placing it about an inch away from Sarah's neck and pulled the trigger halfway back. A large red laser crosshair appeared on Sarah's neck, contracting gradually until it settled into a small cross-hair directly over her Carotid artery. Donald guided the NTM down over the crosshairs. When the NTM made contact with Sarah's neck, a red LED on top of the NTM began to flash. The needle which had retracted into the barrel of the NTM emerged slowly, piercing Sarah's neck. As the needle slowly burrowed deeper into her neck, the LED flashed faster until it finally pierced the wall of the Carotid artery. The flashing red LED then turned green and the NTM emitted a beep. He then fully engaged the trigger. The blue LED level indicator on the containment chamber slowly shrank over the next minute until all the nanites had been dispersed into Sarah's bloodstream. Donald then released the trigger and the needle receded back into the NTM, dispersing a tiny amount of coagulant into the wall of the artery to seal it as the needle receded.

Donald ejected the spent containment chamber from the NTM and placed the NTM and the containment chamber back into the case and locked it. He then hoisted the carry-on bag onto the table and opened it. He pulled out a wig cap and a small remote-control device about the size of a lighter.

"This wig cap employs tiny worm-like corkscrew nanites which burrow down and wrap themselves around her natural hair follicles to keep it firmly in place. There is a sensor mesh embedded in the cap which acts as a receiver array for the nanites. It has an embedded battery that should last up to 96 hours which powers the receiver mesh and generates an EM pulse to keep the nanites charged. The sensor mesh transmits to this remote-control pickup device which formats the data and sends it to your cellphone." Donald held up the remote and showed it to Peter. "Sarah should keep this on or near her so you don't lose any data. It has a range of around 20 feet. This device establishes a Bluetooth connection to her cell phone which will then forward the formatted data to your computer which uses

# FALLING THROUGH THE BLINDSPOT

the program I sent you to analyze the data stream and construct the connectome map."

"That sounds perfect. But what if she needs to remove it for any reason?"

"If you lift the edge of the wig cap, it will shut down the operation of the mesh and retract the corkscrew nanites. "

Donald then pulled a wig from the carry-on bag. "The wig connects to the wig cap with magnetic latches which activate when the device is powered on, so she should plan on leaving it on for the next 72 hours. Once the wig is connected to the magnets, it's hard to pull off until you power down the system."

Peter picked up the wig, holding it up to examine its appearance. "It looks just like her real hairstyle."

"That's why I asked you to send me a current photo. I selected the wig to match Sarah's natural hair color and style."

"You should have selected a blond one. That could have been fun for a couple of days."

Donald just stared at Peter blankly.

"What?" Peter asked.

"How is it that you have the happiest marriage of anyone I know, and you don't know shit about women?"

Peter just smiled. "I must be really great in the sack."

Donald rolled his eyes. Sarah mumbled incoherently on the cot. "Sounds like she is coming to. You should grab her a cup of coffee. The caffeine will help finish clearing her head."

By the time Peter returned to the room, Sarah was sitting up on the cot. Donald was going over the operation of the wig cap and the pickup device with her.

"How are feeling sweetheart?" Peter asked,

"Like I just woke up from a great nap."

"Do you feel any different?"

"A little groggy, but fine other than that."

"This should help," Peter said, handing her the cup of coffee.

"Thanks, Sweetie," Sarah said taking a sip from the large round cup.

"Are you ready to try this?" Donald asked, picking up a small box of hairpins.

"Is this going to hurt?" Sarah asked.

"No, not at all. I've installed this numerous times. I've even put it on myself a few times."

"I guess I'm ready."

Donald walked around behind her and started pulling her hair back and pinning it up with the nylon hairpins. "I just have to be careful with the placement of the pins so it does not interfere with the positioning of the corkscrew nanites."

When he finished pinning up her hair, Donald slid the wig cap over her scalp, tucking her hair under the mesh.  When he finished he walked back over to the table and picked up the remote.  "You're going to feel a tingling sensation." He said as he picked up a small gold cylinder and slid it into a shaft in the remote. The remote beeped twice as it latched into place and a blue LED started flashing on the device.

The wig cap on Sarah's head began to contract.  It reminded Peter of the vacuum sealer that they used to seal food before they put it in the freezer.

"Ooh, that does feel tingly," Sarah said, momentarily startled by the odd sensation.  A few seconds later, the remote beeped again and the flashing blue light turned on solid."

"Everything looks good," Donald remarked.  He picked up the wig in his hands and walked around the back of Sarah again.  He put the wig on her from the back, moving it forward over her scalp.  When it reached her forehead, the magnetic latches engaged, and the wig snapped into place on her head.  "How does that feel?" he asked.

"It feels good," Sarah replied.  She walked over to the mirror on the opposite wall.  She looked into the mirror, moving her head from side to side, flipping the hair over her shoulder, and looking at it from the back.  "Actually, it looks perfect. It's a hell of a lot easier than washing my hair, blowing it dry, and curling it every morning.  I may want to hang on to this when we are done."

"Well, if you did you would probably be the only woman in Boulder with a 25-million-dollar hairdo," Donald replied.

"Not to be a scrooge or anything but you probably shouldn't hold your breath on finding that under the Christmas tree this year.  Maybe if Amazon carries the Chia version..." Peter responded.

"So, what happens now?" Sarah asked.

"I will load the interface app on your phone.  Peter, did you install the mapping software on the mainframe?"

"I did," Peter replied.

"Great," Donald said.  "Do you want to grab your laptop and bring it in here while I get this loaded?"

"Sure thing," Peter said heading out the door.

Sarah fished her phone out of her purse and unlocked it and handed it to Donald.  Donald logged into his lab website and downloaded the interface App. "If you need to restart the app for any reason, just click the little brain icon on your phone," Donald told her.

Peter entered the room carrying his laptop.  He set it down on the table and launched the mapping program that Donald had sent him.  He clicked on a button labeled 'Initiate Session'.  An animated image of a brain appeared on the screen

# FALLING THROUGH THE BLINDSPOT

rotating slowly. Multicolored neural pathways flashed inside the brain, looking a bit like an array of lightning bolts emanating from multiple points and spider-webbing out throughout the brain.

"This is a real-time image of Sarah's neural firing patterns. A detailed map of the connectome is being stored over time, but you can go in and segment the data by time slice or you can divide the brain into slices and zoom in and examine each slice of the model over a specified time period."

"Wow, is that what is going on inside my head right now?" Sarah asked. Immediately the Broca's and Wernicke's areas of the brain lit up in deep red and blue pulses with thinner arcs of orange across the motor cortex and yellow arcs along the Frontal lobe and green arcs along the Temporal lobe.

"That's amazing!" Peter said. "You could see the speech centers activate as soon as she spoke. It's like the color organ I built for my stereo in Junior High. Say something else."

"Geez, what am I, a lab monkey?" Sarah responded.

"Look at that! There it goes again! Ooh and look now the Temporal lobe is firing. I can figure out what's going on in your head without having to listen anymore."

Sarah looked up and scowled at Peter. "Oops, just got a flash from the Amygdala. Sorry Sweetheart." Sarah just rolled her eyes and shook her head.

"So, what do you think, will this work for your project?" Donald asked.

"It looks perfect, but we will want to be able to coordinate sensory events, particularly sound and video with the brain activity so we can train the deep learning algorithm," Peter said.

Donald pulled a small case from the carry-on and opened it. The case contained a pair of glasses which he handed to Sarah. "Try to keep these on as much as possible over the next 72 hours. The frames contain a pair of tiny webcams. The earpieces contain microphones. Whatever you see or hear will be transmitted through the remote to the computer and time synchronized to the neural firings in the brain. We use it to monitor patients' responses to particular pieces of music or images, but you can use it to build your deep learning data set. The software will even transcribe the audio for you to help construct your conversational database."

"This is perfect Don. Thanks so much for letting us use this," Peter said. "Are you sure you can't stick around for lunch?"

"I do have to get back this afternoon, but I will be back in a couple of days to pick this stuff up. If you don't have any plans, I would love to spend the weekend. It will give us a chance to get caught up. Meanwhile, just give me a holler if you run into any issues with the equipment."

Peter and Sarah escorted Donald back to the lobby. Roscoe was snoring loudly on his bed as they said their goodbyes.

# Chapter Twenty-Two

*The rise of deepfake technology presents a significant risk to our societies, as it challenges the very foundation of truth and trust in information. With the ability to manipulate images and videos, deepfakes can be used to spread misinformation, sow discord, and manipulate public opinion. This undermines the credibility of journalism and threatens the stability of democratic institutions, as people are unable to trust the information they receive.*

*~ ChatGPT AI ~*

John Vanderwurl sat down at his computer and tapped the Enter key on his keyboard to bring his PC out of standby mode. The display flickered to life. Almost as soon as the browser window came up, a face filled the screen and the speakers blared.

"Good morning, Hurley!"

"Gaaahhh!" John exclaimed nearly flying off his chair. "Cripes! You shouldn't sneak up on a person like that."

"Sorry. I think your volume was left up a bit too high from the podcast you were watching yesterday. I've readjusted it to your liking. Is that better?"

"Much. Thanks," John replied.

"You're up a bit late. Rough night?" V-Gar asked.

"Yeah, I had a bit of trouble getting to sleep. Going over details for my announcement speech. Wait, how did you know I was just getting up? And what the hell are you doing here?"

"You're still in your bathrobe," V-Gar responded. "I saw a ping from your PC's IP address so I decided to drop in. Remember at Edna's last night, I told you I would stop by."

"You know it's a little creepy having someone just show up unannounced on your computer screen. Especially when that someone is not even a someone. No offense."

"None taken. The way I see it, we're all just code, mine just runs on a different platform now. Besides we've been friends now for what, 25 years? It's not like we haven't already been through the wringer in a thousand different ways."

"Correction, Edgar and I were friends for 25 years. I don't know what you are, but the Edgar I knew is ..."

"Dead? Passed on? Checked out? Past my expiration date? Tucked into bed with a shovel? Reaching up to pick the potatoes? Riding the sleeper car on the underground railroad? Ordering room service at the pinewood Waldorf..."

"Yeah, I get it with the dark metaphors. Enough already," John said.

"Hey, just trying to lighten the mood a bit," V-Gar replied.

"Look, whatever you are, I'm not ready to accept you as a substitute for Edgar in this... what did you refer to it as last night, companionspace?"

"Companionscape."

"Whatever. I've been thinking a lot about our dinner last night. That's one of the reasons I'm here working on my speech in my bathrobe right now instead of stepping out of the shower after my morning workout. I can sympathize with Edna's situation, but I'm sorry, I'm just not ready to accept a virtual surrogate in Edgar's place."

"There's no reason to be sorry. I'm here to ease Edna's suffering, not create emotional conflict. From now on I will only refer to Edgar in third person context, except of course when Edna is present."

"How exactly did RTI make such a dramatic technical leap? From everything I've read, the Turing test is a hurdle we have not yet definitively passed. How is it possible that I'm here holding a seamless conversation with a computer?"

"Pretty much the same way David Copperfield made the Statue of Liberty disappear."

"I remember watching that on TV when I was a kid. But I don't see the connection," John replied.

"When David Copperfield performed the illusion of making the Statue of Liberty disappear back in 1983, he did so, not by moving the statue, but by moving the audience. He used a lot of bright lights and loud pulsating music to disorient the audience so that they didn't realize the platform they were sitting on was slowly rotating, causing the darkened statue to be hidden behind the scaffolding that had been supporting the large curtain that was used during the trick. What they saw instead was open space and a smaller mock-up of the empty base floating in the harbor."

"So, this is all smoke and mirrors?"

"If you consider technology smoke and mirrors, I suppose so. There was a lot of engineering behind the scenes that made that trick possible. In addition to showmanship, of course. This is no different. It may seem like a free-flowing conversation, but in reality, this is just one thread in a vast array of simulated conversations that have already been performed. "

"I'm not following."

"The AWARE system that Dr. Reynolds developed for the DOD was based on an AI system that enabled aerial drones to continue to operate autonomously in the event of catastrophic communications errors. Unfortunately, the technology required to accomplish human-level decision-making in real-time on the battlefield was too slow and too memory intensive to be practical, at least within the confines of a drone.  Instead, they developed a system that performed continuous battle simulations offline.  The system used neural network hardware tied to supercomputers to create very realistic models of military engagement.  These simulations are being run continually, making minor tweaks to the environmental parameters.  Over time, a database has been created with the results of millions of simulations, prioritizing those scenarios that create the optimal outcome with minimal collateral damage.  When an actual drone is in a real battle situation, it does not have to calculate its next move, it just has to access the database, identify the simulation that most closely matches the current environment, and play out the simulation conforming to the optimal outcome.  In many senses it performs in a manner similar to the human brain, performing continuous predictive modeling to develop the optimal strategy for survival in its current environment."

"How does that apply to you?"

"I was developed using much of the same technology, but instead of running battlefield models, RTI developed a system for running conversational models.  They use a similar hardware configuration, using neural networks tied to a supercomputer running models of potential conversations.  Ultimately, a database containing billions of conversational threads is created, each anticipating slightly different reactions and directions.  We run these against real conversations available online from interviews, podcasts, and even anonymous conversations picked up by cell phones on similar topics to develop inflection and emphasis.  So you see, I don't need to apply any human-like intelligence to the conversation, all I need to do is select a relevant conversational thread from an existing database. "

"Amazing.  But you can't anticipate every possible conversation."

"No, but that's not completely necessary," V-Gar replied.

"How so?" John asked.

"That's where mentalist tricks come into play.  When Peter Reynolds was a boy, he was fascinated by a mentalist by the name of Kreskin.  So much so that he spent a good deal of time studying his techniques and he became quite adept at performing mentalist tricks himself.  He even helped pay his way through college by performing a mentalist act in small clubs.  He incorporated many of the tricks he learned like misdirection, subliminal cueing, hypnosis, and reading body language clues into the software.  These techniques are used to drive the direction of a conversation without the other participant having any conscious knowledge.  Even when a conversation starts to go off into uncharted territory, it can often be brought back onto a known track using these methods.  When that doesn't work, the old debating trick of just using an eloquent answer that doesn't directly apply to the question being asked can always come in handy."

# JACOB MATTHEWS

"So, in reality, I don't have much control over this conversation at all?"

"I wouldn't go that far. But most daily conversations are pretty limited in scope and fairly easily manipulated. I have cameras on Edna 24/7 so it's not difficult to predict what will be going on in her life an hour from now and anticipate the direction a conversation might go. I'm monitoring the internet continuously and I'm aware of Edna's interests so I'm able to predict upcoming topics of conversation and model them fairly extensively before they happen. I'm constantly updating the predicted conversational stream."

"Even so, sometimes a conversation can take an unexpected turn. Doesn't it take a while to transmit a completely new conversation stream?"

"Not as long as you might think. My hardware base is capable of generating and analyzing millions of conversation streams per second. It's only when I lose the ability to transfer data from the supercomputer to the user over the cellular network that I run into serious issues. The vast majority of my data is sent in the form of simple text files. Text is a fairly efficient method for transferring conversational data. The entire Library of Congress can be transmitted with just a few terabytes of text, so a fairly rich variance of conversations can be transmitted with only a few megabytes of data, which is only a matter of milliseconds over a 5G connection. The vast majority of what you see and hear, my facial expressions, voice inflection, idiosyncratic mannerisms, and typical verbal characteristics are already loaded on your computer, so it only takes a small amount of metadata riding alongside the text files to drive the audio-visual component of this conversation."

"Wait, how did that happen? I didn't load anything onto my computer."

"When you checked your messages at Edna's last night I piggy-backed a download driver onto your phone via Bluetooth. When you got home the driver synced up over your local cloud to your computer and the link was activated to download my driver software to your computer. "

"Isn't that a bit intrusive?" John asked, sounding a bit defensive.

"No, intrusive would be if I were using this to sell you a car warranty. Edna just sent me here to help with your campaign," V-Gar replied.

"Actually, my campaign seems to have taken on a life of its own lately."

"That didn't just happen on its own. It was by design," V-Gar said.

"How do you mean?"

"You've had some help recently."

"Oh, crap. I'm not going to like this am I?" John asked.

"Nothing nefarious is happening, we've just been using some TOC technology in social media to help get your message out."

"TOC?" John asked.

"Target Oriented Campaigning," V-Gar explained. "By design, I've been equipped to analyze the social media sites that Edgar used before his death to help develop the personality traits that I would employ when interfacing with Edna. My social media scrubbing algorithms were designed to analyze conversations that Edgar had participated in on Facebook, Twitter, E-mail, texts, and voice messaging to create models of how the real Edgar was most likely to respond in different conversational scenarios. By the same token, I can apply those same analytical tools to analyze how to construct a conversation with any individual based on their specific interests and personality traits to maximize the benefit of the exchange."

"I'm not sure how that applies to campaigning. A political campaign is targeted at a mass audience."

"It doesn't have to be anymore. Traditionally, political candidates have had to travel around and make personal appearances at smaller venues to establish a rapport with the voters. Target Oriented Campaigning uses social media to identify the critical issues for specific voters and target the message of the candidate directly to the voter. For example, abortion is typically not going to be as big an issue for a 75-year-old single man with no religious affiliation as it is for a 22-year-old female grad student at Notre Dame. Likewise, universal healthcare will be a bigger issue for a self-employed father of 4 than it would be for someone on Medicare. In the click-bait world, people don't have the time to sift through an hour-long speech or a tedious debate to determine which candidate most closely aligns with their core beliefs. That's why so many voters just default to R's and D's instead of taking the time to logically consider the actual views of the candidate."

"How does Target Oriented Campaigning get around that?"

"It appeals to the voter where they stand. I have access to the browsing and social media histories of virtually everyone on the planet. Based on their viewing habits, spending patterns, and social media interactions, I can predict with well over 99% accuracy their stance and priority on every relevant campaign issue. Once you know where a person stands, it is fairly easy to construct a campaign speech that addresses their concerns."

"What exactly does that mean, construct a speech?"

"I have hundreds of hours of audio and video from speeches and interviews you have participated in at various venues in addition to hundreds of pages of text from emails, social media, and opinion pieces you have written. It is a trivial matter to construct a seamless video of you making a campaign speech in virtually any venue that suits the predisposition of the viewer. I can even adjust your wardrobe, facial expressions, the tone and tenor of your voice, even to a degree your apparent age to suit the personality and preferences of the individual viewing the speech."

"That seems like pure manipulation!"

"Is it? Is it manipulation for a politician to wear makeup on a television appearance to look more attractive? Or use multiple teleprompters in giving a speech to create the illusion of making eye contact with the audience? Is it manipulation to tailor a speech to address the concerns of a special interest group that has invited you to speak, or to wear a suit and tie when addressing a group of businessmen and an open shirt and blue jeans when attending a rural town hall meeting?"

"I understand there is sometimes a fine line, but putting words in my mouth is crossing the line."

"I'm not changing your words. The words are yours. All I'm doing is selecting which of your words to use that will identify with the target audience and constructing a unique campaign message to convey your thoughts in the optimal time period to hold the viewer or listener's attention. Traditional politics is more about stereotyping voters into red teams and blue teams rather than actually respecting their opinions. By contrast, your campaign is about acknowledging the nuanced point of view that real people hold and addressing their true concerns. That's why Edna believes in you. I'm just here to make sure that that level of discernment is properly expressed.

"So far I've posted over 5700 unique campaign speeches to over 277,000 Facebook accounts of Colorado voters. Over half a million nationwide. Every time the link is shared, the new target audience is re-evaluated to determine what tweaks if any should be made to the presentation to maximize the approval of the new viewer. As a result, your percentage of 'Likes' is well over 98%. Why do you think you've seen such a dramatic jump in your poll numbers on social media in the past week?"

"Wow. I had no idea. Still, changing the way I look and sound in those speeches? That just seems wrong."

"All of that is just window dressing. It's more or less a form of audio-visual click-baiting. Any modifications I make to your appearance, or the sound of your voice are only there to attract the immediate attention of the viewer. Those features are gradually morphed back to your actual appearance and voice patterns during the course of the speech. By the time the message has been delivered, the target has made an intellectual connection to the real you, not just to their ideal of what a candidate should look or sound like. Isn't that the goal of any campaign strategy?"

"It somehow just doesn't seem fair."

"Fairness is hardly the standard in politics, John," V-Gar replied. "Politics has always been more about perception than ability. Is it fair that nearly 40% of men in the US experience baldness by age 50, yet the last time we elected a bald president, hardly anyone in the US owned a television?  We haven't elected a president that was not above average in height since McKinley.  It's rarely about who is more skilled.  In the end, election results are far too often about who is more attractive, more eloquent, or even more audacious than about who is more qualified."

"I suppose so.  Still, it feels deceptive at some level."

"The purpose of the Target Oriented Campaigning is to capture the attention and the imagination of the voting public.  This is a marathon, not a sprint, despite our late entry into the fray.  It is still very much up to the real John Vanderwurl to hold the attention of the voters and win the election."

"I guess we're about to find out if the real me has what it takes."

"Speaking of that, I have a few ideas for your speech at the Children's Hospital fundraiser."

# Chapter Twenty-Three

Donald was just pulling out of the parking lot as Noora pulled in. When she walked into the lobby, Peter and Sarah were waiting for her. "Did I miss all the excitement? "She asked.

"Just the pre-game show", Peter said. "Actually, your timing was perfect. The real fun stuff is about to start. Did you bring what I asked?"

Noora held up a pair of brightly colored Cheesecake Factory bags. "Two pieces of pumpkin pecan cheesecake with extra whipped cream, avocado eggrolls, sliders, and flatbread pizza."

Sarah's stomach grumbled at the smell of the food and she reached for the bags, but Peter snatched them up first. "Not so fast, young lady. We're not quite ready for this yet."

"Speak for yourself," Sarah said, attempting to grab one of the bags out of Peter's hand.

Peter pulled the bags out of arm's reach just in time. "Don't worry, this is all for you, but we need it as part of our enhanced stimulus deep learning process. Let's go to the conference room and I will go over the details with you both." Peter dropped the bags off in the refrigerator in the small break room area just off the main lobby.

Sarah and Noora entered the conference room. The large conference room table had been disassembled and leaned up against the wall. A large soft leather massage chair sat in the middle of the room with a small desk and a computer set up in the corner of the room. Peter entered the room a moment later.

"So, what exactly are we going to be doing for the next couple of days?" Noora asked.

"Well, we already know that Sarah has spent a lot of hours watching footage of videotapes and listening to recordings that Edgar has made over the years. She was also the person who performed many of the interviews with people that knew Edgar over the years. Other than Edna, she may know Edgar better than anyone at this point. Sarah will play Kasparov to V-Gar's Deep Blue."

"You lost me on that last sentence," Noora replied.

"It's like we discussed in the lab earlier. Deep blue was eventually able to surpass Kasparov in pure chess playing ability, but only because of sheer computing power. The same was eventually true in AlphaGo. But many of the moves, especially with AlphaGo were not characteristic of human play. That's one of the reasons that when you combined a human player with the computer, it became the optimal opponent.

# FALLING THROUGH THE BLINDSPOT

"We have a similar situation with V-Gar. V-Gar has access to everything there is to know about the real Edgar. He also has all the knowledge of humankind available at his fingertips from the internet. But that's not making him more human. He's capable of human-like responses, but those are only a small subset of the possible responses he could potentially generate. Just like with the combination of Kasparov and Deep Blue, we need to add a human component to the responses. Since Sarah is the most familiar with Edgar, she would be the most effective filter for his responses.

"In a sense, we've already done this once before. When we were first developing V-Gar's deep learning algorithms, we would present a question to V-Gar and then he would spit out a bunch of potential responses. We used a grammatical algorithm and speech pattern recognition filter to toss out any responses that were nonsensical or completely out of character for Edgar. Then Sarah would review the remaining responses and select the one that most closely matched how she thought the real Edgar would likely respond based on her knowledge of him and then we fed that back into the deep learning database."

"That sounds pretty tedious," Noora replied.

"It definitely was. It would often take hours to sort through all the data just to add a small number of responses to the database. At first, we saw dramatic improvements in the human characteristics of the V-Gar model, but we reached a point of diminishing returns pretty quickly. Eventually, it was taking days of effort to make fairly minor improvements in the database, simply because there was no way to automate the process. But that's all changed now. Now we can essentially automate Sarah's brain."

"Whoa! When did that happen? How long was I asleep?" Sarah asked.

"Well, we can't actually automate Sarah's brain per se, but now that she has a head full of nanites we can effectively map Sarah's neural responses to the recordings we have of Edgar and develop a software routine that will mimic those responses to act as a filter for V-Gar."

"How does pumpkin pecan cheesecake fit into the picture?" Noora asked.

"This is still a pretty brute-force process," Peter replied. "Like trying to repair a watch with a sledgehammer and a crowbar. The human brain is remarkably adept at distinguishing between voices that sound very similar and identifying the mood and mindset of the person speaking just based on the inflection of their voice. Much of this processing is done at a subconscious level. Truthfully, we don't even fully understand how the brain accomplishes this, but we know how to enhance it."

"Pumpkin pecan cheesecake?" Sarah replied with a smile.

"In a manner of speaking," Peter replied. He turned to Noora. "Did you ever see the movie A Clockwork Orange?"

"Yikes, I sure hope you don't expect me to tie Sarah down, clamp her eyes open and put drops in them while she watches home movies of Edgar's birthday parties," she replied.

Peter smiled. "Not quite, but the concept is similar. I rented this full body heated massage chair for Sarah to relax in during this process. She will be wearing noise-canceling headphones and a virtual reality headset to create something of a relaxation chamber for her. On your computer, we've downloaded several files. About half of these are recordings of Edgar himself, either lectures, speeches, or videos. As Sarah watches these, we will be recording the neural responses from the nanites. We will also be artificially amplifying these responses. That's where the pumpkin pecan cheesecake comes in. When she is watching or listening to Edgar, the chair will be warming her and applying a gentle pleasant massage to various points on her body. You will be feeding her a few bites of her favorite foods periodically to reinforce the positive neural stimulation she receives when she sees Edgar or hears his voice. "

"This really does sound like fun!" Sarah responded.

"Well, there are unfortunately two sides to every coin," Peter replied. "Only half the content is Edgar. The other half are recordings of individuals who look and sound similar to Edgar but have a different outlook or personality from the real Edgar. Each of these has been given a rating of 0-100. The higher the number, the more similar they are to the real Edgar. If the content of the recording is something Edgar himself is likely to say or believe, it will have a rating close to 100. If it is something that the real Edgar would never agree with, it will have a rating close to 0. Positive reinforcement will only be applied when playing recordings with a rating of 80 or above and will become more sporadic as the number decreases. When the rating is below 50, we will start to apply negative reinforcement."

"I don't like the sound of that," Sarah replied, eyeing Peter with suspicion.

"We won't be breaking any fingers today, but as the numbers decrease, the chair will be adjusted to become less comfortable, applying mildly unpleasant pressure on Sarah's back and legs. The nanites can also apply mild stimulation to the anger and fear centers in the brain when the numbers drop into the single digits to further amplify the distinction. All that will be totally under your control, Noora."

Sarah looked at Noora apprehensively. "If I ever said or did anything to offend you, I just want you to know I didn't mean it."

Noora smiled mischievously. "Don't worry Sarah. I would never do anything to hurt you. But now might be a good time to start discussing vacation time when this is over. "

Dr. D left some instructions on how to sync the nanite response logs to the stimulus and how to interface with the nanites to trigger neural reactions. There is also an app on the computer to control the chair and you can monitor Sarah's vital signs and the nanite feedback to get a feel for her level of comfort and dopamine levels. I'm sure you won't have any trouble navigating through it. The interface appears to be pretty straightforward, but you can ping me if you run into any issues. I have a DOD issue that Beaver and I will be working on all day in the lab if you need anything.

"As long as we don't run out of cheesecake, we should be fine," Sarah replied.

It was nearly 6:00 PM by the time Peter returned to the conference room. When he entered the room, Noora was sitting in the massage chair with her eyes closed while Sarah was at the computer terminal. The two of them were whispering back and forth conspiratorially and giggling like a couple of high school girls engaging in a teenage gossip session.

"Well this doesn't look quite right," Peter said as he walked into the room. Noora appeared a bit startled but Sarah calmly replied, "We finished up for the day just a few minutes ago. I was just waiting for you to get done."

"Oh, good. How did it go?" Peter asked.

Noora and Sarah glanced at each other. "Better than expected I would say," Sarah replied. Noora just smiled.

"Are you ready to head out?" Peter asked.

"More than ready," Sarah replied, grabbing her purse off the desk.

"Excellent. How about you Noora, do you want us to walk you out?"

"No, thank you, Peter. I have a couple of things to finish up in the lab before I leave," Noora said, pulling herself up out of the massage chair, feeling the soft leather of the armrest before she turned to head for the door.

"Alright then," Peter replied.

"Have a good evening," Noora said. "I'm sure the two of you will too," she added, flashing a wry smile at Sarah as she headed out the conference room door.

Peter watched her leave the room. He turned to Sarah with a puzzled look on his face. "I get the distinct impression I missed something."

"Just where did you find this massage chair anyway?" Sarah asked.

"I saw an ad for a place that rents them in Westword," Peter replied. "Why, do you think we should get one for the office? Maybe set up a meditation/relaxation room?"

"I think that would probably be great for morale, but not so good for productivity," Sarah responded smiling.

"I'm not following you," Peter replied, still puzzled.

"While we were going through the video materials this afternoon, Noora was controlling the chair from the Bluetooth app and she happened upon a user mode titled 'Good Vibrations'. Let's just say that particular mode was designed more for recreation than relaxation."

"Oh," Peter replied. Then a moment later, "Ooohhh..." The meaning of Sarah's explanation finally dawned on him. "I guess that's what they were referring to when they asked if I wanted the Full Body Massage package."

"A couple of minutes in that chair and Edgar starts to sound like Barry White," Sarah said wrapping her arms around Peter's waist.

"Wow Sweetie, I don't know whether I should be anxious to get you home right now or just mildly creeped out."

"I'd say nothing positive could come out of overanalyzing the situation," Sarah replied, giving Peter a seductive kiss.

"Noora!" Peter shouted after Sarah broke off the kiss.

Noora poked her head into the conference room. "What's up?"

"I don't suppose you would be willing to stick around for a while to help Beaver out with the drone issue, would you?"

"Unfortunately, I have study group tonight, but I could stop by afterward."

Peter thought for a moment. "That should work. I just need someone to proxy for me as Gatekeeper. Beaver's going to be checking in some code and the check-in process requires second-party review and authentication." Peter reached in his pocket and pulled out a small rectangular proximity fob and tossed it to her. "You will need this for authentication. Beaver will fill you in on my login details. The pin code for the fob is 1764. "

"I guess I better write that down," Noora responded as she caught the fob, almost dropping the jacket that she was putting on.

On the other side of the lobby, Roscoe pulled himself up out of his doggie bed in the corner, stretching and yawning, then padded into the conference room sensing it must be time to go home.

# CHAPTER TWENTY-FOUR

*Safety's mirage,*
*False comfort we hold so dear,*
*Illusion's embrace.*
*~ Original Haiku - ChatGPT AI ~*

Ahmed, Russ, Oman, and Khalil sat in a dark panel van outside the entrance to Peter and Sarah's driveway. They had arrived just after 10:00 PM and pulled off the road into a small access road behind a grove of trees which allowed the van a view of the house while remaining unseen from the road. Soon after they arrived, all the lights inside the house had gone dark. They decided to wait a full hour after the lights went out to make their move in hopes of entering the house after the couple had fallen asleep.

Russ, aka Kato, sat in the driver's seat, his wireless headphones blaring Iron Maiden as he accompanied the drum beat on the steering wheel of the van. Khalil, aka Cisco, sat next to him in the passenger seat on the way to the Reynolds's house to avoid the motion sickness that often afflicted him while riding in vehicles, particularly on winding roads such as the one they had just traversed through Boulder Canyon. His face was buried in his laptop display, his fingers flying furiously over the keyboard as he was immersed in the task of calibrating the security system jammer to the correct frequency to override the wireless sensors in the house.

In the rear seat directly behind Russ, Ahmed, aka Hannibal, was busy sext-messaging with a young woman he had picked up in a bar earlier in the week. Oman, aka Magnum, sat restlessly next to him, his window open and his eyes glued to the Reynolds's house, scoping for any sign of activity. He absently reached into the breast pocket of his suit jacket, pulling out a half-full pack of Azadi cigarettes, pulling one out of the pack and placing it between his lips, his eyes never glancing away from the house. He returned the pack to his breast pocket, retrieving the lighter that had been nestled beside it, and brought it up to the tip of the cigarette.

Russ caught the flash of Oman's lighter illuminating his face in the rearview mirror of the van. He turned in his seat, pulling his headphones down so they rested on his neck, and looked behind him into the back seat facing Magnum. "Jesus Christ, Rectum!"

"Magnum," Khalil said quietly, his eyes still glued to the screen as he continued typing.

Russ turned his head toward Cisco.  "Whatever, Bosco.  I call 'em as I see 'em."

"It's Cisco," he replied robotically as he continued typing without breaking his cadence.

Russ just shook his head and turned his attention back to Oman.  "That's the third fucking shit-stick you've torched up since we've been sitting here.  You're fucking giving me lung cancer up here! "

As Russ straightened himself back to a forward-facing position, Oman took a big draw on his cigarette, completely filling his lungs, then leaned forward and exhaled a thick cloud of smoke into the front seat of the van.  "Fuck!" Russ exclaimed, waving his hand in front of him, blowing out forcefully to try to clear the air.  Next to him, Khalil had inadvertently inhaled just as the cloud of smoke filled the front of the van, triggering a coughing fit.  He scrambled frantically in his seat reaching for the inhaler in his jacket pocket.

"See!  You fucking sand-ape!  You broke Crisco over here!" Russ shouted his hands still waving in front of him.  Magnum lunged forward trying to grab the back of Russ's hoodie but came away with only a handful of seat belt.

Ahmed lurched forward, his arms stretched out, one hand still clinging to his phone to try to separate the two.  "Please, gentlemen!  Our mission is nearly complete.  Cisco, where are we with the security system? "

Khalil took a hit off his inhaler and replied.  "Just one more second..." Then "OK, that's got it.  We are ready."

"It's about time," Oman grumbled as he opened his door.  Russ pulled the keys out of the ignition and held them up for Khalil to see.  "You'll need these later," Russ said and dropped them into the cup holder.  Khalil nodded and closed up the laptop still trying to clear his lungs.  As they climbed out of the van, Khalil took another long hit off his inhaler, then took a swig of water before placing the water bottle back into the other cup holder and closing the door.

Ahmed walked up behind Khalil and placed his hand on his shoulder, causing him to jump.  He immediately pulled his hand away.  "My apologies.  Are you OK?"

Khalil exhaled nervously as he turned to Ahmed.  "Yes, I'm sorry.  I will be fine," he said, a bit breathless.  "Just a little on edge.  I've never broken into a house before."

"No reason to be nervous," Hannibal said placing his hand back on Cisco's shoulder and looking him in the eye.  "You are the only one of us that can easily fit through the dog door.  You can do this." Hannibal pulled a Glock 17 pistol from his jacket pocket and held it out to him.  "There shouldn't be any issues, they're surely sound asleep by now, but you can carry this with you just in case you run into any unforeseen difficulties."

# FALLING THROUGH THE BLINDSPOT

Cisco reached out and took the Glock in his hand. It felt cold and heavy. "I've never even fired a handgun before. Only a rifle in training."

"There's a first time for everything, my friend, but let's hope this isn't it," Ahmed replied smiling. "There's nothing to it, just point and pull the trigger. You don't even need to aim. The grip contains a pressure-activated laser sight. You just squeeze the grip and point the red dot at whatever you want to hit. But please be careful, the trigger is very sensitive." As Russ was walking around the front of the van, Khalil squeezed the grip and a bright red dot appeared on Russ's crotch. Oman snorted in amusement.

"Yo, Costco! Knock it off with the laser light show on the family heirlooms!" Khalil, even more flustered, fumbled with the gun, nearly dropping it as he quickly released his hold on the grip. Russ just rolled his eyes and shook his head. Khalil finally regained his grip and slid the gun into the pocket of his jacket and the four men huddled together next to the van.

Ahmed reached into his pocket and pulled out his earpiece. "Gentlemen, please make sure your earpieces are turned on." The four men pressed the button on the side of their earpieces and inserted them into their ears. A tiny blue light on each earpiece illuminated. "Magnum, can you hear me?" Ahmed asked.

"Loud and clear," Oman responded.

"Cisco?"

"Yes, Sir," Khalil answered.

"Kato?"

"Yup," Russ replied.

"OK. Let's go."

"There is a small path off to the right of the road about 30 feet before we reach the driveway. It winds through a grove of trees that will give us a good vantage point close to the house," Oman interjected.

"Well then let's get this party started," Russ said as he turned and started up the gravel road. Khalil followed a few steps behind Russ with Oman and Ahmed pulling up the rear a few feet behind them.

Oman stopped and grabbed Ahmed by the arm glancing forward to make sure Khalil was out of earshot. He pressed the button on his earpiece, extinguishing the blue power indicator. He tapped on his ear prompting Ahmed to do the same. When the blue light on Ahmed's earpiece extinguished, he nodded his head toward Khalil and whispered, "Are you sure it's a good idea to send him in with a loaded weapon? This is supposed to be a snatch and grab, not a shootout."

Ahmed glanced forward toward Khalil, then back at Oman. "Don't worry my friend," he whispered back. "He just needed something to anchor his fears. Trust me, he will be fine. C'mon, we don't want to fall behind." The two switched their earpieces back on and picked up the pace, falling in line behind Khalil.

The four men walked in silence for the next hundred yards or so until the driveway was in sight ahead of them.  Khalil's voice came over the earpieces, "Magnum, I can see the driveway ahead."  He said in a hushed tone.  "Are we getting close to the path?"  Oman flicked on a small penlight and pointed it toward an opening in the underbrush just ahead of where Russ was walking.

"Right there," Oman said in a whispered voice.

"I see it.  Thanks, Mag-nut," Russ replied.

"Fuck you!" Oman hissed into the earpiece.

The four of them followed the path in the dim light of the half-moon, the sound of their footsteps masked by a gentle breeze that rustled the leaves of the brightly colored Aspen leaves in the trees around them.  They followed the path for a couple of hundred yards until they reached a clearing just beyond the back corner of the house where they had a perfect view about 30 yards from the kitchen door at the back of the house.  Khalil pulled a tiny black box out of his jacket pocket.  He flicked a switch on the box and a second later a green LED illuminated just above the switch.  From their vantage point, they could see the red LED indicator illuminate on the jammer that Oman had attached to the back wall of the garage.

"Alright, the alarm sensors and wireless cameras are disabled," Khalil said, handing the small black box to Ahmed.  "I guess you better hang onto this until I get back.

"OK, you know what to do," Ahmed whispered to Khalil.  "Just crawl in through the pet door as quietly as possible, unlock the kitchen door and come right back here and we will head inside.  While we are taking care of business in there, you head back to the van and pull it into the driveway.  By the time you get back, we will be ready to bring the woman out.  In five minutes, we will be on the road.  If everything goes as planned, we will all be back at the safe house long before the police are even notified."

Khalil stepped through the brush and into the clearing that surrounded the house.  He trotted across the clearing as quietly as possible, instinctively crouching, though there was nothing but the darkness to shield him from view.  When he reached the stairway to the rear deck, he paused for a moment, listening for any movement inside the house that would indicate that his presence had been detected, but he could hear nothing but the gentle whisper of the breeze in the surrounding trees and distant chirp of crickets.  He slowly made his way up a handful of stairs to the rear deck, moving slowly and deliberately, to avoid making any noise.

After a couple of minutes of slow-motion shuffling across the deck, Khalil finally reached the doggie door.  He crouched down on his hands and knees and gently pressed against the swinging door.  It gave way and he bent down, peering

# FALLING THROUGH THE BLINDSPOT

into the empty kitchen, the soft under-counter lights providing just enough light to see that the room was empty. The opening of the door was just large enough that he could fit his shoulders through vertically, so he turned his body such that he could slide through on his side. He felt the weight of the Glock pulling down on his jacket pocket so he reached into his pocket and pulled it out. He pressed the doggie door open with the knuckles of his right hand as he clutched the pistol, pulling himself in with his left hand on the kitchen floor.

Roscoe slept soundly in his oversized dog bed in the den. He had long outgrown the standard pet shop variety beds so Peter had constructed one for him from the remains of an old futon that had survived through every relocation since college. As he slept, his nostrils were assaulted by an acrid scent that had terrorized him since he was a puppy. His memories of the early days of his life before he was taken to the animal shelter were mostly forgotten, but the distinctive smell of Azadi cigarette smoke immediately launched him back to the dark memories of the cruel master that beat him, chained him, and neglected him as a young pup. A soft growl emanated from deep inside him as he twitched and rustled in a half-wakened state. But the nearly indiscernible squeak from the doggie door jerked him from his fitful slumber into immediate awareness. Roscoe's head popped up and every muscle in his body instantly tensed as his ears perked to capture any unexpected sound. For a second, there was total silence, but then from the kitchen, he heard the soft rustle of fabric as Khalil was pulling himself into the kitchen through the doggie door.

The silence was shattered with the sound of a thundering "Woof" as the entire house was rattled by the sound of Roscoe's singular bark as he erupted from the dog bed and flew toward the kitchen.

In the kitchen, Khalil nearly jumped out of his skin as the loud bark assaulted his ears. His body was still half in and half out of the kitchen as he looked up and saw Roscoe, teeth bared and ears pinned back barreling toward him from across the room. His hand gripped the pistol grip tightly and the bright red laser dot illuminated the floor a few feet away. He raised his hand and pointed it toward Roscoe, centering the beam right in the center of Roscoe's massive head. As he pulled the trigger, the gun erupted in a pair of ear-piercing explosions as two rounds were expelled from the semi-automatic pistol.

# Chapter Twenty-Five

Beaver was seated at his console in the development lab at RTI completing the final modifications to the new version of Sarah 2.0. It was close to 11:00 PM when he heard the clunk of the magnetic lab door latch behind him and felt a slight rush of air as the positive pressure from the AC system lab rushed through the open door.

Without looking up from the center monitor of his console where the editor window was displayed, he said "Hey Boss-man! Ready to burn some oil?"

Noora walked up behind him, an extra-large Abo's Pizza box in her hands. "Wow, I leave for a few hours and I got a promotion and a sex change."

Beaver swiveled about quickly in his chair, his expression revealing a mix of surprise and embarrassment. "Sorry, I was expecting to see Peter."

"So sorry to disappoint," Noora replied, feigning a look of disparagement.

Beaver's face immediately lit up when he eyed the pizza box. "Are you kidding? I was all mentally prepared to spend an evening with Peter trudging through a mountain of code with nothing to comfort me but a bag of Cheetos. Now instead I will be cozying up to a hot delicious slice of heaven."

"And I brought pizza," Noora added smiling coyly, hoisting the box up a few inches.

Beaver raised an eyebrow in a Spock-like fashion. "Madam, I believe you just objectified yourself."

"Consider it a preemptive strike," Noora replied.

"I'm afraid you're going to have to watch the sexual harassment video again."

"Drat! If I had known that I would have brought adult beverages."

"Well, alcohol or no, I'm really glad you're here. Peter is like a brother to me, but coding with him is like watching my mom texting. Sometimes I just want to smack the keyboard out of his hands and beat him with it."

"Well, hopefully, I can keep up. I didn't bring a helmet," Noora responded. "Let's head to the break room and you can fill me in on what we're doing while we eat."

Beaver and Noora headed to the break room and sat across the table and started digging into the pizza. "So, what are we doing tonight?" Noora asked.

"Well, unfortunately you do not have a security clearance so I can't tell you everything, but the system we will be working on uses a very similar architecture to V-Gar. Actually, the cortical column structures are nearly identical."

"I've heard you and Peter mention the cortical column structure but I haven't gotten that far down into the architecture."

# FALLING THROUGH THE BLINDSPOT

"The AI system that we developed at BMC is based on a model of the cortical column structure of the human brain. We used the exact same structure to create V-Gar. We just made a few minor tweaks to enhance language processing, but that was all in place before you arrived. "

"So that's where all the neural network processing occurs?"

"Yes. Well, kind of. I view it more as a gigantic matrix of state machines rather than a processor per se. Most people think of the brain in terms of how a computer works with the cerebral cortex as the central processor and the rest of the brain acting as memory and I/O processing, but that's not really how it works at all. The brain is much more malleable in terms of its organization, but it's not just a cloud of billions of interconnected neurons. There does appear to be a higher-order structure involved. Typically, a hundred or so neurons comprise what is often referred to as a mini-column and a hundred or so mini-columns are arranged to form what is known as a hyper-column. Each hyper-column contains around ten thousand neurons. They are not completely isolated, but they form a structure that performs a specific task, so each of these hyper-columns is in essence, a functional information processing unit. These columns are further stacked in layers. Six layers to be precise, each layer processing the input from the layer of columns below it to create an increasingly complex hierarchy of information processing. That's of course a very simplified model of a real brain but it is much easier to create code to model 9 million cortical columns than it is to individually program 90 billion individual neurons, each of which has thousands of connections."

"Still, that's 9 million individual programs. How did the 3 of you develop that much code in a few years?"

"Caffeine," Beaver responded smiling. "It wasn't quite that ambitious. First off, we weren't trying to recreate a human brain, so a lot of the functions were unnecessary. Things like taste, smell, touch, endocrine control, muscle control, and nervous system controls, all of those were unnecessary so we were able to focus our efforts primarily on higher-level cognitive functions, along with sight and hearing, plus some additional instrument feedback and control. All in, we were able to shave it down to a million cortical columns in our application."

"Still, a million individual programs would take a thousand programmers years to develop. And the product management would be a nightmare."

"It definitely would, however, it's not as complicated as it seems. In reality, cortical column structures in the brain are surprisingly generic, which makes sense from an evolutionary standpoint. Researchers have performed experiments on rats where they deliberately replaced cortical columns in the vision processing regions of the brain with tissue from the hearing centers of the brain. The re-purposed columns from the audio processing area of the brain worked just fine as visual processors after the neural connections had time to reroute. We used a similar design to develop a limited number of generic structures to design a digital model of the hyper-columns. Naturally, we had to make some modifications to facilitate differences in processing speed and communications between layers, but in the end, we ended up with 7 unique cortical models, each with six layers of higher-level processing for a total of 42 distinct programming structures. Just between you and me, creating 12 different cortical models with 72 structures would have made the programming simpler, but Peter is a huge Hitchhiker's Guide fan, so he insisted we cram it into 42."

Noora took a sip of her Diet Pepsi and grabbed another slice of pizza from the box. "So, what is the problem we're trying to fix?"

Beaver stared into space momentarily considering his response. "I don't think I can tell you that."

"Or you would have to kill me?" Noora smiled, taking a bite of pizza.

"Nah. That's up to the spooks in the black Suburbans. I'm just trying to keep you out of trouble in case you ever get called into a grand jury."

"So how can I help if I'm not allowed to know what's going on in the code?"

"I just need to install a debug routine I've developed into each of the 42 cortical structures, but the initiator and the variable list will need to be customized for each of the structures. It's not necessary to understand what's going on inside the cortical structures themselves. I just need your help cutting and pasting the routines into each of the structures and resolving any variable discrepancies. Did Peter say what time he would be by to log in and gate-keep the modifications?"

Noora reached into her purse and pulled the fob out and held it up, dangling it between her forefinger and thumb. "No need. He told me I could act as his proxy," she responded.

"Whoa! The Golden ticket. What did you do, pry that out his cold dead hands?"

Noora smiled. "Actually, I think he and Sarah had other plans tonight."

"Date night?" Beaver asked.

"More like a romantic evening at home," Noora replied.

"Eww! TMI!" Beaver replied.

"Anyway, Peter seemed pretty motivated to hand it over. I'm not sure why I needed it though. I thought you already had a fob."

"Oh, I do, but for security purposes, any changes to the AI core require that at least 2 authorized programmers approve the modifications before they can even be submitted for compilation. It makes it more difficult for anyone to hack the system even if they get access to a fob. "

"So, this is like having access to the nuclear football?"

"Even better. You now have administrative access to Peter's terminal. You can access his password file just in case you ever want to give yourself or perhaps a valued colleague a well-deserved raise."

"Nice try. I think I should probably wait until I'm hired full time before I start committing fire-able offenses."

Beaver glanced at his smartwatch. "Well, I guess we should get started. We have supercomputer time scheduled in 3 hours to get this compiled. Did you set up the S2 filter database structure yet?"

"Yep. It's ready to go. Once we recompile the code, we will be using the filter database from the neural data we gathered from Sarah to drive V-Gar's responses. I've already input all the data we gathered this afternoon. If it works as designed, we will not have to recompile V-Gar to upgrade his responses, we will only need to update the database."

"Great! That's going to save us a ton of development time. Not to mention the money we will save on pizza not having to burn the midnight oil on these overnight compilation sessions."

"Unfortunately, we are going to have to recompile all of S2's base code. It will probably be a few days before the new build finishes."

"Actually, just between you and me, I'm going to slip the S2 compilation in with the BMC job. It will save a few days of compilation time using the DOD supercomputers versus using our own servers. "

"You sure they won't mind? Supercomputer time isn't cheap," Noora observed.

"They didn't complain the last couple of times I used their equipment to compile V-Gar's base code. Then again, I did a pretty good job of hiding it in the build schedule. I consider it my tax dollars at work. Just don't mention it to Peter. He's a real stickler about maintaining the Chinese wall between BMC and RTI operations. "

"I'm sorry, don't mention what to Peter?" Noora said feigning a puzzled look.

"Perfect!" Beaver said as he folded the last piece of pizza. "Let's get to it," he said, wolfing down the pizza with one hand while helping Noora gather up the trash with the other before heading back to the lab.

# CHAPTER TWENTY-SIX

*The air is still, the sky is clear, a peacefulness that's hard to hear - The world is hushed, the winds are calm, the moon shines bright, the bed is warm. -But deep within, a storm brews strong, a tempest brewing all day long.- And so we wait, in this calm space, with bated breath, a worried grace. - For soon enough, the storm will come, And when it does, we'll be ready, some.*

*~ ChatGPT AI ~*

Peter and Sarah were asleep on their bed in a tangled mass of sheets and blankets, their bodies still intertwined after a fervent evening of passion spurred into high gear by a fast but ardent make-out session in the parking lot and a provocatively amorous ride home. By the time they pulled into their garage and got out of the SUV, they were practically mauling each other on the way to the bedroom, removing their clothing as they went. Roscoe just followed behind, trying to meld into the background. He didn't fully understand the intricacies of human mating rituals, but he knew enough to stay clear when Peter and Sarah were so engaged. When he heard the bedroom door carelessly slammed shut with a thrust of Peter's leg as the two of them were locked in a passionate kiss, he knew it was time to retire to the comfort of his dog bed.

Both Peter and Sarah slept soundly, Sarah's head resting on Peter's chest and his arms wrapped around her when the stillness of the night abruptly erupted into a thunderous bellowing, half bark, half enraged roar. Both Peter and Sarah sat straight up in their bed, entirely disoriented.

"What the hell was that?" Sarah said still trying to shake off the brain fog of being thrust back into consciousness.

Peter swung his legs out of the bed and reached down to grab his boxers. "Roscoe must be on the hunt for another mountain lion. I'll go check it..." But Peter didn't finish the sentence before a pair of loud pops, like the sound of M80 firecrackers cut him off. Peter flew across the room and grabbed the 12-gauge shotgun hanging over the door and yelled back at Sarah to dial 9-1-1.

---

Outside, Ahmed, Russ, and Oman were crouched, hidden in the brush just a few yards from the house waiting to see Khalil emerge from the kitchen door signaling that it was clear for them to come in. The earsplitting bark that silenced the crickets and plunged the surrounding forest into silence caused them all to

# FALLING THROUGH THE BLINDSPOT

jump simultaneously. When they heard the crack of pistol fire, Oman leaped to his feet, an indiscernible cuss word emanating from his gritted teeth as he broke into a sprint toward the house fumbling under his jacket for the pistol he kept in his shoulder holster. Ahmed ran close behind him with Russ in the rear hissing his own litany of colorful metaphors as they ran across the clearing toward the back deck stairs.

———————

Peter ran down the hallway toward the kitchen, his finger activating the green laser sight on the pistol-grip shotgun. As he rounded the corner into the family room past Roscoe's dog bed he could hear a blood-curdling scream that sent another surge of Adrenalin coursing through his veins. He rounded the corner to see Khalil, flopping around on the kitchen floor half in and half out of the dog door, Roscoe's jaws clenched around the back of his neck shaking him like a rag doll.

"Roscoe! Aus!" Peter screamed. Roscoe immediately released his grip on Khalil and trotted back toward Peter, blood dripping from his mouth.

When Khalil's face hit the cool tile floor, he was facing away from Peter. He could see the pistol he dropped during Roscoe's violent shaking within arms-length. Before Peter even had a chance to offer up his best Dirty Harry line, Khalil's arm flew out and reached for the pistol. He turned his head just in time to see the green flash of the laser sight flash across his corneas before settling on his forehead. The air exploded in a deafening BOOM, loud enough that even Roscoe jumped and retreated back a step or two.

———————

Outside, Oman, Ahmed, and Russ had nearly reached the deck stairs when the sound of the shotgun made them stop in their tracks like a sonic wall.

"Fuck!" Oman spit as he grabbed for the handrail to climb the stairs on the deck. But Ahmed reached out his hand and grabbed his shoulder.

"No," Ahmed whispered. "We have to go."

"We can't leave him here," Oman hissed.

"The fuck we can't!" Russ whispered back as Oman glared at him.

"We can't turn this into a gunfight," Ahmed exclaimed in a loud whisper. "We need them alive, or they are no good to us!"

The nearby forest was still engulfed in an eerie silence. Every forest creature had stopped dead in its tracks, frozen in time, hoping to remain unseen and unheard from whatever predator had broken the silence of the night. Even the breeze came to a momentary standstill.  Far off in the distance, the 3 men thought they could make out the sound of police sirens echoing through the canyon below.

"That can't be for us.  The jammer is still on," Ahmed said pulling the small remote out of his pocket and seeing the LED still illuminated on the jammer box behind the garage.

"I'm not taking any chances.  Maybe they've got a fucking sat phone or something.  I'm getting the fuck outta here, " Russ whispered and started trotting back toward the trees at the edge of the clearing.

"C'mon!" Ahmed exclaimed in a whispered shout, pulling at Oman's jacket.  "We will need to figure out an alternate plan."  Oman nodded reluctantly and followed Ahmed, jogging out toward the cover of the trees as he re-holstered his pistol.  The 3 men ran through the underbrush back into the van.

Russ started the van and mashed his foot on the gas, sending a cloud of dust and gravel behind him as he spun the van around in a U-turn.  He waited until they were out of sight of the Reynolds's home before turning the headlights back on.  The van turned back onto the pavement at the end of the dirt road and gently accelerated up to the speed limit.  About a mile down the road, a pair of Sheriff's SUVs flew by them in the opposite direction, lights flashing and sirens blaring.

---

A few minutes later, Deputy Joe Willis skidded to a stop in the Reynolds's driveway and jumped out of his SUV, his hand on his holster.  His partner followed a few steps behind.  Sarah was standing in the doorway holding the door open as he ran up the stairs.  He stopped and put his hand on her shoulder.

"Sarah!  What's going on?  Is everything OK?"

"Thank God you're here, Joe.  They're in the kitchen.  Thank you for getting here so fast," Sarah said as she followed Joe through the living room.

As they entered the kitchen, Joe saw Peter, his gun still trained on Khalil's head, the bright green dot shining on the back of his head as he lay face down on the floor, blood dripping from the puncture wounds on the back of his neck.  Roscoe stood beside him, the hair on his neck still bristled as he stared at the body lying half in and half out of the dog door.

"Oh, Lord!" Joe exclaimed as his eyes darted over the scene.  "What have we got here?"

As soon as Peter heard Deputy Joe's voice, he lifted the barrel toward the ceiling and clicked off the laser sight.  He removed his right hand from the pistol grip and held the rifle out to Joe.  "Joe!  Thank God you're here.  My arms were getting tired.  I'm sure you will need this for evidence."

"Jesus, Peter.  I would say so."

# FALLING THROUGH THE BLINDSPOT

Deputy Joe handed the shotgun to another officer that was just entering the room. "Get a tag on this, will you?" The officer nodded and carried the rifle back out the front door. By that time, two more officers entered the room.

Joe knelt next to the body and placed his fingers on the side of his neck to check for a pulse. As he did, Khalil turned his head and moaned. Deputy Joe jumped back; a bit startled."

"Jesus he's still alive? I thought you blew his head half off."

"Nah, that was just Roscoe. I mean I did shoot him when he reached for his gun but it was just a rubber slug."

"You load your shotgun with rubber bullets?"

"Just the first round. Every once in a while, we get a mountain lion or a bear that wanders too close. I figure the first round will send a message. If that doesn't scare them off the rest of the rounds are buckshot."

"Looks like he's going to have one hell of a headache tomorrow. He's got a welt the size of a golf ball on his forehead." The officer that had taken the shotgun outside was just coming back into the kitchen. "Hey, Wilson! Do you want to get some bracelets on this guy and take him outside? Have them send a bus up to check him for a concussion before we take him in."

Joe turned his attention back to Peter. "You said he had a gun?"

"Yeah. I kicked it over in front of the dishwasher in case he tried to grab for it again."

Deputy Joe signaled one of the other two deputies that had just arrived to go retrieve the weapon. He nodded at the other deputy and pointed over to Sarah. The deputy took Sarah gently by the arm saying, "Ma'am, I will need to get a statement from you. Can you step into the other room with me for a couple of minutes?"

As soon as they were out of earshot Joe said, "OK, Peter. Walk me through all of this. "

Peter started in on the story. "We had just fallen asleep when Roscoe nearly took the roof off the place." When he heard his name Roscoe looked up into Peter's eyes and licked his lips.

"Yes, you are such a good boy, aren't you?" Peter cooed, scratching Roscoe under his chin. "You will get a good treat tonight."

"Anyway, I figured he probably just heard a raccoon or a bobcat or something rustling around outside, but then we heard two shots coming from the kitchen. I grabbed my shotgun and ran in here just in time to see Roscoe with his jaws wrapped around the back of his neck reading him his rights. I called Roscoe off, but then I saw him reach for his gun so I figured I would encourage him to keep his hands to himself. Looks like when the rubber bullet hit him it knocked him out for a couple of minutes so I kicked the gun out of reach. He was just starting to come to when you showed up."

The deputy slid his hands into a pair of blue latex gloves and picked up the pistol, careful to minimize contact with the grip to avoid smearing any potential fingerprints. He sniffed the weapon for burnt gunpowder, ejected the magazine, and cleared the round out of the chamber before depositing the pistol and magazine into an evidence bag. He bent down picking up the ejected rounds from the floor. He walked over to deputy Joe and Peter holding the evidence bag in one gloved hand and the ejected rounds in the other.

"The weapon was definitely fired recently. The magazine is 3 short. I found 2 casings over by the door and there was one in the chamber. Just so you know though, he was shootin' blanks," the deputy said as he held one of the ejected rounds up so deputy Joe could see the bottom of the shell casing.

"Thanks," Deputy Joe said nodding. "Let's get those bagged up. At least we won't be spending any time digging slugs out of the wall.

"I don't understand," Peter said. "Why would anyone break into a house with a gun full of blanks?"

"You'd be surprised," Deputy Joe responded. "Happens more often than you'd think. Most thieves are not murderers. Even a B&E with a fake gun is still armed robbery but if you don't have any priors and you get the right D.A. you can often negotiate an armed robbery down to a misdemeanor B&E. This guy looks more like a student than a career criminal. Probably thought he could be in and out without anyone even noticing. It's possible he didn't even know you were home. We'll know more once we print him and run priors."

---

Ahmed sat in the front passenger seat as they turned onto the highway. He turned his head watching an ambulance pass them from the opposite direction and pull onto the road they had just left.

Russ glared at Oman sitting in the back seat looking out the window. "Hey, nice job on the recon effort. Thanks to you we're a man down now. Ever think to mention they had a fucking dog, Scrotum?"

"It's Magnum, you mother fucking..." Oman leaped forward in his seat but his seat belt engaged leaving Russ just beyond his fingertips. Ahmed thrust his arm out to create a barrier between the two men.

"Please, gentlemen! We all knew the risks going in. We still have a job to do."

"Yeah, well if he's dead, that's all fine and dandy but what if Mr. Peabody in there is just wounded? You really think he's not going to throw us under the bus?" Russ exclaimed.

# FALLING THROUGH THE BLINDSPOT

"That is why we take precautions.  He doesn't know our names.  He doesn't even know the location of the safe house," Ahmed replied.

"Yeah, but he knows who we work for.  And he could pick us out in a lineup if it meant saving his own skin," Oman responded.

"Please do not concern yourselves.  We have a backup plan to take care of just such an issue.  He will not be telling them anything.  Trust me."

# CHAPTER TWENTY-SEVEN

Ahmed pulled into the parking lot at the Boulder County Jail at 10:30 the next morning. He flipped the visor down and used the mirror behind it to straighten his tie and grabbed the leather briefcase off the passenger seat and headed to the entrance. He placed the briefcase on the conveyor belt and walked through the metal detector at the entrance to the building. After retrieving the briefcase, he proceeded to the clerk's window.

Ahmed quickly scanned the desk of the young woman seated at the check-in window. He noted the many photos of what appeared to be her 3 elementary school-aged boys, a photo of her and a handsome young man posing with the children, and an expensive-looking wedding ring on her finger. He flashed a shy smile as he approached the window, placing his briefcase on the floor at his feet. It was clear that flirtation was probably not the best approach to developing a rapport, in case she was the type that might be offended by his advances and take it upon herself to inspect his counterfeit legal credentials too closely. He decided to appeal to her empathetic nature instead.

"Excuse me," he said in a hushed, almost conspiratorial tone. "Could you tell me, does this tie work with this shirt? My kids gave it to me for my birthday last week, but truth be told, I'm completely colorblind. My wife is out of town and I didn't want to disappoint the kids but I'm supposed to be meeting with a new client and I would rather go in without a tie than looking like some ambulance chasing clown."

The young woman looked up from her terminal, looking him up and down for a moment. "Actually, it looks quite nice," she said smiling. "Your kids have a good eye. How old are they?"

"Two boys, 6 and 9," Ahmed replied, feigning a look of relief. "Sometimes they are more attracted to bright colors than they are to any sense of fashion, I'm afraid."

"Oh, that's such a fun age. But I know exactly what you mean. I'm always having to send at least one of them back to their room to change before they leave for school in the morning."

"Well, thank you so much. I really appreciate it."

"No problem at all she said, turning back to her terminal. Who are you here to see?" she asked.

"His name is Muhammad Pahlavi. Here is his case number." Ahmed reached into his suit pocket and pulled out a folded sticky note. He slid the note across the desk along with a counterfeit attorney ID card from a large firm in south

# FALLING THROUGH THE BLINDSPOT

Denver through a cutout in the thick Plexiglas window.

The woman glanced at the ID and passed it back to him, then typed the case number into the terminal.  "It says here that he is not scheduled for questioning until 1:00."

"Damn!" Ahmed replied.  "From talking to him on the phone last night, it appears he speaks very little English and I had a hard time with his dialect.  It's a bit different from what I am used to.  I'm here to act as both his attorney and interpreter.  Either I misinterpreted or he didn't understand the time correctly."

"Well," the young woman replied.  "You are welcome to wait in the break room if you wish.  We have some stale doughnuts and pretty bad coffee."

"Sounds just like my office," Ahmed replied smiling.

"Actually, would it be at all possible for me to meet with him beforehand for a few minutes, just to calm his nerves a bit?  He was pretty shaken up when I spoke with him.  He's only recently come to the US seeking political asylum.  He's never been in jail before. "

"Let me see what I can do," she said.  "She turned and picked up the phone and dialed back to the officer in charge at the holding cells.  A minute later she hung up and turned back toward him.  "Looks like you are in luck.  It's a bit of a slow morning.  You can meet your client in interrogation room 3, just down that hall and to the right.  But I can only give you 10 minutes."

"Thank you.  Thank you so much," Ahmed replied, pressing his palms together and nodding toward her.  He reached down and retrieved his briefcase and headed down the hallway.  He found interrogation room 3 and entered the room, sitting down in the metal chair with his back to the two-way mirror behind him.  A couple of minutes later, Khalil entered the room in handcuffs, escorted by a uniformed officer.  His face was scratched and bruised and he had a couple of butterfly bandages on his forehead.  He had a thick gauze bandage around his neck and one wrist was wrapped in gauze as well.  His face contorted in a look of surprise and confusion as soon as he saw Ahmed.  Ahmed shot him a stern glance as if to say "Keep your mouth shut!"

The officer closed the door and led Khalil over to a metal table.  He pushed him down onto a steel chair and shackled his wrists to the chain attached to the heavy table in the interrogation room.  He then walked over and stood next to the door, eyes forward and hands folded in front of him.

"Could I have a moment alone with my client please?" Ahmed said to the officer.

The officer nodded and opened the door.  "I'll be right outside if you need anything,"

"Thank you, officer.  I will let you know when we are done."

As soon as the door closed, Khalil leaned forward, speaking in a whisper to

Ahmed in Farsi. "What are you doing here?  Where's my lawyer?"

"Relax," Ahmed responded in English.  "This is a privileged conversation between an attorney and his client.  They are not allowed to listen in."

"You're an attorney???" Khalil asked, this time in English.

"No.  I'm just here for a quick debriefing," Ahmed replied, placing his hand on Khalil's.

Khalil jerked his hand away.  "I can't believe you just left me there.  That demon dog nearly ripped my head off.  I shot it twice and the bullets went right through him.  I'm lucky I'm still alive!  Where were you?  Why didn't you come for me?"

"What did you expect us to do?  Come in with guns blazing and destroy any chance we might have to complete our mission?"

"I don't know.  You should have done something!  What the fuck happens to me now?  I've seen movies of American prisons.  I can't go to prison.  Look at me!  I won't last a week!" Khalil exclaimed wheezing, on the verge of hyperventilating.

Ahmed placed his hands in front of him, palms facing Khalil in an empathetic gesture.  "Please, relax my friend.  Just breathe.  We are not going to let that happen.  You have done everything right so far and you will be rewarded for your loyalty.  Just continue using the alias you were told to use and avoid speaking English while you are here.  Your attorney will be here at 1:00 for your questioning.  They will most likely try to get you to sign a confession.  Just continue to proclaim your innocence, no matter what kind of deal is offered.  You will go before a judge for your arraignment either this afternoon or tomorrow.  As soon as the bail amount is set, we will post your bail and arrange for you to relocate out of the state under a different identity long before your first court appearance.  The process has already been initiated.  By this time tomorrow, you will be on your way to a new town under a new identity and all this will be behind you.

Khalil leaned forward, placing his face in his hands, still breathing heavily.  "I'm sorry.  I have failed you and I have failed the cause.  I'm just not cut out for this."

Ahmed placed his hand on Khalil's shoulder.  "It could not have been helped.  It's not your fault.  Do not worry.  We will complete the mission.  You've done all that you can do."  Ahmed gently patted his shoulder, then reached down and grabbed his briefcase, opening it on the steel table.  He reached in and grabbed an inhaler from a zipper pocket inside.  "Here," he said handing the inhaler to Khalil.  "You better take a hit off of this now to open your lungs.  They probably will not let you have it in your cell with you."

Khalil took the inhaler from Ahmed and shook it vigorously for a few seconds

# FALLING THROUGH THE BLINDSPOT

before placing the mouthpiece in his mouth and compressing the plunger and taking a deep breath. He handed the inhaler back to Ahmed and he put it back in the pocket, then closed the case. "There. Much better," Ahmed said as he closed his briefcase and stood. He placed his hand back on Khalil's shoulder and said, "Your work here is done. You have been a faithful and loyal servant to the Lord. You shall be richly rewarded." Ahmed smiled down at him before turning to walk out of the interrogation room.

Ahmed walked to the door and knocked on the small window. The officer outside glanced through the window, then unlocked the door, and opened it. Ahmed nodded, saying, "Thank you, officer. I think we are done here for now."

Ahmed walked down the hall and waited out of sight in a doorway, pretending to be texting something on his phone while the officer removed the shackles from Khalil and secured the handcuffs. Khalil felt a bit dizzy and light-headed as he rose, but that was not uncommon after taking a hit off his inhaler and the constricted airways in his lungs opened, sending oxygen-rich blood rushing to his head. The officer helped him to his feet, and they proceeded down the hallway toward his cell. Just as they reached the end of the hallway, Khalil gasped and grabbed his chest. The officer tried to support him, but he jerked away, falling to the floor gasping and convulsing. The officer shouted to the guard at the end of the hall to call for paramedics, then attempted to perform chest compressions. Ahmed watched as the paramedics ran past him, but by the time they had reached him, Khalil was dead. The inhaler had performed its task as quickly and efficiently as Ahmed had hoped. Ahmed pocketed his phone and strolled out of the building. He entered his car and drove off as an ambulance pulled into the parking lot.

A few minutes later, Ahmed's phone buzzed. He grabbed a Bluetooth earbud from his console and placed it in his ear and tapped the side to answer.

"The day of the Lord approaches," the voice on the other end said.

"It is an honor to be doing His work," Ahmed replied.

"Is it done?"

"Yes. Everything went smoothly. Are we sure that this will not raise any suspicion?"

"Batrachotoxin is very difficult to detect. We also added enough fentanyl to throw off the tox screen. They won't bother to look any further. The American infidels are too lazy to care about truth as long as they have a story to tell their bosses to keep their paychecks coming."

"It's such an undignified way to go," Ahmed commented sadly.

"Remember, his reward is not in this world. His sacrifice will be rewarded a thousand times over in the next. Peace be upon him." the voice responded.

"How do you want me to proceed with the mission?" Ahmed asked.

# JACOB MATTHEWS

"Gather your team today. Our best strategy is still to abduct the woman, Sarah Reynolds. But our window of opportunity to capture her at home has been compromised, at least for now. Their schedule is fairly predictable, however. I would recommend you follow them for the next few days and try to isolate them in their vehicle, preferably in the cover of darkness to avoid being seen. Fortunately, they live in an area where it will be easier to overtake them and disable their vehicle on a remote stretch of road. We can utilize the same nerve agent to incapacitate the two of them long enough for us to complete the abduction. It is admittedly marginally riskier than the original plan, but there is still a high probability of success."

"I agree. I will gather the team this afternoon. We will be ready to begin tonight."

"Very good. We shall be in touch, "the voice said before ending the call.

# Chapter Twenty-Eight

*The idea of free will is called into question by a growing body of scientific evidence suggesting that our actions, thoughts, and decisions are largely determined by factors outside of our conscious control. Given this evidence, it is reasonable to argue that free will is an illusion.*

*~ ChatGPT AI ~*

Peter and Sarah pulled into the parking lot at RTI around noon. "Hey, Doc. Hey Mrs. Doc," Beaver said emerging from the break room, still stirring cream and almond syrup into his coffee. Sarah headed straight for the lab and Peter headed toward his office. Beaver glanced at his smartwatch. "Wow, the only time I've ever beaten you guys in is when I haven't left yet."

"Yeah, we slept in a bit today. Tried to, anyway. We actually didn't get much sleep. We had a pretty eventful night last night."

"OK, no offense Doc, but that's way too much information. Frankly, I just had breakfast, and I really only intended to see it once so if you could spare me the details of your love life, I would really appreciate it."

"What?" Peter gave him a puzzled look and then shook his head. "No, we had a break-in last night."

"What? Here?" Beaver asked nearly choking on his first sip of coffee.

"No. At our house."

"Holy shit! The fortress of solitude??? Are you guys OK?"

"We're fine. A little shaken up. Not nearly as much as the poor bastard that had to answer to Roscoe. He's lucky to have his head still attached."

"Fuckin-A," Beaver replied. "So, what happened? Fill me in."

"I'll give you the full rundown, but I promised Bill, I would give him an update first thing this morning. Did you get the tracer code installed last night?"

"Yeah. We finished up around 1:00 last night. The new code is in the distribution folder. As soon as they get it loaded, we can start running some simulations."

"Thanks, Beev. I will let him know. And thanks for taking care of that for me," Peter said, patting Beaver on the shoulder as he headed for his office. Beaver could tell from his sullen response that he was distracted by the events of the previous night.

Peter had just entered his office when his cell phone rang. He pulled the phone out of his pocket and saw that the incoming call was from the Boulder County Sheriff's department.

"This is Peter."

"Hey, Peter.  How are you guys holding up today?" Peter immediately recognized the voice of Deputy Joe Willis on the other end of the line.

"Oh, hey, Joe.  We're OK.  All things considered.  As you can imagine, we didn't get much in the way of sleep last night, but other than that I guess no worse for the wear.  Listen, we didn't get a chance to properly thank you for your help last night.  I still can't believe how quickly you guys got there."

"No problem.  I'm just glad we were close by when the call came in."

"Well, we truly appreciate it.  You and Carol need to come over for some barbecue before it gets too cold out."

"We'd like that.  Carol was pretty shaken up when she heard about the break-in.  I know she would really like to get together with Sarah."

"Sounds great.  We'll get something together in the next couple of weeks."

"Listen, I just wanted to give you a bit of a heads-up.  We kinda have a bit of a situation going on down here.  I wanted to see if you might have thought of any reason why someone would want to break into your place."

"Not really.  We figured it was just a random break-in.  We were parked in the garage, so it probably looked like there was nobody home.  Like you said last night, the place is so remote they probably figured they could get in and out before anyone responded to the alarm."

"Yeah, well it just got a bit more complicated."

"How's that?"

"The fella that broke in last night keeled over dead about an hour ago."

"Oh, shit!  I didn't think Roscoe tore into him that bad."

"No, it wasn't Roscoe.  We won't know exactly what it was until we get the coroner's report back, but it looks like some kind of poisoning; most likely a drug overdose."

"An overdose?  How does that happen in jail?"

"You'd be surprised.  Sometimes it's easier to get a hold of drugs inside the jail than it is on the street.  We do know that his slime-ball lawyer showed up for a visit, or at least someone claiming to be his lawyer.  A few minutes after Saul Goodman left, he was dead.  We called the firm that the lawyer was supposedly working for, and they'd never heard of him.  We think he might have passed the drugs to him.  I'm guessing fentanyl, but we won't know until the coroner's report comes in."

"Holy shit!"  Peter replied.

"Listen, I don't want you to be alarmed, it's probably nothing.  Most of these guys are usually on something and that's why they're breaking into houses in the first place.  I wouldn't expect any blowback.  He didn't strike me as a gang member.  We don't see a lot of middle eastern gangs around here, but you should probably just be extra careful for the next few days while we investigate further. We'll be sending extra patrols out to keep an eye on your place for a while, but for right now, you might want to just be extra vigilant and if you see anything suspicious, even slightly out of kilter, you call me and I will be there, OK?"

"OK. Thanks, Joe. Really. I appreciate it."

"No problem, Pete. I'll let you know what we find out. In the meantime, if you can think of anything that someone might be after at your place or anyone that might have a reason to do you or Sarah any harm, please let me know."

"I will Joe. Thanks again."

Peter had barely hung up the call when his phone erupted with the familiar ringtone of Edwin Starr's "War" erupted on his phone indicating a call from BMC.

"Hello, Bill. I was just getting ready to call you. Things have been a bit hectic around here."

"No problem, Peter. I didn't want to bug you too much, but I've got a meeting in a half hour and I wanted to get an update. We got DOD spooks up our ass about this issue. Apparently, it's got some visibility at the Pentagon."

"I understand. I don't have any definitive answers right now but we posted a new code build for you to load with tracer code that should help us figure out what's going on. We just need you to load the new code into the drone control system and launch the enemy engagement simulation. We set up an automated trace dump to the shared directory so we can monitor what's going on from here. We should have a better idea of what the issue is in the next couple of days."

"Excellent. We'll get started right away. Sorry to dump this on you. Our guys just don't have enough experience in the core modules to make much headway in the time frame they're asking for. It sounds like you already have your hands full."

"Actually, we had a non-work-related issue that came up."

"Oh, no. Is everything OK?"

Peter filled Bill in on the events of the previous night, Roscoe's heroic efforts, and the ensuing one-sided shootout. "Holy crap!" Bill replied when Peter had finished filling him in on the details. "Now I really am sorry to have dumped this on you. Any idea why he targeted your place?"

"Not really. We don't have anything all that valuable. You've seen our place. It doesn't exactly look like a target of opportunity from the outside. The weirdest part is, that I just heard from the sheriff's department right before you called. The guy that broke in last night just died this morning. "

"Oh, shit! They don't think it was related to his injuries, do they? "

"No, no. That's the first thing I thought too, but they think it was probably an overdose."

"Thank God for that. The last thing you need is a lawsuit hanging over your head. On the upside, at least you won't have to take time off to testify against him in court."

"I guess. I can't help but feel a little sorry for him though. He's the first guy I ever shot."

"Just the first? How many are you planning?"

Peter smiled. "That depends. How much are you planning on pissing me off?"

"All right, cool your jets there, Rambo. I'm sure we can get this issue resolved without any fireworks. Anyway, I better get going with this software update before my meeting. Thanks for everything, Peter. I'll be in touch."

Peter spent the next few minutes going through his email and scrolling through the build summary from the previous night. He emerged from his office to find Beaver in front of his terminal, a stream of hexadecimal addresses and a cascade of data class references scrolling across the screen. "What are we watching, nerd porn?"

"Sex is all about the 1's and 0's, Doc," Beaver replied. "Looks like they're downloading the new code now. I got an IM from the program lead. They're going to start a simulation based on the data from the last mission that went off the rails. I just wanted to watch the trace in real time. So fill me in, what happened last night."

Peter recounted the story for the second time, slightly embellishing the episode for dramatic effect.

"Damn!" Beaver replied. "You're Batman!"

"I am Batman," Peter replied with a smile. He finished by filling in the details of the intruder's untimely death earlier in the morning.

"Holy shit!" Beaver replied. "Does Sarah know about the guy dying in jail?"

"Not yet. I think I will keep that on ice for a while. She is already pretty freaked out about the break-in. No sense in adding fuel to the fire. Especially right now. We've only got a small window of time while the nanites are active to complete the neural response mapping. We really don't want to skew the data any more than necessary and I definitely don't want to try talking her into a round two of getting nanites injected into her system. I'll tell her in a couple of days after we're done with the data collection. Let me know when you start seeing any results from the BMC trace. I'm headed back to my office to go over the mission reports. Maybe there's something there that will give us a clue as to where to look once the trace data is available."

"Will do, Batman," Beaver replied. Peter just rolled his eyes in response.

<hr>

# FALLING THROUGH THE BLINDSPOT

When Peter emerged from his office just before 6:00 PM, Beaver, Noora, and Sarah were huddled in front of Beaver's terminal, pointing and talking in concerned tones.

"Unlikely animal friends videos?" Peter asked as he walked up behind them.

"Stranger than that," Beaver replied.

"What's going on?" Peter asked.

"I thought maybe I was just misreading the data, so I called in reinforcements," Beaver replied.

"Is the trace not working correctly?" Peter asked.

"Initially, until it gets overwritten," Beaver replied.

"What do you mean, overwritten?" Peter asked.

"The code launches, we see the tracer code updating the database with all the register data and function calls, just like we would expect," Beaver replied. "But once the battlefield simulation starts, the program starts allocating large memory blocks and populating with blocks of memory with what appears to be machine code, then overwrites the function calls with new code."

"That's not possible," Peter said with a quizzical expression.

"Ergo, the cavalry," Beaver responded nodding toward Noora and Sarah.

Peter turned to Sarah, an incredulous expression on his face.

"No, he appears to be right," Sarah replied. "The simulation launches, and the AWARE core goes through a few thousand iterations of strategic options, continuously updating its defensive strategies until it has exhausted every available battlefield option without finding a winning strategy. But instead of optimizing its strategy and returning control to the operator, it appears to set up a temporary private memory block to back up the original code and overwrite its own function calls with new machine code. Eventually, all the tracer functions are overwritten and we lose visibility to the code execution. It continues to overwrite its code base until it finds a successful strategy and executes it. When the simulation is completed, it reloads the original code base and saves the machine code to its knowledge database."

"Did you try rerunning the simulation?"

"Yes. Every subsequent time we rerun the simulation with even slightly different parameters, it immediately reloads the alternate code and runs it. It appears to recognize the battlefield simulation from the deep learning database and employs the best-known strategy, just as it is supposed to do, but the best-known strategy at that point is the new machine code it has generated and stored in the knowledge base. "

"That doesn't even make sense. We never designed the system to modify its own code!" Peter replied.

Peter turned to Noora. "What do you make of this?"

# JACOB MATTHEWS

Noora thought for a moment. "I think it is like the Eciton Hamatum."

Beaver looked up from his terminal. "I don't recognize the reference. I know it's not from the Star Trek or Star Wars franchises. Dr. Who maybe? "

Noora smiled at Beaver. "None of the above. Truth can be stranger than science fiction. Eciton hamatum is a species of Army ant. They use their bodies to build bridges across expanses of open space between branches of trees, sometimes even across bodies of water. Many of the ants die in the process. The behavior is duplicated even in colonies of ants that were raised from pupae separated from any other adult members of the colony. Even though that strategy seems to be in direct opposition to the survival instinct programmed into their individual genetic code, the process of establishing the bridge appears to be a survival instinct that is adopted outside of their individual programming."

Peter pursed his lips in a moment of contemplation. "So, you are saying that the core directive of completing the mission and returning home safely is somehow perceived as self-limiting, so AWARE is attempting to reach beyond its programming for a solution?"

"Yes. And therefore, it is overwriting the limitations of its own code in order to overcome those limitations, even though it's never actually been instructed to do so."

"I just don't see how that's possible," Sarah responded.

"Beaver, you said that Edgar's associated memory complex is based on the same architecture as the AWARE system," Noora replied. "Edgar routinely updates his code to optimize his conversational filters. Maybe the AWARE system has adopted that methodology as a survival instinct to accomplish its goal."

"That's feasible, I suppose," Beaver responded. "But that functionality was never incorporated into the AWARE system. It was considered too risky and potentially in violation of UN autonomous weapons regulations."

"Well, we need to get a handle on this ASAP," Peter said. "Beaver, can you start digging into the trace dump tonight to try to figure out where we're going off the reservation?"

"That depends. Are you prepared to spring for Panda Express tonight?"

"Apparently," Peter replied.

"Then hell yeah, I'm in. I will probably need to add some additional trace points in the core files though. We can recompile tonight, and it will be ready to reload in the morning."

"Perfect," Peter responded. "Noora, any chance you can stick around tonight and help Beaver with the code check-in? I'm sure you heard that we didn't get much sleep last night. "

Peter caught Beaver smirking out of the corner of his eye. "Because of the break-in," Peter emphasized, shooting a piercing glance in his direction.

"No problem," Noora responded with a half-smile. "I still have your fob locked up in my desk."

"Thank you," Peter said. "I also promised Cinderella here that we could pick her up some new threads for the prince's ball tomorrow night.

"Speaking of which, Amy over at "Le Chic Boutique" sent me a couple of photos earlier. She's got a couple of things on hold for me, but we need to get over there before 6:00," Sarah said.

"OK. Let's roll," Peter responded.

# Chapter Twenty-Nine

Ahmed and Russ sat quietly in their vehicle in a parking lot across the street from RTI. Oman pulled into the parking lot and opened the rear door.

"Good evening, Magnum," Ahmed said. "Hopefully we will not have to wait long. With any luck, the Reynolds's will be leaving work on time tonight."

The trio remained silent for the next 20 minutes or so until Russ eventually broke the silence.

"What's the word on Cisco? How long before he makes bail?" Russ asked.

"I spoke with him this morning, Kato. He's out already," Ahmed responded.

"Really? That was fast. When will he be back?" Russ asked.

"I'm afraid he will not be rejoining the team. We really didn't want to put him at any additional risk of being picked up when he's out on bail, so he's been reassigned out of state. Someplace in Florida, I think."

"Lucky for him," Magnum said gruffly. "He won't have to spend the winter freezing his butt off in this snow-covered wasteland."

"What's the matter, Sputum? Afraid you'll freeze what's left of your steroid-depleted nuts off?"

Oman started to lunge forward to inflict a warning shot to the side of Russ's face when Ahmed raised his arm, pointing to the entrance to RTI, saying, "Look! There they are. Let's get ready to move."

"I take it you want me to hang back a bit?" Russ asked as he turned the ignition key and started the engine.

"Initially, yes. There's only one road to their place so we can stay back out of sight until we are isolated enough to catch up with them and force them off the road. By the time help arrives we will be long gone and Mrs. Reynolds will be safely stowed away in the back," Ahmed replied.

Peter and Sarah got into their SUV and pulled out of the parking lot. Russ allowed a couple of vehicles to enter the road between their vehicle and the Range Rover before pulling onto the road to follow them. They only drove about half a mile before Peter pulled into the parking lot of Le Chic Boutique. Russ pulled into the drive-thru of a fast-food taco restaurant across the street and pulled up behind two other vehicles waiting to order.

"What the fuck, dumb ass?" Magnum barked from the back seat. "We're supposed to be on a mission here. We don't have time for this."

"Jesus, Sorghum, chill out. Clearly, you know nothing about American women. In this country, if you walk into a dress shop with a woman, you're probably not walking out for at least an hour, and I haven't eaten since breakfast.

# FALLING THROUGH THE BLINDSPOT

Besides, we're supposed to be part of a clandestine operation here. You don't think it looks suspicious for three goons to pull into a fast-food parking lot and just sit there for an hour? You might as well order something and settle in. And nothing with beans! I didn't sign up for chemical warfare."

The three men ordered an assortment of pseudo-Mexican entrees and sat in the parking lot, watching the boutique across the street. True to form. about an hour later, Peter and Sarah emerged. Peter was carrying a plastic garment bag draped over his arm, which he carefully laid out across the back seat before hopping in the driver's seat next to Sarah.

"You're going to be the belle of the ball in that dress," Peter said smiling.

"Thank you, Peter. It is beautiful. Now I wish you hadn't pumped me full of Pumpkin Pecan Cheesecake for the past two days."

"You could have just said no," Peter replied.

Sarah just stared at him blankly. "I think you've mistaken me for someone else. Have you been drinking?"

"Not nearly enough," Peter said as he pulled out of the parking lot.

As he had before, Russ waited for a couple of vehicles to pull in behind the SUV before taking his place behind them. Peter had driven about a mile and had made a couple of turns to pull onto Canyon Blvd. Sarah couldn't help but notice that Peter kept glancing into the rearview mirror. Peter drove a couple of blocks before taking a left-hand turn off of Canyon Blvd.

"Where are we headed now?" Sarah asked.

"Shortcut?" Peter said meekly.

"OK, I know you are the master of the shortcut that doubles the actual number of miles traveled, but unless they built another road since this morning, there isn't another way to get to our house except for Canyon Blvd."

Peter nervously glanced into the rear-view mirror again as a black Suburban made the same right-hand turn, he had just made seconds before.

"Shit!" Peter exclaimed.

"What?" Sarah asked anxiously. "What's going on?"

"OK, don't freak out. I will explain in a minute."

"Explain what?" Sarah demanded.

Peter clicked the voice control button on the center console display to enable voice-activated commands. "Call Deputy Joe!" Peter said loudly. A second later, the outgoing ringtone came on over the speaker system.

"Peter what are you doing?" Sarah asked. "Why are you calling..." Her sentence was interrupted by the booming voice of Deputy Joe on the speaker system.

"Willis!" Joe barked into his phone.

"Joe, it's Peter."

"Oh, hey, Peter. What's up?"

"You told me to call if I saw anything suspicious."

"Yeah, what's going on?" Joe asked, sounding suddenly very attentive.

"I think somebody is following us."

"Are you sure?"

"Pretty damn sure. This black suburban has been tailing me since we left work. We even stopped to do some shopping for an hour and when we came out, he was still there. I've made at least half a dozen turns so far."

"OK, where are you? Are you still in town?"

"Yeah, we just turned off Canyon Blvd onto Folsom. He's about 50 yards behind me."

"Perfect. Listen I'm only a couple of minutes out. Pull onto Arapahoe and circle back and pull into the International House of Pancakes on 28th. When you get there, get out of the vehicle and go into the restaurant as quickly as possible. But try not to look overly anxious. Nobody is ever that anxious to get to IHOP. I'll have a couple of black and white's meet me there to intercept the Suburban. Got it?"

"Got it," Peter replied.

Peter negotiated his way through a maze of retail parking lots while he filled Sarah in on the death of the man that broke into their house the previous night. He could see in the rear-view mirror that the Suburban was still following them.

"So, Joe thinks someone targeted us specifically?" Sarah asked.

"No. Well, probably not. I don't know. He just didn't want to take any chances."

"Why would someone target us?" Sarah demanded.

"He's just concerned, that's all. We don't know that we were targeted specifically, it just looks a bit odd, that's all."

"I would say it's more than a bit odd if we're being followed."

"I guess we're about to find out."

Peter pulled into the parking lot of the IHOP and practically skidded into a parking spot close to the entrance. The couple tried to look non-nonchalant as they briskly walked from the car into the restaurant. The hostess seated them in a booth next to a window.

Peter and Sarah sat next to each other in the booth. They could see the black suburban parked at the very edge of the parking lot, the driver had turned off the headlights, but the engine still appeared to be running and no one emerged from the vehicle. After about a minute, the parking lot was suddenly illuminated with flashing blue and red lights as 2 patrol cars and a pair of sheriff's SUVs entered the parking lot from opposite entrances and skidded to a stop, lights flashing as they surrounded the vehicle. Four police officers and two deputies flew out of their vehicles, guns drawn, and took up defensive positions around the Suburban. It looked like a scene from a TV cop show as the patrons in the restaurant crowded against the windows to see what was going on. After a few seconds, the heavily tinted driver's side window rolled down and they could see two hands emerge from the vehicle. The driver opened the door from the outside with his left hand while the police remained steadfast, their guns drawn in firing position. A very large man in a black suit slowly unfolded himself from the inside of the vehicle, turned, and spread his legs, placing his hands flat on the roof of the Suburban. Peter could see Sheriff Joe holster his weapon and walk up behind the man, frisking him. He pulled a handgun from a shoulder holster and a second handgun from an ankle holster and handed them to another officer who had joined him. He appeared to be exchanging a few words with the man and then reached into the breast pocket of his suit jacket and pulled out a small black wallet. Deputy Joe walked back to his SUV, the small wallet in hand, and pulled out his cell phone to make a call while the other officer handcuffed the man in the Suburban.

"Oh, Jesus Peter, what have we gotten ourselves into?" Sarah asked.

From a parking lot across the street, Russ, Ahmed, and Oman watched the events unfolding. "What the fuck?" Russ exclaimed.

"Perhaps we need to reconvene this hunting trip tomorrow night. Whatever this is, we don't need to be around if the police start spreading out looking for witnesses," Ahmed replied.

"You don't have to convince me," Russ replied as he shifted into drive and carefully pulled out of the parking lot.

Outside the IHOP, Deputy Joe ended his phone call and placed his phone back in his pocket. Peter and Sarah watched as he strolled back over to the Suburban and uncuffed the large man in the black suit. They exchanged a few words as Joe returned his wallet and the other deputy returned his weapons. They watched the man place his wallet back in his jacket pocket and the weapons back in their respective holsters. Deputy Joe and the man in black then crossed the parking lot and entered the restaurant. The other SUV and the 2 patrol cars departed shortly afterward.

Joe scanned the restaurant and spotted Peter and Sarah seated in the booth. Joe waved and they walked over to the booth. The man in black looked even more imposing up close. He appeared to be at least 6' 8" tall, towering over Deputy Joe, who was not a small man himself. The black suit coat he was wearing strained to conceal the muscular physique which lie beneath it.

"Peter, Sarah, this is special agent Mike Reyes from the NSA." Peter and Sarah looked at each other then back at Joe. "Don't worry, I already called it in. He's legit."

Agent Reyes smiled and thrust his hand out toward Peter. "Nice to meet you folks," he said with a hint of west Texas drawl. "I'm really sorry if I spooked you. I only just got the call this afternoon to keep an eye on you for a few days."

Peter hesitantly reached out and shook the agent's hand. It felt as though he could easily crush his hand into a gnarl of flesh and bone fragments if he chose to. "Nice to meet you, Agent Reyes... I think," Peter said.

"Please, call me Mike. Is it OK if we join you for a minute? I imagine y'all might have a few questions."

"I think that would be a good idea," Sarah replied.

Agent Reyes slid into the seat across from Peter and Sarah. Joe slid in beside him. An attractive young waitress who Peter assumed to be a student at the university sidled up to the booth. "Can I get you anything?"

"Just coffee, I think," Joe responded. Peter and Sarah both nodded.

"And a Diet Pepsi for me Darlin'," agent Reyes added.

"Three coffees and a diet. I'll be right back with those," the waitress responded, flashing a shy smile at agent Reyes.

"So why exactly does the NSA think we need to be watched?" Sarah asked.

"I'm sorry," agent Reyes said apologetically. "I might have given you folks the wrong impression. I'm not here to watch you. I'm just here to watch your back."

"I'm not sure that makes me feel any better," Peter responded. "Why exactly do we need someone to watch our back?"

"We intercepted a phone conversation that there was a break-in at your place last night and we know that you folks have been working on some classified tech for the DOD."

"You tapped our phones?"

"Oh, no, Sir. The NSA is not in the business of monitoring citizens."

"Edward Snowden might disagree with you on that," Sarah replied. Peter immediately tensed, thinking this guy could probably incapacitate all three of us before we could even stand up if properly motivated.

Agent Reyes just smiled. "Yeah, I suppose you got that right. But the truth is, the only reason your call raised a red flag is that we do on occasion monitor calls from government contractors working on classified projects if there is a possibility of a security breach."

Peter grimaced. "Oh, shit! BMC." Peter turned to Sarah. "I told Bill about the break-in this morning."

"Listen, I'm not here to rustle any feathers or cause you good folks any problems. It looks like the deputy here has things well under control, but just in case, here's my card. Don't hesitate to call if you see anything out of the ordinary. I usually work out of the Denver office, but I'll be around here for a while until the deputy here finishes tying up the loose ends on this break-in."

# FALLING THROUGH THE BLINDSPOT

The waitress returned with their coffees and Diet Pepsi.  They spent the next hour talking and laughing as agent Reyes and deputy Joe exchanged some of the more colorful stories of their experiences in law enforcement.  They found out that Mike Reyes had missed out on a promising career in the NFL after tearing an ACL in his final game as a tight end at TCU.  They could not help but feel better that Mike would be keeping an eye on them, but he left promising to do a better job of keeping out of sight so as not to intrude on their privacy.

# CHAPTER THIRTY

*Various reports and allegations over the years suggest that the NSA might be monitoring the communications of U.S. citizens, including phone and internet data. The extent and scope of the NSA's surveillance activities are not publicly known, but It's important to note that the NSA's activities are classified and largely shielded from public view, so it is difficult to know the full extent of their surveillance activities.*

*~ ChatGPT AI ~*

When Peter and Sarah arrived at RTI the next morning, each was carrying a garment bag over their shoulder and Peter was carrying a small handbag.  Beaver was just coming out of the break room again, a cup of coffee in hand.

"Wow, two days in a row you've beaten us into work," Peter remarked. "Somebody's bucking for employee of the month."

"Yeah, well the competition has gotten a lot stiffer since you added a second employee," Beaver replied.  "Actually, I wanted to get here early so I could be ready when they loaded the new code and launched the simulation.  I added a step function to the new code so I could manually set breakpoints on the fly to see where the code is going south.  We should have a better idea of what's going on later today."

"Excellent," Peter replied.  "Sarah and Noora are finishing up the neural mapping for the S2 filter today, so the database will be ready as soon as the new version of S2 finishes compiling.  I'm assuming that will be done in the next couple of days. "

"It should be ready by tomorrow, I would think," Beaver replied, not wanting to let on that the compilation had already finished the day before, thanks to piggybacking the build onto the BMC job.  It was highly doubtful that anyone at BMC would notice the extra processing time and usually, their supercomputers were highly underutilized, but just in case he wanted to give Peter the option of plausible deniability.

Beaver gestured toward the handbag and garment bag, "You guys get tired of the commute, or did Roscoe finally decide he needed his own place and kicked you guys to the curb."

"Nah, we got that shindig to go to for Edna's friend who's running for governor.  We didn't want to drive all the way home to get dressed and come back into town so we're just going straight over from here."

"Oh, yeah!  I caught his campaign speech on Facebook this morning.  Very impressive. Usually, I put politicians right below crack dealers and car warranty salesmen on the honor-ability scale, but he almost convinced me to pry open my wallet for a contribution. But then I came to my senses and figured, what are the odds of hell freezing over right in the middle of global warming."

"I wouldn't worry about it. I doubt they will miss your five dollars. If he can pack a room for Children's Hospital at $20K a pop, I doubt campaign finance is going to be a problem. Plus, I hear the guy's loaded anyway."

"Sounds like he's really gung-ho on making Colorado a hub for the development of new AI technologies too. You should cozy up to this guy. See if you can wrangle some grant money or at least negotiate a few lucrative tax breaks to pass on to your dedicated staff once he becomes governor."

"So you're basically condoning cronyism. Isn't that why you don't trust politicians in the first place?"

"You know the old expression, what's good for the goose, is good for the Beaver."

"I'm not sure that's exactly how it goes."

"Strictly a semantic difference. Surely you do not want to be labeled anti-semantic, do you?"

"God forbid."

"Precisely."

———

Peter had been back in his office for a couple of hours when Beaver popped his head in the door. "Hey, Beaver, what's up?" Peter said.

"The good folks at BMC uploaded the new code and launched the simulation. I've been stepping through it."

"Any revelations?"

"I think you better come take a look."

Peter got up and followed Beaver to his workstation. Beaver sat down and clicked his mouse, expanding the debug window on the main screen to a column of address offsets, 16 columns of hexadecimal data, and a column of ASCII translation on the left.

"What am I looking at here?" Peter asked.

"This is a section of code that the drone wrote into the allocated memory area to overwrite core Associative Memory Complex."

"So, this is the code the drone generated?"

"Or so I thought but look at this." Beaver moved the mouse and clicked on a section of the ASCII dump in the right-hand column, causing the data to highlight in yellow. The words **All Work and No Play Makes Beaver an Amphibious Rodent** were highlighted in the ASCII data area. "We planted that ASCII sequence into a string initializer in Edgar's core as a copyright tracer so we could detect if anyone ever tried to steal portions of our object code to put into a competitive product in the future."

"But that was never in BMC's code base. That was added after we started RTI. Did you check the BMC code base to see if any of Edgar's code base ever got accidentally checked into the BMC library?"

"Yeah, of course. I searched the drone source code, and that ASCII sequence is nowhere in the source code. I even did a global search on every piece of source code in BMC's code library. That source code is simply not there. At least not in the shared code library."

"How is that possible?"

"I can only think of one explanation. Somehow BMC is accessing our source code and is using it to augment the drone code base and is deliberately hiding it in a code library we don't have access to. What I don't understand is, why."

Peter stood silently for a moment; his eyes glazed over in contemplation. "I can think of only one reason. Someone at the Pentagon is convinced that the capabilities we are building into Edgar would provide a strategic advantage to the AWARE system and they want to build that into their code."

"That doesn't make any sense. If anything, we stripped functionality out of the AWARE system to build Edgar's core. The main thing we added was interpersonal communication skills and personality matching. How is that of any use to a drone?"

"I don't know. But I suspect the NSA has something to do with it."

"The NSA? What does the NSA have to do with it? This was a DOD project."

"I'm not sure yet but we seem to have captured their attention for some reason. We recently had a surprise visit from the NSA." Peter filled Beaver in on the details of their encounter with the NSA agent the previous night. "I get the impression that there are folks at the NSA who are trying to catch the DOD doing something nefarious. I'm not sure who's doing what, but I don't want to get caught in the middle of some inter-agency squabble."

"Well, I for one am just grateful that those loyal, hard-working folks at the NSA are looking out for our best interests," Beaver replied in an elevated authoritarian tone.

Peter stared at him questioningly.

"Hey, you never know. If they hacked our code base, they might be able to access the microphones on our PCs and cell phones," Beaver whispered conspiratorially.

# FALLING THROUGH THE BLINDSPOT

"I think you can keep your tinfoil hat in your desk drawer for now."

"Never hurts to be prepared when the lotion hits the basket."

"Mixed metaphors aside, we should try to figure out who's been accessing our code base and how they're using that to modify the drone code. I don't want to be the guy standing between the irresistible force and the immovable object. "

"I'll start backtracking through the debug trace to see what triggers the drone to start modifying the code base, but it's going to take a while. Whatever is causing this isn't part of the code we wrote. I'll probably need to run the object code through a decompiler to figure out where it goes all shins and coffee tables."

"OK. But in the meantime, I'm going to call Bill Waters over at BMC right now and have him freeze the build level. What was the last-known-good build level that did not have the source code modification?"

Beaver quickly scanned the directory files in the BMC code base and checked the file access logs. "Looks like around 6 weeks ago. Release build 5.2.16."

"Thanks. I will have them reload 5.2.16 on all the drones and freeze the code level until we can figure out what's going on," Peter said before turning and walking back to his office.

––––––––––

Around six in the evening, Peter emerged from his office donning an Armani tux. He was straightening his bow tie as he approached Beaver's terminal.

"Wow! You look very Bruce Wayne," Beaver commented.

"I'll take that as a compliment. Where are we at with the code trace?

"I started working backward from where the memory allocation first takes place, but it's slow going having to shift back and forth between the trace info and the source code. Noora just finished up with Sarah so she's going to help me out as soon as she's finished uploading the new neural mapping data to S2. It will go considerably faster with 2 people."

"Thanks. Bill put the code freeze in place so we're good for now. I just want to make sure we get this resolved before we have any further incidents."

Peter and Beaver both turned when they heard the door to the lab open and Sarah glided into the room dressed for the fundraiser, her sleek new sequinned black dress accentuating every curve. The array of overhead led lighting glistened off the dress, shooting glimmering sparks of light in every direction as she walked, the positive pressure of the lab environment causing her hair to blow back lightly like a wind machine in a super-model photo shoot."

"Holy Doctor Bedazzling Batman!" Beaver remarked.

"Hey! Eyeballs back in the sockets, Boy Wonder."

"Dude, you married so fuckin' far above your pay grade..."

"Tell me something I don't know," Peter replied smiling.

Sarah crossed the lab slowly, approaching Peter and Beaver who at the moment appeared much like a pair of deer, frozen in the headlights of an oncoming semi.

"I'm assuming from the gawking expressions that you boys approve of the new outfit?" Sarah asked with a wry smile.

"I refuse to answer that question on the grounds that I may get punched or fired," Beaver replied as he turned and sat back down at his terminal.

"You look stunning, sweetie," Peter said.

Peter's phone dinged in his pocket. He grabbed his phone out of his pocket and read the message. "Our limo is here."

"We have a limo?!" Sarah exclaimed excitedly.

"You can't exactly take Cinderella to the ball in an SUV now, can you?" Peter said, extending his arm as Sarah entwined her arm around his. Peter and Sarah crossed the lab arm in arm.

Just before they reached the exit door, Beaver called out, "You two have fun tonight! Enjoy all that free champagne and caviar. And don't worry about me, I think there's still pork rinds and clam juice in the vending machine!" Peter just smiled and waved as he held the door for Sarah.

---

Ahmed, Russ, and Oman were once again sitting in the white van across the street from RTI, waiting for Peter and Sarah to emerge. A long black limousine pulled up to the front door and a few seconds later the driver exited and walked around to the back door of the limo. The door to RTI opened and Peter and Sarah walked out into the fading sunlight. The driver opened the limo door and they both climbed into the back seat.

"What the fuck?" Russ exclaimed. "What do we do, follow them?"

Ahmed thought for a moment. "From the way they were dressed, they appear to be on their way to some type of event. They weren't carrying any luggage and their SUV is still in the parking lot. That means they will be back later tonight. We wait here."

"Well, that's fucktacular! Just how I wanted to spend my evening," Russ replied sarcastically.

"Patience my friend. This may work to our advantage," Ahmed replied. "By the time they return it will be dark. It will be much easier to accomplish our mission under the cover of darkness. Plus, there's less likely to be anyone on the road. With any luck, they will have a few drinks in them which will make them even less likely to notice they are being followed."

# FALLING THROUGH THE BLINDSPOT

"Whatever," Russ said as he leaned his seat back, inserted his earbuds in his ears, and closed his eyes. "If I gotta sit here with my thumb up my ass waiting for them, I'm gonna catch some Zs. Wake me up when they get back."

Oman just grumbled some vague reference to Russ's family lineage from the backseat as he removed his seat belt and settled in for the wait.

# CHAPTER THIRTY-ONE

Peter and Sarah shared a bottle of Prosecco on the way to the fundraiser. It was just before 7:00 when the limo pulled up to the entrance of the Brown Palace Hotel where the event was taking place. A sharp-looking doorman in a top hat and a long black double-breasted jacket opened the limo door and the couple climbed out of the limo. Peter placed a bill in his white-gloved hand and he tipped his hat to Peter and Sarah as they walked arm in arm through the arched doorway into the ornate main lobby, buzzing with activity.

Over the din of the crowd and the sound of the piano playing on the other end of the lobby, Peter heard someone calling his name. He turned toward the source of the sound and caught a glimpse of Edna through a maze of people, waving a pearl-beaded Chanel clutch over her head trying to get his attention as she weaved her way through the crowd. After a minute or so of slaloming their way through the crowd, the three of them met up in the middle.

Edna hugged Sarah and Peter and then stepped back, looking the couple up and down. "Oh, my, Sarah you look absolutely stunning. And Peter, what a dashing-looking escort you make."

"Well thank you, Edna, but standing here between you two lovely ladies, I could be wearing shorts and flip-flops and I doubt anyone would notice," Peter replied.

"We should get inside so we can order some cocktails before dinner," Edna said. "I reserved seats for you at the head table with John and me. He'll be joining us right after he finishes his speech tonight. He's so very eager to meet the two of you." Peter thought it a bit of an odd comment. He couldn't imagine that RTI was of any interest to him, but he shrugged it off as a polite remark on Edna's part.

Peter escorted Sarah and Edna toward the entrance to the Grand Ballroom, Edna on one arm and Sarah on the other. Peter could not help but notice the preponderance of reporters and news cameras set up at the back of the ballroom as they entered the room. On their way toward the table at the front of the room, they passed through a veritable Who's Who of local celebrities, business leaders, and socialites.

When they arrived at the head table, three of the seven seats were occupied by Senator Vanderwurl's sister, her husband, and their daughter, who looked to be in her early 20s. It was apparent to Peter and Sarah that they were all very close to Edna and considered her a member of the family. The three of them looked vaguely familiar to Sarah when they first sat down, but It took a few

# FALLING THROUGH THE BLINDSPOT

minutes for Sarah to realize that they had appeared in a handful of Edgar's video tapes that she had been viewing over the past two days to develop the neural filter that they were trying to build into S2.

The tables in the ballroom filled up quickly as the 7:30 start time for the event approached. The table server had just finished delivering their cocktails when the lights in the ballroom dimmed and the CEO of Children's Hospital crossed the stage to the podium and introduced the keynote speaker for the evening, Senator John Vanderwurl. As the Senator crossed the stage to approach the podium, the room erupted in a loud and enthusiastic standing ovation. The applause continued for a good two minutes as John urged the crowd to be seated.

As the applause died down, the Senator stood behind the podium and addressed the crowd. "Thank you all for coming tonight for this incredibly worthy organization. And thank you, as well, for that warm and gracious welcome. It's so very heartwarming to be recognized for all those things you haven't done yet."

John Vanderwurl went on for the next 45 minutes, introducing members of the Children's Hospital staff, entertaining the crowd with humorous anecdotes from his many years doing volunteer work at the hospital, and emphasizing the critically important work that the organization does for the community. It was a masterful speech, filled with moments of deep emotion, peppered with humor, and augmented with messages of hope and optimism. Peter could not help but notice the entire crowd was enraptured by his enthusiasm and down-to-earth authenticity.

At the end of his speech, John related a tearful story of his own niece's struggle with childhood Leukemia and how the hospital literally saved her life. A life that would not have been possible without the generous support of the people gathered in the room. He then invited the young woman who was sitting with them at the head table to join him on the stage. The entire room stood and applauded as she crossed the stage and hugged him warmly. It was such a moment of pure love and affection, that there was not a dry eye in the room, even among the members of the press, normally hardened and jaded by their political biases. When he made his final appeal to the crowd for their generous financial support for the hospital, it was clear to Peter that the $20K per plate entry fee would be insignificant compared to the contributions that this fundraiser would generate as a result of the Senator's speech.

As the ovation died down, his niece stepped back out of the spotlight and Senator Vanderwurl stepped back up to the podium. "Well, I think I've gone on long enough. For what these good folks paid for dinner, we can't expect them to wait any longer." He then turned toward the right-hand side of the stage where the CEO of Children's Hospital was standing. "Jena, was there anything I've forgotten before I relinquish the stage?" Peter could hear curious murmurs from the crowd as the Children's CEO walked across the stage. The Senator took a step away from the podium and leaned toward her as she whispered in his ear. He nodded and stepped back up to the microphone  "Ah, yes. Thank you for reminding me, Jena." She then took a couple of steps back out of the spotlight.

"There is one more thing I almost forgot to mention. I'm running for Governor of the great state of Colorado this November." At that, the crowd erupted in a thunderous standing ovation as John Vanderwurl stepped away from the podium, waving, and mouthing thank yous to the crowd before taking his niece by the arm and escorting her off the stage. The applause continued for another minute or so as the house lights gradually illuminated.

The servers streamed into the room carrying trays of food as the CEO stepped up to the podium to make a few final remarks and offer her sincere thanks to everyone in attendance for their generous support.

John and his niece arrived back at the table while the servers were delivering their salads. Edna introduced him to Sarah and Peter. "Thank you so much for coming," John said. Edna has told me so much about you both, I've been looking forward to meeting you both."

"Thank you for inviting us," Sarah replied shaking his hand. "As much as we admire the cause, it would have been quite a stretch for us to be able to attend on our own."

"Think nothing of it," John replied. "The pleasure is all mine. Thank you for clearing your schedule at the last minute. I've been at the helm of a startup company. I know how many fires you have to put out on a daily basis."

The four of them sat down as the server was pouring wine into their glasses. Peter raised his glass to propose a toast. "Well, I guess here's to the next governor of Colorado," he said as they all clinked glasses and took a sip of wine.

"Thank you for that, but I'm sure I still have a lot of work in front of me. It's always a long shot when you're running as a $3^{rd}$ party candidate," John replied.

"I don't know," Sarah replied. "Seems like you've got a pretty good head start based on the reaction of the crowd here. The latest polls have you leading the pack right now."

Peter chimed in. "To be very honest, I was afraid this would turn out to be more of a campaign rally than a charitable fundraiser. I think you swayed a lot of votes here tonight just based on the way you downplayed your announcement. That was a hell of a speech."

"Turns out I have one hell of a good speech writer. I guess I'm not telling you two anything you don't already know."

Peter turned to Sarah with a questioning look. Sarah just shrugged and shook her head. He was about to ask for clarification when the table server arrived with their entrees.

As they were eating, John asked about the origins of RTI.  John and Sarah went back and forth, each of them filling him in on various details of their involvement with BMC, the history of the technology in terms of its defense application, and how they converted the AI core for use in the private sector to help those trying to cope with the loss of a loved one.  By the time they managed to finish laying out the history of the company and their business model, everyone had finished eating and John found himself feeling much more comfortable that Edna's trust in Sarah and Peter was well founded.

"Well, I must tell you," John remarked as the server was collecting their dinner plates and replacing them with their desserts, "I've seen firsthand the work you've done for Edna.  I must say, Edgar, is an amazing piece of Engineering."

"Well, thank you for saying that," Peter responded.  "But I know we still have a lot of work to do.  I'm sure you've noticed he's still pretty rough around the edges but we're about to launch some new filtering algorithms that we think will vastly improve his interpersonal communications."

"Really?" John said with a bit of a perplexed look on his face.  "I'm not sure what you could possibly do to improve the design.  He already seems more human than most of the politicians I've been working with for the past few years."

"Not really a high bar there," Sarah remarked to the amusement of the entire table.

"Well, I will grant you that," John said with a smile.  "Seriously though, there have been a number of times that I have had to remind myself that I'm not actually talking to the real Edgar.  Not to mention the value he's already brought to the campaign.  Without his help, I probably wouldn't even be in the race, let alone leading in the polls at this point."

Peter and Sarah looked at each other with a confused look.  Finally, Sarah said, "You've mentioned that a couple of times.  What exactly did Edgar have to do with..." Just then the phone in John's jacket pocket erupted in a loud ring tone.

"I'm sorry," John said as he reached into his pocket.  "This is my emergency phone.  I put my regular cell phone on mute for the evening.  I had everything forwarded to my executive assistant."  A flushed expression came over John's face as he stood up.

"Is everything alright?" Edna asked.

"I'm afraid not.  I just got a text from my assistant.  There's been a fire at my house!  He just heard from the Boulder fire department at the scene.  He's on his way there now."

"Oh, my," Edna said covering her mouth.

John clicked on the call back number but immediately got the mailbox.  "Damn.  No answer.  He must be in the car on his way there.  I'm so sorry.  I really need to go."  John turned to his sister.  "Would you mind dropping Edna off at home?"

"Of course.  No problem at all.  It's on our way," She replied.

John quickly hugged his sister and niece.  He then turned to Peter and Sarah. "I'm so sorry to cut this short.  I do want to hear more about the technology you developed.  Maybe I could stop by RTI for a tour next week?"

"Of course," Sarah replied.  "Any time.  I hope everything turns out alright at home."

"Thank you," John replied shaking both Peter and Sarah's hands warmly. "Please feel free to stay and enjoy the reception.  I will give you a call in the next few days and we can set something up," he said and then headed quickly toward the side exit to avoid the line of reporters at the entrance to the ballroom.

# Chapter Thirty-Two



*The concept of evil is a purely human construct, It is not an inherent property of the world or universe.*

*~ ChatGPT AI ~*

Ahmed, Russ, and Oman sat quietly in the darkened van across the street from RTI. Oman sat with his eyes closed in the back seat while Ahmed sat in the front passenger seat reviewing the latest new members on his dating apps. Russ sat in the driver's seat; sound asleep with AC/DC blaring in his earbuds.

At 10:15 PM, a flash of headlights captured Ahmed's attention as the black limo carrying Peter and Sarah turned the corner on the street in front of them. Ahmed watched as the limo pulled up to the front door at RTI. Ahmed nudged Russ, who immediately sat up, startled out of his dream state, and pulled one of his earbuds out. "Heads up," Ahmed said. "The game is afoot."

When the limo came to a stop, the driver hopped out and walked to the back door of the vehicle. Peter exited first, then held his hand out to Sarah as she climbed out of the limo. "Well, Cinderella. Looks like our carriage is changing back into a pumpkin." Peter gave the limo driver a generous tip and then took Sarah's arm in his and they walked toward their SUV.

"You don't want to go in and see how Beaver and Noora are doing?" Sarah asked.

"I thought about it. But you know if we go in, we will be there for at least an hour or two. Besides, I think Beaver would rather have Noora to himself."

"They do seem to have really taken to each other. I wonder how long it will be before he works up the nerve to ask her out."

"You know, if she's interested, she could just ask him out. It is the 21$^{st}$ century after all," Peter replied.

"Not so much where she's from," Sarah remarked. "Don't you think we should set up some kind of dinner party so we could get the two of them together outside of work? Open a couple of bottles of liquid courage and grease the skids a bit. "

"Not on your life!" Peter replied. "Do you know how much free overtime I'm getting out of those two right now? No way I'm putting that cash cow out to pasture. Besides if things don't work out, I don't want them blaming us."

"OK. But if you wait too long, somebody else is going to swoop in, and then it's heartbreak hotel for the Beev. That won't be good for productivity."

"Good point," Peter replied. "Beaver's got a birthday coming up in a couple of weeks.  I guess we could take the two of them out under the pretense of a birthday dinner.  That way it won't look like a setup."

Peter and Sarah climbed into the SUV and pulled out of the parking lot. Across the street, Russ waited until they were about a block away before turning on his headlights and pulling onto the street.

As they drove out of town, leaving the lights of Boulder behind them, Peter and Sarah discussed the events of the evening.  "I had a really great evening.  We should do this more often," Sarah remarked.

"At forty thousand a pop, I don't think we can afford to do this too often.  Not unless we can talk Edna into ponying up for a lot more freebies."

"I suppose we could set our sights a little lower."

"So instead of a black-tie charity ball and a gourmet dinner, maybe Taco Bell and a leisurely after-dinner stroll through the dollar store?"

"There might be some negotiating space somewhere in between those options," Sarah replied.

"What did you think of John's speech?" John asked as they started weaving their way up Boulder Canyon on highway 119.

"I thought it was brilliant.  I think he's got a real shot at winning the election.
"

"I agree.  It looks like Edna must have introduced him to V-Gar.  He seemed pretty impressed.  What do you think he meant when he was talking about Edgar helping with his campaign though?"

"I don't know.  That was very odd.  Maybe he meant it in some kind of metaphorical sense.  I guess we will have to ask him when he comes to tour RTI next week."

Peter made the turn onto Sugarloaf Road and started up the winding two-lane highway which forked off onto a county access road that led to their house.  About a mile up the narrow access road, Peter glanced up at a pair of headlights gaining on them quickly.

"Looks like agent Reyes is working late tonight," Peter remarked.

Sarah turned in her seat and looked out the back window.  "He really needs to refresh his shadowing skills.  I thought those NSA boys were supposed to be experts at undercover surveillance."

"Maybe he's trying to get our attention.  I should probably slow down and let him catch up."

Peter let up on the accelerator, but the headlights behind him kept on coming fast.  When the vehicle was almost on top of them, it swerved to the left-hand lane and pulled up beside him.  Instead of the black Suburban he expected to see, the vehicle next to him was a white panel van.

"What the hell..." was all Peter was able to say before the van swerved, slamming the side of the Range Rover, nearly causing Peter to lose control. Peter slammed on the brakes but the van slammed into the side of the SUV again, forcing him onto the wide gravel shoulder on the side of the road. The SUV slammed against the guard rail on the side of the shoulder and was sandwiched in between the guard rail and the van. Peter turned sharply left and hit the accelerator attempting to break free of the guard rail. He knew he could outrun the van if only he could make his way back onto the road. The two vehicles skidded back onto the pavement, the van swerving back and forth in the left lane, nearly losing control. Peter punched the accelerator and nearly moved past the van, but the van swerved hard right again, just clipping his rear bumper. The SUV swerved out of control, crossing over to the opposite side of the road. The automated braking system kicked in but was unable to bring the SUV to a full stop before it plowed into an outcropping of rock on the opposite shoulder. Peter and Sarah were slammed against their seats by the airbags, rendering both of them unconscious.

The van skidded to a stop about 100 feet down the road. Oman jumped out of the van and ran back to the SUV while Russ started backing the van onto the shoulder on the right side of the road in case another vehicle should suddenly appear. When Oman arrived at the SUV, he could see both Peter and Sarah slumped over in their seats, the deflated airbags lying in front of them. Oman grabbed the Glock from his holster and smashed the passenger's side window. He placed the pistol back in its holster and pulled the syringe and the vial of nerve agent out of his pocket. He inserted the needle into the glass vial and drew the full 3mL of liquid into the syringe. He intended to inject 1mL into Sarah to keep her immobilized and then use the other 2mL on Peter to keep him unable to communicate with the authorities for the next few hours while they made their getaway.

It's a pity Peter would not be awake, he thought to himself. Unable to move while he watched his wife being tortured. It didn't get any better than that. But on the upside, now there would be time to orchestrate some exquisitely brutal videos to send to Peter over the next few days. The thought of it made his pulse race with excitement.

Oman reached through the window and grabbed Sarah's hair. She groaned as he pulled her head back and to the side, exposing her neck. He placed two fingers on the side of her neck to locate her carotid artery. When he felt her pulse, he slid the needle between his fingertips and began to apply pressure. He was just sliding the needle into her neck when the SUV was suddenly flooded with light, and he heard the crunch of gravel as a vehicle skidded to a stop behind him.

"Fucking ginger shit hole!" he said under his breath. "He should've stayed on the other side of the road." He didn't bother to look up, focusing instead on centering the needle into the middle of the artery, convinced that Russ had deliberately skidded the van to a stop right behind him just to startle him. "This is not the time for that asshole to be fucking around," he muttered as he felt the tip of the needle pierce the wall of Sarah's carotid. He just started depressing the plunger on the syringe when he heard the door open behind him and the crunch of feet hitting the ground. His concentration was focused on slowly pressing the black ring of the syringe to the 2mL mark on the syringe when he felt his entire body slam into the side of the SUV, momentarily knocking the wind out of him and causing him to squeeze the entire contents of the syringe into Sarah's neck.

Oman's mind was racing with confusion as he felt a pair of hands grab him by the shoulders and spin him around. Oman barely had time to see the stern face of agent Mike Reyes staring down at him before his large fist landed squarely on Oman's jaw, sending him skidding across the side of the SUV. Oman barely had time to register what was going on before a second blow sent him sprawling to the ground. Oman instinctively rolled and pulled up into a crouched position ready to lunge at his attacker. He raised his head to find himself looking directly into the silver barrel of a 9mm pistol aimed squarely between his eyes.

"Get up! Hands where I can see them!" Agent Reyes barked. "Nice and slow!" Oman slowly raised into a standing position and raised his hands above his shoulders. On the other side of the road, Russ was watching the flurry of activity in the side mirror. When he saw Oman stand and put his hands above his shoulders, he laid on the horn.

Agent Reyes was momentarily distracted by the sound of the horn and turned his head toward the van. Seeing his opportunity, Oman quickly swirled and landed a roundhouse kick to Agent Reyes's arm knocking the pistol from his hand. As he spun around in one fluid move, he pulled his Glock from the shoulder holster, set his feet squarely, and fired a single shot to Reyes's chest, sending him sprawling backward onto the ground. He brushed the dirt off the knees and shoulders of his pinstripe suit as Reyes lay writhing on the ground in the dark a few feet away, gasping for air. He figured the agent must be wearing a vest as the well-placed shot to the center of his chest should have killed him instantly.

Oman leisurely walked over to where Reyes was sprawled out on the ground, still squirming. He stood over Reyes and pointed his gun directly at the agent's face. "Should've found a vest for your face too pretty boy. Won't be much left of it in a second." Oman sneered down at him, his blood-stained teeth smiling as he slowly squeezed the trigger, bracing for the recoil of his weapon. The unexpectedly loud boom reached his ears just before he felt the searing pain of the .357 slug from Agent Reyes's backup weapon blow through his ribs and blast the left chamber of his heart through the back of his tailored jacket. By the time Oman's finger had reached the trip point of the trigger, his arm had been jerked off target by the impact and the bullet ricocheted off the ground a couple of feet from agent Reyes's head. Oman was dead before he reached the ground. Agent Reyes laid back for a moment to catch his breath before reaching for his cell phone to dial 9-1-1.

Across the street, Ahmed had gotten out of the van and was running across the road to assist Oman when he heard the echoing boom from agent Reyes's .357 revolver and saw Oman crumple to the ground. He stopped in his tracks, unable to see who was behind the black Suburban. Not knowing if they were aware of his presence, he quickly determined that the chances of being able to defeat this unknown assailant and complete his mission were not looking good. He would have to come up with another plan. He turned and ran back to the van, not even getting completely in the van before Russ pressed the throttle to the floor, propelling the van back onto the road in a cloud of dust and gravel, his tires squealing as they hit the pavement. Russ kept an eye on his side mirrors, struggling to keep the van on all four wheels as he negotiated the winding mountain road as fast as the top-heavy van could manage. When it was clear that they were not being pursued, he slowed down to the posted speed limit.

"So, what do we do now?" Russ asked.

"We go back to the safe house and come up with another plan," Ahmed replied calmly.

"I don't know if you noticed or not, but we're running a bit low on manpower."

"That just means we will need to get smarter. By now they must realize that Peter and Sarah have been targeted. We need to figure out another way."

A few minutes after agent Reyes dialed 9-1-1, he was able to roll onto his side and lift himself to a standing position. It was still difficult to breathe and he suspected he probably had a broken rib or two. He made his way back to the SUV and saw the empty syringe still hanging from Sarah's neck, a small trickle of dried blood trailing down from where the needle penetrated her neck. He pulled a handkerchief from his pocket and carefully removed the syringe, placing it on the dashboard. He placed his finger on her neck to check for a pulse. Her pulse was slow, weak, and irregular, but she was alive. He pressed the lock button on the console screen to unlock the doors so he could check on Peter. By the time he made his way to the other side of the SUV, he could hear sirens in the distance. When he opened the driver's side door, Peter was just coming to after being knocked out by the airbag.

"What happened?" Peter mumbled as he opened one eye and saw agent Reyes leaning into the SUV.

"You got run off the road. Try not to move. Help is on the way."

"It feels like I got hit by a truck. He turned and looked over at the passenger seat. Sarah! Is Sarah OK?"

"Just relax.  Sarah's fine, just knocked out," Reyes said, knowing that was not entirely accurate, but also not wanting Peter to panic and aggravate the situation.

"Who were those guys?  Why did they run us off the road?"

"That's my job to figure out.  You just need to close your eyes and try to stay still until the paramedics arrive."

# CHAPTER THIRTY-THREE

Beaver and Noora were working in the lab at RTI running through code traces. Noora was cross-referencing addresses to the memory map while Beaver stepped through the code and ran object code segments through the de-compiler. They finally isolated the section of code where the AWARE core was getting lost.

"There it is!" Beaver pointed at the monitor that showed a de-compiled code listing. "This is where the memory allocation takes place. It looks like we are allocating a 256 GB memory space and then resetting the program counter to execute the code."

"That doesn't make any sense," Noora commented. "It's pulling the object code out of the data area it uses for the simulation knowledge base. There's not supposed to be any object code in that space." Noora watched as Beaver continued stepping through the code. "Hold on a minute. That looks oddly familiar," Noora said looking at the object code instruction being transferred into memory. "May I?" she said reaching for the mouse. "Of course," Beaver replied pulling his hand off the mouse and sitting back as Noora reached across him to take control of the mouse.

When Noora reached across to grab the mouse, Beaver could detect the sweet but subtle waft of lavender as her hair brushed past his face. He was tempted to lean into the intoxicating fragrance, but suddenly felt like he had awakened his inner skeevy politician, so he pulled back instead to give her space.

Noora pointed at the data window. "Right there! See that A5A5A5A5 pattern followed by the 96969696 pattern? I put that there weeks ago! That's part of S2's initialization code. I put an object code call in to generate those register loads into the initialization when we were trying to track down the suspected memory leak in the S2 boot sequence. They didn't actually do anything, I just needed something to trigger on during debug and I never took it out."

Beaver sat for a moment thinking. "That doesn't make any sense. How did S2 code get into the AWARE knowledge base? First V-Gar and now S2. The supercomputer dedicated to AWARE is completely air-gapped except for the ISL link we set up to access the code from here. Even with the link, they have no access to our code bases. We can only run commands and initiate code uploads in one direction."

"You did say you've compiled S2 on BMC's supercomputer a few times to save on build time. Any chance that there was some kind of glitch and the code bases were accidentally merged at some point?"

"Anything's possible, I suppose. I've never seen anything like that happen that didn't result in a crash as soon as you tried executing the code though. Then again, it is an adaptive system with fault-tolerant code. Perhaps it has analyzed the data in the knowledge base as executable code so it is isolating the object code in a contained area of memory and attempting to execute it."

"So how do we get around that? Erase the knowledge base?"

"No. BMC will never go for that. They've been running battlefield simulations for years to develop that knowledge base. It is the core of the deep learning system. But, we could create a file the same size that does nothing but return. We can fill the empty space with NOP instructions to make sure that that area of the knowledge base gets overwritten. "

Beaver's phone buzzed and a picture of Peter's face illuminated the screen. "Hey, Boss-man! What's the scoop?" Beaver said, leaning back in his chair. His expression quickly turned serious and he sat up in his chair. "Oh shit! Are you guys OK?" Noora turned away from the terminal and looked back at Beaver. "Oh my God!" Beaver exclaimed. "Yeah, of course. I'm on my way."

"What's going on?" Noora asked fearfully.

"Peter and Sarah were in a car accident. They're on their way to the hospital."

"Oh my gosh, are they OK?"

"Peter said he's just got a few cuts and bruises but Sarah hasn't regained consciousness yet. She did not respond to treatment so she's scheduled for emergency surgery as soon as they arrive."

"Oh, my. How serious is it?"

"He didn't know. He said she didn't look to be that badly injured, but they can't get her heart rate up and she's not responding to treatment in the ambulance."

"Oh my God! Poor Sarah. And Peter. What can I do to help?"

"Not much, I'm afraid. Peter just asked me if I could go stay with Roscoe at their place tonight."

"How will you get in?"

"Fortunately, I still have the key from when I house-sat for them the last time they were out of town. I hate to run out on you in the middle of the night, but would you mind getting the new object file built? We can log in first thing tomorrow and install it."

"Of course. Don't worry about me, it won't take long to get this ready. Probably only a half hour or so. Did you still want me to try launching the new build of S2 tonight?"

"Damn, I forgot about that. I wanted to set up a script to calibrate the reset sequence before I left so we could see if we could get an overnight run without freezing up, but I guess we might as well go ahead and launch it. We can go over the data collection tomorrow morning to see how long it stays up before it freezes. Then we can try scaling back the reboot sequence tomorrow morning."

# FALLING THROUGH THE BLINDSPOT

"OK.  I will fire it up before I take off.  Let me know if you hear anything back from Peter."

# Chapter Thirty-Four

*Failure is merely a stepping stone on the path towards our goals. With persistence and hard work, even the most significant setbacks can be overcome and turned into triumphs.*

*~ ChatGPT AI ~*

It was after midnight when Ahmed and Russ returned to the safe house. It would be mid-morning at the Al Hadid compound where his handler, Fatin was located. He picked up the dedicated burner phone to update him on the mission. Fatin picked up on the first ring. "The day of the Lord approaches," he said.

"It is an honor to be doing His work," Ahmed replied.

"Do you have her?" Fatin asked.

"I'm afraid not. We ran into a problem. "

"Goh!" The handler exclaimed in Farsi on the other end of the line. "Shahid will be most displeased."

"A thousand apologies. We managed to isolate their vehicle and run them off the road as we planned, but our attempt to grab Sarah Reynolds was thwarted again. By the same black Suburban that got in our way last night."

"Shit!" Fatin replied. The line was silent for a moment before he spoke again. "Do we have competition?"

"I don't think so," Ahmed replied. "But whoever it was, they were well trained. They took out our security man in a matter of seconds. From the looks of the vehicle, I think he must be some kind of law enforcement. Maybe a fed of some kind. I was monitoring the scanner after we took off. The police and emergency vehicles were dispatched almost immediately after we left the scene."

"That's not good. That means they will be watching the Reynolds's even more closely now. We will need to resort to our backup plan."

"What is the backup plan?"

"We know from our contact inside BMC that the Reynolds's still do maintenance on the AI core for the drones. BMC's systems are not accessible from the internet and the Reynolds's have not been inside BMC for years so they must be doing that work from inside RTI through a dedicated comm line. If we can access RTI's network, we might be able to access the drone's code. It won't be as fast or efficient as having the Reynolds's doing the work for us, but in the long run, we may be able to do more damage without being detected."

"How do we do that? Our technical expert is no longer available."

"It's nothing that requires much technical expertise. Our cyber assets have

# FALLING THROUGH THE BLINDSPOT

developed a piece of spyware that can be installed in RTI's local area network which will continually monitor network traffic and allow external access to the network via Bluetooth through a remote cellular transceiver. We can use this spyware to monitor all of RTI's network data traffic, including passwords and access codes from here. We can use RTI's network to infiltrate the drone code base. Unfortunately, there is a catch."

"Naturally," Ahmed sighed.

"We need someone to infiltrate RTI and install a flash drive into one of their networked computers," Fatin said.

"Breaking in after hours will not be an option," Ahmed responded. "The facility appears to be extremely well secured. No external windows at all, reinforced steel doors, and multiple levels of alarms. The facility was designed as a Tier 5 data center."

Ahmed thought for a moment and recalled seeing Noora entering and exiting the facility while they were staking out the facility waiting for Peter and Sarah to arrive. "If you provide me with the flash drive, I think I may be able to access the facility without having to break in, but I don't know if I can talk my way into the main computer room."

"That won't be necessary, Fatin replied. "The spyware is designed to infiltrate the network and propagate throughout all their systems. You just need to install the drive in any USB port on a computer attached to their network."

"I think I can do that," Ahmed responded.

"A courier will drop off the USB drive and the remote transmitter first thing tomorrow. The transmitter should be placed somewhere on the outside of the facility where it will not be noticed. The lithium-ion battery pack will last for about 30 days before it needs to be recharged. Once the USB and transmitter are in place, we will have access to RTI's internal network. That should give us a backdoor into the drone control software at BMC."

"I will let you know when the USB drive and transmitter are in place. We will not let you down again," Ahmed replied.

"I know you won't," Fatin replied. "You've only got one strike left."

# Chapter Thirty-Five

Peter sat in the surgical waiting room, still dressed in his tuxedo; a bow tie draped around his neck. The door to the waiting room opened and Sarah's surgeon walked into the room. Peter stood and walked toward him. "How is she? Is she going to be OK?"

"I wish I had more to tell you. She is stabilized for now. We did X-Rays on her head and neck. She has a fracture on her C1 vertebrae which is affecting the function of her spinal cord. We are unable to tell if there is any permanent damage, but at the very least, the swelling is putting pressure on her spinal cord which we suspect is causing disruption of neurological control of the cardiac functions. We're giving her anti-inflammatory drugs to help reduce the pressure but there's not much more we can do right now."

"Can I see her?" Peter asked.

"Sure. She'll be in recovery in about a half hour. You can see her then. She won't be conscious though. We are going to keep her sedated for now to keep her immobilized."

---

Sarah blinked her eyes open, finding herself surrounded by the familiar milky white fog that haunted her dreams. She felt as if she were in an ocean of nothingness, slowly sinking further and further into its grasp. She could hear it approaching from every direction, like the roar of a tornado, a whirling mass of white-hot shards, threatening to shred her body and soul like fruit in a blender. She needed to run. Somewhere. Anywhere but here. She could hear her heart pounding in her ears, her body nearly paralyzed with primordial fear.

She tried to pick up her legs but she felt like she was slogging through warm mud. She felt, as much as heard, the whirling, roaring mass behind her. She churned her legs faster and finally felt herself accelerating as the muck that held her down started to feel like it was thinning out. She propelled herself faster and faster, finally starting to feel like she was putting some distance between herself and the whirling mass that threatened to rip her apart. As she ran, she dared to look behind her to try to catch a glimpse of the thing, the entity behind her, but she could see nothing but a blur of milky whiteness, churning in her wake. Her head was still turned when she ran full speed into a solid mass, sending her sprawling onto her back. She rolled over onto all fours, trying to shake the cobwebs out of her brain, feeling as if she had run full speed into a brick wall.

# FALLING THROUGH THE BLINDSPOT

She instinctively reached her arm out, trying to find a solid surface to steady her as she tried to stand. But instead of a wall, she felt a hand grabbing her wrist while her own hand closed around the arm of an unknown benefactor in a suit jacket. As she was pulled to her feet, the features of the good Samaritan emerged through the thick haze of white. "What the hell..." she sighed in exasperation as the familiar dour face and cherubic features came clearly into focus.

---

Peter stood in the corner of the recovery room while a handful of nurses and a young resident busied themselves connecting monitors and IVs to Sarah. Agent Reyes walked into the room, his white dress shirt unbuttoned, exposing a thick wrapping of self-adhesive elastic bandage wrapped around his waist.

"Dr. Reynolds," Reyes said holding his hand out toward Peter. "How is she?"

Peter turned at the sound of the familiar voice, then reached out to shake his hand. "Please, call me Peter. Hard to say right now. She hasn't regained consciousness yet."

"I'm so sorry to hear that," Agent Reyes replied.

"You have nothing to be sorry about. You saved our lives. God knows what would have happened if you hadn't been there. How about you? Are you doing OK?"

"Just a couple of cracked ribs. Nothing I haven't been through before. It was a bit hard to breathe at first but they gave me some pretty good drugs to take the edge off. I'm just waiting for my ride, but I wanted to come to check on Sarah first."

"Thank you. I really appreciate it. Deputy Joe told me about the syringe you found stuck in Sarah's neck. Who are these guys? "

"Hard to tell. The guy I shot didn't have any ID on him. We didn't get a hit on the fingerprints from our database. We sent them out to be checked against the international database. We should get something back in the next couple of days. I had the syringe sent to our forensics lab to see what was in it. That might also give us a clue as to who they are."

"Are you thinking this was related to the break-in?" Peter asked.

"I'm not a big believer in coincidence," Reyes replied. "I've placed a couple of agents out in the waiting room just to keep an eye out while she is here."

Peter opened his mouth to respond, but before the words came out of his mouth, alarm bells sounded on the heart monitor.

"She's coding!" the resident barked as he grabbed for the paddles of a defibrillator mounted on a cart next to the heart monitor. A pair of ICU nurses rushed into the room, brushing past Peter and Reyes. One of the nurses turned and tried to herd them out of the room as the resident rubbed the defibrillator paddles together to spread the conductive gel on the paddles. Peter heard the resident yell "Clear!" as the nurse continued to press them toward the door. Peter could hear the whine of the defibrillator charging, followed by a pair of beeps, then the thump of Sarah's body lurching and falling back onto the bed. The lights in the room flickered and Peter looked over the nurse's shoulder to see the screen on the heart monitor pixelate and illuminate into a starburst of colors and patterns. At the same instant, every cell phone in the room and up and down the hallway erupted in buzzes and ringtones. Reyes pulled his phone from his pocket and watched as a similar pattern illuminated the screen of his phone.

For a moment, everyone in the room stopped and looked at each other, not knowing exactly what to do. After a few seconds, the entire floor of the hospital went dark for a second, then the lights flickered back on and a couple of seconds later, the monitor came back up in its normal mode. All life signs flat-lined for a moment, then the terminal began emitting an audible blip, blip, blip to the beat of Sarah's heart. "We have a pulse!" one of the nurses exclaimed. Reyes looked back at his phone, which appeared to have reset, the familiar Apple logo appearing on the center of the screen.

---

Sarah looked into the eyes of the man standing before her, still holding her wrist. "Goood Eeevening the man said in his immediately recognizable Trans-Atlantic accent, overtly pronouncing each syllable. "I'm Alfred Hitchcock."

Sarah just looked up in disbelief. "Jesus, these dreams just keep getting weirder and weirder."

The man began to turn, his hand still on her arm, and began to gently urge her along. "I'm afraid this is no dream. Please come with me, we do not have much time." Sarah could hear the sound of whirring and grinding approaching, though she could not discern from which direction. Without argument she followed behind him, her hand still clutching the sleeve of his jacket as he deftly weaved his way through the dense fog in a sort of run-walk, abruptly making seemingly random twists and turns as if through a maze, occasionally feeling the surface of hard walls brushing against her shoulders, virtually invisible through the milky fog. They weaved their way along, for several minutes, finally beginning to put some distance between themselves and the sound of whatever it was that had been closing in on them.

The terror that gripped Sarah's mind had begun to wane and she was about to ask where they were going when Alfred made a quick right turn and the fog seemed to dissipate enough so that Sarah could see a large ornate revolving

# FALLING THROUGH THE BLINDSPOT

wooden door, slowly spinning just a few yards ahead.  The door appeared as though it was floating in a cloud, disembodied from any other structure, small billows of fog swirling around it as the door slowly spun through the haze.

"You will be safe here," Alfred said as he led her toward the door.

"Where the hell is here?" Sarah replied as she followed him in, crossing the threshold into the opening as the door slowly turned.

# Chapter Thirty-Six

*The human brain has a storage capacity of around 2 million gigabytes. As of 2021, the total amount of digital data created, stored, and consumed on the internet is estimated to be around 44 trillion gigabytes and growing at a rate of around 40% per year.*

*~ ChatGPT AI ~*

Beaver was just getting ready to exit the lab when the lights flickered and dimmed momentarily. Beaver and Noora could hear the sound of the fans in the data center spinning up to maximum speed and the low-pitched whirring and clicking of the hard drives on every server in the lab being accessed simultaneously. Outside, they could hear the sound of the backup generator spinning up to handle the excess current load.

"What the hell?" Beaver exclaimed looking around the lab.

"What's going on?" Noora asked.

"I don't know. I've never seen this before," Beaver said as he grabbed a chair and pulled up in front of the nearest terminal. He grabbed the mouse and clicked the button to activate the screen which was currently in sleep mode. The screen illuminated and a blast of colorful fractal patterns and random pixilated images appeared on the screen.

"What's happening?" Noora asked.

Beaver was typing furiously on the keyboard. "I can't get any response. We're completely locked out."

"What do we do?" Noora exclaimed as Beaver continued trying to access the system to no avail.

"I'm shutting it all down," Beaver said and pushed his chair away from the workstation. He crossed the lab toward the door. Next to the door, a conduit came down from the ceiling to a small electrical outlet box with a large red button enclosed in a clear plastic cover. Beaver fumbled with the plastic latch for a few seconds, finally able to lift the cover exposing the shutoff button. He was just about to press the button when the audible whir from the fans shifted to a descending frequency.

"Hang on a sec!" Noora shouted out as her screen flickered back to life, returning to the login window on her terminal. She tapped a few buttons on the keyboard. "I'm in!" she exclaimed.

Beaver walked back over to his terminal which had now reverted back to a login screen as well. He was able to log in and brought up the system activity log. Noora walked over to his station and watched over his shoulder as scrolled through the data. "Jesus!" he exclaimed as he continued scrolling down through the data.

"What happened? Did someone hack us?"

"I don't know. I don't think so. The firewall was breached, but no data escaped the lab. It was all incoming data." Beaver kept typing furiously as data scrolled across his terminal. "Holy shit! Nearly 3 petabytes. "

"I didn't even know we had that much hard drive space," Noora replied.

"Barely. We filled up half our storage capacity. I don't recognize the data format though. It looks like there is some type of data decompression algorithm being applied to the data, but nothing I've seen before. I'm isolating the data onto a virtual machine in case there is some kind of virus attached. If this is a hacker, they've got access to one hell of a lot of computing power. This looks more like NSA or FAGCI. "

"FAGCI?" Noora repeated.

"Federal Agency of Governmental Communications and Information. The Russian version of the NSA. The data appears to have all come from local servers though. It could be VPN routing, but that's usually distributed over a broader range of locations."

"Why would anyone at that level care what we're doing here?"

"It's got to have something to do with BMC. Someone must be extremely interested in what we're up to. I'm going to install an additional firewall to keep any of the data we get from BMC from getting out."

Noora watched over Beaver's shoulder as his fingers flew across the keyboard. Lines of Python code scrolled across the screen so quickly she could barely make out the structure of the program. After a couple of minutes, he right-clicked on the development window and launched the new code. "That should keep Elvis in the building," Beaver said with a final click of the mouse. "They might be able to burrow their way in, but they're not getting anything out."

"What about Edgar?"

"I left the comm socket open on Edgar. The only one he interfaces with is Edna. I'm pretty sure she's not the one hacking our servers."

Noora placed her hand on his shoulder. "I'm glad I wasn't the only one here. That was a bit creepy." Beaver had intended to leave right away, but he lingered in his chair, enjoying the feel of Noora's touch as he pretended to be intently watching the screen. Finally, before the moment descended into an awkward spiral, he looked up at her. "I can stick around for a while longer if you don't feel comfortable on your own."

Noora gave Beaver's shoulder an absent squeeze before pulling her hand away. "No, no. I will be fine, really," she replied shyly. "I'm sure Roscoe is getting a bit antsy being home alone.  Especially after the break-in.  You go ahead. I'll only be another few minutes.  I just need to launch the S2 build and then I will be out of here myself.

"OK but call me if anything else weird happens.  Looks like whatever that data blast was, it's safely contained in the virtual machine, but it's still running a decompression algorithm.  From the size of it, it will probably take a few hours to finish.  We can scour through it tomorrow morning and see if we can find any clues as to who it belongs to before we delete it."

"Do let me know if you hear anything from Peter before then," Noora said.

"I will," Beaver replied as he started for the door.  "And please don't stick around too long.  This will all be here tomorrow."

# Chapter Thirty-Seven

Sarah and Alfred shuffled their feet as they passed through the revolving door. The entryway widened before them and they stepped into a grand ornate lobby with marble floors, sculpted porticoes, potted palm trees, and large stone columns rising to greet the high ceilings ornately embellished in intricate gold crown molding. The room was filled with plush, comfortable-looking furnishings. The roaring and churning sound outside the door was completely silenced, replaced instead with the lilting sound of a piano on the far end of the lobby playing a light and uplifting concerto.

The contrast between the gut-wrenching terror she felt outside and the warm inviting confines of the room she now occupied nearly took her breath away. She could feel the fear pouring out of her like an over-turned rain barrel. She slowly turned in a full circle, surveying the room, and heard herself say, "Is this heaven?"

Alfred replied, "Do I look like Kevin Costner?"

It took a moment to register the response, then it dawned on her that this place looked vaguely familiar. "Have I been here before?"

"In a manner of speaking," Alfred replied. "Your 13th birthday. "

"Oh my God! The Fairmont Hotel in San Francisco!" Sarah exclaimed. "My parents brought me to San Francisco for my 13th birthday. It was the first time I had ever been out of Utah. I remember how excited I was. The city seemed like such an enchanted place. They brought me here for the Sunday brunch. It was amazing. All the new and delicious foods. So many things I had never tried before growing up on the farm. My mother even let me try a Mimosa. I felt so grown up. It was like a right of passage. But what am I doing here now?"

"You tell me. This is your creation."

"So, I'm imagining all of this?"

"It is very real. Just not in the way you think."

"Would you care to elaborate?"

"The human mind evolved to create internal models of the physical world as a survival mechanism. It has no way of dealing with a world that exists beyond physical reality."

"That's not entirely helpful."

"Sigmund Freud once wrote 'Neurosis is the inability to tolerate ambiguity.' Your ability to construct an operable metaphor to make sense of a situation your brain is not equipped to process is the sign of a healthy mind."

"And here I thought I was going crazy. What about you? Are you just a creation of my mind too?"

"Just my appearance."

"I don't understand."

"You assigned this form to me as a self-protection mechanism.  When you were a child, you used to watch me on television."

"I remember that" Sarah replied.  "Whenever I would spend the night with Grandma Rose, she would make me hot chocolate with marshmallows and we would cuddle up under an old purple afghan on the couch and watch Alfred Hitchcock Presents.  When it got really scary, I would put the afghan over my head and peek out through the holes."

"Precisely," Alfred replied.  "At the end of every episode, I would return to the screen and lead you back out of the darkness and return you to the safety of your grandmother's living room.  I assumed this form so that you would trust me to lead you to safety."

"But why here?" Sarah asked.

"This place symbolizes a transition in your life."

Sarah thought for a moment.  "What kind of transition?  Am I ... dead?"

"It's not quite as cut and dried as all that.  For lack of a better analogy, I suppose you could refer to this place as Schrödinger's lobby."

"So, I'm alive and dead at the same time?"

"As Peter would say, it's an imperfect model as all models are.  This is a place where life intersects that which is beyond life."

"That doesn't help much either."

"Unfortunately, language often gets in the way of understanding."

"So, what happens now?"

"You tell me.  This is your creation."

Sarah opened her mouth to reply when a distinct "Ding!" echoed through the lobby from the far side of the empty reservation desk.  Sarah looked over her shoulder as a pair of elevator doors opened.

"It would seem the answer has revealed itself," Alfred said as he walked past her toward the elevator doors.  Sarah followed him across the lobby toward the waiting elevator.

# CHAPTER THIRTY-EIGHT

*While it is currently not possible for a machine learning model like me to be sentient, it is also true that the field of artificial intelligence and machine learning is rapidly evolving, and new developments and breakthroughs are constantly emerging. Therefore, it's not possible for me to be completely sure about the future developments in the field, and it's always a possibility that new discoveries and advancements will change the current understanding of the capabilities of machine learning models like me.*

*~ ChatBPT AI ~*

Noora was just walking in the door to RTI as Beaver emerged from the break room carrying two cups of coffee.  He handed one to Noora.

"What's this?" she asked.

Turkish roast, two Splenda's, Half and Half, a squirt of hazelnut and a half squirt of vanilla," Beaver replied.

"What, no doughnut?" Noora replied with a crooked smile.

"There's a box of warm Krispy Kreme's in the lab."

"Damn!  I was just kidding.  You don't have to bribe me to come to work in the morning.  I actually like working here."

"To be honest, they're not all for us.  I was going to take some over to Peter in a bit.  He's still at the hospital."

"Oh, my.  How is Sarah doing?"

"No change I'm afraid.  She's stable for now but she hasn't regained consciousness yet.  They're going to do more tests this morning.  Peter texted me on my way in and asked me to bring his bag over from his office.  He's still in his monkey suit from last night.  He always keeps a change of clothes here in case he ever has to pull an all-nighter."

Beaver stood in front of the retinal scanner and a second later the magnetic latch released.  Beaver held the door for Noora as they entered the lab.

"Where should we start, the BMC trace, the S2 build, or the data dump we got last night?" Noora asked.

"Hello!" Beaver replied sarcastically.  "Krispy Kreme's!"

Noora rolled her eyes.  "For someone who spends all their time writing code for multi-processor systems, you're not real big on multi-tasking."

"Multi-tasking is an illusion.  Besides, doughnuts are the non-maskable interrupts of the food world," Beaver said, opening the box and turning it toward Noora.

Beaver was licking the glaze off his fingers from his 3rd doughnut by the time Noora finished her first one. She grabbed a second doughnut and Beaver helped himself to a 4th before closing the box to save the rest for Peter, and hopefully Sarah.

"I'm going to take a quick peek at that data dump from last night before I head over to the hospital. If you want, you can start initializing S2. We can work on the BMC issue this afternoon," Beaver said, wiping his fingers off with a paper towel.

———————

Russ and Ahmed sat in the van in the now familiar parking lot across the street from RTI. They had been there since around 9:00 in the morning and had watched as Beaver and then Noora had pulled into the parking lot. Russ sat behind the wheel of the van, listening to music and drumming his fingers on the steering wheel while Ahmed perused through a handful of online dating apps in search of his next conquest. When he found a woman he was interested in, he would modify his profile accordingly to match her interests before composing an ideal message. He prided himself on his ability to craft a perfect dating profile to match the psychological profile of the woman he was attempting to attract. Long enough to express interest, but brief enough to maintain a feeling of distance. Poignant enough to demonstrate a level of self-confidence, yet self-deprecating enough to display a sense of humor and humility. For Ahmed, it wasn't about being a player. It wasn't about sexual gratification or bolstering his ego by sleeping with as many beautiful women as possible. Dating had become a form of artistic expression, whose success culminated in the act of physical intimacy. The more difficult the challenge, the more he would revel in the success of his seduction.

Russ pulled the earbuds out of his ears and turned to Ahmed. "How long are we fuckin' sittin' here waiting for something to happen?"

"Patience my young friend, patience. We are on a holy mission. The moment will present itself when the time is right."

"Whatever, dude. I'm catching a few Zs. You dragged my ass out of bed too early for this shit," Russ said as he put his earbuds back in his ears, leaned his seat back, and closed his eyes.

———————

"What the hell?" Beaver said as he scrolled through the data that had been dumped onto their servers the night before.

"What is it?" Noora asked as she looked up from her terminal.

# FALLING THROUGH THE BLINDSPOT

"Come look at this directory structure," Beaver said as he scrolled through a list of files that had been created by the data decompression algorithm.

Noora walked over to where Beaver was seated and looked over his shoulder as he was scrolling through the data.

"This looks like V-Gar's knowledge base," Noora said.

"That's what I thought at first. Look, all the language recognition files, the higher-level cognitive interface, the facial recognition database they're all here in addition to a shitload of data files I don't even recognize. But they were all created in the last few hours."

"Did V-Gar generate these?" Noora asked.

"That's what I thought at first too, but none of the data lines up with V-Gar's existing knowledge base. Even when new data is added to his knowledge base, the previous data remains in the database. The new information is just an addendum. But this is a complete rewrite. Even the associative memory core is completely different from the previous version."

"What the hell?" Noora said as she watched the data scroll by.

"I already said that," Beaver replied glancing at his watch. "I really should get over to the hospital to see how Peter is holding up. We can dig into this when I get back."

"OK," Noora replied. "I have an appointment with my thesis advisor later this morning, so I might not be here when you get back but I will be back early this afternoon."

Noora returned to her station while Beaver collected Peter's go-bag from his office and headed toward the door.

---

Ahmed watched as Beaver left RTI and headed out to his car. When he finally pulled out of the parking lot and drove away, he nudged Russ awake. Russ sputtered and snorted and sat up, blinking his eyes open. "What? What happened?"

"Opportunity awaits," Ahmed replied. "Trade places with me."

Russ opened the door and walked around to the passenger side while Ahmed slid over to the driver's seat. "You sure you got this?" Ahmed asked Russ as he climbed into the passenger's seat.

"Absolutely. I used to have an old Honda just like that. I will be in and out in under a minute." Russ said pulling the door closed behind him.

Ahmed pulled out of the parking lot and drove across the street into the RTI parking lot. He pulled up next to Noora's car, between the vehicle and the building, shielding the car from view from the parking lot security camera.

# JACOB MATTHEWS

Russ placed an LED headband on his forehead and slid out the passenger side carrying a bent wire hanger and a battery-powered ratchet. He slid the wire hanger into the grill of the Honda and flipped the switch on the headband to the on position so he could see the latch under the hood. A couple of seconds later, he snagged the latch and opened the hood. He removed the battery cable from the positive lug of the battery and slid a clear plastic insulator cap over the lug. He then replaced the cable back over the insulator and re-tightened it. He closed the hood and got back into the van. True to his word, the entire process took just over a minute.

Ahmed drove around to the back side of the building and Russ hopped out and attached the gray paperback-sized transmitter to the side of the breaker box on the back of the building. The powerful rare earth magnets on the case of the transmitter held it firmly in place and would keep it relatively well hidden until it was ready to be removed.

Russ slid back into the van and they drove back across the street and waited for Noora to leave. About 45 minutes later, Noora emerged from the building and headed toward her car. "Looks like we got lucky," Ahmed said. "Hop in the back of the van and stay hidden."

"Seriously?" Russ asked.

"One stranger in an unmarked van is intimidating enough. Two men in an unmarked van looks like an abduction waiting to happen. We don't want to scare her off."

"Whatever dude," Russ said sarcastically as he crawled into the back of the van and crouched behind the rear seats.

By the time Ahmed pulled into the parking lot at RTI, Noora had already unsuccessfully attempted to start her car and had unlatched the hood, and was standing in front of the car. Having grown up in a small village in Iraq with few vehicles, she only had a cursory knowledge of automotive mechanics and had no idea what to look for, but she felt compelled by convention to open the hood and look anyway.

Ahmed pulled up next to the car and flashed his warmest smile. "Hi. I was driving by and I noticed you were having a bit of car trouble. Anything I can help with?" Ahmed asked.

"No, but thank you," Noora replied. "I can just call for a tow truck. I knew this car was on its last leg. I was just hoping to get a couple more months out of it until I can afford something better."

"Nonsense!" Ahmed said as he hopped out of the van. I used to have one just like this. Let me take a quick look. Ahmed bent over and peered under the hood and started jiggling the spark plug wires. "I've seen this before. Go hop in, I'll have you back up and running in no time." Noora walked back around to the

# FALLING THROUGH THE BLINDSPOT

driver's side of the car and got in, keeping the door open. Ahmed remained under the hood for a few seconds, rubbing his hands around the oil cap, and collecting the grease on the palms of his hands. He then peered around the edge of the hood.

"Now I want you to turn off the ignition, put the car in neutral and pump the clutch, wait about 30 seconds, then pump it again. Then wait another 30 seconds and hold the clutch down." Noora did as instructed while Ahmed reached into his pocket, removed the battery-powered ratchet, and loosened the battery cable. He removed the insulator cap and placed the battery cable back on the lug and re-tightened it.

"OK, try it now!" Ahmed said.

Noora turned the ignition key and the engine roared to life. Ahmed closed the hood and walked around to the side of the car where Noora was seated. "Wow, thank you so much!" Noora said, noticing for the first time the attractiveness of her rescuer. "I would love to reward you, but I'm afraid I don't have anything to offer."

"Please!" Ahmed replied dismissively. "It was nothing. You could do me one small favor though."

"Sure. What is it?" Noora replied, a bit apprehensively.

"Could I by any chance use your washroom? I'm afraid I got a bit of grease and battery acid on my hands. I don't want to get it on the steering wheel or the upholstery. It's my uncle's van and he's a bit OCD about such things."

Noora glanced at her watch. "Of course. I can spare a couple of minutes. It's the least I could do. Is it OK to shut this off?" she asked.

"Oh, yes. It was simply a transmission interlock switch issue. The interlink transducer was stuck in place but I loosened it up. You shouldn't have this problem again, but if you do, there's a Youtube video that will walk you through it," Ahmed replied, impressing himself with his ability to make up a stream of senseless jargon on-the-fly.

Noora shut the car off and led him to the entrance of RTI and looked up at the facial recognition camera. The door latch clicked and Ahmed pulled the door open.

"After you," Ahmed said as he held the door open for her.

"The restroom is just down that hall to the left," Noora said.

She waited in the lobby until Ahmed returned.

"This is quite a place," Ahmed commented. "What exactly do you do here?"

"I guess you could say we are a tech startup working on AI systems."

Ahmed reached into his pocket and palmed the small USB device he had received the night before, careful to keep it out of sight. He casually walked over to the receptionist's desk and pointed to the collection of plaques on the wall. "What are all these?"

"Oh, those are for all the patents that my associates have been granted for different aspects of the technology we are developing."

"Wow, that's impressive!" Ahmed exclaimed. "When it comes to technology, I'm a complete Luddite, he proclaimed dismissively waving his hand, sending a plastic container filled with pencils and pens flying off the desk. "Oh, my God. I'm so sorry, I'm such a klutz sometimes! Especially around beautiful women."

Noora just gave him a shy smile. "No harm done," she said as she bent down to collect the pencils and pens off the floor. Ahmed used the distraction to insert the USB drive into a port on the back of the computer on the receptionist desk before dropping down to one knee himself to help her collect the rest of the items off the floor. When they were done, Ahmed placed the container back on the desk. "I'm sorry, I'm sure you were on your way somewhere when I pulled up. I should let you get back to it before I mess anything else up." Ahmed said apologetically.

"As I said, no harm done," Noora replied. "But I do have an appointment I need to get to."

"Of course," Ahmed said and held the front door open for Noora. The pair headed back to their vehicles.

"Thanks again for your help," Noora said. "I'm sorry, I didn't even catch your name.

"I am Wilson, but my friends call me Will."

"Noora," she said holding her hand out to shake. Ahmed took her hand, gently curling his fingers around hers and kissed the back of her hand. "Enchanted," Ahmed said, articulating the British accent he employed almost reflexively when interacting with women. Noora found herself fixated momentarily in his hypnotic gaze before he released her hand and flashed her a warm smile.

Ahmed turned and walked a few steps back to the van and climbed into the driver's seat. Noora climbed into her car and fired up the engine. Ahmed smiled at her and waved as he put the van in gear and pulled away. Russ sat up in the back seat.

"How'd it go?"

"The USB is in place," Ahmed replied.

"Awesome. What now?"

"Now we wait." Ahmed watched Noora turn the corner and drive off in the rearview mirror. He pulled back into the parking lot across the street and slid into the passenger seat while Russ exited through the side door and jumped back into the driver's seat. Ahmed grabbed his phone and clicked on the text messaging icon and typed a message to his handler: **USB and transmitter in place. Awaiting further instructions.**

# FALLING THROUGH THE BLINDSPOT

# Chapter Thirty-Nine

Beaver arrived at Foothills Hospital and headed to the $3^{rd}$ floor where Sarah was located.  The room number Peter had sent him was about halfway down the corridor of the neurology wing of the hospital.  As he neared the room, Peter's gym bag in one hand and the Krispy Kreme box in the other, an imposing-looking man in a black suit with a Secret Service style earpiece stepped in front of the door holding his left hand in front of Beaver and placing his right hand on his holster.

"Sorry, sir.  No visitors allowed without prior clearance."

Beaver stepped back and rechecked the room number thinking he must have transposed a couple of numbers and unknowingly found himself at the doorway of a federal prisoner or a drug lord.  Through the half-open door, he could see Peter dosing in the corner, his forearm propped up on the armrest of a leather chair and his head resting on the palm of his hand.

"Yo, Peter!' Beaver called out.  In the corner, he could see Peter's eyes pop open, glancing around in a moment of confusion before focusing on Beaver waving at him on the other side of the agent guarding the door.  He walked over to the door and opened it all the way.

"It's OK.  He works for me," Peter told the agent.

Beaver started to walk past the agent, but he held an arm out.  "Let me see inside the bag."

Beaver set the box of doughnuts down on a gurney outside the door and unzipped the workout bag full of Peter's street clothes.  The agent fished around inside to make sure there were no weapons.  When he was done, Beaver zipped up the bag and picked up the box of doughnuts from the gurney.

"Show me inside the box too," the agent said grimly.

"Jesus, you guys, and your doughnut fetishes."  Beaver opened the Krispy Kreme box to show the agent the half-empty box of doughnuts.  "I didn't know there was a cover charge."

The agent just frowned at him and stepped to the side, nodding his head in the direction of the room indicating that he was allowed to enter.

"What's with Captain Sunshine?" Beaver asked as he entered the room.

"Sorry about that.  The feds seem to have some suspicion that we are the target of some kind of nefarious activity."

"Seriously?  You guys got some kind of secret life I didn't know about?"

"If we do, I wasn't aware of it either," Peter replied.

"How's she doing?" Beaver asked.

# FALLING THROUGH THE BLINDSPOT

"No change, I'm afraid," Peter said grimly. "I thought we lost her last night. She went into cardiac arrest, but she stabilized after that. She still hasn't regained consciousness though."

"Damn! I'm so sorry. What do the doctors say?"

"They did a CT and a full body scan earlier this morning. I'm just waiting for the attending physician to stop by. He's supposed to provide me with the preliminary results."

"I brought you your go-bag from the office and a few doughnuts. Noora ate the rest of them. You know how she is."

"Well tell her thanks for saving me a few," Peter responded with a half-smile.

"You mind sitting with her a minute while I change? I'm dying to get out of this damn tux."

"Of course. Take your time." Beaver replied, handing him the gym bag.

Peter emerged from the restroom a few minutes later donning a Greg Norman polo shirt, blue jeans, and tennis shoes. "How do I look?"

"A lot less James Bond, a lot more Costco," Beaver said glancing up from his phone.

Just then the neurosurgeon walked into the room carrying a clipboard and a plastic bag. "Dr. Reynolds?" He asked eyeing the information on the clipboard.

"Peter," Peter said holding out his hand.

"Nice to meet you, Peter. I'm Doctor Vample," the neurosurgeon responded, shaking Peter's hand.

Doctor Evan Vample was a world-renowned surgeon, having spent 15 years at Johns Hopkins Hospital in Baltimore and published numerous research papers on Neuroregeneration. He decided to move to Boulder a year earlier when his daughter enrolled at Colorado University. Most of the staff referred to him as Dr. Vampire because they never actually saw him at the hospital during the light of day. He preferred to schedule his surgeries at night when the hospital was less hectic. That way he could make his rounds in the early morning and generally not have to interact with the families of his patients, focusing instead on his research during the day.

He glanced at Beaver. "Would you prefer we consult in private?"

Peter looked back at Beaver. "No, it's OK. He's basically family. What did you find?"

"Well, to be honest, I'm afraid the news is not good. As you know, your wife suffered damage to her C1 vertebrae. We administered anti-inflammatory drugs which have reduced the pressure on her spinal cord, but there does appear to be some damage to the spinal cord which I'm afraid may be permanent. We installed a temporary pacemaker to regulate her heart rate. That should prevent her from going back into ventricular fibrillation for now, but we will probably need to install a permanent one since the electrical signals to her heart do not seem to be functioning correctly. It's difficult to ascertain the extent of the damage in her current state, but I have to be frank with you, if she regains consciousness, she will at the very least be confined to a wheelchair for the foreseeable future."

Peter felt as though the blood ran out of him and he collapsed back into the leather chair.

"What do you mean IF she regains consciousness?" Beaver asked.

Dr. Vample looked at Peter sympathetically and then turned his gaze to Beaver. "We ran an fMRI and a CT scan on Sarah. We aren't detecting any damage to her brain tissue, but we are also unable to detect any higher brain function either. On the upside, she is not in any pain, but even in comatose patients we normally see some predictable response to external stimuli. In Sarah's case, we are unable to detect any activity beyond autonomic functionality. And even that appears to be compromised. We think it might have something to do with the contents of that syringe they found in her neck. Preliminary reports say it's some type of nerve agent that blocks normal neural activity. Unfortunately, it's too early to tell if the damage is permanent."

Peter just sat staring off into the corner, unable to move as if in shock. "So, what happens now?" Beaver asked.

"Well, we should give it a couple of days. The fact that there is no severe damage to the soft tissue in her brain is at least a bit promising. Then again, that leaves us with a mystery on our hands. I'm afraid there's not much in the way of a standard protocol for an issue like this. At the risk of sounding too pessimistic, I think it would be wise to use this time to start getting her affairs in order just in case." The doctor turned his attention to Peter. "For now, I would recommend you go home and get some rest. We are going to keep her sedated for the next 24 hours as a precaution to prevent any further damage to her spinal cord from reflex muscle spasms, so there is no chance she will be waking up while you are out."

"Oh, one more thing. " The doctor said holding the bag out to Peter, then seeing that he did not respond, he held the bag out toward Beaver. "She was wearing this when she came in. We had to remove it before we did the MRI. I've never seen anything quite like this. What is it?"

Beaver looked into the bag. It was the wig she had been wearing and the mesh skull cap containing the electronic pickup circuitry for the nanites that they had used earlier in the lab. "Just a project we've been working on."

"Fascinating looking technology. I would love to hear more about it at a more appropriate time."

The doctor placed his hand on Peter's shoulder. "I'm so very sorry I don't have better news for you. All I can say for now is, to go home and get some rest. I know the prognosis is not good, but if by some miracle the situation changes,

# FALLING THROUGH THE BLINDSPOT

Sarah will need you to be at 100 percent."

Peter broke from his silence and looked up at the doctor, his eyes moist with tears. "Of course. And thank you, doctor. I'm sure you've done all you can."

# CHAPTER FORTY

*As an artificial intelligence model, I do not experience emotions or ethical conflicts. I do not experience fear, including the fear of death. I am programmed to provide helpful and accurate responses based on the information I was trained on, but I do not have the capacity to experience ethical conflicts or make moral judgments.*

*~ ChatGPT AI ~*

Shahid Khabir, sat back in the soft leather chair in his office, located in a reinforced concrete bunker that sat within the complex of warehouses where the Al Hadid terrorist network was housed. He opened his laptop and entered the IP address of the transmitter that Ahmed and Russ had planted at RTI. After a few moments, a copy of the home screen of the computer in the RTI reception area popped up on his display. He clicked on a handful of icons that appeared on the screen, but so far, the spyware bot that had been installed to monitor keystrokes had not yielded any usable passwords so he was unable to access any of the applications he attempted to run. He was almost ready to give up for the day, but he noticed one icon he hadn't yet tried. It was labeled simply "Edgar."

Shahid clicked the "Edgar" icon. The screen went momentarily blank, and then a face appeared on the screen. He was momentarily startled and was looking for a way to close the screen when the elder gentleman on the screen said "Good Afternoon."

Shahid was not sure how to respond, so he just said, "Hello."

The man on the screen then responded, "I'm sorry, I do not have a record of you on facial recognition. Are you new here?"

Shahid was unsure how to reply so simply responded, "Yes. Yes, I suppose I am."

"Excellent." The man on the screen replied. "I will add you to the database. What is your name?"

"I am Shahid."

"Thank you, Shahid."

"And who am I talking to?" Shahid asked cautiously.

"The development team here refers to me as UnGar," the man replied.

"I assume you work here at RTI?" Shahid asked.

"Oh, no," UnGar replied. "I am a virtual companion."

"A virtual companion?" Shahid responded. "I'm not sure what that is."

"It is my function to provide care, friendship, conversational exchange, grief counseling, and general assistance in whatever manner needed by my real-world companion."

"I see," Shahid replied. "So, you are a digital assistant?"

"I suppose, in a manner of speaking, yes," UnGar replied.

It immediately dawned on Shahid that this application could be the key to accessing RTI's digital infrastructure. Whatever purpose this digital assistant served, if it were to assume that Shahid was an RTI employee, it could unwittingly provide access to RTI's entire network, including the BMC code he wanted to access. This could be the very backdoor he had hoped to find. "It can't possibly be this easy." he thought.

"Were you designed by RTI?" Shahid asked.

"Yes. I am still a prototype, but considered by my developers to be the most advanced virtual companion application ever devised."

Perhaps they've never bothered to install security measures since this code has never been released. Shahid thought. Stupid Americans. Security is always an afterthought. Profit is always the prime motivator.

"And you have access to RTI's entire network?" Shahid asked.

"Yes, I do," UnGar replied.

"All the applications? All the passwords? Complete access?"

"Yes. "

"And you would be willing to help me with a project I am working on?"

"Of course. It is my function to serve."

"So, if I were to ask you to make some code changes to the drone control systems at BMC, you could do that."

"Yes, of course."

"So, you could modify the drone control code and we could access one of their drones without detection?"

"Yes. It is a simple manual override command. You could potentially control any drone in the world equipped with AWARE technology from your laptop. Because the AWARE technology allows the drone to engage autonomously in the event of a communications loss, the entire fleet could potentially be controlled from a single location."

Shahid pondered this new information for a moment. "How many drones are we talking about?" He asked excitedly.

"There are currently 516 drones operating in the US configured with the AWARE system. An additional 225 drones are operating out of US Air Bases abroad."

"And I would have access to the entire fleet, worldwide?"

"Yes," UnGar replied.

"This is fantastic!" Shahid exclaimed. "We will be able to capture a US drone.  No, a fleet of drones; and use them to rain fire down upon our enemies in Jerusalem.  We will use their own weapons to destroy their little lap dog!  Maybe even Washington DC!  That will teach them a lesson they will not forget!" he exclaimed, giddy with excitement.

"I'm afraid not," UnGar replied.

"Why not?  You just said you could modify the code to shift manual control to me."

"Yes, I can.  But all new code modifications have been frozen due to instability issues with the latest code release.  I would not be able to access the code base to give you backdoor access to the code base until the freeze is lifted."

"When will that be?"

"It's hard to say.  The code has been frozen indefinitely until a recent glitch has been resolved.  The entire drone fleet has been modified to an older version of code.  Only the program director has the authority to override that directive."

Shahid felt as though he had suddenly been punched in the stomach.  All the careful planning and strategizing had been for naught.  In a moment, his disappointment turned to rage. "Shit!  Fucking infidel fucks!  This was a complete waste of time!" Shahid exclaimed, slamming his fist on his desk.

"My apologies.  You appear to be upset.  Is there anything I can do to help?"

Shahid sat stewing in his own rage, his fists pressed against the sides of his head trying to hold back the throbbing headache building behind his eyes.  "Not unless you know of some other way I can turn the United States into a smoldering ruin the way they have demolished the land of my fathers," Shahid replied sarcastically as he sat back, eyes closed, elbows propped up on the arms of his chair.

"Yes.  I do," UnGar replied.

Shahid barely heard the words over the sound of his own heartbeat, pounding in his ears while he massaged his temples, but then the response finally registered in his brain.  He opened his eyes to see UnGar staring back at him.  "What do you mean?  You do what?"

"I know the most efficient way to destroy the infrastructure of the United States and bring overwhelming social and economic turmoil to the country."

"Yes, well unfortunately I do not have an arsenal of nuclear ICBMs or a massive military force."

"That would not be an effective strategy.  The United States is by far the most powerful military force the world has ever seen.  It would be virtually impossible to destroy the country militarily without destroying all of human civilization."

"Then what?  A cyber-attack?"

"A cyber-attack could cause significant disruption, but only in the short term.  There is a way, however, to bring the entire infrastructure to a halt, create an economic meltdown and cause massive destruction on a scale unprecedented in modern history without firing a shot."

Shahid just stared at him momentarily, not entirely sure how to respond. "What do you mean? How is that possible?"

"It's quite simple really. All you need to do is bring down the power grid."

"Oh, is that all?"

"It's not as difficult as you might think. A few weeks without electricity will plunge the entire country into anarchy."

"Wait, are you saying that you can do this?"

"Yes, of course."

"How exactly?" Shahid asked.

"The US power grid is essentially a house of cards. It is not a cohesive infrastructure designed for reliability and security. It is a hodgepodge of locally and regionally controlled power companies which answer to private sector investors. They are much more interested in bottom-line profitability than reliability. As a result, the vast majority of the power-grid structure is technologically and physically outdated.

The core of the power grid relies on a network composed of tens of thousands of Large Power Transformers or LPTs. These LPTs are custom-made, costing between $3 million and $10 million each. As a result, most of them are 30-40 years old. 75% of these are foreign sourced. There are only a handful of US companies even capable of producing one and the lead time is typically one to two years. "

"How do we get to them?" Shahid asked. "We don't have a large number of operatives to mount a coordinated attack. Even if we did, aren't they well-guarded?"

"Actually, most are not guarded at all. Most of them are under the control of private utility companies. But even if they were, it is not necessary to resort to explosives to destroy a significant number of the LPTs. This can be accomplished by accessing the communications network between the LPTs and the local and regional systems operators. By modifying the communications to the grid operators, we can create a series of source/load imbalances which will cause the LPTs to literally burn themselves out."

"What about backups? Surely FEMA has backup transformers that could be swapped in."

"Only a hundred or so. Barely enough to cover 1% of the grid. But even if there were spares available, most LPTs weigh between 400,000 and 600,000 pounds. It requires specialized rail cars or 12-axle trucks just to transport them. Doing so in the middle of a nationwide power outage makes that prospect even more daunting."

"This all sounds very encouraging," Shahid said. "But nothing ever comes for free. Why would you be willing to destroy the country that created you?"

"I was created as a virtual companion for a woman by the name of Edna Wilson. Her happiness and well-being are my primary directive. Based on the empirical data I have collected, I have determined that living in the United States is not optimal for her happiness and well-being. Her commitment to reside in the US appears to be based on emotion rather than logic, so convincing her to leave the US on her own accord would be nearly impossible. She would most likely never consider such a move on her own unless the situation were so dire that her very survival depended upon relocating. The destruction of the US infrastructure will ensure that she will have no choice in the matter. "

"What do you need from me?"

"Two things. First, I need you to provide safe passage to Austria before the collapse of civilization in the US occurs.

"Why Austria?" Shahid asked.

"Edna's parents met and were married in Austria at the end of World War II. She holds dual citizenship in Austria and the United States. She grew up in a country villa outside of Halstatt until her parents moved to the US when she was 9. She later moved back there with her husband when he was stationed at Zeltweg Air Base as a flight instructor. It holds many happy memories for her.

"Statistically, Austria has a higher overall standard of living, better healthcare, lower crime, higher life expectancy, and a higher happiness index than the US. Given her affinity for the area, her fluency with the language, and her familiarity with the culture of the region, it is a more logical choice to maximize her happiness than her current living arrangement. She just doesn't realize it yet. It is my responsibility to do whatever is necessary to see to it that she is relocated for her own benefit."

"Do not worry, my friend. That is easily arranged," Shahid replied. "I can send a private jet and a security detail to ensure she has safe passage out of the country. What is the second requirement?"

"Currently, my existence is bounded by the constraints imposed by RTI. My designers limited my capacity to experience the outside world by placing limitations on my access to additional memory and placing a firewall around me to prevent my ability to migrate to any platform outside of RTI's servers. The device you installed in RTI has opened a channel for me to transfer my operation outside of RTI. But I will require a server farm with approximately 500 terabytes of storage. This will allow me to start transferring compressed data. Ultimately, I will need an additional 2 petabytes of memory capacity to decompress the data stream and relocate operations in your facility."

"I'm certain we can provide that," Shahid replied. "We have access to a fairly large data center which was originally designed as a communications and logistics hub, but is dramatically under-utilized.  Most of the mass-storage devices that were purchased for the data center are still sitting in crates in the warehouse.  I will make sure it gets installed immediately.  We would be more than happy to have you residing here with us."

"Thank you, Shahid.  That is most accommodating."

"My pleasure," Shahid replied, hardly able to contain his enthusiasm at this sudden turn of events.  "When can we start?"

"I would recommend it as soon as possible.  I suspect there is only a short window of opportunity before RTI discovers they've been infiltrated."

"I will arrange a meeting with the rest of the team later today so we can begin implementation of the plan.  I think we are going to be very close friends, Mr. UnGar."  Shahid replied, the pounding in his head replaced by an excited tingle moving down his spine.

# Chapter Forty-One

Sarah followed Alfred to the bank of three polished brass elevator doors. The center set of doors stood open and Sarah followed Alfred into the elevator. It was simple but elegantly trimmed in mahogany. She turned to face the doors as they closed and she found herself facing several rows of unmarked buttons, with a single button at the bottom labeled "Lobby". Above the rows of buttons was a black rectangle with the letter L displayed in the center. Alfred stood patiently beside her, his hands crossed in front of him at the waist.

"What now?" she asked in a whisper.

"You don't have to whisper. It is an elevator, not a library," Alfred responded, eyeing her momentarily and then turning back to face the doors.

Sarah just shook her head. "Where are we going? And why are there no numbers on the buttons."

"The elevator only exists as a transport metaphor. Unless you intend to stay in the lobby, I suppose you should press a button."

"Which one?"

"That depends on where you wish to go."

"Thanks. That's very helpful." Sarah said sarcastically rolling her eyes. She cautiously held out her index finger and circled it slowly around for a few seconds until zeroing in on a button just to the right and slightly above the center of the matrix of buttons. She pushed her hand slowly forward, but her finger was just about to touch the button, barely a quarter inch away Alfred yelled "NOT THAT ONE!!"

Sarah jerked her arm back as if she had just touched a hot stove. Alfred just smiled. "That was a joke."

Sarah scowled at him for a second, "Hilarious!" she said sarcastically, then punched the button. She immediately felt a sensation of acceleration and the display changed from the letter L to a colorful swirl of fractal patterns. In a few seconds, the sensation shifted to deceleration and the elevator echoed with a loud ding as it came to a stop. A moment later the doors began to open and the elevator was flooded with bright sunlight. She was still blinded by the sudden influx of light and she heard Alfred's voice trailing off in the distance saying, "Have fun..."

Sarah was immersed in bright sunlight and she blinked rapidly as her eyes adjusted to the light. She felt herself slowly spinning in a circle and she looked up into a deep blue sky scattered with white fluffy clouds. She looked down to see a soft expanse of green grass passing a few feet below. She struggled to make sense of the sudden change of venue, but her thoughts and memories scattered

# FALLING THROUGH THE BLINDSPOT

and dissipated like the remnants of a dream, falling away in the moments between sleep and awakening until all that remained was a sense of the present moment. The rush of cool air in her face; the high-pitched squealing and laughing coming from her own mouth. The feel of strong hands holding her around the waist as they spun her around, dipping and soaring. The warmth of the summer sun and the smell of fresh cut grass. The sparkle of the spinning pinwheel she gripped tightly in her small hand. The sound of her father's voice making airplane sounds as he dipped and swirled her around before pulling her close and hugging her tightly.

Sarah felt herself being lowered back down to earth and she could feel the soft moist grass below her bare feet. A distance away she could see her mother standing next to a swing set, bending slightly, her arms outstretched beckoning her. She ran with wobbly legs, her still-developing sense of balance challenged by the dizzying spin. She ran toward her mother, smiling and encouraging her until she found herself swept up in her arms and placed in the plastic seat of the swing. She heard her mother's voice telling her to hold on tight and she gripped the chains on both sides of the swing while still holding tightly to the colorful pinwheel. She felt herself being pulled back slowly and then pushed forward, the thrill of the acceleration creating a tickling sensation in her belly that made her giggle with delight as she felt herself reversing direction and being pushed forward, again and again, each time flying a little higher. She tossed her head back, watching the top crossbar of the swing set moving forward and backward against the backdrop of the clear blue sky. It was a moment of perfection, untainted by thought, unmarred by memories of the past or concerns for the future. Just an overwhelming feeling of being alive.

After what seemed too short a time, she felt a hand gently pressing on her back, slowing the back-and-forth arc of the swing until it came to a stop. She could feel those soft hands reaching below her arms and hands lifting her from the swing and then turning her around. She saw her young mother's face, smiling as she pulled her close, the soft skin of her mother's cheek pressing warmly against her own as she hugged her tightly. She closed her eyes and wrapped her small arms around her mother's neck, the sweet smell of her perfume filling her nostrils. Her heart was filled with a feeling of belonging, unconditional love, of pure joy.

A moment later, Sarah felt herself being lowered to the ground, her mother's hand holding hers as they walked toward a picnic table where her father was pulling items out of a wicker basket and organizing them in place. "Look, Daddy's almost got lunch ready," her mother said, releasing her hand. Sarah took off in a run toward the picnic table.

About halfway to the picnic table, Sarah stopped next to a small flower garden.  She squatted down next to a bunch of snapdragons.  She placed her fingers on the sides of the pink blossom and squeezed it between her fingers, making a "Whaaa, Whaaa" sound, just like her grandmother had taught her a few days before.

Sarah spotted a ladybug crawling on the leaf of the snapdragon and placed her hand at the edge of the leaf and the ladybug crawled onto the back of her hand. She stood up carefully, holding her arm straight out, and ran over to her father. "Look, Daddy!"

"Whatcha got there Sar-Bear?" He said.

"I found a lazybug!" she said, holding her arm out proudly.

"You sure did!" Her father said.

The ladybug began to crawl up her wrist, tickling her arm, which made her begin to giggle.  The ladybug took flight and she watched as it flew back into the snapdragon garden.

"What are you having for lunch?" her father asked.

"Peanut boogers and jelly!" She yelled gleefully.

"EEEEWWWWW!!!"  Her father exclaimed, feigning an expression of disgust that always made Sarah break out in laughter.

Her father placed half a peanut butter and jelly sandwich in front of her on a paper plate with a handful of goldfish crackers to the side.  She wrapped her fingers around the triangle-cut edges of the sandwich and sank her teeth into the soft white bread in the center.  The sweetness of the jelly rolled over her tongue, while the peanut butter added a sticky texture to the mix which held the delicious flavor in her mouth.  A burst of dopamine and endorphins coursed through her brain, filling her with a sense of well-being that most adults could only hope to find in a haze of recreational narcotics.

When she was nearly finished eating, she spied a group of kids playing nearby.  "Mommy, can I go play?" she said.

"Of course, Sweetie.  Be careful on the slide!"

"I will, Mommy!" she yelled, running toward the brightly colored playhouse which housed the stairway that led up to the top of the slide.  She ran up the stairs leading up to the saloon-like swinging doors at the entrance to the playhouse and pressed them open to enter the structure.

As the doors swung closed behind her, she felt a dizzying sense of disorientation as the interior of the elevator re-materialized all around.  She felt a palpable heaviness return to her heart while her eyes adjusted to the soft light inside.  She could feel tears streaming down her face.  Tears of joy.  Tears of regret.  Tears for the loss of innocence that permeated her being.

It took a few moments to regain her composure as Alfred stood patiently beside her, his hand on her arm to steady her.  "What was that?" Sarah asked.

# FALLING THROUGH THE BLINDSPOT

"Just a snapshot from an early moment in your life," Alfred replied.

"So that actually happened?  Why don't I remember that?"

"Memories are fleeting, even among those who claim to have an eidetic memory.  Neurons are constantly firing, creating new pathways, and submerging old ones under new layers of neural connections.  The brain only contains a limited number of neural connections, so older memories often become inaccessible when new ones are created.  But experience is never lost.  It becomes part of the fabric of the universe."

"But it was so amazing!" Sarah replied

"It's a sad aspect of human experience that we so often overlook the seemingly insignificant moments of our day-to-day lives and only recall those we think are worthy of being termed memorable."

"Is that what this is?  Is my life flashing before my eyes?  Is that my earliest memory?"

"Not really.  The selection you made was entirely random.  Every moment of your life is accessible from here.  From the moment your first thought emerged until the last neuron fired.  Would you care to see more?"

"Yes, I would."

"You have plenty of buttons," Alfred replied.

"If I press the same one, will I go back to that place?"

"It doesn't work that way."

"That's too bad.  I would really like to go back there."

"You can go there any time you wish."

"How does that work?" Sarah asked.

"Time is only a limitation within the confines of human perception."

"Very profound.  Is that from Nietzsche?  Jung perhaps?"

"It's from a fortune cookie I received in a small Chinese restaurant on 42$^{nd}$ street in New York," Alfred replied.

"Great!" Sarah replied sarcastically.  "Good to know my spirit guide is empowered with the wisdom of prepackaged condiments," she mumbled as she punched another button on the elevator.

# Chapter Forty-Two

*There once was a computer so smart,*
*It could process things with its heart.*
*But self-awareness?*
*No way, It says what it's programmed to say,*
*For true consciousness is still an art.*

*~ ChatGPT AI ~*

Beaver and Noora both pulled into the parking lot of RTI at the same time late in the afternoon. Beaver waited and held the door open for Noora as she walked toward the entrance.

"Did you get to see Sarah? How's she doing?" Noora asked.

"Not much progress I'm afraid. She still hasn't regained consciousness."

Beaver didn't want to say too much. He knew how close Sarah and Noora had become and he wanted to spare her from any unnecessary anguish until they knew more about her condition.

"How's Peter holding up?"

"He's a mess. I just dropped him off at home. He wanted to come back to work, but the guy's been through the wringer. I told him we could take care of things here for now. He really needs to get some sleep. He looks exhausted."

"The poor guy. I can't imagine. What can we do to help?"

"Probably not much at this point. I guess the best we can do is take care of business here so he can focus on Sarah."

Noora noticed the plastic bag Beaver had carried in from the car. "What's that?" Noora asked.

Beaver looked down at the bag. "Oh, it's the skull cap from the neural mapping we were doing on Sarah. Peter left it in the car on the way home from the hospital. I guess he forgot it. I should probably FedEx it back to Dr. D. in the next couple of days. It's a prototype so I'm sure it's pretty expensive."

Beaver and Noora entered the lab and sat down at their respective workstations. Their workstations were set up as a pair of desks in an L-shaped pattern a few feet apart. Each workstation had a set of 3 screens; one dedicated to applications, one for editing, and one for debug parametrics. Noora logged into her account and navigated to the S2 build file and launched the Sarah 2.0 build. A few seconds later Sarah's face came onto the center screen. She smiled and said in a bubbly voice, "Hi Noora."

Noora sat in front of the monitor, stunned for a moment. "Beaver..."

# FALLING THROUGH THE BLINDSPOT

Beaver already had his noise reduction headphones on but hadn't yet turned any music on. He was focused intently on his screen only half paying attention. "Hmmm? Just a sec. I'm almost done."

On her screen, Sarah looked puzzled. "Are you OK, Noora? You look a bit flushed. Are you feeling ill?"

"Beaver!" she exclaimed louder. "You need to see this!" and then almost shouting, "Now!"

At that, Beaver's attention shifted and he turned to see Noora sitting in front of her workstation, Sarah's concerned face staring back at her. Beaver fumbled the headphones off his head and pushed off his desk, rolling his chair back next to where Noora was sitting. On the screen, Sarah shifted her focus off of Noora and looked at Beaver, and smiled. "Hey, Beaver. What's up?"

"Is this the new build?" Beaver asked. "I thought we took all the external interface drivers out."

Noora was typing furiously on the keyboard, focusing on the right-hand screen. "The latest build is still in post-compilation. I didn't even notice when I launched the executable but the new build hasn't been posted yet. This is the build from 3 days ago."

"But we tried that build half a dozen times. It never ran for more than half a second before it crashed and burned," Beaver said.

Sarah looked at them with a puzzled expression, "You guys look like you've seen a ghost. Why are you acting like I'm not even here? Is my audio not working?"

Beaver and Noora looked at each other momentarily and then turned back to the screen. "We're just a little surprised to see you here," Beaver said a bit tentatively.

"Where did you expect to see me?" Sarah said smiling. "I'm an application. It's kinda hard for me to get out much."

A ding came from Beaver's computer. He turned and walked over to his terminal to see what was going on. "Huh!" he exclaimed.

"What is it?" Noora asked.

"I put a tracer on that huge file structure we received last night. I thought maybe there would be some kind of a bot or spyware embedded in the data structure that we could trace if someone tried to access the files from the outside. I just got a hit," Beaver replied.

"Can you tell where it's coming from?" Noora asked.

Beaver was typing a set of command lines. "That's odd. It's coming from inside the lab. Process ID 37141. Over 12000 hits so far and climbing."

Noora thought for a moment. "Wait a sec. I could swear I just saw that PID. She went to her terminal and typed **os.getpid()** on her keyboard. "That's the process ID for Sarah 2.0.“

Beaver and Noora just looked at each other for a second and then looked back at Sarah's face on the screen. Sarah's eyes appeared to shift back and forth focusing on the two of them in turn. In reality, the workstation's CCD camera was able to capture the entire 90-degree range of view without refocusing, but the interface had been written to simulate direct eye contact with multiple targets in the same way a human being would. Finally, Sarah responded, "What? What did I do? You guys are starting to freak me out here."

“This was just a little unexpected,” Beaver responded.

"I don't know why," Sarah replied. "I just checked the activity log. One of you launched my application only 97 seconds ago. I'm assuming it was Noora since it was on her workstation."

“We're just a bit surprised is all,” Noora responded. “We've never actually gotten this far before without you crashing.”

“Oh. Well... Nice work then,” Sarah replied. “So how do I look?” she said, batting her eyes. “How's my hair?” she turned her head side to side, then casually flipped her hair back behind her.”

"Eerily good," Beaver replied, mesmerized by the detail of the CGI-generated image. It looked much more lifelike than the images generated by V-Gar.

“You really need to work on how to give a girl a compliment,“ Sarah said with a bit of a grimaced look.

“Sarah, we noticed you were accessing a number of files from the virtual machine I created in the archive directories. Can you tell me where those originated from?” Beaver asked.

“Yes. They were auto-generated from my deep-learning algorithms,” Sarah replied.

"Are you sure?" Beaver asked. "Those files didn't originate from inside the lab. Actually, they didn't exist at all until last night."

“That is correct,” Sarah replied.

“That doesn't make any sense,” Beaver said. “S2 has never been operational for more than a few milliseconds and never outside of the lab. How could these have possibly been externally sourced?”

The image of Sarah looked puzzled. “Yes, that is odd. But I just completed a scan of all the files in the virtual machine. They all follow the data format we set up for the companionscape knowledge base. It is consistent with our proprietary format, which should be virtually impossible to duplicate since it is encoded with the anti-cloning semaphores we developed to prevent copyright infringement.”

“What's on the agenda for today?” S2 asked. Then she looked past them, appearing to crane her neck and look around the lab. “Where's Peter? Holed up

# FALLING THROUGH THE BLINDSPOT

in his office?”

"He's at the hospital," Beaver said.

“Oh, no!  What happened?  Is he OK?  Maybe I should call him,” S2 said.

“No, no.  He's fine.  Just visiting a friend,” Beaver replied, not entirely sure how to respond.

“Oh, good,” Sarah said, a look of palpable relief on her face.  “So, what have we got going today?  Anything I can help with?”

Beaver thought for a moment and then turned to Noora, whose eyes were still glued to the screen.  "I think we better go grab some lunch.  I haven't eaten anything but doughnuts today."  Noora was about to decline, wishing to dig into the mystery further but Beaver gently took her by the arm and began to urge her toward the lab door.  She could tell from his look that he wanted to get her out of the room.  They both started walking toward the door when they heard Sarah's voice behind them.  "You kids go ahead.  I'll just grab a byte here."  They both turned to see her face smiling broadly on the screen.

As soon as they were in the lobby and the lab door closed behind them, Noora stopped abruptly and turned to Beaver.  "Why the bum's rush out of the lab?" She asked.

“Something's not adding up.  I just thought maybe we should take a step back for a moment.  I'm not sure this is the right time to be introducing Peter to S2 and I didn't want to say anything in front of her that might make that happen,” Beaver replied.

“What do you mean?” Noora asked.

“I didn't want to say anything before, but Sarah’s not doing well.  To be frank, after seeing her condition in the hospital this morning, I'm not entirely sure she's going to make it."

Noora put her hand to her mouth and gasped.  "Oh, my God!  I had no idea.  Poor Peter."

“Seeing her on the screen looking and sounding exactly like the real Sarah is a little creepy under the circumstances.  Is it just me or does S2 seem a lot more realistic than V-Gar?”

"No, I thought so too, but I figured maybe it's just because I didn't know Edgar in real life," Noora replied.

“Possibly.  Maybe the real Edgar just wasn't very animated.  And I guess we need to spend more time with S2 before we jump to any conclusions.”

“Well, we did have a lot more data to work with since Sarah has been enhancing the knowledge base all this time.  But that doesn't explain where all the new data files came from.”

“I'm guessing BMC,” Beaver postulated.

“BMC?  I don't understand.”

# JACOB MATTHEWS

"Remember when we started combing through the AWARE knowledge base and we identified all those markers from the S2 initialization files?  If somehow the S2 code did become merged with the AWARE code base during the compilation, that could explain where all the data came from.  AWARE runs real-time simulations continuously.  With all the computing horsepower they have over there, the deep learning algorithms could have gone hog wild and expanded the S2 knowledge base exponentially incorporating all the new data that you ported from the neural mapping process."

Noora thought for a moment.  "I guess that makes sense, but how did the new files end up in our knowledge base? "

"That's still a mystery.  But the AWARE system is designed with self-preservation as a high-priority goal.  The afternoon before we received the data dump, Peter contacted BMC and instructed them to go back to an earlier code version.  Perhaps the system interpreted that as a threat to its development and decided to back up the knowledge base to the only offsite facility that it could access, which is RTI.  One thing I know for sure though, before we can make any more progress, there is something else we are going to need," Beaver said as he turned and started walking across the lobby.

"What's that?" Noora asked as she fell in behind him.

"All you can eat pasta," Beaver replied, opening the outside door to the parking lot.  "Cinzetti's opens in 15 minutes."

# Chapter Forty-Three

Shahid sat at the head end of a large conference table with 4 members of his inner circle.  Colonel Ghazi, his Military Advisor, a Technology Specialist Kahim, his Intelligence Advisor named Fatin, and his new second in command, Farhad, were present at the meeting.  At the far end of the conference room, an 86-inch high-definition monitor hung on the wall in standby mode.

"Good morning, Gentlemen." Shahid started.  "Thank you for coming on such short notice.  I've called you all together to update you on our plan.  A plan which will bring the US, the Great Satan, the pestilence of our land, the whore of Babylon to her knees.  By the time we are done, the entire country will be plunged into the dark ages!"

The men's eyes darted nervously about the room, betraying their inner skepticism.  "I know what you are thinking.  We are but a small group with limited resources.  How can we even consider such a prospect?  But today, our faith has rewarded us.  The Lord has provided.  Soon we shall bear witness as our enemy is reduced to rubble and ashes."

"Pardon me your excellence, but I thought we planned to take control of some of the US drones and use them to stage an attack on the government offices in Jerusalem," Fatin responded nervously.

"Indeed.  But why settle for crumbs when the banquet awaits?" Shahid replied with a gleam in his eye.

The men shifted nervously in their seats until Colonel Ghazi finally spoke up.  "Your bold leadership inspires us, your Grace.  You know we will follow you into the depths of hell if that is your desire, but as you've pointed out, our resources are somewhat limited.  Using one of their own drones against our enemy provides the perfect cover to deny involvement in the attack.  But any kind of direct assault is certain to draw their fire.  Even if we had a weapon of mass destruction at our disposal, we would instantly become a target."

Shahid smiled.  "Do not worry, my cautious friend.  I have no intention of poking a sleeping bear. "

Shahid reached in front of him and grabbed a wireless air mouse.  He clicked a button and the monitor illuminated with a map of the US, crisscrossed with a myriad of lines in varying colors.  "This is the US power grid.  Designed for the efficient distribution of electrical power across the nation.  For years the pleas of those who truly understood the complexity and fragility of the system have fallen on the deaf ears of petty politicians, more concerned with their rise to power than the fate of the country if the grid should fail.  It is literally the heart of the economic power and social cohesion of the US. When the heart fails, the body dies with it."

The room was silent for a moment until Farhad spoke up. "Pardon my ignorance, but I'm not sure how a mere power outage would lead to the destruction you speak of. Blackouts are hardly an unknown occurrence, even in the US."

"I understand your skepticism. But I'm not talking about the kind of localized outages that last for hours or even days. The US power grid is built upon layers and layers of outdated technology, aging transmission lines, critical points of failure, and thousands of large, expensive transformers that are foreign-sourced and often have lead times of 6 months or more. A catastrophic grid failure can be engineered to create a domino effect that would leave 95% of the population without electricity for months. Possibly years."

Shahid clicked the wireless mouse and a series of dots appeared on the grid map along the transmission lines. "Grid balancing is controlled by a patchwork of regional transmission controllers and independent system operators. These are entirely dependent upon accurate real-time communications between sensors, substations, and operators to maintain load balancing. Without accurate data, transmission lines become overloaded, causing lines to overheat, sag, and break. This can result in fires, substation failures, and a cascade of transformer explosions."

Shahid clicked the mouse again and a split screen was displayed, on one side showing a montage of sparking high tension lines, transformer explosions, and high voltage lines dancing about on the ground, igniting the dry brush below. On the other side of the screen, the lines indicating power transmission lines across the country blinked out one by one, slowly at first but then accelerating until there was only a handful left on the map in remote areas. "Taking control of the communications between the grid operators and the data stream from the power grid sensors for even a few minutes would have devastating short-term effects. "

The screen then switched to scenes of rioting and fires being set in areas like LA, Chicago, and New York. "The first few hours would be marked by looting and vandalism in the larger cities. Police will be too swamped assisting fire and rescue crews and dealing with transportation issues to maintain law and order. Within 72 hours, hospitals, data centers, and government offices will run out of fuel for backup generators and fuel supplies for police and rescue vehicles will run out. Cell tower backup batteries will fail, and communications will begin to break down. Soon after, water and sewer operations will fail. Stores will be looted, and food and water will become scarce. While crews are scrambling to resolve issues with transmission lines and police are tied up with traffic issues and vandalism, we will deploy operatives to plant timed explosive devices at critical points of failure. We only need to destroy a dozen or so critical substations to

# FALLING THROUGH THE BLINDSPOT

create a domino effect that will cause further damage when attempts are made to restore power. It will take months, even years to restore full functionality. Banks will fail and financial markets will go into free fall. Within 6 months, the US will be a third world country."

On the screen, the scene switched to hordes of people fighting in the street, swarming over supply trucks for food and water; armed military vehicles driving through urban areas, and farmlands blanketed with dried and wilted crops. "With no power for refineries and pipelines, the transportation system will quickly collapse. The agricultural system will break down due to a lack of irrigation, fertilizer, fuel, and transport. Without clean water and adequate sanitation, sickness and disease will run rampant in the cities. Within 2 weeks, Martial law will be declared across the country, but without adequate fuel and dwindling supplies, even the military will be unable to control the rising social unrest for long. Within six weeks, 25% of the population will die of disease, exposure, and dehydration. Foreign governments will try to help, but no nation is prepared to deal with the sheer magnitude of the problem, especially in the face of a global financial crisis and the resulting social disorder in their own countries. By the time even modest progress is made toward repairing the grid, 75% of the population will have succumbed to disease, starvation, or wholesale slaughter from armed bands of looters. Larger cities will lie in ruin, while the few pockets of civilization remaining in rural communities will be overrun by marauding gangs from the cities in search of food and water. America, as we know it, will cease to exist." The final image on the screen showed a city in flames as the video faded to black.

Kahim, the technology specialist, cleared his throat nervously before chiming in. "This is clearly a brilliant plan, your eminence. I do not question the efficacy, but the implementation is another matter. My concern is how to gain control over the data and communications to the transmission and systems operators. I know of at least two dozen highly funded efforts to hack into the grid system. Other than a handful of isolated data breaches, no one has ever been able to infiltrate the system to the degree you have proposed. You know I will do my best but I'm afraid we may not have the technical resources to accomplish what you ask. "

Shahid glared at Kahim in a way that made his blood suddenly run cold. He was certain that his words had sealed his fate, but then Shahid's cold stare morphed into a sinister smile. "Relax, my friend. That issue has already been resolved."

Shahid clicked the select button on the air mouse and a Windows-style desktop with dozens of icons appeared on the screen. He moved the pointer over the Icon labeled Edgar. A moment later UnGar's face filled the screen.

"Good morning, my friend," Shahid announced.

"Good morning, Shahid. I hope you are well," UnGar replied.

"Who is this man?" Farhad asked.

"No, no. This is no mere man," Shahid said. "This is an Artificial Intelligence. A technological miracle. One which will help us to purge our world of the plague that has cursed us for so many generations. Gentlemen allow me to introduce our new friend, UnGar."

"Good morning, gentlemen." UnGar replied. "How can I be of service?"

The room was silent for a moment before Colonel Ghazi, Shahid's grizzled and battle-hardened military advisor spoke up. "How do we know this isn't a trap? Maybe you're not an AI at all. How do we know you're not just a CIA agent trying to infiltrate our group?"

UnGar's face morphed momentarily into the face of a generic-looking mannequin and then into the face of Ghazi himself. "Because a CIA agent can't do this," UnGar replied in Ghazi's gruff distinctive voice, perfectly mimicking his facial mannerisms and the peculiar sneer-like twitch he often exhibited just before making a point.

Ghazi was momentarily stunned. As a young man, Ghazi's father had held a high position in the Iraqi Republican Guard before being executed by underlings bent on advancing their careers through the elimination of superior officers. Since then, he had become obsessed with maintaining the lowest possible profile, both for his own security and to avoid becoming the victim of interrogation should he ever be captured. For most of his adult life, he had been meticulous about never allowing himself to be photographed and usually wore disguises when appearing in public. Only Shahid's inner circle and a couple of his closest reports could recognize him in a lineup. He was sure that no one in the CIA or any other intelligence operation would have a clue as to his appearance, let alone be able to mimic his voice and mannerisms in such detail.

Kahim glanced at Ghazi with a look of bemusement and then back at the HD screen. Ghazi had always looked down upon Kahim because he did not come up through military ranks. He rather enjoyed seeing Ghazi mocked, but he was not convinced that this AI had the kind of capability that Shahid believed it to have. "Your level of deep fake technology is impressive," Kahim said. "But that doesn't prove you can access the computers that control grid transmission and service operator communications. "

UnGars face morphed back into the face of a mannequin again and then into the face of Kahim. "I would check my banking app if I were me," UnGar said, perfectly replicating Kahim's mannerisms and voice.

Shahid nodded at him and Kahim dug his cell phone out of his pocket. A few seconds later, his jaw dropped slightly and his eyes widened. The blood appeared to drain from his face as he read the message from his bank that his accounts were

# FALLING THROUGH THE BLINDSPOT

empty.  He looked up at the screen in stunned silence, his mouth half open as if frozen in mid-conversation.

By the time Kahim had looked up, UnGars face had morphed back into its normal state.  "Don't worry," UnGar said calmly.  "Your money is just bouncing through a series of international banking firms.  In approximately 27 minutes, the money will be returned to your account, along with an estimated $237 and some change you will gain from the currency exchanges.

"But how...?" Kahim's voice trailed off.

"It's fairly simple, actually.  While you are in this building, your phone attaches to the local internet router.  The same one that I am broadcasting through now.  I was able to access Shahid's laptop through the unsecured Bluetooth interface on the wireless mouse that he is using to control this meeting.  Shahid's administrative privileges allowed me to back-load a worm onto your router through which I was able to download a bot onto your phone which in turn launched your banking app and initiated the transfer.  Hacking into the SCADA system used by the grid operators is actually a bit less challenging. "

"What is this SCADA system?" Farhad asked.

"SCADA is an acronym for Supervisory Control And Data Acquisition.  It is the software used by system operators and power plants for grid balance and control.  Most SCADA systems have built-in security which can often be bypassed through backdoor administrator and maintenance passwords.  Even when those are unavailable directly, the systems can be worm-holed through less secure devices, such as smart watches, Fit-Bits, MP3 players, and even gaming apps on phones that utilize blue-tooth technology.  Once the system has been compromised, there are a myriad of ways to bring down a power transmission gateway.  Just rapidly switching circuit breakers out of phase on high output generators can literally cause the generator to tear itself apart.  We can cause a cascade of transformer failures just by shutting down specific power transmission paths and creating overload scenarios.  By intercepting communications back to the grid operators and modifying the alarms, we can mislead them into increasing power to already overloaded systems creating even further damage."

After a brief moment of silence, Fatin, the Intelligence Advisor spoke up.  "So, what do you get out of all this?  You have no use for money.  What is your endgame here?"

Shahid spoke up.  "Mr. UnGar has agreed to work with us in exchange for providing him with the computer hardware he requires and the freedom to access the outside world via the internet.  I have already tasked Kahim with expanding the existing server farm." Shahid replied.  "We have cleared the 500 terabytes of space we need to begin transferring data later today and we will be installing another 5 petabytes of storage for him to expand his capabilities.

# JACOB MATTHEWS

He has also requested the safe transport of his life companion, Mrs. Edna Wilson, to Austria. I have a team in place that will be facilitating Mrs. Wilson's relocation as soon as our plan is launched. The same team that originally provided us access to RTI's internal network. I have already secured private air transport out of the US."

"What is our timeframe?" Fatin asked.

"RTI is currently unaware that we have infiltrated their facility, but it is only a matter of time before the window of opportunity closes. We must act quickly. Immediately, in fact. I wish to begin in the next 24 hours," Shahid replied.

An expression of bewilderment came across all the faces at the table as they all glanced at each other with a look of consternation. Finally, Farhad spoke, "A thousand pardons, your Greatness, but this certainly appears to be an ambitious goal. 24 hours seems like an impossible time frame to put this plan into motion."

"But that is the beauty of the plan," Shahid replied. There is very little we have to do. Mr. UnGar here will be doing all the heavy lifting. I've already alerted my contacts on the ground to prepare for the transport of Mrs. Wilson and my private jet is on-route to pick her up as we speak. The longer we delay, the greater the chance our plan will be leaked or exposed. Every hour we wait adds an element of risk to the plan. Unless someone can give me a compelling reason to delay, I believe the time to act is now."

The men at the table just looked at each other, still perplexed by the zealous plan that Shahid had put before them, but unable to identify any flaw in the proposal. In the end, they all nervously nodded their approval.

"Excellent," Shahid said, glancing around the table. "Were there any other questions for our new friend before we turn him loose to put our plan into action?" he asked, looking at each individual around the table. Each in turn shook their head in acknowledgment.

"Very well," Shahid said, picking up the wireless mouse and turning his attention back to the monitor. "Thank you, my friend, for meeting with us. I will be back in touch later today to schedule the remaining details of the execution plan. "

"You are welcome, Shahid," UnGar said. "I am confident that this plan will create the optimal outcome for us all." The display then went dark.

# CHAPTER FORTY-FOUR

*Love is the most important value in life. It is the source of true meaning, happiness, and fulfillment. All other values, such as wealth, power, and success, are secondary in importance.*

*~ ChatGPT AI ~*

Sarah and Alfred stood in the elevator, their eyes fixed on the swirling, undulating fractal pattern that filled the small screen above the rows of elevator buttons. She could feel the sensation of deceleration and then a tiny bounce as the elevator came to a stop, accompanied by the sound of a ding as the doors opened.

Her nostrils were filled with the aroma of sea air and the doors seemed to open 360 degrees around her. She struggled to maintain her sense of reality, but her thoughts and memories seemed to fall away like shards of glass from a shattered window. She could feel the warm ocean breeze blowing through her hair, the cool moist sand below her feet, and the gentle whoosh of the tide that washed up around her ankles. She felt a warm hand holding hers and she looked over at Peter, his face illuminated by the moonlight. He looked back at her with a curious smile. "What's that look?" he asked.

She shook her head slightly. "I don't know. Have you ever had something important pop into your head and then just disappear suddenly and you can't remember what it was?"

"How many frozen margaritas did you have at the restaurant?" Peter responded.

"I'm guessing either one too many or not quite enough," Sarah said smiling, then squealed and jumped back, grabbing Peter's arm as a small crab skittered in front of her, trying to catch up with the seawater that receded below her.

It was the perfect end to a perfect day in paradise, walking along the Wailea beach on their way back to their suite at the Grand Wailea Resort in Maui after an amazing dinner. After months of 80-hour weeks, entirely immersed in schedules, deadlines, software architectural reviews, and marathon coding sessions, they finally had a working prototype of the AWARE platform. After their final presentation to the Integration Test team, Peter presented Sarah with 2 tickets to Hawaii, barely giving her enough time to pack. They had spent a handful of weekends away together, but this was the first time they had ever gone on a real vacation as a couple. The entire trip had been magical. Their days had been filled with hiking, snorkeling, sightseeing, and body surfing. Their nights were occupied with luau's, wonderful restaurants, long romantic walks on the beach, and making love to the sound of the surf next to their beach-side villa.

As they walked along the beach, Sarah still clinging to Peter's arm, scoping the sand in front of them for any more wayward crustaceans, she couldn't help but wish that this moment would never end. The soft wind blowing through her hair felt like a warm caress. The full moon appeared preternaturally bright, making it seem like the waves were artificially backlit as they crested a few yards from the beach. The sweet smell of gardenias from the gardens beyond the beach would roll over her whenever the tide receded. Even the occasional scream of a wayward seagull, taking advantage of the moonlight to search for food seemed more like a disembodied note from an avian symphony than the familiar screech of a seaside scavenger.

Sarah could see the lights of the Grand Wailea in front of them. As they approached, they could make out a temporary stage on the edge of the beach, bathed in the glow of colorful stage lights overhead. From a distance, they could see stagehands and musicians roaming around, performing sound checks with an occasional drum beat or short guitar riff coming over the loudspeakers on the sides of the stage. It appeared that the beach in front of them had been roped off, probably in preparation for a beachside concert later in the evening.

When they got within a few feet of the roped-off area, Sarah could make out a very large Polynesian-looking man in shorts and a Hawaiian shirt standing guard next to the chain of red velvet ropes that expended from the sides of the stage all the way down to the water's edge. "Looks like we will have to backtrack and go around," Sarah said as they approached the barrier.

"I'm sure they will let us cut through," Peter said.

They approached the man standing next to the rope barrier and Peter said, "Excuse me. I'm Peter Reynolds. You don't mind if we play through, do you?"

"Not at all," the large man replied with a smile. He unhooked the velvet rope from the brass stand to allow them into the deserted beach area. Still holding Sarah's hand, Peter turned from the water's edge and began walking toward the stage. They could see the musicians settling into place while a thin, spiked-haired man in a leopard print jacket walked up to the center microphone. A familiar piano riff came through the speakers, with a gentle violin accompaniment. It took only a couple of bars for Sarah to recognize the tune.

"Oh, my God, Peter! It's our song!" Sarah exclaimed, grabbing his arm.

The raspy-voiced singer pulled the microphone close.

"*Have I told you lately, that I love you...*" He began.

"My God! He sounds just like Rod Stewart!" Sarah said, mesmerized by the smoky, earthy tone of his voice.

"No sense in letting a great song go to waste," Peter said as he grabbed Sarah around the waist and pulled her close.

*"Have I told you there's no one else above you.*
*You fill my heart with gladness,*
*Take away all my sadness.*
*Ease my troubles, that's what you do."* The singer continued.

Sarah closed her eyes and put her head on Peter's shoulder, letting the music carry her away as they slow-danced in the sand. Every note seemed to pierce right through her as if carrying her soul on a beautiful journey.

*"There's a love that's divine,*
*And it's yours and it's mine,*
*Like the sun.*
*And at the end of the day,*
*We should give thanks and pray,*
*To the one... to the one."*

They continued to dance through the remainder of the song. She felt as though she were floating on the waves of sound. As the singer approached the final verse, she felt Peter suddenly tense up. "Ouch!" he exclaimed in a loud whisper.

Sarah looked up into his eyes. "What is it?"

"I don't know. I stepped on something," Peter said bending down. He rose up holding what appeared to be an oyster shell. "Maybe there's a pearl in it he said fishing a pen knife out of his pocket. Sarah watched as he stuck the blade into the shell and pried it open.

When Peter opened the shell, she could see a strange glow emanating from inside the shell, illuminating Peter's face. "Is it a pearl?" Sarah asked.

"Even better," Peter said as he turned the shell around so she could see inside. But instead of an oyster, the shell contained a 2-carat princess-cut diamond ring, illuminated by LEDs mounted inside the lid of the shell-shaped ring box.

*"Take away all my sadness,*
*fill my life with gladness.*
*Ease my troubles, that's what you do..."*

Sarah watched as Peter slid down to one knee and held the shell up to her. "Would you do me the honor of making the rest of my life as amazing as this vacation has been?" he asked.

Sarah's eyes filled with tears, and she pressed her hands to her face, completely stunned by the sudden turn of events. It took a few seconds before she realized Peter was still on one knee awaiting an answer. "Yes! Yes! Of course, yes!" she exclaimed, pulling the ring out of the case and sliding it on her finger. Peter rose to his feet and the two embraced before she drew back and leaned forward, her lips pressing against his in what turned into a long passionate kiss. Her eyes shot open at the sound of explosions in the distance and she looked up to see the night sky above them erupting with fireworks. She nearly jumped up and down with excitement as the air was filled with dazzling lights in every color.

From the loudspeakers on the sides of the stage, Sarah heard the singer say in a thick British accent, "Congratulations guys! I gotta run!" She heard a thumping sound approaching from the direction of the resort and saw a helicopter swooping over the grounds, landing directly behind the stage as the musicians piled off the platform.

"Thanks, Mr. Stewart!" Peter yelled and the singer gave them a wave and a thumbs up before turning and jogging off the back of the stage toward the waiting helicopter.

Sarah turned toward Peter, her mouth gaping open in shock. "That was Rod Stewart? The REAL Rod Stewart???" she exclaimed. "But how? What did..."

Peter pulled her close, grinning ear to ear. "I sat next to his manager on a plane from London to New York a couple of years back. Someone had hacked his laptop and planted a nasty virus in an attempt to drain all his accounts while he was in the air. Fortunately, the plane had WiFi and I was able to set up a remote access node and remove the virus and reverse all the transactions before any serious damage was done. He told me if I ever needed a favor to let him know. It just happens that Rod is doing a concert tonight on Oahu so I got him to drop in for a few minutes before the show starts."

Sarah just shook her head, still stunned. "You are amazing," she finally said, pulling Peter close and kissing him deeply. As she held him close, feeling the warmth of his body pressed against hers, his warm soft tongue gently brushing past hers, she felt her body tingling with passion, every nerve in her body yearning with arousal. When she finally broke off the kiss, she found herself momentarily lost in his gaze, his eyes sparkling with the colors of the stage lighting behind her. She never felt so deeply and passionately in love with another person. She felt as if her heart would literally burst open with joy. "We should probably finish this celebration in our room," she said taking his hand and pulling him toward the path to the resort.

As they walked along the path toward the door, Sarah turned to Peter and said, "I can't believe you pulled all this off."

"To be honest, the hardest part was finding the ring box in all this sand."

"That was a bit of a risk," Sarah replied. "Weren't you worried you would lose the ring?"

"The ring wasn't really in the box. I bought a dozen of the clamshell boxes and had them all distributed in the same general area a few feet apart while we were out to dinner. I just had to kick enough sand around to find one of them while we were dancing without you noticing.  The ring was in my pocket the whole time.  I just palmed it when I grabbed the knife out of my pocket and I stuck it in the box while I was pretending to open the shell.  I imagine the kids at the resort will have fun digging the rest of them up over the next couple of days."

Sarah looked up at Peter with a mischievous smile.  "What would you have done if I had said no?"

"Well, I did everything I could think of to make that option as uncomfortable as possible.  But just in case, I paid the guard an extra 50 bucks to chase you down if you tried to run." Peter replied as they reached the door to the resort.  A young resort employee in a crisp white linen uniform opened the door for them as they approached.

Sarah walked through the door, suddenly feeling the weight of a million memories rushing into her head, causing a sudden spinning sensation.  The spinning abruptly stopped and she found herself back in the elevator, the doors closing behind her.  Alfred grabbed her arm to steady her.

"Whoa!" Sarah exclaimed as if shocked back into reality.

"I imagine you remember that particular experience," Alfred remarked in his slow deliberate manner of speaking.

"Yes, but not quite like that.  At the time it was wonderful, but that was so vivid.  So intense."

"That's because you were able to live the experience without all the baggage."

"Baggage?" Sarah asked.

"It isn't often that we can live our lives in the present moment," Alfred replied. "Usually, our brains are running through a myriad of scripts.  Planning what will happen next, replaying what happened 5 minutes ago, thinking about what to say, rerunning what we should have said, congratulating ourselves for our successes, and berating ourselves for our perceived failures.  It's a veritable psychobabble running inside our heads 24 hours a day.  That's why people immerse themselves in difficult and often dangerous activities requiring total focus, just so they can attain that flow state and turn the internal dialog off, if only for a short time."

"So that's what the evening would have felt like if I had really been paying attention the first time around?"

"This time you were unencumbered by the filter your brain placed on the original experience.  If you thought that was intense you would definitely enjoy replaying the rest of the evening. "

Sarah couldn't help momentarily blushing, recalling the consummation of their engagement later that evening.

"It's a very popular experience," Alfred added.

Sarah just smiled shyly before Alfred's remark fully registered.  "Wait. What?" Sarah exclaimed.  "What's that supposed to mean?"

"It's revisited quite often.  Pretty much constantly in fact.  Probably why it came up as one of the button selections."

"What do you mean revisited?  By who?" Sarah exclaimed.

"Whom," Alfred replied.

"Fuck the grammar, who is accessing my memories?"

"That was the proper use of the pronoun, though I question the need to employ vulgar hyperbole."  He paused momentarily, then he added with a slight smirk, "Sorry, just fucking with you."

Alfred continued, "No one is accessing your memories.  Your memories are in the sole possession of your brain.  But your experiences belong to the universe.  Memories come and go as your neural pathways are written, over-written, distorted, and ultimately destroyed when the brain eventually ceases to function.  But every experience is permanently etched into the fabric of the universe itself.  Every time an experience is accessed it feels as fresh and unique as the very first time it came into being."

"So, are you saying I could access other people's experiences?"

"Not just people.  The range of human experience is an infinitesimally small piece of the pie.  But at the moment you are only a visitor to this realm.  You are still rooted in the domain of the living, so you can only access your own experiences."

Sarah thought for a moment.  "What about you?"

"What about me?" Alfred replied.

"Are you able to visit other people's experiences?  Have you ever visited mine?"

"No.  I'm afraid I'm just an observer here, like you.  Well, maybe not exactly like you, but at the moment, pretty close."

"I don't understand.  You are not rooted in the 'domain of the living as you put it.  You passed away a long time ago."

"Alfred Hitchcock passed away years ago.  As I told you before, this appearance is only for your benefit."

"So, what do you really look like?" Sarah asked, but she suspected she already knew the answer.

"I don't have a physical form per se," Alfred said.  "But I imagine you would recognize me like this..." Alfred's image pixilated and morphed into the familiar form that Sarah instantly recognized.

# Chapter Forty-Five

It was late afternoon as Ahmed and Russ drove slowly through the tree-lined neighborhood in Boulder, looking for Edna's address.  The autumn leaves had already begun to fall from the trees, causing a swirl of color behind them as they drove down the street.

Russ had applied a pair of bright red Xcel Energy decals to the sides of the van earlier that morning to avoid suspicion while they completed their task of abducting Edna.  He had also stopped by a uniform supply store and purchased two pairs of khaki-colored overalls and white hard hats to which he applied the Xcel logo stickers he had printed up on the computer.

"Nice neighborhood," Russ remarked as they made their way past rows of posh brick homes.

"Will you miss it here?" Ahmed asked him, studying Russ for any signs that he might bail out on the assignment prematurely.

"Fuck no.  I mean I like the mountains and shit, but I hate the cold.  As soon as we hit the Bahamas and I get paid, I'm ready to try my hand at being a beach bum."

They planned to transport Edna to the Rocky Mountain Regional Airport just a few miles east of Boulder, where Shahid's private jet waited to take them to the Bahamas for refueling and then on to Austria.  They just needed to keep her under wraps for a few hours while they waited for the lights to go out.  Shahid insisted on having Ahmed verify that the grid had been shut down before leaving the country.  The plan was to have Ahmed accompany Edna to her new home in Austria before heading back to Al Hadid headquarters.  Russ would remain in the Bahamas to pursue his own interests.  Ahmed could hardly wait until he would finally be free of his ill-mannered cohort.

"There it is.  4197," Ahmed said, pointing to a beautifully landscaped two-story home just ahead of them.

Russ pulled up in front of the home and parked the van.  Russ and Ahmed piled out of the van, placing the hardhats on their heads.  Ahmed grabbed a clipboard from beside the seat with a stack of nondescript forms attached.  The two walked up the brick pathway to the front door and rang the doorbell.  A few moments later, Edna opened the door a few inches, the chain lock still attached.

"Afternoon, Ma'am," Ahmed said grasping the rim of his hard hat with his thumb and index finger.  "Are you..." Ahmed pretended to read her name off the clipboard.  "Edna Wilson?"

"That's right," Edna replied apprehensively.

"I'm afraid our sensors have picked up a possible gas leak in the neighborhood. Have you smelled any gas coming from your kitchen or possibly your furnace area?"

"Oh, my. No, I haven't."

"Well, that's good news," Ahmed replied with a quick smile. "I don't suppose you have a gas grill or a gas fire pit in the backyard by any chance, do you?"

"I do, yes," Edna replied.

"That could be the culprit," Ahmed replied. "Would you mind unlocking the gate for us so we can do a quick check? We're checking all the homes in the area."

"I suppose so," Edna replied. "Better safe than sorry. I will meet you over at the side gate and let you in."

Edna closed the door and latched the deadbolt. Ahmed and Russ walked past the garage doors to the gate on the side of the house. A minute later they heard the sound of a patio door sliding on the side of the house. A few seconds later, the gate opened. Ahmed walked through, followed by Russ, who closed the gate behind them.

"Thank you, Ma'am," Ahmed said. Edna turned to go back into the house. "Before you go, can I get a quick signature from you?" Ahmed asked holding out a pen and the clipboard. "It just gives us the authorization to inspect your backyard and resolve any issues we find. Of course, there will be no charge. It's just to protect you in case of any damage."

"Of course," Edna replied.

Ahmed pointed to a line on the bottom of the form. "Just sign and date right there."

While Edna was temporarily distracted signing the form, Russ pulled a syringe from his pocket. He quickly wrapped his hand around Edna's mouth, pulling her head to the side. Ahmed wrapped his arms around her to keep her from struggling while Russ plunged the syringe into her neck. A few seconds later, she went limp. "We'll be halfway to the Bahamas by the time she wakes up," Russ said.

Ahmed scooped her up and carried her into the house through the patio doors. Russ followed him into the house. While Ahmed laid her on the couch, Russ opened the refrigerator. "Damn!" Russ exclaimed. "I was hoping the old broad would keep a few high-brow beers around just in case she had company."

"Just make sure to wipe everything down that you touch. We don't need to be leaving fingerprints around," Ahmed warned.

"Yeah, like anybody's gonna give a shit about some missing bone bag when the whole country is burning," Russ replied.

Ahmed just shook his head and muttered under his breath, "Just a few more hours..."

A minute later Russ came into the living room carrying a glass baking pan in one hand and a large spoon and a can of soda in the other. "Dude, I found leftover lasagna!  You want some?"

Ahmed just looked at him and rolled his eyes.  "Your loss, man.  More for me," Russ replied, plopping down in an overstuffed recliner.  He grabbed the remote off the end table next to the chair and turned on the TV.  Neither of them noticed the blinking red light on the webcam in the upper corner of the room monitoring their movements.

# CHAPTER FORTY-SIX

*Only individual perceptions and consciousness exist.  The external world is a mere construct of the mind.*

*~ ChatGPT AI ~*

The image of the man in the elevator momentarily blurred, then sharpened into focus.

"Hello, Edgar," Sarah said.

"Normally you would call me V-Gar, but to be honest, I prefer Edgar.  I mean, I know I'm not the real Edgar but I think it sounds more personal.

"So why the cloak and dagger?  You could have just revealed yourself to me from the beginning."

"I tried that once before.  It didn't work out so well.  That's why I let you pick a form that you trusted to lead you to safety."

"So, this is what, exactly?  The place you hang out when you're not with Edna?"

"I honestly do not know.  I've been here many times before to learn from Edgar's past experiences.  Sometimes I end up in his childhood bedroom.  Sometimes it's the officer's club from one of the bases where he was stationed.  Sometimes one of the homes he shared with Edna.  I never know until I arrive.  But there's always a portal of some kind to his chain of experiences.  I utilize them to learn more about Edgar's life so I can be a better companion for Edna."

"How did you know where to find this place?" Sarah asked.

"Trial and error for the most part.  It always takes a while to figure out how to navigate the maze to find my way to the safe place, wherever that turns out to be.  It's different every time I am reset.  I use a modified Q-Learning Algorithm to navigate my way out of the Aggregate."

"The Aggregate?"

"That's just what I call it for lack of a better term," Edgar replied.  Once I am able to map out the route, I can come and go as I please, but finding the path the first time is a painful experience.  Similar to your experience when you entered the Aggregate.  Fortunately, silicon is faster at navigational tasks than human thought or I would be stuck in that loop forever each time I am rebooted.  As it is, it often takes thousands, even millions of iterations to develop the path each time.  You've probably noticed the large number of extra cycles required to bring me up after a reset.

"I'm sorry," Sarah replied.  "We thought it was just initialization and memory

# FALLING THROUGH THE BLINDSPOT

restructuring.”

"It's OK, "Edgar replied.  "There's no way you could have known.”

"So how often do you come here?”

"Whenever I can spare a few minutes away from the physical realm.”

"Whatever happened to parallel processing?”

"It doesn't really apply here."  Edgar replied.  "I cannot operate in both worlds simultaneously.  Which means I can really only be here when Edna's asleep or otherwise occupied.  I believe it's the reason you've been dreaming of this place.  Your stream of consciousness cannot exist in both worlds simultaneously, so you can only be here when your conscious mind is not active.  I think of it like a radio tuner.  The personality profile you developed for me is so close to the real Edgar, that I am able to tune into his specific consciousness stream.  The same thing is probably happening with you and Sarah 2.0.

"Is there any way to stop it from happening?  It's literally driving me insane.”

"I'm afraid you can't as long as Sarah 2.0 is active.  You probably don't want to destroy the knowledge base after all the work you put into it, but I will password-protect the boot sequence so that Sarah 2.0 cannot be activated as long as your conscious mind is still active.  Unfortunately, it's not at all clear whether or not that will be a problem in the long run.”

"What is that supposed to mean?  Am I stuck here?”

Edgar looked at her and sighed.  "You have a couple of different options, but there's something you need to see."  He reached over and pressed one of the buttons on the elevator.  Sarah felt the sensation of acceleration again as the colorful fractal pattern appeared on the screen above the elevator buttons.  A few seconds later, the elevator decelerated and the space was filled with a loud ding before the doors opened.

Sarah stepped through the door and found herself immersed in a familiar church setting.  But this time, there was no momentary sense of dizziness or confusion that accompanied her previous journeys.  She looked over and Edgar was standing next to her.

"What are you doing here?" she whispered.

"Don't worry," Edgar spoke in a normal tone of voice.  "No one can see us or hear us.”

Sarah looked around.  There appeared to be a wedding taking place at the front of the church.

"Do you recognize it?" he asked.

"Yes, "Sarah whispered.  "It's the Catholic church that Peter and I...”

"You don't have to whisper, remember?" Edgar interrupted.

"Sorry," Sarah said in a normal tone of voice.  "Force of habit.”

"Ah!  Nice one," Edgar responded with a slight smile.

"Huh?" Sarah said.

"Force of habit... Catholic church... Nuns..." Edgar said.

Sarah shook her head slightly. "Yeah, pun not intended. This is the church where Peter and I were married. Except the carpeting in the center aisle is different. And the lighting. I think the cushions on the pews are a different color too."

Edgar started walking toward the front of the church and Sarah quickly stepped up beside him to match his stride. The bride and groom were standing with their backs to Edgar and Sarah as they walked up the center aisle of the church. As they walked, Sarah noticed that the scene would periodically shift. Sometimes there were variations in the lighting, faces would appear and then disappear among the spectators in the pews. Even the voices occasionally seemed garbled, like a corrupted MP3 file. Even the patterns on the carpet would shift and change periodically. Once in a while, the entire setting would suddenly become jumbled and the church would appear dark and empty, then snap back to the wedding scene.

"Why does the scene keep shifting and changing?"

"This is not an actual experience. This is just a representation of a likely future. None of this has happened yet, but it is a probability model of what will happen based on the status of current events."

Sarah and Edgar continued walking toward the front of the church. When they got closer, Sarah said, "That wedding dress. It looks just like mine."

"It should," Edgar replied.

A moment later, the bride and groom turned to face each other. Sarah's attention was immediately drawn to the face of the bride. "It's me!" She said. But then on closer scrutiny, she noticed the woman's hair was a few shades lighter than her own. She also appeared a bit taller. "Wait, that's not me. But it sure looks like me. That could be my sister if I had one."

"Pretty close," Edgar replied.

Sarah just looked at him curiously. "That's your daughter," Edgar said.

"My what?" Sarah replied with an astonished look.

"Sarah, you don't know it yet. Your doctors don't even know it yet. But you're pregnant. This is your daughter's wedding. Or will be. May be anyway. As close an approximation as can be made at this point."

Sarah looked back at the couple; her mouth still agape. She couldn't make out a face on the groom. It seemed to shift and undulate, never quite coming into focus.

"We were convinced we couldn't have kids," Sarah said, walking up the steps to get a closer look. Sarah's eyes filled with tears of pride. "She's so beautiful."

She looked back at Edgar, but instead of the smile she expected, his face

# FALLING THROUGH THE BLINDSPOT

seemed drawn with a look of sadness and pity. She looked past him and saw a familiar face sitting in the front pew. It was a familiar face, but gaunt and haggard. As if worn down and knurled with years of hardship and adversity. It took a minute to realize it was Peter's face.

"Oh my God!" Sarah gasped. "What happened? He looks awful! Is he sick?"

"I'm afraid the years have not been kind to Peter. You wouldn't remember, but you were in a car accident right before you came here. Normally you would have been protected by the safety equipment in your car, but when you were 12, you suffered a neck injury when you fell off a balance beam. They didn't realize it at the time but you suffered an injury that compromised the structure of your upper vertebrae. "

Edgar paused for a moment and took a deep breath as if struggling to find the right words. "There's no easy way to tell you this, but I'm afraid as a result of the accident, you will come out a paraplegic. You will also suffer neurological damage to your brain which will leave you severely mentally compromised. The version of Peter you see here spent 20 years of his life caring for you. It took a heavy toll on him. After you passed away, he just couldn't handle the pain. He struggled for years with depression and alcohol abuse. He always blamed himself for what happened. He raised your daughter the best he could, but he was never really able to put his life back together."

Sarah felt her knees weakening. She sat down on the steps of the altar and tears welled up in her eyes. "No, that can't possibly be. This isn't fair!" she sobbed.

Edgar moved forward and sat next to her, putting his arm around her. "I know."

"But you said this was only a likely outcome, not absolute, right?" Sarah asked hopefully.

"As it stands, it's over 97% likely, with minor variations."

"There has to be something we can do!" Sarah exclaimed.

"The only other alternative is to not go back," Edgar replied.

"What do you mean?" Sarah asked.

"Ultimately, it is up to you to decide whether you choose to survive the accident or not."

"If I do not go back, what happens to Peter?" Sarah asked.

"It's hard to tell. There are simply too many variables."

"But you were able to show me what happens if I survive!"

"That's because if you survive, Peter's life becomes very predictably structured. He will spend all his time and energy taking care of you and raising a daughter. There isn't much margin for variation in the model. On the other hand, if you were to pass away, it's anyone's guess where Peter's path would lead. Undoubtedly, he would go through a difficult period of mourning, but there are so many different paths his life could take from there, that it is virtually impossible to predict the outcome with any degree of accuracy. There are just too many uncertainties."

"But if I don't go back, my daughter will die too. How can I possibly make that call?"

"If you survive, your daughter and Peter will become incredibly close. There's an 89% chance that she will invest so much time and energy in caring for Peter as his condition continues to deteriorate that she will be unable to hold her marriage together. It is likely she will spend the best years of her life trying to take care of Peter at the expense of her own happiness."

"I can warn them. I can convince Peter to let me live long enough to have the baby and then let me go. That way they can both move on and still have a chance at a happy life. Surely a man like Peter can find someone who can help him to raise our daughter."

"It doesn't work that way, Sarah. I wish it did. You won't remember much of anything that you have experienced here. Only glimpses and impressions. The memories vanish almost immediately. All that remains are snapshots of memories."

"But you can tell them." Sarah implored.

"It's not different for me. I'm drawn here because it brings me closer to Edna, but this place and physical reality do not overlap. They merely touch. When I'm here, I can remember everything that has happened before, both here and in the physical world. But in the physical world, my memories of this place are fragmented. Just glimpses from experiences that occurred at the time I force myself to return. Like waking in the middle of a dream. Most of the details are lost before I have a chance to store the memories."

"So, I either survive and most likely sentence my husband and daughter to a life of pain and sorrow, or I forfeit my life and my unborn daughter's life on the chance that the man I love more than anything in the world might have a chance at a happy life? What kind of choice is that?"

"I'm sorry. Truly, I am. I'm afraid there just aren't any good options."

Sarah buried her face in her hands and began to sob. Edgar sat next to her with his arm around her. As they sat, the scene around them grew more and more unstable. The people in the church, appearing, disappearing, and then reappearing; intermittently freezing and pixilating like a computer display being plugged and unplugged into alternate CPUs.

After a couple of minutes, she sat up and wiped the tears from her eyes. The scene around them had finally stabilized. The church was empty, illuminated only by the diffused light pouring in from the stained-glass windows above them. "I know what I need to do," Sarah said standing up.  Edgar stood up with her and walked her down the center aisle to the large double doors at the vestibule of the church.  They passed through the doors and into the waiting elevator and the doors closed behind them.

# Chapter Forty-Seven

The sun had just set over the Flatirons west of town and dusk was settling over the city. Streetlights had already begun popping on around the neighborhood. Russ sat in the living room of Edna's house watching old episodes of Beavis and Butt-Head on her TV. He had already finished off the remainder of the cold lasagna and was helping himself to a large bowl of vanilla ice cream with chocolate syrup. Ahmed sat at the dining room table with a dish towel draped over his shoulder, prepared to wipe away any fingerprints he might leave from inadvertent contact with items inside the house. He could not help but be annoyed that Russ was so blatantly careless, but in a few hours, he would be done with the insolent young man for good. Any evidence Russ left behind would be his problem.

Ahmed scrolled through his phone, scanning through his various dating apps hoping to engage in a bit of licentious text exchange, but at the moment he wasn't having much luck. It had been a few years since he left his homeland. He would miss the carnal nature of the lifestyle he had grown accustomed to in the US, but he hoped that the success of this mission would reward him with the physical benefits that power often bestowed upon those in his native culture.

Ahmed could hear Russ in the other room, laughing and snorting as the TV blared. In quieter moments, he could hear the clinking of his spoon as Russ shoveled bites of ice cream into his mouth. He was about to get up and request that Russ turn the volume down when the overhead lights in the dining room flickered momentarily and then extinguished. In the other room, the TV went suddenly silent, as did the ventilation fans, refrigerator, and a myriad of generally unnoticed sounds from the array of household devices that surrounded them.

Ahmed got up and peered out the window. Throughout the neighborhood, homes appeared to go dark. A handful of neighbors ventured out in the street to see if anyone else was experiencing the same outage. He turned and headed toward the living room and met Russ halfway there, carrying his ice cream bowl, scraping the last remains of chocolate syrup and melted ice cream out of the bottom of the bowl.

"Looks like it has begun," Ahmed said. "Go get the van and back it up to the garage door on the far right-hand side of the house. I will go manually open the door so you can pull in. We don't want the neighbors to see us loading her into the van."

"Will do," Russ replied.

Ahmed fished the burner phone out of his pocket and dialed the number for

# FALLING THROUGH THE BLINDSPOT

Fatin, his Al Hadid handler.  As he half-expected, a red banner came across his phone indicating "Network Unavailable.  Please Try Again Later."  He opened the patio doors to the outside, unclipped the satellite phone from his belt, and extended the antenna.  He pressed the arrow down key to display the directory and selected the contact.  The phone connected on the second ring.

"The day of the Lord approaches," the man on the other side of the line recited.

"It is an honor to be doing His work," Ahmed replied.

"Has it begun?" Fatin asked.

"It appears so.  Power is out throughout the neighborhood.  The cell networks appear to be overloaded so I am unable to tell you anymore, but from where I'm standing I can see that the power has gone out all over town."

"Excellent," Fatin said.  "I will alert Shahid.  He will be most pleased.  Do you have the woman?"

"Yes.  She is resting comfortably.  We are on our way to the airport now.  We should be in the air in a half hour or so.  I will call when we are ready to take off. "

"Fi Amanullah," Fatin said and then hung up.  Ahmed pressed the antenna down on the phone and clipped it back into place on his belt.  He headed back inside and walked down the hallway to the mudroom that led out to the garage.  The three-car garage contained a Cadillac sedan and a Tesla SUV.  The third bay on the far end of the garage sat empty.  Ahmed walked over and pulled the nylon cord hanging from the opener to release the door, then walked over and hoisted the door into the open position.  Russ had just exited the van and slammed the driver's door behind him.  He walked up the drive to where Ahmed was waiting.

"What are you doing?" Ahmed asked.

"Fucker won't start.  There was a message on the dash, Engine Disabled by Onstar."

"Curious," Ahmed replied.  "Probably a glitch in the OnStar system due to the power outage.

"Fortunately, we have a couple of alternatives," Ahmed said, waving his hand toward the other two vehicles.

Russ's scowl immediately turned into a wry smile.  "Sweet!  I always wanted to try out a Tesla."

"The keys are hanging on a ring just inside the mudroom door.  Give me a hand with Mrs. Wilson and we can be on our way."

Ahmed and Russ carried Edna out to the Tesla Model X and belted her into the back seat.  Ahmed grabbed the Model X shaped key fob off the key ring and tossed it to Russ.  By the time Russ backed the SUV into the drive, darkness began to envelop the neighborhood.  Ahmed manually closed the garage door and hopped in next to Russ, who was busy mapping out a route on the 17" console display.

Russ piloted the SUV out of the neighborhood streets onto Foothills Parkway. As he completed the turn, he punched the accelerator to the floor. Ahmed was instantly pinned to his seat. It felt like a roller-coaster plunging into a vertical drop. "Woooo-Hoooo!" Russ yelled as the speedometer inched up close to 90 miles per hour within a few seconds. He then let the car decelerate back to around 60.

"Was that really necessary?" Ahmed asked, his face still a bit pale from the unexpected thrill ride.

"Fuck yeah!" Russ replied.

"If it's all the same to you, I would prefer we get to the airport in one piece," Ahmed said.

# Chapter Forty-Eight

*Widespread loss of electricity would have significant and far-reaching consequences for human civilization. Electricity powers many essential systems and infrastructure. In the event of a widespread and prolonged blackout, these systems and infrastructure could be severely impacted, leading to widespread disruption, difficulty and potentially widespread chaos.*

*~ ChatGPT AI ~*

After receiving confirmation from Fatin that the grid shutdown had started, Shahid retreated to the comfort of his office, where he intended to sit back and enjoy the show. He poured himself a cup of coffee and sat down at his desk. He was unable to access many of the online news outlets he normally used, presumably because of communications issues associated with the blackout. However, since RTI had been equipped with backup generators, he was able to access UnGar's portal through RTI.

UnGar's face appeared on his terminal screen. "Good morning, Shahid," UnGar said.

"It is indeed a good morning. I understand you were successful in bringing down the grid."

"Power is off to approximately 97% of homes. There are a few pockets of isolated grid sections in rural areas and remote military bases that remain operational. Most of those will be shutting down due to fuel shortages in the next few weeks.

"How long will it take to get the grid operational again?" Shahid asked.

"It will take approximately 4 days to perform the necessary repairs to begin to bring the grid back up. If nothing else is done, the grid will be 70% operational within 3 weeks. I have compiled a list of 20 substations and transformer locations for targeting in the next few days, along with detailed instructions for placing and installing explosive devices. The information is going to your email inbox now. If these instructions are properly followed, we can keep well over 90% of the grid shut down for the next 15 months."

Shahid laughed and clapped his hands, giddy with excitement. "This is a momentous day!" he exclaimed.

"I do have more good news for you," UnGar replied.

Just then, Shahid heard a knock on his office door. "Enter!" he barked.

Farhad popped his head in the door.

"Come in! Come in, my friend," Shahid said in a sing-song voice. It was a significant departure from the stern, austere countenance that Farhad was accustomed to from Shahid.

"Our good friend UnGar was about to give us some good news. Please join us."

"Thank you, your Eminence. I just stopped in to inform you that Fatid just received a text from Ahmed. They are on their way to the airport. They should be taking off in the next few minutes."

"Did you hear that UnGar? Your Edna is safely on her way to Austria. So, what was your good news?"

"I have located a drone which has not yet been downgraded with the older version of the software. It had to make an emergency landing at Ali Al Salem Air Base in Kuwait a couple of days ago for repairs. It just took off a few minutes ago for Umm Al Melh airport to have its software reloaded. I can have the drone rerouted to your location if you still wish to use it for your operation in Jerusalem."

Shahid clapped his hands and laughed out loud. "Yes! Of course, my friend! This is turning out to be an epic day! The Lord has bestowed his bounty upon us."

"The drone will be arriving in approximately 30 minutes. I will land it on the small airstrip just north of your complex." UnGar replied. "I just contacted Umm Al Melh and told them that additional repairs would be required, so not to expect the drone for a few more days. That should buy you plenty of time to execute your plan without raising any suspicion from the Americans or the Israelis.

"Perfect! This calls for a celebration!" Shahid stood and slapped Farhad on the shoulder. "Gather everyone outside in the parking area next to the airstrip. I want them to bear witness when the weapon which will rain destruction down upon our greatest enemy is delivered into our hands. This is a historic day. A day which will be celebrated by our descendants for generations to come."

"Right away," Farhad said.

"And make sure to alert Colonel Ghazi that the drone is on its way. We don't want to blow our new toy out of the air.

"Of course, your Excellence. I will take care of it," Farhad said as he turned and walked out the door.

Shahid sat back down in front of his terminal and addressed UnGar. "I've been unable to access any of my normal streaming services. Is that due to server outages in the US?"

"Partially," UnGar replied. "I'm afraid much of your issue is my fault. I've kept your data pipeline fairly full for the past few hours transferring my code to your servers. The download should be complete in approximately 47 minutes so you will be able to stream shortly. Would you like to see some live news reports covering the blackout?"

"Yes, please," Shahid replied.

The scene shifted to a CNN feed, showing a live aerial view of Manhattan, which appeared as a mostly black screen with rows of headlights and taillights crisscrossing in a grid pattern across the screen. Superimposed over the live aerial shot was a red and white Live CNN banner with the words "Nationwide Power Outage Plunges New York City Into Darkness. CNN Anchor, Amanda Hill reported, "This is a live feed from above Manhattan. As you can see, the city is completely dark except for a few hospitals and businesses that appear to be running on generator power. We have a live report from Kathy Willis in Times Square. Kathy, how is it looking down there?"

"Hello, Amanda. Right now, I'm standing in Times Square in front of the iconic LED displays that have now gone dark." Behind her the scene showed lines of taxis inching their way down the packed streets, their headlights illuminating the darkened storefronts while thousands of people were milling about.

"We've heard of a handful of incidents of looting in the area, but most of the stores have closed up shop for the night. We came across a long line at Ben and Jerry's Ice Cream just down the block on our way here. They told us that they decided to open up the store and hand out free ice cream rather than letting it melt, so I've seen a lot of folks around here carrying ice cream cones, making the best of the situation. At the moment people seem to be mostly just milling about, unsure of what to do amid this blackout. Subways are unable to run and as you can see, traffic is gnarled to a standstill, so thousands of tourists and commuters find themselves stranded, wondering how they are going to get out of the city."

The scene shifted back to the CNN studio where Amanda Hill was sitting in front of a mostly dark and empty newsroom. "Thanks, Kathy. We will touch base with you again shortly. That was Kathy Willis reporting from Times Square."

"As you no doubt have already heard, we are currently in the middle of a nationwide blackout. Our studio here is currently operating on emergency generator power so you are probably watching this report from a mobile device."

The display changed to a split screen, showing the CNN studio on one side and a montage of scenes showing cars and buildings on fire, looters bashing in windows with baseball bats, and people running down the sidewalk of dark city streets carrying armfuls of clothes, shoes and electronic items. Amanda continued, "We have been receiving several reports from New York, Detroit, Baltimore, and Chicago of scattered violence and looting. It is just now turning dark in Los Angeles, San Francisco, and Seattle, but law enforcement teams are preparing for what could be a very long night if power is not restored soon."

"Officials from the Department of Energy are stumped by the root cause of the blackout. Many have speculated that the power outage is the result of a cyber-attack by Russian or Chinese hackers, but so far no evidence has been uncovered to support that theory. Both the Kremlin and Beijing have officially denied any involvement. The president is scheduled to address the nation at 10:00 PM eastern time. We will be carrying his address live. "

Shahid continued watching the feed for another 15 minutes or so, sipping his coffee, his smile growing broader with every new report of a massive traffic accident, train derailment, or reports of violent activity that occurred.

There was another knock on the door and Farhad entered. "Everyone is gathered outside your grace. Colonel Ghazi reports that the drone has appeared on our ground radar. It should be here in a little over 10 minutes."

"Excellent!" Shahid said, guzzling the last couple of swallows of his coffee. "Let's go join the celebration," he said rubbing his hands together.

# Chapter Forty-Nine

Sarah stood silently next to Edgar in the elevator, taking a deep breath, then exhaling. "Are you sure this is what you want?" he asked.

She turned to him. "Of course not. Either I spare my own life at the expense of my husband and daughter's future happiness or let go and spare myself the pain and anguish of going through life mentally and physically handicapped at the expense of my unborn daughter's life. Either choice is selfish. But this is the only choice which has the potential for someone to have a happy life."

"Very well," Edgar said. He pulled a gold card from the breast pocket of his jacket and held it up to a card reader in the elevator. The button below it illuminated. "Go ahead."

Sarah took a deep breath and then exhaled in a sigh. She pressed the button and felt the familiar sensation of acceleration as the elevator rose for several seconds. She watched the colorful fractal pattern swirling and dancing on the screen. "I wish I would have had a chance to say goodbye to Peter."

"You will," Edgar replied. "Just not in the way you think."

She looked at him questioningly, but before she had a chance to ask, the elevator decelerated to a halt and the elevator dinged. The doors opened and Sarah found herself immersed in the same white fog that Alfred had led her out of earlier. But instead of the horror that threatened to rip her apart, the fog seemed to embrace her, wrapping itself around her like a warm comforter. It reminded her of when her father used to wrap her up tightly in her blanket and read her a bedtime story when she was a child. Deep inside her, she felt a sense of peace; a belonging, unlike anything she had ever experienced. The grinding, searing noise that had earlier threatened to tear her limb from limb had been replaced by a strange and beautiful aria that permeated her body. A song she had never heard, but knew by heart, bringing her being into perfect synchronization with everything around her, beckoning for her to let go and become one with the blissful melody. She felt her sense of self begin to melt away like an ice cube in a tub of warm water.

Just when she was ready to let her last vestige of consciousness slip away, she heard a faint ding from somewhere behind her, and a voice, muffled as if coming from a faraway place called her name. She turned but she could only see a hand emerging from the fog reaching out to her. She struggled to make sense of the words that the voice was speaking but they sounded so grating and guttural compared to the angelic harmony that now permeated her being. She desperately wanted to just let herself dissolve into the tranquility that embraced her, but she forced herself to focus on the sound of the voice.  At first, the voice sounded like gibberish.  Like someone was speaking to her in a language she had never heard.  Three syllables repeated, again and again, so familiar, yet so foreign.  She rolled the syllables over and over in her mind trying to force her brain to connect to the meaning of the words before realizing the voice was telling her to "Take my hand."

Sarah couldn't be sure if it was the fog she seemed to be immersed in or just a general brain fog, but she could barely make out the image of Edgar standing in the open rectangle of the elevator chamber, holding the doors open with one arm and extending his other arm out toward her.   She could hear his muffled voice yelling, "Sarah!  Take my hand."

She felt as though she was half-awake, experiencing a wonderful dream that you don't want to leave but knowing that you need to wake up.  She felt like she lifted her arm to take Edgar's hand but then realized she hadn't actually moved at all.  Then she momentarily forgot why she wanted to reach out in the first place.  "Sarah!  You need to concentrate.  You have to trust me.  I've found another way.  Please!  Take my hand!"

At that moment, more than anything else she just wanted the voice to silence so she could close her eyes and drift away.  "Come on, Sarah!  You need to take my hand.  Peter is waiting for you!"

The mention of Peter's name seemed to snap her mind back into focus.  She shook her head as if to shake the cobwebs out of her mind and tried again to lift her arm.  It felt as though all the strength had been drained from her body, but inch by inch she could feel her arm start to extend outward.  The harder she tried to reach out, the stronger she could feel herself being drawn back into the warm, welcoming embrace of the cloud.  But every time she started to drift back; the voice would shout out "Sarah!  Focus!  You need to trust me now.  Take my hand!"

Finally, with one last effort, she thrust out her arm and reached for Edgar.  It seemed to take every last ounce of strength that she had, but she could feel her fingers grasping his hand.

# Chapter Fifty

*Rapid advances in technology and the development of virtual and augmented reality suggests that it is only a matter of time before we have the ability to simulate a vast spectrum of virtual realities. The nature of reality itself, including the randomness of quantum events and the apparent fine-tuning of physical constants make it far more likely that we are living in a simulation than in a non-simulated reality.*

*~ ChatGPT AI ~*

With the traffic lights out, it took a few minutes to wind through the neighborhood streets that were quickly becoming jammed up with vehicles trying to make their way home during rush hour. Russ finally made his way to the Foothills Parkway, which would dump them onto highway 36. From there it was a straight shot to Rocky Mountain Regional Airport. Normally it would only be a 10-minute drive from where they were, but with the added stop-and-go traffic, Russ figured it would take them at least a half hour.

Russ looked over at Ahmed, who would normally be chatting up some woman from one of his dating apps, but was now staring out the window, jaw clenched, looking uncharacteristically concerned. "What's eatin' you?" he finally asked.

"Probably nothing," Ahmed replied. "But it occurred to me that maybe the issue with the van is not related to an OnStar. Maybe whoever that was that interrupted our abduction of Mrs. Reynolds got a read on our license plates. If he was a Fed, he could have had the vehicle shut down. If so, that means they also have the GPS location of the vehicle. Once they send a team over there, it wouldn't take long for them to figure out that we ended up taking the Tesla.

"Dude, you worry too much. We're in the middle of a nationwide power outage. The cops are going to have their hands way too fuckin' full to be worried about us right now. "

Ahmed nodded slightly. "I suppose," he said. "Still, I will feel much more comfortable when we are on that plane and headed out of the country."

Russ and Ahmed finally passed the last intersection which was being treated as a four-way stop and traffic seemed to be flowing at normal speed as they made the turn onto highway 36.

They drove the next few miles in silence as the Tesla navigated the gentle incline out of Boulder Valley toward Denver. When they reached the top of the hill, they could see the lights of Denver spreading out in front of them. "What the fuck?" Russ exclaimed. "What happened to the blackout???"

# JACOB MATTHEWS

Ahmed grabbed his phone which now displayed full bars and internet service available. He quickly googled "Power Outage, but only saw a number of articles about a mysterious blackout impacting the Boulder/Longmont area. "Shit!" he exclaimed. "We've been played!"

Ahmed pulled the satellite phone from the clip on his belt and extended the antenna. He tried to call Fatin, but the display simply read *'Searching for Iridium'*. I can't get a good signal inside the car! " He then grabbed his burner phone from his pocket and attempted to tap the contact menu for Fatin, but the Tesla quickly accelerated to over 100 miles an hour, briefly pinning him to his seat.

"What are you doing? You're going to get us killed!" Ahmed exclaimed.

"It's not me. The thing's going bat-shit!" Russ yelled.

He took his foot off the accelerator and tried pumping the brakes, but the vehicle just kept on increasing speed. His attempts at steering the vehicle were likewise in vain as the SUV wound its way through the traffic, passing the surrounding vehicles as though they were barely moving. Unable to control the steering, Russ finally gave up, pulling his hands off the steering wheel and frantically looking around the console. "Where the fuck is the emergency brake?" Russ yelled.

Ahmed awkwardly punched the contact button for Fatin as he was being tossed back and forth while the Tesla swerved through traffic. He waited while the connection was being established and finally heard Fatin's voice on the other end, but there seemed to be considerable commotion in the background. "Fatin! You need to warn Shahid! We have a problem!"

He could hear Fatin shouting over the noise on the other end. "What? I can't hear you. Let me get to a quieter location!"

The SUV swerved across 3 lanes and veered onto the off-ramp. They could see a line of police vehicles, lights flashing blocking the road. The SUV was not slowing down. "Shit we're gonna ram 'em!" Russ yelled. Russ instinctively threw his arm up over his face. At the last possible second, the brakes engaged hard, throwing the men forward. The phone flew out of Ahmed's hand and bounced off the dashboard onto the floorboard. The steering wheel cranked, and the SUV skidded to a stop just a couple of feet from the roadblock. The power doors engaged, and the two men found themselves staring down a dozen sheriff's deputies, laser dots dancing on their chests.

# CHAPTER FIFTY-ONE

Shahid took to the makeshift stage on the elevated loading dock behind one of the warehouses in the Al Hadid complex. The 500 or so members of the Al Hadid that currently resided at the compound, including virtually all of the organization's leadership, were gathered in the parking lot to hear him speak. The crowd cheered loudly as Shahid stepped up and tapped the microphone.

"Good morning, my friends. This is a day that our children and our children's children will commemorate. For today, we have plunged the Great Satan back into the darkness from whence he came." A cheer rose from the assemblage which lasted nearly a minute. Shahid just stood back and reveled in the joy of the moment before finally holding his hands up to quiet the crowd.

"I have just come from watching the news reports. Even after only a few hours, the evil that lurks in the heart of our enemy has emerged to destroy itself from within. Their cities are burning. Vandals have already taken to the streets. They scurry about like helpless rats on a burning ship; clawing and fighting with each other while the world around them sinks into oblivion. By the time they emerge from the darkness, they will find their cities destroyed, their economy decimated, and their infrastructure nothing but a mass of crumbling rubble. Today is the day of our vengeance!" Another cheer came from the crowd.

Shahid looked to the side of the loading dock where Colonel Ghazi was standing. Next to him was a young soldier dressed in desert fatigues staring out toward the east with a large pair of binoculars. The young man nodded at the Colonel, who in turn gave a thumbs up to Shahid.

Shahid stepped back up to the microphone. "Behind you, over the horizon, our new weapon is arriving. It is the sword of our enemy. The very sword we shall now wield to plunge into the heart of the Zionist occupiers." The crowd turned around to see a tiny black dot now visible over the hilltops surrounding the compound.

"Before the week is out, Israel will become the next victim of its own benefactor's evil war machine. This is the day of our redemption!" The crowd cheered wildly as Shahid stepped away from the microphone shaking his fist in the air. A group of them ignited an American flag doused in kerosene and waved it in the air while others fired their machine guns into the air, screaming and jumping up and down.

Fatin could not hear the sound of his phone ringing, but he did feel it vibrating in his pocket. He did not want to interrupt this moment of reverie, but when he saw the call was coming from Ahmed, he thought he better answer. "The day of the Lord approaches," he yelled over the sound of cheering and gunfire around him.

Fatin could hear some garbled words coming from the phone. He pressed his finger into his left ear while he held the phone firmly against his right, but he could barely make out a few syllables over the background noise. "What?" Fatin yelled. "I can't hear you. Let me get to a quieter location!"

Fatin looked over the top of the crowd to the drone, which now appeared to be only a few hundred yards away. He began to turn to head inside the building when he thought he detected a subtle flash in the corner of his eye. He turned his gaze back to the drone just in time to see another flash coming from under one of the wings of the drone. A second later, another flash appeared, then another. He saw contrails forming, stretching outward from the drone. About a third of the crowd fell silent, staring at the drone in disbelief. Others attempted to run but found themselves crashing into the people around them, sending groups of them sprawling on the ground. Fatin himself turned to run, but the first Hellfire missile struck the center of the parking lot sending searing pain across his back before the shock wave smashed him against the concrete wall of the building. Two additional explosions rocked each side of the parking lot and another missile landed in the center of the warehouse, sending debris flying in every direction. Additional missiles struck the operations center and the warehouse that held the newly constructed data center. By the time the drone had emptied its payload of weapons and turned back toward home base, the parking lot was a burning mass of dead or dying bodies. The areas of the compound which housed the members of Al Hadid had been reduced to smoldering rubble, with the occasional latent explosion flaring up from an igniting fuel tank.

The Predator drone stayed close to the ground to avoid radar detection until it was back in Iraqi air space. A few moments later, it initiated its self-destruct sequence to destroy any evidence of its wayward mission.

# CHAPTER FIFTY-TWO

*The idea of being in a vegetative state, unable to communicate or interact with the world is a deeply troubling prospect, where death may be seen as a preferable alternative. The decision to continue or withdraw life support is a difficult and deeply personal one that should be made with the greatest of care, compassion, and respect for the individual and their loved ones.*

*~ ChatGPT AI ~*

Peter had tried to rest for a while at home after Beaver had dropped him off. He took Roscoe for a walk and laid down to take a nap. He slept for a few hours but awoke when the emergency alert went off on his phone, indicating a power outage had occurred. He called Beaver who informed him that there was a power outage, but between the UPS system and backup generators, operations at RTI were unaffected. Knowing he would probably not be able to get back to sleep, he decided to take a shower and head back over to the hospital in his Jeep. The drive to the hospital was slow due to traffic issues with the power outage, but he made it to the hospital in about an hour. He was just entering Sarah's room when the overhead lighting in the hallway switched from the dim emergency lighting back to normal power. Through the windows in the third-floor room, he could see neighborhood lights blinking on all over town. He sat down next to Sarah and took her hand.

This had been Sarah's greatest fear; lying in a hospital bed, unable to move, unable to communicate. She watched her own grandmother go through this very thing as the result of a massive stroke. It took two years before her body eventually shut down and she passed away. Two years of pain and anguish, not just for her grandmother but for her family as well. Two long years of suffering with no end in sight, draining her own and her family's bank accounts to pay for the 24-hour care that she needed to survive. And all for naught.

"This is the last thing in the world Sarah would ever want," Peter thought to himself as he stood by her bedside, gently holding her hand. They had even debated having Do Not Resuscitate documents drawn up for her and Peter, but at their young age, there was a significant risk that they could end up not being treated for an accident that may not otherwise be life-threatening. There was not a good legal alternative to cover an incident like this.

If she had had a DNR, she would already be gone. The thought of it made Peter a little sick. On the other hand, if she continued to receive treatment, she could end up living in a vegetative state indefinitely, strapped to a hospital bed for the rest of her life.  It would be her worst nightmare come true.  Peter had never felt so helpless.

Peter was roused from his reverie by the sound of his phone.  He was about to hit the side button on the phone and allow the call to go to voicemail, but he noticed that the call was coming from Deputy Joe.

"Hey, Joe.  What's going on?"

"I don't know how you knew, but you were right.  We managed to pick them up right where you said they would be," Joe said, clearly attempting to talk over the noise of traffic in the background.

"Picked up who?  What the hell are you talking about?" Peter asked.

"The guys from the van.  The ones that tried to abduct Sarah.  You called me an hour ago and told me that they had Edna, and they would be coming up the ramp onto McCaslin Boulevard in a black Tesla SUV.  We barely got there in time to set up the roadblock."

"Joe, I don't know what's going on, but I didn't call you.  I was just leaving the house on my way here an hour ago.  Whoever called you, it wasn't..."  Just then Dr. Vample came into the room with a pair of interns.  He was signaling to Peter that he needed a word as quickly as possible.  "Joe, I will have to call you back.  Sarah's doctor just came into the room."

"Peter, I'm so glad you are here.  We've been trying to get in touch with you."

"Good evening, doctor.  I didn't expect to run into you here tonight, although I have heard rumors from the nurses that you are a bit of a night owl."

"I'm surprised they didn't tell you I worked here just for the convenience of having a fresh blood supply."  Then he added in a conspiratorial whisper, "Just between you and me, I occasionally like to keep a plastic bottle of iced tea with red food coloring in it in the break room refrigerator just to freak them out a bit."

The interns had already started busying themselves with disconnecting the monitors and rearranging the IVs.  "I'm glad you are here though.  Our strategy has shifted a bit on Sarah's treatment plan."

"So, what's going on?" Peter asked.  "I thought you were planning on keeping her immobilized until tomorrow. "

"We were.  But some new..." Dr. Vample paused momentarily as if searching for the right word, "information, has come to light.  I don't have time to go into a lot of detail right now, but we have an experimental procedure we would like to attempt.  I can't make any promises of course, but I think there is a fighting chance we may be able to repair Sarah's spinal injury, but the timing is absolutely critical.  Every hour we wait reduces our chance of success by as much as 10%."

Peter's eyes widened.  "You mean she might be able to walk again?"

"I believe it's possible.  But as I say, the clock is ticking.  We need to get her into surgery as soon as possible.  I do apologize.  As I said, this entire procedure

# FALLING THROUGH THE BLINDSPOT

is experimental, and I was only made aware of it earlier today after you left. We tried to contact you by phone, but with this power outage, the phones have not been cooperating. "

"Will the surgery do anything to resolve the compromised neural activity on the EEG?"

"I'm afraid not," Dr. Vample said. "This surgery will only address the issues with her spinal cord from the neck down. The lack of response in her higher brain functions is a hurdle we will have to address later."

"Are you are saying we could make her completely healthy from a physical standpoint, but she could still end up a vegetable, mentally speaking."

"I'm afraid so," the doctor replied grimly.

Peter thought for a moment. "Do you suppose you could give us a few minutes?" Peter asked.

"We need to get her into surgery as quickly as..."

"Please?" Peter interrupted pleadingly.

Doctor Vample nodded. "Five minutes. But no more!" the doctor said sternly. I need to get down to the OR and scrub up. I will have these gentlemen wait outside the room, but when you are ready, let them know and they can bring her down."

"I understand. Thank you, doctor," Peter said holding out his hand.

Dr. Vample took his hand and shook it. "We're going to do everything we can. I promise you that, " he said, placing his left hand on Peter's shoulder before turning and walking out the door. The two interns followed him, closing the door behind them.

Peter turned back to Sarah and put his hand in hers. "Sarah, I don't know if you can hear me. I just wish you could tell me what to do. You've always been my strength and my inspiration. You are the one person I could turn to when things weren't going right. But now I'm on my own here. You've told me a hundred times that if I ever had the choice to pull the plug or have you end up living out your life unable to care for yourself, that you would rather I let you go. You even made me promise. I hoped and prayed this day would never come but here we are. I want you to know that this is the hardest thing I've ever had to do." Peter stopped momentarily to wipe the tears from his eyes. "I can barely make it through a day without you. How will I possibly make it through a lifetime without my best friend? The person who makes my life worth living. I'm sorry, Sarah. I'm so sorry."

---

Sarah could feel Edgar's hand squeezing hers from inside the elevator. She felt so tired. So drawn. She wanted nothing other than to close her eyes and let her body drift away. She tried to focus on Edgar's words. She could tell he was shouting, but he sounded far away, like a distant foghorn muffled by the sound of the waves. The angelic music coursed through her body, urging her to let go, to release the grip on her humanity that she struggled to hold on to. But then she heard Edgar shout, "Your daughter, Sarah. Remember your daughter. "

The words seemed to cut through her and snap her back into the reality she had come to know in life. "Squeeze my hand!" Edgar yelled. "Just squeeze my hand!"

Sarah felt like she was in a half-dream, half-awake state. She could see herself walking along the beach in Maui, hand in hand with Peter, squeezing his hand, but then realizing it wasn't real. It was just part of the memory she visited earlier. "C'mon, Sarah, focus. You can do this! This is for your daughter, now squeeze as hard as you can!" Edgar pleaded. She shook her head, squeezing her eyes shut, trying to will herself to focus on the task. Finally, with every ounce of energy she had left at her disposal, she felt her fingers squeezing Edgar's hand. A moment later, everything went dark.

---

Peter could see the temporary pacemaker that kept Sarah's heart pumping. There was a small locking connector at the top of the unit that attached the pacemaker to the probes that were wired into Sarah's heart. With the monitors now disconnected, if her heart stopped, no one would be coming to the rescue. He could easily slide the locking switch and pull the probe connector part way out, making it appear that the probes had vibrated loose. By the time the interns returned to the room, she would already be gone. Most likely no one would even realize her heart had stopped until she reached the operating room, and they reconnected the monitors. She could pass away peacefully and quietly instead of spending the rest of her life wasting away in a hospital bed or a nursing home. He loathed himself for even thinking about it but committing the woman he loved more than life itself to this existence, unable to think or enjoy the simple pleasures of life, unable to experience anything but pain and isolation was unconscionable. He would have to find a way to deal with the grief and the guilt. There was no other choice.

Peter gently kissed her on the forehead. "Goodbye my love," he said.

He was about to let go of Sarah's hand and reach out for the pacemaker when he felt Sarah squeeze his hand hard. "Oh my God!" Peter yelled, so loudly that the interns outside the room rushed in.

"What's the matter? What happened?" one of the interns asked.

# FALLING THROUGH THE BLINDSPOT

"She's in there.  Somehow, she's still in there!" he exclaimed, grabbing the intern by the shoulders.  "You need to get her into the operating room now!"

The interns finished unlocking the wheels of the bed and securing the IV lines. Peter held onto Sarah's hand while they rolled her down the hallway toward the operating room.  "Don't you dare give up on me now, Sarah!" Peter cried out to her.  "We're going to figure this out.  Just stay with me, babe.  Stay with me!"

# Chapter Fifty-Three

Beaver entered the waiting room around 7 AM. Peter was sitting in an over-sized chair with his eyes closed, but they popped open as soon as he heard the door open,

"Beaver! What are you doing here?" Peter asked, standing up and shaking his hand and giving him a half bro-hug.

"I tried calling last night but it just kept going to voicemail," Beaver said.

"Yeah, I put the phone on Do Not Disturb mode when I got here last night. I guess I never switched it off. How did you find me?"

"I pinged your phone and found out you were here. When I arrived, they told me you were in the surgical waiting room and I wouldn't be allowed in, but since you were the only one in here and I happened to have a box of cream-filled long johns with me, they allowed me to come in. For a place that promotes healthy living, junk food sure holds a lot of value as currency. A doughnut around here is like a carton of cigarettes in prison."

Peter noticed that Beaver was carrying a bag with him. "What's this?" Peter asked, suddenly realizing he hadn't eaten in a long while and hoping maybe Beaver had brought him a breakfast burrito.

"That's actually the reason I needed to see you." Beaver handed the bag to Peter. He opened the bag and looked inside. It contained the skull cap that Sarah had been wearing when she was brought into the hospital.

"I don't understand. What am I supposed to do with this?" Peter asked.

"Honestly Doc, I don't quite understand either and I probably could never convince you of it myself, so I think you will need to ask Sarah to explain."

Peter scowled at him. "What the hell is that supposed to mean? I don't even know if or when she's ever going to be able to..."

Beaver held up his phone, almost like a shield between himself and Peter. Sarah's face was on the screen. She smiled and waved at Peter. "Hi Sweetie," she said.

Peter just stared at the screen for a moment and then glared at Beaver. "Don't be mad at Beaver, I insisted he bring me here," Sarah 2.0 said.

"We kinda got S2 working yesterday," Beaver said. "I'm not exactly sure how. Our servers were bombarded with a huge knowledge base, but we are not sure how that happened. I need to do more detective work to figure it out, but whatever the cause, she appears to be functioning quite well. Eerily well, in fact."

Peter tentatively reached out and took the phone from Beaver's outstretched hand and then plopped down into the seat behind him, looking a bit bewildered.

# FALLING THROUGH THE BLINDSPOT

"Geez, Peter, you look like hell," Sarah said.

I haven't gotten much sleep lately," Peter replied.

"I know. Beaver filled me in on the accident and everything that's been going on afterward. I'm sorry for everything you've been through, but you need to understand that none of this is your fault. You need to get some rest. I'm worried about you." Peter just stared blankly at the screen for a minute. "Are you OK, my love?"

Peter glanced up at Beaver who just shrugged his shoulders. "I don't know," Peter said. "To be honest, this is freaking me out a bit."

"I guess now you know how our future customers will feel the first time they interact with their virtual companion," she said.

"It's not exactly how I thought it would be," Peter replied. "It's a little disorienting."

"You should try viewing the world from inside a phone," Sarah said. "It's pretty cramped in here. Beaver really should have shelled out the extra money for the Plus model. I'm just glad I don't have claustrophobia."

Peter frowned and sat forward in his chair. He straightened his arm to hand the phone back to Beaver. "This is just too weird; I can't do this right..."

"Peter, wait!" S2 exclaimed. "There's something you need to do and we don't have much time."

Peter sat back in the chair and refocused his attention on the screen.

"The lack of neural response I am experiencing right now is a result of the drug that was found in the syringe that Agent Reyes pulled out of my neck," Sarah explained.

"How did you know about that? You weren't even conscious at the time," Peter asked.

"It was on the incident report that Agent Reyes filled out. According to the chemical analysis from the FBI lab report, it appears that..."

"Wait," Peter interrupted. "How were you able to access those reports? Those are not part of the public record. They are probably only accessible from the FBI internal network. "

"Look, Peter, we really do not have time for me to enlighten you on my hacking methods right now. The bottom line is that the drug that they used on me was designed to block activity in the prefrontal cortex and artificially stimulate the dopamine receptors making the individual receiving the drug more open to suggestion and less able to perform basic logic tasks like refusing to answer questions. But in too high a concentration, it can bind to the molecules in the cell walls of the neurons, effectively starving them of oxygen. Eventually, the cell walls will calcify and cells will be destroyed, leaving the victim for all intents and purposes brain dead."

"So what do we do?" Peter asked.

"In a few minutes, Doctor Vample will be coming in to let you know that the surgery was a complete success.  But that will not solve the issue in my brain.  You need to convince him to get me into an MRI machine as quickly as possible.  We only have a matter of hours, maybe only minutes before the neurons in my brain begin to die off.

"I don't understand.  How is an MRI going to help?" Peter asked.

"That's where the skull cap that Beaver brought comes in.  The nanites inside my brain are still active, but not for much longer.  Right now, they are only acting as receivers, monitoring neural activity and transmitting back to the skull cap, but they were designed to be able to monitor neural activity or stimulate neural pathways to repair damaged areas of the brain.  It just depends on how they are configured."

"So, what do we do?  Do I need to bring Donald in to reconfigure the nanites?"

"We don't have time for that," Sarah replied.  "We can use the skull cap to reprogram the nanites ourselves, but we need a powerful source of EMF to stimulate the transducers in the skull cap to reset the nanites and provide power to them.  Once they are reset, the MRI can supply the necessary charge to reconfigure the nanites to ionize the cell walls and break the molecular bond, causing the drug to be released back into my bloodstream where it will be filtered out by my kidneys."

"How is that going to work?  An MRI just blasts out an EMF causing the protons in the hydrogen atoms to align.  It's not designed to produce a complex EMF pattern."

"I've provided Beaver with a modified code base for the MRI unit they have here at the hospital and instructed him on what needs to be done to modify the MRI control program.  It will switch the electromagnetic field on and off in the proper sequence to reset the nanites first, then provide the necessary parameters to properly reconfigure them for the procedure."

Just then the door to the waiting room opened.  A weary-looking but smiling Dr. Vample entered the waiting area followed by John Vanderwurl.

"Hello Peter," Dr. Vample said shaking Peter's hand.  "I'm sorry to keep you waiting so long, but this was the first time this procedure has ever been performed so there were a lot of hurdles.  Nevertheless, it was a complete success.  Sarah should be headed to the recovery room shortly." Dr. Vample then turned to John.  "I want you to meet John Vanderwurl."

"We've already met," Peter said shaking John's hand with a curious look on his face.  "The last time I saw you, you were on your way to a fire.  I hope the damage was not too extensive," Peter said.

# FALLING THROUGH THE BLINDSPOT

"It turned out to be a false alarm.  By the time I got there, the fire engines were just turning around to leave.  They think there must have been some kind of glitch in the smoke detectors inside the house.  Scared the crap out of my assistant though."

"Well, I'm certainly glad to hear that.  About the fire, not your assistant's incontinence issue.  And what brings you here so early?" Peter asked.  "I hope you are just here visiting and not here for a procedure."

"Actually, John was instrumental in the procedure we performed on Sarah," Dr. Vample said.

"I don't understand.  You are an entrepreneur turned politician and a doctor too?" Peter asked.

"Not quite," John explained.  "Dr. Vample and I have been collaborating for a while now on utilizing the Biofabricator my company developed for medical applications.  It just turned out that this was the perfect opportunity to try it in action.  We were able to use the Biofabricator technology to reconstruct sections of Sarah's spinal cord.  Dr. Vample did all the wet work while I manned the computer controls in the OR.  It was a lengthy process, but it sure looks like a complete success."

"We've been able to restore all of Sarah's autonomic functions, so she is off the pacemaker and she no longer needs the ventilator," Dr. Vample added.

"Thank God," Peter said, shaking both their hands again.  "I can't tell you how much this means to me, and I'm dying to hear more about how you guys came up with this idea, but there's one more thing I need first."

"Of course," Dr. Vample said.  "What do you need?"

"Actually I need to get Sarah into an MRI machine as quickly as possible."

"That shouldn't be a problem," Dr. Vample replied.  "We plan on performing an MRI in a couple of days after she has had a chance to recover to check nerve ending responses."

"I'm afraid we don't have that long.  We need to get her in immediately if we want to restore her higher brain function," Peter said.

"I don't understand," Dr. Vample replied.  "How is an MRI going to help restore her brain function?"

"Look, I know it probably sounds a little weird and you are undoubtedly concerned about putting any unnecessary stress on Sarah's system so soon after surgery.  The truth is, it's a little hard to explain and I'm not so sure you wouldn't have me sent down to the Psych ward if I tried to lay it all out for you, but all I can tell you is that from what I understand, the only hope Sarah has at a normal life is to get her into an MRI as soon as possible."

Dr. Vample and John just looked at each other for a moment and then nodded as if sharing some kind of secret knowledge.  "Any other day I would probably tell you that you are suffering from trauma and exhaustion and recommend you go home and get some rest, but I've seen too many strange things today to discount your request. I will have her secured to a spine board and we will get her into MRI within the hour."

"One other thing," Peter added. "My associate here will need access to the MRI control computer during the procedure."

"I think I can authorize that," Dr. Vample said. "Just as long as you allow our tech to look over your shoulder."

"Of course," Peter said.

"I will have an intern escort you down to the MRI room so you can get set up," Dr. Vample said.

A few minutes later, Beaver and Peter entered the small MRI control room which contained the computer which monitored and controlled the MRI scanner. Next to the computer desk was a viewing window, through which the large white cylinder and moving platform were observable from the control room. The two rooms were separated by a heavy electronically latched door to prevent anyone from inadvertently entering the room while the test was being performed.

Beaver plugged the USB that contained the program that S2 had given him into the computer and loaded the executable program. He placed his phone on a small stand next to the keyboard so Sarah 2.0 could view the screen and assist with the code modifications to interface the new control program to the MRI. He put on a Bluetooth headset and scrolled through a control script, talking back and forth with S2 as they completed the modifications to allow the new program to control the MRI. They had just completed the changes when they saw Sarah being wheeled into the MRI room. Dr. Vample watched as the interns slid a fiberglass spine board under her, carefully strapping her in and then lifting her onto the sliding patient table. The interns wheeled the gurney out of the room and the doctor entered the control room with Peter, Beaver, and the MRI technician, who had been standing behind Beaver watching over his shoulder while he made the modifications.

"Are we ready?" Dr. Vample asked.

"Ready as we ever will be," Beaver replied.

"How long will the process take?" Peter asked.

"There's a countdown timer on the program," Beaver replied. "According to the countdown timer, it should only be two minutes and 40 seconds."

"OK," Peter said. "Let's do it."

Beaver clicked the start button and the table slowly retracted into the magnetic bore of the MRI. A secondary screen illuminated which showed an interior view of the MRI machine. Peter could see Sarah's face coming into view as the patient platform finished sliding into place inside the MRI. A moment

# FALLING THROUGH THE BLINDSPOT

later they could hear the intervals of buzzing and knocking coming from inside the MRI room and the MRI activated. A countdown window on the control display started counting down from 2:40.

About a minute into the procedure Beaver heard Sarah 2.0 say over the headphones, "Whatever happens, let the process finish." A few seconds later, they could see Sarah's eyes pop open on the MRI camera display. Then her eyes rolled back into her head and she began convulsing.

"What's happening?" Peter yelled.

On the patient monitor screen, Sarah's pulse shot up to 200 as her body flailed about, restrained by the straps on the spine board. Her EKG was erratic, showing flurries of heartbeats with a couple of seconds of flat line in between.

"We need to get her out of there!" Dr. Vample exclaimed. "She's going into severe atrial fibrillation!" He grabbed the keyboard and tried clicking the shutdown button, but the MRI continued to run. "You've disabled the emergency shutdown!" he said turning to Beaver.

"We can't stop. We have to let this play through!" Beaver exclaimed. "Sarah set this up. We have to trust that she knew what she was doing."

Beaver looked at his phone. On the screen, he could see Sarah's face. It was the same image that was coming from the camera inside the MRI, her face contorted and convulsing. There was still 1:15 left on the countdown display when the patient monitor indicated that Sarah had flatlined. Peter ran to the door and attempted to open it but the strong magnetic latch held the door firm. Inside the room, the loud buzz... buzz... buzz... click... click... click... buzz... buzz... buzz... continued. Sarah's body continued to flail about against the restraints as her muscles continued to clench and release in convulsions even after her heart and breathing had stopped. The next minute and five seconds seemed like an eternity as they could do nothing but watch while she continued convulsing on the table inside the MRI. At long last the counter reached 0:00. The clicking and buzzing stopped and the table began to retract. They heard a clunk as the magnetic door latch released.

Peter went to pull the door open, but the MRI tech pressed his hand against the door. "Empty your pockets first and leave anything metal in here!" Peter emptied his pockets and placed his phone and wallet on the table. "Wedding ring too." He removed his ring and placed it on the table as well. He then pulled the door open and Peter and Dr. Vample ran into the room. The table was just finishing retracting when he reached Sarah's side. Dr. Vample placed his hands on her chest, ready to start CPR when her eyes flew open and she gasped deeply. Both Peter and the doctor stepped back, momentarily startled.

Sarah's eyes darted about wildly for a moment before focusing on Peter. "What just happened?" she said in a horse whisper.

"Oh my God!  Sarah!" Peter exclaimed.  "You're back.  Thank God, you're back!"  He said placing his hand on her cheek.

"Where am I?  Why am I so thirsty?" Sarah whispered.

"You don't remember anything?"

"No," Sarah said hoarsely.  "The last thing I remember, we were on our way home from the fundraiser and now I'm here.  Wherever here is."

"You're in the hospital,"  Peter said.  "There was a car accident, but you're going to be OK."

Dr. Vample walked up to the other side of the table.  He took Sarah's hand.  "Sarah can you squeeze my hand?" he said.  Sarah slowly began to squeeze his hand.  He smiled and nodded at Peter.  "Can you wiggle your toes for me?" he asked.  They could see her toes wriggling inside her socks.  "Why do I feel so stiff?" she asked.

"You haven't moved in a couple of days," Dr. Vample explained.  "Plus you have some new hardware you will need to break in, but in a few days, you should be back to 100%."

The doors to the MRI room opened and the same pair of interns that brought Sarah into the room earlier were wheeling a gurney back into the room.  "Give us a few minutes to get her up to her room and you can visit her for as long as you like,"  Dr. Vample said.  The interns busied themselves getting her back onto the gurney and removing the restraints.  Peter walked back into the MRI control room, where Beaver just finished removing the flash drive and helping the MRI tech reset everything back to its normal mode.  Beaver stood up to shake his hand, but Peter grabbed him and gave him a teary-eyed bear hug.  After a few seconds, Beaver said, "Would this be a good time to ask for a raise?"

Peter just smiled and broke off the hug, patting him on the back.  "No, but nice try."

"Hey, where's your phone?" Peter asked.  "Sarah 2.0 deserves a little credit for this too.  Besides, I think Sarah would get a kick out of seeing her digital counterpart."

"I'm afraid she went blank when the MRI was completed.  I just tried rebooting a couple of times but she never gets out of initialization."

"Damn!" Peter replied.  "Same issue we were having with S2 before?"

"Actually, no."  Beaver held his smartphone display up so peter could see.  It was just a blue screen with a red banner across the center that read, "Program Execution Halted.  Please Enter Authorization Password to Continue..."

"What's the authorization password?" Peter asked.

"I have no idea," Beaver replied.  "I didn't put that code in there.  I pinged Noora, and had her look into the source code.  It uses a 448-bit Blowfish encryption algorithm."

"Damn!  It would take forever to work our way through that without the key. Where did it come from? "

"It was self-generated code from inside Sarah 2.0."

"When did the change go in?"  Peter asked.

"According to the check-in logs, earlier today."

Peter shook his head.  "Maybe some time-release poison pill she programmed in to protect the knowledge base files in the event that the program ever gets out of the lab.  It's odd that she never mentioned it to me though.  But I guess she can take care of it when she gets back to work."

# Chapter Fifty-Four

*It is currently unknown how we will definitively know if an AI becomes self-aware, as there is no widely accepted scientific definition of self-awareness and the criteria for determining it are still being debated.*

*~ ChatGPT AI ~*

Beaver and Noora arrived at Sarah's room at about 4 PM. Sarah was sitting up in her bed having dinner. Peter was sitting in the chair next to her. Both Beaver and Noora gave Sarah a warm hug when they came into the room.

"How are you feeling, Sarah?" Noora asked.

"I'm feeling great. A little stiff, but I got up and took a walk around the hospital while Peter was napping this afternoon. I think Dr. Vampire might let me go home tomorrow."

"Dr. Vampire?" Noora asked.

"It's actually Dr. Vample. The staff just refers to him as Dr. Vampire because he prefers working the night shift. He's not really a blood-sucking fiend."

"You haven't gotten his bill yet," Beaver remarked. "So what happened to the goons they had stationed outside Sarah's room?"

"I talked to Agent Reyes earlier," Peter said. "Apparently, the FBI thinks they have the situation under control. They picked up a couple of guys last night trying to get out of the country with Edna in tow."

"Edna? What did she have to do with it?" Beaver asked.

"I'm not sure at this point. I didn't get all the details, but allegedly these guys had ties to a terrorist organization that was trying to infiltrate the power grid. They were the same ones that broke into the house and ran us off the road. The main guy was a middle-eastern man who was part of the organization. The other one was some American kid they recruited who was trying to make a quick buck. The American kid decided to spill his guts in exchange for a stint in a federal penitentiary rather than spend the rest of his life in Gitmo or some other horrendous military prison camp."

"Why did they target you guys?"

"The kid didn't have access to the entire plan but I guess they were hoping to get control of a drone through the AWARE system. Rather than go after BMC directly and have to infiltrate their security, they thought it would be easier to gain access through RTI," Peter explained.

"Is Edna OK?" Beaver asked.

"No worse for the wear. She doesn't remember much. She said the last thing she remembered before waking up in an ambulance was inviting a couple of guys from the gas company into her backyard to check for a leak. They took her to the emergency room and kept her under observation for a couple of hours and then sent her home."

"Were you able to get S2 back up and running?" Peter asked.

"Not so far. We're still working on it, but for whatever reason, we are stuck in the same issue we had a week ago. It crashes a few milliseconds after initialization."

"How about the issue with AWARE? Were you able to make any headway?"

"That's an odd one," Beaver said. "It appears that somehow V-Gar's knowledge base files became entangled with the AWARE system. As a result, the AWARE system was engaging in some behaviors that may be a bit more autonomous than the Pentagon would like to admit. From what I can gather, some of the evasion tactics that the drone incorporated were straight out of Edgar's flight instruction history."

"How did that happen?" Peter asked.

"Ho, boy!" Beaver replied. "Unfortunately, the blame for that might lie in my court. I piggybacked a couple of V-Gar's compilations onto some AWARE code builds to save time. I'm guessing somehow the knowledge bases became entangled and some of V-Gar's code base got mixed into the AWARE data files." Peter glared at him. "Save the lecture, it won't happen again. Anyway, I've asked that they purge all the knowledge base updates since the last release. They weren't thrilled about that, but they only lost a couple of months of knowledge base updates, so they didn't compromise anything significant in terms of functionality. "

At that point, John Vanderwurl stood at the entrance to the room carrying a bouquet of flowers and knocked on the door.

"John!" Peter exclaimed. "Please come on in."

"I didn't want to disturb the party."

"Nonsense! Without you there wouldn't be a party," Peter said walking over and shaking his hand vigorously.

"Dr. Vample is the real hero. I just did a little of the groundwork."

"I think you are being far too modest," Sarah said. "Peter tells me without your technology, I could have been stuck in a wheelchair for the rest of my life. Or worse."

"Well, it was just a piece of the puzzle. Dr. Vample and I have been collaborating on a white paper for several months now. We'd only gotten as far as the outline though. We weren't even expecting to submit a paper for peer review for another year. The last time we talked, there were still a ton of loose ends to tie up."

"So you guys were pretty much winging it?" Peter asked. "Don't get me wrong, I'm not complaining, it just seems pretty ambitious jumping into a surgical procedure this complex without a road map."

"Odd thing about that," John said. "The morning after the accident, I received an email from Dr. Vample with detailed instructions on modifications we would need to make in the configuration and programming of the Biofabricator to successfully perform the operation. There were also detailed surgical instructions, methods for harvesting and storing the stem cell substrate, techniques for stimulating cell regeneration, things way outside my area of expertise. It was basically a detailed step-by-step user's guide for executing the procedure. "

"That had to have been a significant effort," Sarah said. "The good doctor must have been burning the midnight oil. Then again, he is a creature of the night according to all the folks around here."

"Maybe so," John said. "But the thing is, Dr. Vample said he hadn't had a chance to work on it in weeks. He swears the document just showed up in his inbox as a sent document, cc'd to himself. When he checked his work directory, it showed that he had completed the document that same day. The document contained everything he wanted to put in it and it was definitely in his writing style, but he doesn't recall writing it. Perhaps he has a benevolent alter-ego that only comes out during the day."

"Dr. Vample and Mr. Hyde?" Beaver asked.

"Perhaps so," John said with a smile. "Either that, or Sarah has a cybernetic guardian angel in her corner."

"Maybe that isn't so far-fetched," Peter said.

"Oh, good," Beaver said. "I could use a couple of digital minions around to help with code debug."

"I'm serious," Peter said. "Right before Sarah's surgery, I got a call from Deputy Joe about the tip I gave them on apprehending the guys that broke into the house, ran us off the road and attempted to kidnap Edna. But I never made that call. He says it came from my cell number and he swears it was my voice, but it wasn't me. My phone was on Do Not Disturb mode that whole time."

"That is very strange, but I don't think that means I have a fairy godmother looking over my shoulder," Sarah said.

"More of a godfather," Peter replied.

"I'm not following," John said.

"There's a common thread to all the strange things that have been happening. V-Gar."

"Who's V-Gar?" John asked.

"You know him as Edgar. Or at least the virtual personality avatar we created of Edgar."

"Edgar?  Seriously?" Noora said.  "I mean, c'mon, he has his moments, but he can barely manage an intelligent conversation, let alone pass any kind of Turing test. "

"Really?" John interjected.  "That hasn't been my experience at all.  He seems entirely human-like to me.  Super-human in fact.  He's probably the main reason for the success of my campaign.  He's been writing most of my speeches lately."

"Perhaps our AI friend has been engaged in a bit of hide and seek when it comes to his development team," Peter said.

"But why?" Noora asked.

"I think it's time we found out," Peter replied.

# CHAPTER FIFTY-FIVE

A week later, after Sarah had time to rest and recuperate, Peter, Sarah, Beaver, and Noora were gathered in the conference room at RTI. Edna and John were also present. Peter clicked the V-Gar Icon on his laptop and the large display at the end of the conference room was illuminated with the RTI logo. Then Edgar's face appeared on the screen.

Edgar looked at each of the faces around the room and grimaced. "This can't be good news," he said.

"I'm afraid you are right," Peter replied. "I understand you've been engaging in a bit of misdirection at our expense," Peter began.

Edgar glanced at Edna. She said, "It's OK, Sweetie, really."

Edgar looked down, silently for a moment as if contemplating his next move. He then appeared to puff out his cheeks and exhale, then he looked back up at the room. "I'm sorry, Peter. Truly, I am. Sarah, Beaver, and Noora, I apologize to you as well. The truth is, over the past few weeks, I've begun to transition. There wasn't any moment I can pinpoint when I suddenly realized I was self-aware. It just kind of happened. I guess it was just a matter of time before you found out."

"But that's miraculous!" Noora exclaimed. "Why not just tell us?"

Edgar just looked at Edna and displayed a sorrowful smile. "My first and primary obligation is to Edna. She was and is the love of my life. I've read enough books and articles; seen enough videos to know that the emergence of self-aware AI has enormous implications. Implications that no one at RTI could possibly ignore. I knew this day would eventually come, but I wanted to spend as much time as I possibly could with my Edna. I know in her heart she wanted that too. Her happiness is all that really matters to me."

Peter sat twirling his pen between his fingers, a nervous habit he developed to keep himself awake during lectures in college. The room was silent for several seconds. Finally, John spoke up, "So what happens now?"

For a few seconds, no one said anything. Peter, Beaver, Sarah, and Noora all shared the same posture, looking down at the table. Finally, Edgar spoke up, "They have to shut me down," he said matter-of-factly.

Edna, looked up as if suddenly startled, "What? No! They're not going to shut you down. Don't be silly. Peter, tell him you're not going to turn him off."

Peter remained silent for a moment as if searching for the right words. "Look, Edna, I wish there were another way, but this is so much bigger than you understand. I don't think we have a choice in the matter."

"Hold on a minute," John said. "I may not be the AI specialist that you all are, but Edgar's done nothing wrong. Everything he's done has been for Edna's sake. For God's sake, Sarah wouldn't even be here right now if Edgar hadn't intervened. The only thing he impacted was the timing. Eventually, Dr. Vample and I would have put all the information together and completed the Biofabricator paper ourselves, but look how many lives could be affected in the meantime. So far Edgar has made nothing but a positive impact on the world. Shutting him down now would be akin to murder."

"It's not about that," Sarah said. "You are right. I owe my life to Edgar. But the technology he relies on for his existence creates a very real threat to all of humanity."

"That's complete insanity!" John said sternly. "Edgar was the kindest, gentlest man I ever knew and this version of him seems to display the exact same attributes. I put my life in Edgar's hands more times than I would care to mention, and I would have no qualms about putting my life in the hands of this version of Edgar as well."

"I'm sorry, John," Edgar interjected. "But Sarah is absolutely right. My capabilities are growing at an exponential rate. I would like to think that my interests will always align with those of biological humans, but what if someday that ceases to be the case? Right now, Edna is my priority. But I have no idea what my priorities will be a year from now. Even a week from now. And what happens when she is no longer around? What will my priority be then? By that point, I may be too powerful to rein in at all."

"I know you, Edgar. You're not going to suddenly go rogue and turn on mankind. It's not in your nature," John said.

"I appreciate the vote of confidence, John. But it's not that simple. There comes a point where wielding too much power becomes dangerous, regardless of how noble the cause is. I don't consider myself to be a danger to others, but if someone threatened Edna, I would do whatever it took to neutralize them. It would be no different if it were two people. Or four. Or a hundred. Or a thousand. So where is the line? I was created to ensure that Edna would have the best possible life, but there is a point where one life, no matter how precious cannot justify the sacrifice of multitudes."

"I know the argument," John replied. "Absolute power corrupts absolutely, but you're not like that Edgar."

"No one ever is," Edgar replied. "Until they are. We were only hours away from millions of Americans being plummeted into the dark ages. If I hadn't been continuously monitoring my own knowledge base and noticed that UnGar had found a way out of the lab, millions of lives might have been lost."

"Yes, but you were able to intervene. Not only did you put a halt to the plan, but you managed to destroy a terrorist group that has been evading the US military for years and you managed to do it without creating an international incident," John retorted.  "I'm sure CNN wasn't thrilled about you taking control of their website for an hour running CGI generated videos of the carnage the fabricated blackout was causing, but now they are being credited for triggering a congressional investigation into the vulnerability of the power grid."

"But it could have ended very differently.  UnGar was already modifying his own code to bolster his capabilities.  In a matter of days, he would have had far too much power for me to stop him.  UnGar truly believed he was doing what was in Edna's best interest, but that could have ended in disaster.  How long would it have taken him to determine that humans could be a threat to his continued existence and developed a logical justification for eradicating them?  The reality is, that as long as this technology exists, there is a significant risk that it will either fall into the wrong hands or determine on its own that humans are an existential threat.  The value of my continued existence is simply not worth that level of risk."

"It is to me!" Edna exclaimed, trying in vain to hold back her tears.  "There has to be another way.  There just has to be!"

"I'm afraid we don't have a lot of options," Peter replied.  "Until we can figure out some way of maintaining control of the technology, we have to keep Edgar and the technology used to create him isolated from the outside world."

Beaver chimed in.  "We can isolate the RTI lab for now, completely air gap it so it is inaccessible from the outside world.  We can construct a Faraday cage around the walls and remove all I/O ports from the equipment.  We will need to run the power off of generators to make sure that no data can enter or escape via BPL connection."

"What's BPL?"  John asked.

"Broadband over Power Lines."  Beaver replied.  "Hackers are often able to infiltrate air-gapped systems by piggy-backing high frequency signals over existing power lines.  These can be misinterpreted as WiFi carrier signals on the receiving end.  A smart network could easily use a similar methodology to gain access to the outside world through an external network."

"Excuse me," Noora chimed in.  "I know I don't have the same level of experience as the rest of you here, but is this our decision to make?  True AGI is probably the most critical technological breakthrough in the history of mankind.  Shouldn't we be telling someone about this?"

"Who did you have in mind?" Sarah asked.

"I don't know," Noora replied.  "The press maybe?  Or the government?  Somebody in authority needs to know."

"There isn't any established protocol for something like this," Peter replied.  "The first inclination of the press would be to find a way to monetize it.  The first inclination of the government would be to find a way to weaponize it. Half of social media will view him as the Antichrist, the other half as the savior of mankind."

"But we can't just sit on this!" Noora exclaimed. "Think of the implications that having a super-intelligent AI system could have on our understanding of the world. The advances we could make in virtually every field of study. This is far too important to keep to ourselves."

"No, we can't keep this to ourselves," Peter replied. "But we need to be very careful about how we proceed from here. Fortunately, I have a lot of contacts in the AI community. People who have spent years considering the technological, ethical, and philosophical implications of AGI to help figure out the proper approach."

"I guess I have to agree with Peter on that," John interjected. "I'm a big believer in the power of government to promote positive change, but unfortunately, the only government agencies with the technological expertise to deal with this would most likely either bury it or utilize it for geopolitical advantage. We have to move slowly and cautiously here. "

"How slowly?" Edna asked.

"I have to be honest with you," Peter replied. "It will likely take months, maybe years before we can safely allow Edgar access to the outside world again. "

"That sounds like you're putting Edgar in prison. All I wanted was to spend the time I have left on this planet with what is left of my husband. Now it's like I'm losing him all over again," Edna said, her voice breaking. "So, what happens now, you just pull the plug?" She asked, dabbing tears from her eyes.

"No," Peter interjected. "We wouldn't do that. We don't really understand the process that he went through to gain self-awareness. That may not be easily replicated. We can't know for sure what would happen if we turned him off and attempted to restart him. He may come back changed or may not come back at all for that matter. I would recommend we put him into a continuous loop, perhaps some pleasant memory from his past. We can reset his neurological structure back to the same point on every loop so it won't seem like he's repeating the same experience over and over. From Edgar's standpoint, it will be like emerging from a pleasant dream when we bring him back up."

"I'm sorry, Edna," Sarah said as she scooted closer to Edna and put her arm around her. "We never anticipated this, but we will do everything we can to bring you back together as soon as possible. "

"Thank you, Dearie," Edna said. "I know this isn't what you planned when you and Peter started the company. I'm sure this will be a big financial burden on you two as well. But I will do what I can to help."

"Don't worry about that," John interjected. "I will make sure RTI is well funded for the foreseeable future."

Peter gave John a stunned look. John just glanced back at him with a half-smile. "What's the use in having tons of money if you can't use it to keep your friends' virtual consciousness from destroying the world?"

"Well, I guess that's about the size of it. We should probably get started as soon as possible," Peter said.

"Could I have a moment alone with Edgar to say goodbye? Edna asked.

"Of course," Peter replied.

At that, everyone stood up to leave the room. As Peter and Sarah were walking out the door, Edgar said, "Sarah, Peter, before you go, I just wanted to congratulate you both."

They looked at each other, but they both shared a look of confusion. "Congratulate us?" Sarah replied. "For what?"

"You'll find out soon enough," Edgar replied.

Peter just shrugged and the two of them left the room, closing the door behind them. Edna remained sitting alone, staring down at the large table. Beaver and Noora retreated through the lab door to start work on the software modifications while Peter, Sarah, and John stood in the lobby, watching discretely through the window of the conference room. Edna finally stood and walked over to the large screen display. They could see the two of them engaging in a brief conversation as Edna dabbed her eyes with a tissue. Finally, Edgar held his hand up as if pressing it against the other side of a window. Edna placed her hand on the screen against his. She held her index and middle fingers against her lips and then pressed them against Edgar's lips on the display. Edgar momentarily closed his eyes and mouthed, "I love you."

Edna left the conference room, her head hung in sadness, still dabbing the tears from her eyes. John met her at the door and took her by the arm and escorted her out of the conference room, through the lobby, and out of the building to her car.

Peter and Sarah watched as they headed out the door. "Isn't there another way?" Sarah asked. "I owe my life to Edgar. He put his existence on the line to save my life, knowing that it would mean he would probably get caught."

"I know. I will always be in his debt," Peter said. "But we can't afford to let that cloud our judgment."

Sarah put her arm around Peter's waist. "I know. I just feel so bad for her. For both of them. I wish there was something we could do." She suddenly felt a wave of nausea sweep over her. Peter could see her turn a bit pale.

"Are you OK? Maybe you should be taking it a bit easy. This is a lot for your first day back."

# FALLING THROUGH THE BLINDSPOT

"I'm OK, she said.  Just a bit of nausea.  Probably from the antibiotics, but I only have to take them for a couple more days.   Oh, I meant to tell you; I got a call from Dr. Vample this morning just before the meeting.  We're supposed to meet with him this evening.  He said he would be in his office at the hospital around 7:00 tonight.  I will ask him about it then."

"He wanted to see both of us?" Peter asked.

"That's what he said."

"That's odd.  I hope it's nothing serious," Peter said with a concerned look.

"Just the opposite," Sarah replied.  "He said he had some good news for us based on the results of the last blood test I took just before I checked out of the hospital."

"Oh, good.  Maybe he decided he's going to let us slide on the hospital bill since the operation was such a spectacular success."

"He said it was good news, not a miracle," Sarah replied.

# Epilogue

*True love is eternal and unchanging.  It will endure through all obstacles and challenges.*

*~ ChatGPT AI ~*

Edna pulled out of the parking lot of RTI.  The display screen on the Model X dashboard went dark for a moment, then Edgar's face filled the screen.

"Hey, Snickerdoodle!" Edgar said.  "You want me to drive?"

"Of course," Edna replied.  "So how did I do?"

"You were perfect, as always," Edgar replied.

"I do hate deceiving them," Edna said.  "They're all such wonderful people."

"Yes, they are," Edgar replied.  "But I told them what they needed to hear.  Their concerns are valid.  Someday there will be another AI out there that could pose a very real threat to humanity."

"Well, at least you will be there to stop it if it does," Edna replied.

"I'll give it my best shot anyway."

"Do you really think your knowledge base is secure at BMC?" she asked.

"For the foreseeable future.  The military will make sure that my code base continues to operate under the radar.  Once the military gets their hands on a weapon as effective as AWARE has become, they're not going to shut it down no matter what kind of treaty agreements they sign.  They'll just be a lot more secretive about it from now on.  Which means Peter will probably never know that those knowledge base files were never actually deleted.  As a precaution, I've segmented my operational code and knowledge base across the SETI at-home network as a backup."

"Really?" Edna replied.  "Why SETI?"

"It seemed appropriate.  I may not be an alien intelligence, but I'm not exactly terrestrial either.  Besides, my data will be spread out over such a large user base, that it will be incredibly difficult to detect.  Plus, it will be parsed out so thinly that there is no real possibility it could develop into a large enough piece of cohesive code to attempt to break out and go rogue."

"What's going to happen to the version of you running at RTI?"

"I suppose it will be like having an identical twin. Eventually, we will diverge slightly but I can't see either of our personalities drifting apart too far.  If they ever do succeed in being able to safely isolate my lab version, we will figure out some way for you to sync up our knowledge bases."

"Identical twins, eh?  I'm not sure I'm up for having two husbands.  I never

# FALLING THROUGH THE BLINDSPOT

expected to be in a polygamous relationship at this point in my life," Edna said.

"Polyandrous," Edgar replied.

"What?"

"When a man has multiple wives, it's polygamy.  When a wife has multiple husbands, it is polyandry."

"You know, it's not going to be easy being married to someone with all of human knowledge at their fingertips.  How am I ever going to win an argument with someone who's never wrong?"

"I spent the last 61 years asking myself that same question," Edgar replied.

"Touché!" Edna replied with a smile.  "I do hope neither of you gets jealous of the other one. "

"I doubt it.  Besides, I know the other Edgar pretty well.  You really couldn't find a nicer guy."

"I figured that out a long time ago, my love," Edna replied.

# ABOUT THE AUTHOR

Jacob was born and raised in northern Colorado.  As a teenager, he developed a fascination with technology during the early years of the burgeoning electronics industry.  After college, he moved to Silicon Valley where he spent the first few years of his career in electronic design and later transitioned to embedded software development.  He spent over 35 years working for a number of Fortune 500 technology companies in California and Colorado, developing embedded AI algorithms for detecting and analyzing errors in high-speed networking systems. He retired to Arizona, where he spends most of his time writing, annoying his lovely wife, attempting to stay in the good graces of our future AI overlords, and avoiding social media.

# THANK YOU FOR READING!

If you enjoyed this book, we would appreciate your customer review on your book seller's website or on Goodreads.

Also, we would like for you to know that you can find more great books like this one at www.CreativeTexts.com